JUSTICE DONE

JUSTICE DONE

A Daniel Jacquot Thriller

Martin O'Brien

– 10 –

Sometimes the law fails…

MOBUK
PRESS

Design: ConnorCorcoran Design
Author photo: Gavin Shaw

www.martinobrienthrillers.com

The Daniel Jacquot Series

The Waterman
*"Well-drawn, and strongly flavoured. Rich, spicy,
and served up with unmistakeable relish."*
The Literary Review

The Master
*"Martin O'Brien creates a sexually charged atmosphere
that is as chilling as it is engaging."*
The Sydney Morning Herald

The Fifteen
*"Well written and compelling. Tight plotting, lyrical descriptions
and excellent characterisation mean Jacquot is here to stay."*
The Daily Mail

The Angel
"French country life has never been so fraught with sinister atmosphere."
The Rough Guide to Crime Fiction

Confession
*"O'Brien's evocation of the hot, vibrant and seedy port in which everyone
seems to be either a cop or a criminal, and sometimes both, is as masterly
as Ian Rankin's depiction of Edinburgh."*
The Daily Mail

Blood Counts
*"Chief Inspector Daniel Jacquot of the Marseilles Police is fast becoming
one of my favourite fictional cops."*
The Daily Mirror

The Dying Minutes
*"A wonderfully inventive and involving detective series
with vivid French locales creating the perfect backdrop.
Jacquot is top of le cops."*
The Daily Express

Knife Gun Poison Bomb
"A strikingly different detective, Jacquot walks off the page effortlessly."
The Good Book Guide

Talking To The Sharks
*"One of the very best books I've read in a long time…
Utterly and brilliantly entertaining."*
Goodreads

Also by Martin O'Brien

All The Girls
(Non-Fiction)
"A classic among travel books."
Auberon Waugh, Books & Bookmen

Lunching The Girls
"Unexpected flavours in a highly-seasoned thriller."
Amazon/Constant reader

Writing as Jack Drummond

Avalanche
*"Big, high-pitched disaster novels
don't come much more thrilling than this."*
The Daily Mirror

Storm
"A classy old-school thriller."
The Daily Sport

Writing as Louka Grigoriou

In The House Of The Late Petrou

*"A captivating story and a real page-turner from start to finish,
with a twist when least expected."*
Amazon Reviewer

For my dear friends
Jane McCulloch,
and Carlie Tufnell

Marseilles
April 1992

1

It had to be a good car. A Mercedes, Jaguar, or BMW. A good Audi, or Volvo. Top of the line Renaults or Citroëns, but VWs and Japs only at a pinch. And a saloon or hatchback, not one of those high-sided four-wheel-drives. It was always easier to bend down, than look up. More intimidating, too. But never a sports car. Too low, too cramped. Too fast off the stop.

That was the kind of car which the 'tapper', Adam Loum, was waiting for that Thursday evening in the shadows of the Joliette overpass. A good car. A promising car. And it didn't have to be new either; just clean, looked after, regularly valeted. That said a lot. But no passengers. Just the driver. A woman, preferably. The older, the better. Women were so much easier than men; less likely to argue the toss, especially if they had a child strapped in a kiddie seat.

And traffic lights, of course. There had to be traffic lights. A successful 'tap' couldn't be done without lights. Like the set just fifty metres from where Adam waited. Overheads on a cable, posts left and right, and the smaller sets at driver height. Red, amber, green. But this time of night, just the red and the green. Forty-seven seconds between them. Stop. Go.

It was chill now and darkening fast, the dull drone of home-bound traffic on the overpass lessening with every quarter-hour. Possible now to hear the passing of individual cars rather than the constant drone of many. But down on the old coast road the traffic was always slower, more sporadic. Local traffic coming in from L'Estaque for a night on the town, or lorries turning out of the docks, heading for the autoroute slip roads.

Adam had been waiting an hour, leather cap pulled down tight, fur collar up, woollen scarf tucked in behind the jacket zipper. Eyes on the road.

1

Leaning against one of the V-shaped concrete supports that held the overpass. Left shoulder. Right shoulder. Or squatting down, back against the cold stone, feeling the throb of overhead traffic hum between his shoulder blades, the pleasing ache in his thighs and ankles. Time enough for three roll-ups worked with mittened fingers, lit with his brass Zippo, the flame cupped against a breeze shifting in over the quays from the Golfe du Lion, each browned stub flicked away or stamped out with the toe of his boot.

Sometimes he got the car he wanted quickly, but usually he had to wait. An hour mostly, maybe two. Any time between seven and nine. Before seven it was too busy. After nine, too quiet and too dark to see the driver. And just the one strike. Good or bad, you couldn't hang around after you'd made your move. Take what you can and scram.

Tonight he had to get it right. Seven thousand minimum, or he'd wake up tomorrow with a busted nose and broken teeth. Or worse. Courtesy of Burak's boys.

They always came in pairs, the Burak boys. The Algerian brothers who'd take tea after the business was done; the Albanians with their baby teeth and pink gums who looked like they could do some serious damage if they felt like it; and the two French guys, one of whom really did do damage, and loved any excuse. Midnight they'd be at his place, whichever pair turned up, and he'd better have the money. The three thousand he owed, the two he needed for another deal, and the rest to see him through until the next time he came down to Joliette.

Cash, if he was lucky.

Credit cards, if he could get a number.

Jewellery, if the stones were good or the gold thick and heavy. Earrings, bracelets, necklaces, rings, watches.

Which also made a woman driver the better bet.

2

Adam was reaching for the makings of another rollie when the port gates across the road and back from the lights swung open – a sharp, shuddering metallic grating as an eighteen-wheeler wheezed out from the loading bays. Up in the cab, illuminated by the dashboard instrument panel, he could see the driver – a bald man with a drooping walrus moustache that covered his mouth – hauling the wheel round, casting left for traffic before pulling out onto a clear stretch of road. The lights were green, but Adam knew that he'd never straighten up and make the cut before they turned red. Which they did. And the lorry juddered to a halt, half on the road, half off, hydraulic brakes hissing with irritation.

It was then that he saw the car, way back on the road from L'Estaque, but coming up fast. A dark colour. Green or blue or black, he couldn't tell yet. A Mercedes, he was certain. A big one, with those twin vertical headlights and that signature mesh grill. He nodded, pushed back the rollie makings into his trouser pockets. Forty-seven seconds on red down to forty now, but the lorry pulling out would add another twenty to that, might even delay the Merc for another red.

All the time he needed.

And nothing behind the fast-approaching car. Nothing coming from town either. Just the half-turned container truck, and the Merc dipping down at the front as the driver stood on the brakes, rear brake lights blazing. An SEL 600, by the look of it; top of the range.

And in a hurry.

Adam squinted into the gloom.

Yup, the 600. With the big V8 engine. Couple of thousand kilos. Solid, heavy, but still fast.

The kind of car a man would drive. A chauffeur even. Which wouldn't be good.

3

But it wasn't a man behind the wheel. He could see that now. It was a woman. Low in her seat, a headscarf cinched around the chin. Blonde hair. And on her own. Just what he'd been waiting for.

He looked around, saw nothing, saw no one; slipped his right hand into his jacket pocket, wrapped his mittened fingers round the butt of his 9mm Makarov and started forward.

This was going to be an easy one.

2

Camille Dupay's hands gripped the steering wheel. She had taken the wrong slip road, come off the Joliette overpass too soon. She needed to get back on the autoroute, which meant following the coast road in to town until she could find her way onto it again. She'd had an hour to make the journey when she left the house in Malmousque – easily enough time to do what she'd been told – but she was cutting it fine now. Eighty-thirty, the man had said. By the entrance to the old marina past Bassin Quatre. A yellow-topped bin by the phone kiosk. And it was already eight-fifteen. She'd have to put her foot down if she wanted to get there on time. Still possible, but please God, she prayed, don't let there be any more delays, any more wrong turns.

She was nervous, that was all. Tight as a wound spring. Hardly surprising, given the stakes. Who wouldn't be nervous? But she was excited, too; heart thudding in her chest. And so relieved. Soon the nightmare would be over. Her boy would be back; home again, safe again. She could almost feel him in her arms; the tickle of his soft blonde hair, his plump little cheek pressed against hers, the smell of him… Lucien, Lucien, Lucien. Just ten years old, but the sweetest little boy. So loving, so attentive. A Mama's boy, Alain always said. But then he would say that. She didn't mind, she understood. And so, she knew, did Alain. Because he was the one who'd organised the money, counselled against any police involvement, told her they must do exactly what was asked of them. Just a single call to the bank, no questions asked, and Alain's pigskin briefcase packed with neatly banded bundles of 500-franc notes. *Banque de France.* Yellow, like a dim gold. The head of Blaise Pascal, with beaked nose and sleepy eyes, his features set with a suitably thoughtful expression.

Camille glanced at the dashboard clock. Nearly eight-twenty, but she could see the sign ahead, pointing back to the autoroute. She'd make it. Traffic was light now. There would be no real hold-ups. Three, maybe four more kilometres – not even that – and she'd be there. On time. Drop the case in the bin. And drive away. That's all she had to do. By the time she got home, there would be instructions where to find Lucien. The man had promised that. Her boy would be home before she knew it. And the nightmare would be over.

But the nightmare was just beginning.

A set of lights up ahead, maybe two hundred metres distant. On the green. Just a few metres short of the slip road for the autoroute and L'Estaque. She put down her foot and the Mercedes surged forward. She could make it, she could make it... But then, from the right, a container truck swung out in front of her, half-turned, trying to make the lights like her, but brought up short by the change back to red. Without that truck she'd have made it, for certain. But now she had to hit the brakes, slow the car, grit her teeth and hiss with impatience.

Seconds ticking by. Delay, delay, delay...

Camille didn't see the man at first, stepping from the shadows of the overpass. Only as he came towards her. A fast, loping stride, shoulders hunched, hands in jacket pockets. For a moment she thought he was just crossing the road, coming between her and the back of the truck. But he came up beside her, leaned down to the window.

Was he lost? Did he need directions?

But not here, she realised. No one asked for directions here, and she knew in an instant what the man wanted. And as she thought it, she saw the man's hand come out of his pocket with a gun, saw its muzzle tap against her window.

Instinctively she looked in the rear-view mirror. Thought to reverse, swing out and away before he had time to do anything. But the gun changed things. There would never be enough time. He'd shoot for sure.

Or maybe the gun wasn't loaded? Just a bluff, a prop, perhaps even a kid's toy…?

Was it worth the risk? For Lucien?

The muzzle tapped again. A solid sound. Louder this time. More insistent.

A real gun, not a toy.

She nodded, held up a hand. *Okay, okay…*

She wound down the window, heart beating fast, blood pulsing cold.

"Watch," said the man, his big tombstone teeth surrounded by thick purple lips and a tightly-curled and pointed black goatee. "Earrings, necklace, bracelet, rings," he continued, as she loosened the clasp on her Ebel and worked it off her wrist. Had it not been for the briefcase under her seat, and her appointment in L'Estaque – fast approaching – she might have tried to bargain with him, plead with him: her mother's ring, her grandmother's bracelet; such sentimental value. But she didn't waste any time. She did as she was told, with trembling hands, and dropped everything into his lined pink palm. Then she showed her hands, turned them – bare fingers, bare wrists…

6

"That's it. *C'est tout*," she said, as he shovelled her jewellery into his jacket pocket.

He peered past her, to the passenger seat, bent sideways to check the rear, and then looked down at her knees. Pressed together, to hide something.

"You forgettin' de bag, lady," he said, with a widening, teasing smile. "Give it me now, slow and easy," tapping the Makarov's barrel on the window sill.

Up ahead there was a wheeze of air brakes and Camille saw the lorry begin to move, turning into lane. The lights had changed. Red to green.

In a second she could stamp her foot down, get out of there, leave all this behind her. She was still in gear, toes on the clutch, ready to go. Just a few more seconds for the lorry to straighten, start off, and give her room to accelerate away.

"What case?" she asked, voice quaking.

"Them one there, unner de seat."

"It's nothing," she said.

"I be de judge on that one. So pass it up, lady, afore I done lose me patience."

She saw him look away, glance ahead at the lorry, then back the way she had come. In her rear-view mirror she could see a set of headlights approaching. He'd have to go now; he couldn't risk staying there with the gun in his hand. And she'd never give up the case…

"Now, or I tek 'im mesself." He swapped the gun into his left hand and reached for the door handle, tried to open it. But it was locked. "Open de damn door, lady, or I…"

But she didn't wait for him to finish. Pretending to reach down for the case, she let out the clutch, slammed down on the accelerator…

And the car leapt forward, then stalled with a jerk.

7

The man stepped back, pirouetting like a matador. But then, with the speed of a snake strike, he reached in, slipped the lock, and swung the door open, pushed his hand between her legs.

"No," she screamed. "No, no, *no*... You can't. You *can't* have it."

With one hand she reached for the ignition, scrambling to restart the engine, and with the other she beat her fist against his shoulder, his head, tried to grab for his arm. But he was too strong for her, with too much leverage, and she felt the arm push between her thighs, sensed his fingers clasp the handle of the case and start to drag it out, forcing her legs apart, pulling it up between them, his leather cap against her face, the sour scent of drink and tobacco.

Not bothering with the ignition now, she wound both arms around his body, clasping him as tightly as she could, pulling him down on top of her, headscarf sliding over one eye. Anything to stop him getting away, screaming now for someone to help her, wrestling for possession of the case. Falling back on the passenger seat and trying to get her feet under him, to kick him away.

It was then she heard the gun shot, muffled between their flailing bodies but still a deafening blast. Followed by a red-hot, hammer-like punch to the top of her leg. And a warm wet flow that seemed to pulse out, unbidden, unstoppable, between her thighs.

Urine? Blood? Which was it?

But it didn't matter.

Her body went loose, her arms lost any strength, and she felt her assailant pull free of her, nothing she could do to stop him now, the briefcase swinging from his hand, banging against the door jamb as he scrambled out of the car, turned, and ran.

He'd shot her. When she pulled him down on top of her the gun had been trapped between them, and just – gone off. He hadn't meant to do it. His finger had been forced back against the trigger. Otherwise, he'd have used the butt on the side of her head. No need to shoot. The gun was just encouragement. But he had. He'd shot her. She'd made him. Somewhere in the leg; top of the thigh, by the look of it. Blood spreading quickly into her cream slacks as he pulled away from her. Probably straight through; no meat on those legs. Safe enough if the bullet didn't hit a bone or sever an artery. But not his problem now, thought Adam, hurrying up Bartholomé, keeping to the shadows, and heading for home. If she hadn't struggled it never would have happened. Just hand everything over, lady, or pay the price. A simple enough deal. Her call. But some people just didn't get it.

Of course, a briefcase always caused problems.

They'd give him their jewellery quick enough, maybe a quibble here and there, but a briefcase was different. People always argued about a briefcase. Papers, documents, plans – work-stuff that couldn't be replaced, wasn't insured. Sometimes it wasn't worth the bother, but you never knew till you took a look inside. He'd had no time to check the one he'd pulled from the Merc, but it felt heavy, solid. Which wasn't necessarily good news. Last time he'd felt that kind of weight, it had been some writer's manuscript. Six hundred pages. He'd read the first few chapters – a *roman policier*; not bad – and wondered if the guy had a copy. Adam reckoned not. He'd handed over his watch and wallet easy enough, but there was no way he was going to part with the case. After the usual tug and shove, the butt of the Makarov slammed against the side of his head had decided it.

Back in his basement flat on Daumier, Adam locked the door behind him, closed the curtains and switched on the kitchen light. Briefcase on the table, pockets emptied. The Ebel watch, one gold wedding band, and an engagement ring with a single diamond, a linked gold bracelet set with diamonds and sapphires, a necklace of smaller diamonds and rubies, and what looked like a pair of pearl studs.

Good stuff, best he'd seen in a while. Must be ten grand's worth, maybe twenty – easily enough for Burak. And if he kept back the watch and diamond ring, he'd have all he needed to keep him going a couple more weeks. Maybe longer. Unless…

He turned to the briefcase.

No combination, thank God. He hated combinations. Had to take a claw hammer to the hinges. Waste of time. This one was a dark brown pitted leather, with shiny brass clasps that snapped up when he pushed aside the slide buttons.

He lifted back the lid, and he blinked.

Lost his breath for a moment.

Blinked again.

A warm gold glow in the overhead light.

Collared bundles of notes neatly, tightly, stacked.

Sweet holy fucking mother, Mary…

Which was the moment someone knocked on his door.

Burak's boys. Early.

4

Daniel Jacquot's day began with questions. A lot of them.

He opened his eyes and looked around. Where was he? Whose bed? Whose room? A house, or an apartment? And how had he got there?

These questions eased their way into his dawning consciousness through an aching fog of dry-mouthed, head-wringing weariness. Unable to make any real sense of his surroundings, unable to even raise his head from the pillow without piercing hammer blows of stiffening pain at the back of his skull, and a corresponding drumbeat behind his squinting eyes, Jacquot lay still and tried to remember what he had done to end up here – wherever it was – and in this sorry state.

A combination of factors, he realised.

His birthday, his promotion. Good enough reasons to celebrate, but it had clearly got out of hand.

It had started the previous afternoon in the squad room at police headquarters on rue de l'Évêché. A call from Yves Guimpier, head of the Marseilles *Judiciaire*'s Serious Crime Unit, after Jacquot had wrung a confession from the baker, Audois, that, yes, he had poisoned his bitch of a cheating wife with an overdose of Nembutal, planting the empty pill bottle in the glove compartment of her lover's car. Along with a pair of her knickers in the boot, and her mascara in a door pocket.

He'd made a good fist of covering his tracks but Jacquot hadn't been convinced. That eye-flicking downward look when the questions turned tricky. That was the giveaway. Desperate to find a way out, some reasonable excuse, but finding none. And when Jacquot had asked Audois about the mascara receipt in his wallet from the pharmacist on rue Beaugard, the man was finished. A good result, five days from the body turning up in a builder's skip in the Borély car park to Audois' committal to a holding cell at Baumettes prison on the outskirts of the city.

But there was more.

Guimpier had been brief. With Chief Inspector Guderoi suspended and no one to head the homicide squad, he'd decided to give Jacquot a crack

11

at it. He'd have preferred one of the older hands, he said – Al Grenier, the longest serving in the squad, or the ex-Legionnaire Claude Peluze – but he knew that neither would take it. Married men, Guimpier explained, and he had shrugged. Wives could be difficult. And having their husbands at home with the kids often made up for any financial consideration. So Jacquot got the nod. Single, no children, and a good record to date.

"So don't mess it up, and let me down," Guimpier had said, leaning over this desk and shaking Jacquot's hand. "…Chief Inspector."

Jacquot had been expecting a word of thanks for nailing Audois, but had no inkling that a promotion was on the cards. On previous occasions, when Internal Affairs had taken a look at Guderoi, the wily old bastard had somehow managed to wheedle his way out of it, until a whisper of complicity in the re-sale of confiscated drugs had stuck. And now Jacquot was stepping into his shoes. He'd had no idea…

But the boys in the squad had. When he came out of Guimpier's office, they were waiting for him: Peluze and Grenier, Pierre Chevin and Luc Dutoit, Etienne Laganne, Charlie Serre, and Bernie Muzon. A couple of crates of beer from Hamid at Café-Bar Al-Andalus across the road, and a chalk-scrawled *Bonne Anniversaire, Capitaine*, on the cork-board where normally the photos of crime victims and suspects were pinned.

That's when the drinking began. A Friday evening, nothing to interrupt their weekend with Audois banged up in Baumettes.

And this was where he'd ended up.

Carefully easing himself up in the bed, Jacquot wedged his elbows under him, and looked around. A woman's bedroom, that was certain. A dressing table crowded with a scatter of brushes and make-up, the warm, sinuous, and slightly familiar smell of perfume, a pair of black stockings draped over the back of a chair… But a throbbing pain in his head and neck had him slide off his elbows and ease himself back down onto the pillow. He closed his eyes, then opened them again, looked at the ceiling. Trying to piece it all together.

As far as he could remember, they had stayed in the squad room until the beers were finished. Claude and Al had headed home, Chevin and Laganne had dates so he'd joined Luc, Charlie and Bernie for a quick one at Les Voiles down on the *quai*. Where they met up with a couple of boys from Vice and headed across the port to Bar de la Marine.

And that's where the remembering got harder.

The sequence... The beers and the pastis kicking in.

Glasses raised to his birthday and promotion. To Audois, at Baumettes. To that *salaud* Guderoi, and his suspension. And to a lot more, he was certain.

But after La Marine, what then?

Did he get something to eat somewhere? A steak at Gassi's? Something in the kitchen at Molineux?

Without thinking Jacquot started to shake his head, but it was a movement he swiftly regretted.

Merde. This was not the way to start his first free weekend in a month.

Or maybe it was.

Except he was alone.

Whoever's bed this was, whoever's flat or house it was, there was no sign of them.

But who was it? What had he done, or who had he met, to find himself here? Was it someone he knew, or someone he'd just bumped into... along the way? A chance meeting that had ended up here?

But there was nothing he could see, or hear – save a soft hum of traffic beyond the shutters – to provide any clues.

13

And then, with a soft bleating, the phone beside him started up.

Should he answer it, he wondered? Would his voice work? He coughed, tried *merde* again, and realised he could still speak. He reached out an arm and lifted the phone from its cradle.

"Hey there, did I wake you?" The voice was soft and warm. She could have been in the bed beside him, save the muted sounds of an office in the background.

"I just surfaced," Jacquot managed, trying to place the voice.

"That's why I didn't call earlier. You were out for the count."

"I hope I behaved myself…"

"No complaints; everything as advertised. I'm just calling to let you know that my girlfriend finishes her shift at midday and she won't be happy if she comes home and finds you in our bed." The tone was still light, but business-like now – no pauses, no uncertainty. Apologetic, but firm. And no room for manoeuvre.

"Girlfriend?"

"Monique, she works *Urgences* at La Timone. She'd be very cross with me. I hope you understand."

"Of course, no problem."

"And thanks, I enjoyed myself. It was fun. You were… fun."

The past tense was plain enough for Jacquot. It might have been fun, but by the sound of it there wasn't going to be a replay any time soon.

C'est la vie.

5

An apartment, not a house. In a nineteenth-century Haussmann-style block, balconied and ornately railed, on avenue Sadi. A glance from the bedroom window was enough to tell Jacquot that. The kind of building that had stone-floor landings, wide runnered stairs, and a caged lift that in summer would keep the air moving and the block's interior cool. As was the way with Haussmann, the apartment was high-ceilinged and spacious, with ornate cornicing, lime-washed panelling and bevelled double doors.

After a quick shower – more shampoos and conditioners and body washes than he'd seen in a long time – Jacquot snooped as he dressed. Just the one bedroom, a large sitting room with three sets of shuttered windows overlooking the street, and an open-plan kitchen dining room set on the light well. On the salon bookshelves a mix of fiction, modern history, and biography, and on the coffee table larger format books on interior design, the Impressionists, body art, and classic cars. Music was equally diverse – classical and rock – with albums neatly shelved above a state-of-the-art Neimeyer hi-fi. In the kitchen, he found only almond milk or soya milk, so he filled a glass with water from the tap, looking at a selection of photos pinned to a cork-board and magnet-trapped on the fridge door as he drank: two young women – one in her thirties, wiry black hair and deep Moroccan tan; the other a few years younger maybe, with shoulder-length blonde hair and freckles. Dancing in a night club, on a beach in bikinis, at a restaurant table, making faces in a photo booth.

For the life of him, Jacquot had no idea which of the two he had shared the bed with. The older one or the younger. The blonde or brunette.

By the time he closed the apartment door behind him and rang for the lift, all he could say with any certainty was that if one of the two girls was a nurse at La Timone, then her companion had the kind of job that brought in enough money to cover the rent. He might have heard the clatter of typewriters and distant chatter in the background but he'd bet his first month's pay as a Chief Inspector that the woman who had phoned him wasn't a secretary. Stepping out onto the street he paused to read the name card on the Entryphone.

Apartment Six. M. Fontaine/S. Laronde, printed in a black copperplate. Blonde or brunette, there was no telling. Just the name, S. Laronde.

Tugging up his collar, squinting at a weak mid-morning sun in a thin blue sky, Jacquot set off for home, going through the options: Sophie, Solange, Sylvie, Simone, Suzanne, Stéphanie, Sonia… But he was brought up short when he turned out of avenue Sadi onto rue de la République. A pile of black bin liners on the corner had toppled over and the usual fresh salty scent of the harbour and open sea was replaced by the sweet rotting stench of garbage. One of the bags had split open and a fly-ridden spill of fruit peelings, soiled nappies, pizza crusts and other domestic waste covered the pavement. Nearly a week into the city's refuse collectors' strike, and its effects were beginning to be felt, and smelled. But better now, thought Jacquot as he stepped around the spill, than in summer. Two years earlier a month-long strike in August had filled the city with a throat-gagging reek, and more rats than tourists.

Twenty minutes later, as he turned the corner into place des Moulins on the heights of Le Panier, Jacquot saw the squad car outside his door; two uniforms with their backs to him, talking to his concierge, Madame Foraque. A nail-clipping over one and a half metres, the only things visible between their arms were her black beret and a spray of wiry, hennaed hair.

"*Voilà, il arrive,*" he heard her say when she caught sight of him, and the two cops turned, gave a loose salute.

"Chief Inspector Jacquot?" asked the senior of the two men, two stripes on his shoulder tab. It was the first time Jacquot had been addressed in his new rank. Word got round quickly.

16

He nodded.

"We've been looking for you. Do you have a car, or can we give you a lift?"

6

At police headquarters on rue de l'Évêché the squad room was busy, all the previous day's faces in attendance, some of them – Luc and Charlie and Bernie – looking as gravely hungover as Jacquot. Phones ringing, distracted waves, cigarette smoke, Styrofoam coffees from Hamid's Al-Andalus café. It didn't take long for Jacquot to find out what all the fuss was about.

Al Grenier, unshaven, tie loose in his collar, filled him in as they made their way to Guderoi's old office. And now Jacquot's office.

"Robbery gone wrong. A tapper, by the look of it. Around eight last night on Joliette. Victim, Camille Dupay. Thirty-eight. Shot in the leg and bled out. Taken to La Timone, but didn't make it."

The name seemed familiar, drifting into focus through Jacquot's splitting migraine mist. "Dupay? The Dupays? Opera?"

"And DupayCorp, up on Vacon. The big boys in town," said Grenier, nodding to the closed door ahead of them. "And the lady's grieving husband, Monsieur Alain Dupay, would like a word." He gave Jacquot a sly grin, and handed him the file he'd been carrying; a green initial incident report. The name 'Dupay, C.' had been felt-tipped onto the top-right corner. "He's been here an hour. A tidy piece of work. Good luck."

Alain Dupay was standing by the window, his back to the door, looking out at the seagulls wheeling around the striped heights of the Cathédrale Sainte-Marie Majeure. He was dressed in a trimly tailored blue suit, tall and slim, with light grey hair cut short to the neck, and when he

17

turned from the window Jacquot saw a similarly clipped grey beard pointed at the chin, set in a tanned face that was long and sharp and hard. Well into his forties, maybe early fifties, Jacquot guessed, with deep vertical lines that started at the point of his cheekbones and disappeared into his beard. It was difficult to imagine a smile creasing those thin, tight lips, or twinkling in his icy, flint-blue eyes. Shoulders back, chin up, there was no mistaking his remarkable presence. He seemed to fill the room, and for a moment it felt to Jacquot as though he was visiting Dupay's office rather than the other way round. But it was just a moment.

"Monsieur Dupay. My name is Chief Inspector Jacquot. I will be in charge of the investigation."

"Someone needs to be," said Dupay. A pleasant enough observation, but edged with threat, the voice soft but dangerous.

"I am sorry to hear about your wife, monsieur. She will be missed," said Jacquot, not wishing to be drawn, coming round Guderoi's desk and pulling out the chair, sitting in it for the first time. There was nothing on the desk save a telephone which he wished would ring, to give him some time to gather his thoughts. He put down the file, which somehow made the desk look even emptier.

"You knew her?"

"Only by reputation, you understand. The Opera, her charities…"

Dupay left the window and sat at Jacquot's desk, crossed one leg over the other and tugged at the crease in his trousers. The movement, and the subsequent raising of the trouser hem, revealed a bright red sock in a highly polished black shoe.

"So, perhaps you could let me know what happened, monsieur. Last night."

"I have made a statement already. Do I have to repeat myself to every police officer I meet?"

Jacquot spread his hands, said nothing. He could have, but he chose not to. Instead he looked his visitor over, took a bead on the man. This was a familiar routine, and one that usually provided Jacquot with everything he needed to know. First impressions. Exactly what kind of person sat across the desk from him.

In Jacquot's world, there were three kinds of people. Men and women alike. An instinctive assessment that had never failed him. The ones he liked immediately, the ones who could go either way, or, the third type, the ones that he disliked instantly, no possible chance of redemption. And in Jacquot's mind, at that precise moment, there was not a shadow of doubt that the man sitting opposite him was irretrievably, irredeemably, in this last group. The two of them could be stranded together on a desert island for a decade, but they would never be friends. In Dupay, it was the bored, effortless sense of entitlement that rankled; the sense Jacquot had that he considered himself better than those around him. His looks, his bearing, and his elegant tailoring – the red socks, particularly – didn't help. And it wasn't just the money; he'd have been like that, Jacquot suspected, without a *sou* to his name. Rich or poor, a bully. Brutish. Selfish to the core.

Dupay sighed, his jaw clenching. "Camille was coming home from L'Estaque. She stopped at a set of lights and it appears someone tried to rob her. Perhaps there was a struggle… She was shot in the leg. A lorry driver called the emergency services but by the time the ambulance arrived she had lost a lot of blood and was unconscious."

"And what was your wife doing in L'Estaque, if you don't mind my asking?"

"I believe she was visiting friends."

19

"So, she was driving home, stopped at the lights, and was robbed?"

"That is what I said, yes."

"Why wasn't she on the overpass? It's a much quicker route back to the city. And safer."

Another sigh, a shrug. "Who knows? She was not the most confident driver. Maybe she missed the slip road, and just carried on."

Jacquot nodded. It seemed reasonable enough. It was just… there was something missing. Something not quite right. But it was just a feeling. Maybe, thought Jacquot, his weariness was getting the better of him; or maybe Monsieur Dupay was digging himself more firmly into the role that Jacquot had reserved for him. As Grenier had said, a tidy piece of work.

"Do you have contact details for these friends your wife was visiting? It might be useful to talk to them."

Dupay started to shake his head, exasperated. "Chief Inspector, my wife had many friends, many acquaintances, outside our own social circle. Charity people, people she came into contact with in the course of her work, I'm sure you understand." Though it was quite clear to Jacquot that he thought no such thing.

"So, you don't know who she was visiting?"

"No, I don't."

"When did you last see your wife?"

"Yesterday evening, just before she left for L'Estaque."

"And you expected her back at what time?"

"She didn't say. I didn't ask. We had no commitments last night. I assumed she would be back for supper. Around nine."

Jacquot flipped open the file, glanced at the single page. "You live together in Malmousque? Are there staff? Children?"

"We have a son. Lucien. *En effet*, my stepson. Ten years old. From Camille's first marriage. Her husband died in a car accident. And a nanny, Trudi."

"And they are currently at home?"

Dupay nodded.

"And how, might I ask, did you hear of the hold-up, the shooting?"

"I received a call from the police. There were no papers to identify Camille so they traced the car registration. By the time I got to the hospital it was... too late."

For a man who had lost his wife, Alain Dupay seemed remarkably calm and ordered. No sign that Jacquot could see of any sadness or sense of loss. And certainly not grieving, as Grenier had suggested. He seemed somehow... disconnected. Not that Jacquot was surprised. He knew that people dealt with loss in different ways, and it wasn't the first time he had seen this kind of dislocation. For some, grief was best dealt with privately. But nevertheless...

"Well, thank you for your time, monsieur. As soon as we have any leads we will be in touch. In the meantime, please accept..."

Without waiting for Jacquot to finish, Dupay got to his feet, the chair legs grating on the floor. He stood straight and stiff, black eyebrows beetling down over cold blue eyes.

"I want him found, Chief Inspector. Whoever did this, I want him found quickly, and punished. To fit the crime. The full weight of the law. You understand?"

Jacquot got to his feet, slipped his hands into his pockets. He knew there would be no handshaking.

"Of course, monsieur. And that is what will happen. We will find him."

"Good. Please make sure of it."

It wasn't a request.

7

Standing in his office doorway, Jacquot watched Dupay stride across the squad room and head for the lifts. He had waved aside the usual offer of a squad car to take him home; he had his own car and would drive himself. And good riddance, thought Jacquot.

"Nice chat?" said Grenier, coming up beside him.

"I've had more fun in a morgue," Jacquot replied, as Dupay pressed for the lift. "The man is…" He searched for the right description, but words failed him.

Grenier filled in the gap. "*Con* is the word you're looking for, my friend. Solid gold. Twenty-four carat. Before you arrived we sent out for one of Hamid's coffees, but he just looked at it and asked for a cup and saucer. Like we do silver service here…"

"But you managed to find something."

"The saucer was Laganne's ashtray, and the cup for his toothpicks. But we gave them a rinse."

Jacquot smiled. Across the room the lift arrived, Dupay stepped in, and the doors slid shut.

"So, what have we got?" asked Jacquot, ushering Grenier into his office.

"Right now, not a lot," Grenier replied, taking Dupay's chair while Jacquot perched on the edge of his desk. "We're waiting on ballistics for the gun and forensics to finish up on the car, and checking through rap sheets

22

for known Joliette pranksters. Some low-life tapper looking to cover his next fix, so there's no shortage of likely applicants."

"Do we know what was stolen?"

"The usual. Rings, bracelet, necklace, earrings, and watch. Dupay gave us a list – what he remembered her wearing when she left for L'Estaque."

"Any purse or wallet – credit cards, cash?"

Grenier shook his head. "Dupay said she'd left them at home."

Jacquot frowned. "I don't know many women who'd leave their purse at home when they go out."

"Nor me, more's the pity," he said, with a grin.

"What about the lorry driver who called it in? Did he see anything?"

"Just a shadow, really. A man. Leather jacket, hat, scarf, jeans. Nothing out of the ordinary."

"Did he see the hold-up?"

"Nothing. Out of sight; the wrong angle for his side-mirrors. It was the gun shot that alerted him; said he saw the guy running north, up towards Bartholomé. Reckons he was carrying a briefcase, but can't be certain."

"Briefcase? There was no mention of a briefcase, was there?"

Grenier frowned. "Just jewellery, I think. I'll go check."

Which meant one of three things, thought Jacquot, as Grenier lumbered back into the squad room. Either the gunman was carrying his own briefcase – unlikely; or it belonged to Madame Dupay, and her husband didn't know about it; or he did know about it, but hadn't reported it stolen. For whatever reason.

After just ten minutes in Dupay's company, Jacquot knew which of the three options he favoured.

8

As Dupay negotiated a snarl of traffic around the Vieux Port, he couldn't quite make up his mind about the policeman, Jacquot. He certainly cut an impressive figure; tall and well-built, with shoulder-length wavy brown hair caught in a ponytail, and the most startling green eyes creased with laugh lines, the cheekbones high, the jawline strong, with a mouth made for smiling. The only feature slightly out of kilter was the man's nose, bent at the bridge and lightly scarred, a long-ago bad break that had not been properly set, Dupay guessed. But, like any imperfection, this one somehow served to make his looks even more striking. Beautiful, yet not quite perfect. It was an alluring combination.

There was, too, an easy grace about him, the way he moved, the way he spoke, with a soft, confiding drawl, someone who was comfortable in his own skin yet somehow unaware of the effect he had on people. It was clear, Dupay decided, that women would find him attractive, and men, too, for that matter. What concerned Dupay after their initial meeting was the man's youth, maybe twenty years younger, and his possible lack of experience. There was a lightness in his behaviour, an annoying insouciance that would never be tolerated at DupayCorp, a sense that he wasn't really paying attention, or wasn't too bothered by what had happened. Dupay wanted his wife's murder properly investigated and he had not been convinced, on first acquaintance, that this young man was up to the task. He was also vaguely suspicious that the cop didn't like him. The man might have put on a show of professional solicitude following Camille's death, but there was something beneath the politesse that grated. A certain… edge. Just a shadow, moving silently below the surface.

With an impatient beep at the driver ahead of him, stalled at a set of lights on Paradis, Dupay swung past him as green changed to red and turned down rue Vacon. Indicating to the left he brought his Mercedes up over the kerb and down into the basement parking lot beneath his office. He glanced at his watch. Twenty minutes late, thanks to the delays at the *Judiciaire*. And Dupay did not like being late. It was a weakness, and in his world there was no room for weakness of any kind.

Up on the fourth floor, his assistant, Delphine, greeted him as he stepped out of the lift. She took his jacket, handed him a file, and told him that his team was waiting for him in her office.

He didn't think to tell her that a little over twelve hours earlier his wife had been shot and killed in a random hold-up. She would find out soon enough, and right now he could do without any hollow displays of sympathy and condolence.

He had work to do, and would tolerate no shortcomings.

9

It was more than spring, but not quite summer yet on Jacquot's first full day as Chief Inspector. The blue in the sky had thickened and darkened since he'd stepped out of S. Laronde's apartment block on avenue Sadi, the sun had a little more bite to it, and a light breeze from the Golfe du Lion had swept away the worst of the stench of refuse. When he reached the corner of rue Baptiste and stepped onto the Quai du Port, he went from a shaded street into the full glare of the sun, and its gentle warmth swept across his face, slipped into his jacket, across his shoulders. Seagulls soared and screeched, and for the first time that day he felt a little more human.

Jean-Paul Salette was waiting for him at his usual table at Chez Loisette. The old harbour-master was dressed in his working kit. A light blue

Levi jacket, cuffs turned back, elbows patched, a faded black t-shirt, black cotton drills and dusty cream espadrilles. Every inch of skin was tanned and lined and his grey hair cut to a bristle on the scalp. The eyes were a piercing aquamarine, and the hand that lifted the glass of pastis in Jacquot's direction was as worn and hard as a piece of old timber. For twenty years he had sailed on deep-sea trawlers with Jacquot's father, Vincent, and when Vincent was lost at sea, Salette had stepped into the father's shoes, keeping an eye on the boy, helping him, directing him… for his oldest and dearest friend.

Jacquot pulled off his jacket, hung it on the back of the chair and sat down. A waitress came to the table with a bowl of *soupions* and a basket of warm bread. Salette picked up one of the tiny fried cuttlefish by a crisply stiff tentacle and popped it into his mouth.

"You're late. I ordered."

"Food before friends."

Salette nodded. "Always more reliable. And you look like shit, by the way. Oh, and Happy Birthday."

Jacquot nodded, reached for a *soupion*. "I'm afraid I can't make our trip," he said, quietly, knowing how disappointed the old boy would be.

Salette nodded, lips turned down. As though he'd known the weekend they'd planned wasn't going to happen. "Sometimes you need to walk away, Daniel. A break. And it's just an overnight."

"Not this time," said Jacquot. "I'm sorry to let you down. I was looking forward to it."

"The boat's ready. Supplies on board."

Jacquot shook his head, noting that the ache behind his eyes had reduced significantly. "We've got some work on. A tapper."

"What's new? Same as every day in Marseilles."

"Not this time."

Madame Loisette herself appeared at their table, a mass of black dyed curls held in place by a canary yellow headband. Her blouse was the same shade of yellow, the material thin enough to see the black straps and cups of her brassière, and its frilled front low enough to reveal a brown slice of freckled cleavage. She may have lost the firmness and roundness of youth, but the contents of her black bra moved with a full and enticing sway as she slid two wooden platters onto the edge of their table. A thick wedge of sizzling *entrecôte* on each, a sprinkle of sea salt still visible, and a pile of twisted golden *frites*.

"*Bon apétit, mes amis. La spécialité de la jour. Mais seulement pour vous deux.*"

Salette gave her a smile, took her hand and kissed it.

"You still get a bill, J-P," she chided, in a rich smoker's voice. "A kiss doesn't come close."

"It's a good place to start, *minette*."

"Enough of the pussycat, you old rogue. Just dip a *frite* in your mayonnaise, why don't you? At your age it's probably as much as you can manage with any dignity."

"And I would do so happily if I wasn't dying of thirst," said Salette, rattling his glass on the table top.

"Pastis or wine?" she asked Jacquot, turning away from Salette, but not before she'd snatched the glass from his hand, even if he hadn't finished the last of it.

"Water," said Jacquot.

"The Vallon des Glauges," said Salette. "Mates rates."

Madame Loisette gave a dismissive grunt and headed back to the bar, a tight black satin skirt giving luscious form to hips swaying between the tables, a skirt that had no need of the corset-tight black belt she wore. Salette

27

watched her go with a low-lidded growl of appreciation, and then turned to Jacquot, fixed him with a frown.

"Water? Did I hear right?"

"A rough night. A rougher morning." Jacquot picked up his steak knife and cut through a corner of the meat, revealing an interior the colour of Madame Loisette's lips. He speared some *frites* to accompany the meat, and popped the forkful in his mouth. Hot, juicy, salty. His cheeks puckered.

"A tapper, you said?" Salette had done the same with his steak, and sighed at the taste.

"Joliette. A woman driver shot."

Madame Loisette returned with their Vallon des Glauges, pulled the cork and splashed the wine into their glasses. "*Et voilà, messieurs,*" she said, and then, looking at Jacquot, "The tap's broken, *chéri*, you'll just have to make do."

"So, what's different? Anyone we know?" asked Salette, as Madame avoided his slap on her backside and left them to it.

"Camille Dupay."

Salette frowned, then placed the name.

"You're joking?"

"I wish I was. Shot in the leg. They got her to the hospital, but she didn't make it."

"A big name. Who's running the operation?"

"You're looking at him."

Another frown from the old man. "What about Guderoi?"

Jacquot spread his hands.

"He's gone?"

"Wednesday. Suspended without pay, pending further enquiries."

"So there is a God. What a piece of low-life scum…" And then Salette paused, a forkful of dripping *entrecôte* half-way to his mouth. "Don't tell me you're his replacement?"

Jacquot nodded. "Chief Inspector."

There was a moment's silence as Salette took in this news. He put down his fork, nodded his head, and tightened his lips. And in that moment Jacquot could swear that the old boy's eyes appeared to glisten with tears. But with a clearing of the throat, and a gulp of wine to swallow away the lump, Salette was back to normal.

"They didn't have anyone better for the job?"

"It appears not."

"*Bouf…* Same old, same old… Well, good luck is all I can say. You better work fast or they'll have your head on a plate. The Dupays are big. Family and self-made. *Formidable*."

"I met the husband this morning."

"Cold as ice," said Salette. "Has the biggest yacht in the marina, and knows it. Dutch built. Sixty metres. The *Lucien*."

"His stepson?"

"That's right. Poor kid."

Jacquot frowned. "How so?"

"What do you call it? Down syndrome. Lovely little boy, but…" Salette spread his hands. "It's one of Madame Dupay's biggest charities. Bigger than the Opera, the homeless refuges, the hospices. They organise care facilities, family support, accompanied trips all over. And every summer, fifteen of these kids get invited aboard *Lucien*, three one-week cruises through the season. Five of the poppets per cruise, with parents. You wouldn't believe it."

The steaks were finished, the last of the *frites* dispatched. Coffees were ordered, the bill called for.

"My treat," said Salette, wiping his mouth with a napkin, letting out the tiniest belch. "We'll do the trip another time. Right now, you'll have your work cut out. Any help you need, you know where to find me."

10

Jacquot was half-way down rue Baptiste, walking back to police headquarters with the warming, bloody taste of steak in his mouth, when the stutterer, Chevin, drew up ahead of him in an unmarked squad car, leaned over to open the passenger door.

"Forensics came up with a p-p-print," he told Jacquot, pulling back out into traffic. "On the Merc's door lock and handle. An old f-f-friend. Adam Loum."

"That's quick," said Jacquot. "We have an address?"

"It's where we're headed now. Back end of Belsunce. Thought you'd want to t-t-take a look."

"Ballistics?" Jacquot knew it was absurdly early for any ballistic report, but with Dupay involved there was no telling what might be achieved.

"Single bullet retrieved from the d-d-driver's seat of the victim's car, and a matching shell casing found in the p-p-passenger f-f-footwell. Both with Loum's prints. Confirmed as a 9x18mm Makarov. Possibly Russian, but given the rifling t-t-twist more likely Bulgarian. That's what Ballistics say."

Jacquot whistled. "Any idea who fast-tracked all this?"

"The chief's at his d-d-daughter's wedding in Grenoble, so it's got to be s-s-someone higher up."

The dashboard radio crackled. It was Laganne. "We got Loum. He's not going anywhere."

Seven minutes later Chevin pulled in behind the flashing blue lights of three squad cars double-parked on rue Daumier, a narrow terraced street in the tenth *arrondissement* that fed a few blocks further on into the busier boulevard Constance. The houses on both sides of this scabbed and potholed road were identical, two floors of patched *crépi* and dusty windows, with flat roofs and sagging TV aerials, squatting behind overflowing wheely-bins and low walls spiked with spear-tip railing.

Charlie Serre was looping a yellow chevroned 'Police' tape between a set of these railings either side of a steep flight of metal steps that led down to a basement flat. A crowd had gathered on the other side of the street, and some of the neighbours were leaning from their windows.

"Is he dead?" someone called out, the voice carrying down the road like an echo.

"About time," came a closer, gleeful, reply.

Jacquot looked up at the faces. "Get some names, Charlie," he said, lifting the tape and starting down the steps. "Do the rounds."

"Claude's already on it. He's taken one side of the street, Luc the other."

At the bottom of the steps, Jacquot pushed open a glazed door set with ornamental ironwork and ducked into the flat. The air was still and warm, and smelled of stale pizza, beer, and cigarettes. Drawing aside a bead curtain he found himself in a low-ceilinged sitting room with a barred single sash window looking out onto the steps he'd just come down, a room just large enough for two worn velveteen armchairs and a television on a coffee table. The floor was carpeted but any pile or pattern had long been worn away. The walls were papered in a pale stripe and bare, save a sun-faded tourist poster

31

above one of the armchairs. A beach scene, leaning palm trees, and the words *"Visitez La Gambie, Petite Perle de L'Afrique"*.

Two doors led off this room, and both were open. Through the first, Jacquot could see an unmade bed, a bathroom beyond, and Bernie on his knees going through the contents of a chest of drawers. The second doorway led into a kitchen, a small cramped space with three wall cabinets, a sink, fridge, microwave oven, and a square formica-top kitchen table set with three white plastic garden chairs. Al Grenier was leaning against the sink, Laganne smoking a cigarette in a weed-strewn yard outside the open kitchen door, but what drew Jacquot's eye was the pooling spill of scarlet blood on the lino floor beneath the table. And the body it had come from, slumped back in one of the chairs.

"Dead a few hours. Late last night at a guess," said Grenier.

Adam Loum's head was tipped back, eyes closed and swollen to slits, nose bent and broken, parted lips showing bloodied gums and the jagged stumps of his front teeth. No question about it, thought Jacquot. He must have been held to sustain injuries like that; one behind the chair, gripping the man's arms, the other doling out the punishment. So two, maybe more, assailants.

But it wasn't fists that had killed the Joliette tapper. It was steel. A sharp blade had sliced open his throat from ear to ear. With the head flung back, the killing wound looked like a clown's grinning mouth, the exposed red flesh marbled with severed white tubing, the blood-matted point of his goatee sitting above it like a tuft of reddish hair. Blood had sprayed across the table with the initial slice through the jugular and deeper carotid arteries, and had then pulsed down over Loum's grubby white sweat shirt as the blood pressure dropped, streaming through the slats in the seat of his garden chair and onto the floor. A quick way to go. A minute, with the carotid. Maybe a little more. But the beating would have taken longer.

Jacquot looked at the tilting head and opened throat – the skin around the bloodied gash an ashen grey, the spread of blood darkening on Loum's chest, the scrawny arms hanging loose at his side – and he saw again not just the wounds, but the emptiness.

Always the same, he thought. Just hollow. Something that resembled a living, breathing body, but one now deprived of the spark that made it all work. Cold, still, sometimes stiffened with *rigor*, these victims never failed to register with him. In chairs, like Loum. On beds, floors, and pavements, in cars, gardens and woods, in baths, swimming pools, the sea… wherever that last breath was drawn. He'd seen other *flics* shrug, and tell anyone who asked that you got used to it, just a part of the job, seeing some mangled body. But Jacquot knew they were playing it hard, trying to put some distance between them and each new grim discovery; just a kind of defence mechanism. The truth was, no real cop ever got used to it. The senses never dulled, the horror never lessened. Familiarity went just so far.

Jacquot wondered how many dead bodies he had seen? Men and women, old and young – battered, stabbed, shot, drowned, burned, strangled, poisoned… There was no end to the ways and means. Children too. After nearly ten years with the *Judiciaire*, say a dozen or more murders a year, Adam Loum would likely be well past the hundred mark. Jacquot couldn't put an actual figure to it, couldn't hope to remember them all, but he'd never forgotten the first one. A young girl crumpled in a gutter after being thrown from a window by her pimp, eyes wide and staring, broken limbs splayed at sickeningly unnatural angles, blood puddling, flies swarming. He was fifteen, not even a cop. As for the rest…

"Murder weapon?" asked Jacquot, pulling out a chair, checking it for blood before sitting down.

"He's got a few knives in the drawer there, the usual stuff," Grenier replied, "but nothing sharp enough. Whoever did it came prepared."

"Any sign of the Dupay haul?"

"Nothing so far," said Bernie, joining them in the kitchen. "I've been through his drawers, cupboards... not a thing."

"The briefcase?"

Grenier shook his head.

"Gun?"

Another shake of the head from both men.

"So someone pays a visit, sees the haul, and takes off with it. Puts Loum down because that's the easiest option."

"Makes sense," said Grenier.

"The question is, did they know he had what he had?"

"Tappers work alone. Maybe some friend called by? Maybe someone he owed money to? He's got track marks. A dealer maybe?"

Jacquot pushed back his chair, squatted down and turned one of Loum's arms; pushed up the sleeve of his sweat shirt. A staggered line of angry pinprick puncture marks tracked up the inside of his elbow.

"You find any kit?"

"The usual," said Bernie. "In a bedside drawer."

"Is he married? Girlfriend? Ex?"

"Rap sheet doesn't mention any relationship. No kids, nothing."

Jacquot was about to straighten up when his eye was caught by something in the pool of blood beneath the table. He got down on his knees and peered at the dull scarlet puddle, smoothly rounded at its edges where the blood had begun to clot and dry. A few centimetres in from the edge was

34

what looked like a tiny bump in the surface. A tooth, he wondered? He reached forward, put a thumb and forefinger around it, and lifted it out. The blood was cold and sticky. He stood up, went to the sink. Grenier moved aside.

"You got something?"

Using the side of his hand, Jacquot turned on the tap. Water gushed out and he held whatever it was under the rinsing stream.

"Would you look at that," said Grenier, peering over Jacquot's shoulder.

A pearl. More grey than cream.

With a gold spike.

An earring.

11

It would be Jacquot's last call of the day.

After dropping Chevin at police headquarters he'd taken the squad car, driven round the old port and followed the road for Malmousque. The pearl earring he'd found in Loum's basement flat had been sealed in an evidence bag and was lying on the passenger seat beside him.

The Dupay residence was at the end of a cul-de-sac, a walled estate rising up the side of a hill and overlooking the coast. The stone-block walls were high enough, and the gardens beyond them well-stocked enough with cypress and palm, to hide all but a corner of a distant pantiled roof. Jacquot drew up at a set of closed wood gates, reached out and pressed the call button on a wall-mounted entryphone panel.

"*Oui?*" A woman's voice.

"Chief Inspector Jacquot, to see Monsieur Dupay."

nts later the wood gates parted, slid smoothly and soundlessly

...usings, and Jacquot followed a winding drive through well-tended grounds to the Dupay residence. Two floors, wedding-cake white, with pale blue shutters and an elaborately worked wrought-iron balcony running the length of the upper floor. On the raised ground floor, shaded by the balcony above, was a wide cream marble terrace that ran from corner to corner, furnished with cane armchairs and sofas, and reached by a balustraded rise of stone steps. An impressive property, turn-of-the-century, Jacquot guessed, with at least a hectare of land. A good address, and no mistake. The kind of home you'd have to be a very successful businessman to own.

The high, panelled front doors opened before he had reached them and a maid in black dress and white apron smiled, welcomed him with the tiniest curtsey, and ushered him into an open-plan salon whose far wall was a set of sliding glass panels that led to a rear terrace where Dupay was on the phone. Dressed in a light blue polo neck and darker blue cotton chinos, he turned, gestured for Jacquot to join him, then carried on with his call as though there was no visitor to consider.

Which gave Jacquot time to take in, and savour, the quite extraordinary view, better by far than any he'd seen in Marseilles. Only the belvedere heights of Notre-Dame de la Garde came close. To his right, in the far distance, the sun had set behind the headlands of the Côte Bleue, leaving a deep gold and scarlet sky that the waters of the Golfe du Lion seemed to mirror, its shifting breadth gilded and rosy, and the rocky shores of the usually sun-blanched islands of Frioul turned a shadowy blue in the evening light. Ahead, and to his left, a striped toothbrush lawn sloped down to a line of palms, and above these he could see the twinkling promenade lights of Prado and the distant chalky bluffs of Mont Redon darkening in the evening light. Even the air was different here, he decided, taking a deep breath. No city fumes, no foul smell of refuse, just the calming scent of a freshly mown lawn and a silent, churning sea.

"Chief Inspector."

Jacquot turned quickly, a little surprised by the interruption. For a moment he'd forgotten where he was, and why, and who he'd come to see.

"Monsieur Dupay... My apologies... My attention was... I'm afraid your view got the better of me."

"A fine prospect, is it not? And a good time to be here, to see it like this. It was Camille's favourite time of day." Dupay's voice was as tight and brusque as it had been that morning in Jacquot's office, with no real sense of interest in the view, and nor, Jacquot noted, with any particular softness when he mentioned his wife's name. "So," he said, catching Jacquot's arm and steering him towards the salon, going in ahead of him when they reached the glass doors. "How can I help you?" He glanced at his watch. "I have a meeting to attend in town, so...?" He had perched himself on the arm of a long leather sofa, while Jacquot stood.

"I'd be grateful if you could identify this piece of jewellery, monsieur," Jacquot replied. Down to business suited him fine. He reached for his pocket, drew out the plastic evidence bag with the earring he'd found, and handed it to Dupay. "We believe it may have belonged to your wife."

Dupay opened the bag, shook out the earring into his palm and stared at it for a few moments. He picked it up, turned it in the light, his fingers long and delicate, the nails finely manicured.

"My wife's, yes. No question." He dropped the earring into the bag and handed it back to Jacquot. "There will be a note of it somewhere – a receipt, a description, for insurance, if you need it?"

"That would be useful, monsieur."

"And where was it found?"

"In the home of the man who robbed her."

"And killed her, Chief Inspector." A cool, cold correction. "So, you have found him? You have made an arrest?"

"He's dead."

Dupay frowned, considered this. He seemed disappointed, as though a deal had gone wrong and he'd failed to get what he wanted.

"So, that's it? The investigation is over?"

Jacquot nodded. "All we can do now is try to find whoever killed him, and then locate the rest of your wife's jewellery. Do you have any idea of its value?"

Dupay spread his hands. "It will be with the insurance details, the exact value, but I would say somewhere around two hundred, three hundred thousand. Thereabouts. Maybe more."

"I would also like to know if your wife owned a briefcase, and if she had it with her last night?"

"Of course she did, a birthday gift from me. But whether she took it with her... I really can't say." Dupay gave Jacquot a long level gaze, then got to his feet. "But, of course, I will check with Trudi, our nanny. I'm sure she can tell us. So, if that's all, Chief Inspector?"

"Thank you for your time, monsieur. I will let you know if there are any developments."

To which Dupay nodded, as though it was only to be expected, not worth saying. And, as if on cue, the maid in black dress and apron re-appeared to show Jacquot the way out. Their meeting was over. He'd been dismissed.

Back in his car, leaning forward to turn on the engine, Jacquot looked up at the house. There were no lights from the windows on the upper floor, just dark rectangles beyond the balcony railings. No sign of the boy, Lucien. And no sign of the nanny, Trudi. Strange, thought Jacquot. At a little after eight it was surely too early for bed, and a ten-year old would certainly still be up, watching television, or playing? Some noise, from somewhere in the house; some activity, some sign of a child's presence – a discarded toy, a colouring book, some clothing. But there had been nothing. As if Dupay and the maid were the only people in the house.

Perhaps the boy had been sent to stay with friends, or relatives? But if he had been, he'd only just gone. Earlier that day, Dupay had told him the nanny and boy were at home. And that's surely where he should have been, at a time like this, after his mother's death; surely, he should have been there with his step-father? To be comforted by him.

Jacquot started the car and turned easily in the forecourt, gravel crunching under the tyres, and headed back down the drive. When he reached the entrance, the gates were opening, and as he turned onto the road he watched them in his rear-view mirror as they started to slide shut behind him.

And *bonsoir* to you, too, thought Jacquot. He was pretty sure he'd never felt such a lack of sympathy for anyone.

12

Madame Foraque, Jacquot's concierge, was waiting for him when he returned to his apartment on Place des Moulins. Or rather, she came bustling out of her *conciergerie* before he'd closed the front door behind him. She was in her seventies, with a tangle of red frizzy hair held under any number of different hats and caps (the brown beret she wore this evening a favourite), a powdered face, rouged cheeks, and eyes as thin and sharp as scalpel blades.

39

Winter or summer she favoured the same outfit: a man's shirt buttoned to the neck with extravagant velvet bows in place of a tie, a woolly angora cardigan which she wrapped around herself rather than buttoning, tucking her hands into its pockets or under her arms to hold it in place, a dark skirt that reached almost to her ankles, thick crumpled stockings, and soft-soled slippers that never made a sound on the hallway tiles.

"You didn't think to let me know?" she began. "Out all night, and not a word. And then those two *flics* turning up this morning, hammering on my door. And all I've got is Salette telling me you're too busy to go sailing with him. Called it off. Broke the old boy's heart, you have. How he was looking forward to it, I tell you. And for what?"

Jacquot knew there was no way he could reach the stairs without an explanation, but Madame Foraque hadn't finished.

"It's that Dupay woman, isn't it? Dreadful. Heard it on the news. And all her good work for those poor children, the homeless, and everything else. Sometimes what the good Lord plans is beyond our understanding. And you, of all people, to run the investigation. Salette told me. And you just a slip of a boy. Pah!"

"A Chief Inspector slip to be precise. I thought you'd be pleased."

"Pleased? Staying out all night like you do. It's more worry than I can think on. And you'll be needing your sleep now, if you're to deal with that Dupay fellow. Slippery piece of work, if ever there was one. And his wife such an angel." Madame Foraque shook her head. "And there's another thing beyond our understanding."

Like Dupay, Jacquot glanced at his watch. Maybe it would work on Madame Foraque. It didn't.

"Pah! No time to sail with old Salette. No time to talk to your caring *concierge*. If that's the way you want it, *tant pis* is what I say. Good riddance,

40

too." And with that, Madame Foraque tightened her cardigan, gave a shrug of her shoulders, and tottered back to her door. "And don't forget, rent's due Monday. Or else."

An hour later, Jacquot mashed out the joint he'd been smoking, left his narrow rooftop terrace and went to bed – staring at the ceiling, watching the play of headlight beams from passing traffic, and hearing far off the long mournful hoot of a merchantman heading for sea.

A slippery piece of work indeed, thought Jacquot, and closed his eyes.

13

Saturday morning, early, Jacquot tiptoed across the tiled floor of the hallway, eased open the front door with the care of a cat burglar, and slid out onto Place des Moulins. He'd even managed to slip an envelope with his month's rent under her door without alerting her. A good start to the day, he decided, as he walked across the square and turned to the right, trotting down a flight of steps onto rue des Muettes. Hands in his pockets, collar up, under a sky the glittering silver of fish scales, Jacquot followed a familiar criss-cross of cobbled alleyways until he reached the wider, busier thoroughfares of rue Sainte-Françoise and rue de l'Évêché. Twelve minutes from bedroom to desk. An agreeable commute.

He supposed he shouldn't have been too surprised to find the third-floor squad room so busy, so early in the day, given the murder of Madame Dupay not thirty-six hours earlier, and the discovery of Adam Loum's body just the day before, but the bustle was more than he'd expected.

"Full house," he said to Laganne.

"Any minute now, just Charlie and 'Stut-Stut' to show up," Laganne replied, chewing a toothpick as he followed Jacquot to his office. 'Stut-Stut' was how they all referred to the stutterer, Chevin, but only when he wasn't within earshot. If he was, you were on your own.

"Anything new?"

"Just the quickest forensics and ballistics reports in the entire history of mankind." Laganne dropped the files he'd been carrying on Jacquot's desk. "Phoned through yesterday, with written reports this morning."

Jacquot scanned the sheets. "Makarov 9mm; prints for the tapper, Loum, on the shell and casing. Anything else?"

Laganne shook his head. Nothing they didn't already know.

"But what we do have is two address books," he continued. "One fancy, one not. The first, the fancy one, was found in the glove compartment of Madame Dupay's Mercedes. Suede cover, gold page trim, some Paris outfit – Gucci? The other one just a dog-eared notebook, by the phone at Loum's place. The boys are going through them now... the usual follow-ups."

Jacquot knew the pitch. Name by name, calling up one number after another. With the news of Madame Dupay's murder in the newspapers, on TV and radio, it was unlikely that any of his team would have to break the news of her death. Instead they would make the usual enquiries – what was your relationship with the deceased? When did you last see Madame Dupay? How did she seem? Eighty per cent of these enquiries over the phone would come to nothing, provide no positive lead. Those names that remained on the list, those of interest, would be asked if an officer might call around?

That was how it would go with Madame Dupay's friends. Professional, polite, and courteous. It would be an altogether different approach with Monsieur Loum. No phone calls, just a trawl through Records to check the names in his address book, to see if anything came up. And if it did, it wouldn't be a phone call to start the ball rolling, it would be a visit. Fist to the door. Early morning.

"Who's handling the Dupay list?"

"Who do you think?"

Jacquot nodded. He needn't have asked. Al Grenier and Claude Peluze, the two elder statesmen of the squad room, the pair of them with soft, comforting voices and, when needed, some reliable old-school manners.

As for Loum's contacts, it would be Charlie or Luc in their black jeans and leather zip-ups who'd be banging on doors. With 'Stut-Stut' and Bernie providing back-up.

"You need anything?" asked Laganne, turning for the door.

"A killer, maybe two?"

"Leave that to you, boss."

14

The Records Office for the Marseilles *Judiciaire* was in the basement of police headquarters, on Jacquot's side of the building's central courtyard. A long, low-ceilinged room lit with fluorescent panels and pavement-level wired windows, lined with filing cabinets as grey as oyster shells, and furnished with rows of metal-framed library shelving that ran the length of the room, each shelf packed with boxes of filed case-work. Along one section of wall stood a line of micro-fiche readers. Five screens, five counters, and five swivel chairs neatly nested, now rarely used. The office was run by Sergeant Lefèbre, who'd taken a shotgun blast to the leg ten years earlier. Rather than opt for an early retirement and generous pension, the old boy had elected to stay on. He was a widower, with kids who'd grown up by the time his wife died, so rue de l'Évêché was as much his home as the three-bedroom apartment he owned on rue des Refuges. A shorter commute than Jacquot's by about eight minutes.

Of course, Jacquot could have used the new desk-top computer that had been installed in his office the previous afternoon to access any information he might need, but that Saturday morning he decided that a visit to Lefèbre in the basement might prove more productive. The old trouper's days in charge of the Records Office might be coming to an end any time now, but he was as much a fund of knowledge as the contents of any filing cabinet or library shelf, or indeed any computer. There was nothing he didn't seem to know. As though he had read every file, every newspaper micro-film stored in that basement, and remembered every word and image. And he prided himself on the fact. Not many of the boys upstairs bothered to visit Records any more. Increasingly, there was no need. But Jacquot had always had a soft spot for the man, and Lefèbre for Jacquot. And Jacquot knew that Lefèbre would give him all he needed.

Jacquot found him at his desk, a sturdy walking stick hung over the back of his chair and a hinged calliper over the left leg of his uniform trousers. He was tall and bulky, with a slight stoop, a tight crop of rippled grey hair, twinkly grey eyes, and a cleft in his chin that you could hide a file in. For all his subterranean existence he had a healthy tan to face and hands. When he wasn't at his desk he fished from the breakwaters of Joliette, and it showed. It didn't take long to notice that the old boy's desk-top computer was unplugged.

"I'd stand and salute, if I could do it quickly enough," said Lefèbre, as Jacquot pushed through the swing doors that led to his domain. "Chief Inspector, I hear tell."

"News travels fast, even down here."

44

"Faster upstairs, by all accounts, and in every regard. Damn computers everywhere. But every now and then, you know, word filters down to these shadowy depths."

"I brought you a coffee, from Hamid's. White, two sugars, right?" Jacquot put the lidded Styrofoam cup on the desk, and reached for his cigarettes, offered one, which Lefèbre took and lit.

"Coffee and a cigarette. Now I know I'm going to have to work for my living," said Lefèbre, eyeing Jacquot suspiciously, but with a hint of a grin. Blowing out a plume of smoke. Clearly pleased that someone still needed him.

"Dupay. Alain and Camille. Ring any bells?"

"Cathedral bells. Deafening." He tipped the lid off his coffee, stirred it with a pencil.

"And?"

"Where would you like me to start?"

"Wherever or whenever it gets interesting."

"Then we should start at the beginning. Take a chair, Chief."

Jacquot did as he was told, made himself comfortable, and lit a cigarette.

"Two families," began Lefèbre. "One rich, one poor. Madame Dupay is a Guichot-Navarre. *Ancien régime*, back past the revolution. Landowners, mostly. Here, and in Spain. After her mother's death, when Camille was thirteen or fourteen, she was brought up by her father. A war hero, big in the Resistance. Every gong going. But a daredevil, a gambler. What was left of the family's money and holdings he lost through a poor business head and extravagant tastes. When he died back in the seventies, Camille discovered the true extent of those tastes. After she'd settled up his accounts, she was left with a small apartment on the Vieux Port. *C'était tout.*"

45

"How old?"

"Early twenties… thereabouts."

"She's done well."

"A worker. And smart. Everything her father wasn't. After his death she started as a cleaner – a *femme de ménage*, would you believe? – but within a couple of years she'd set up her own agency for property maintenance. Private contracts to start – apartments, houses, holiday homes from here to Cassis – and then corporate and State. In ten years she'd sold the apartment on the Vieux Port and moved into a penthouse out on Kennedy."

"And met Dupay."

"Who's her second husband. The first died in a car crash, leaving her a single mother. Dupay was one of her first corporate deals. An office block off Paradis. That's where it started."

"And Dupay?"

"Always a sharp operator. But a real *mec*, too; a piece of work. Grew up wild in Toulon where his Dad was a market trader. Learned all the tricks, he did, or rather the important one. How to make money. One way or the other. If he has any scruples, he uses them to link his cuffs. The rest of him is as cold as iced fish."

"No record?"

"Not a thing."

"So how do you know all this?"

"I grew up in Toulon, too. My dad was a cop. Well, coastguard to be precise. So there were plenty of stories doing the rounds. This, that, and the other. Got into some serious smuggling, he did, shifting contraband, but there was never enough to have him bless the court with an appearance."

"And his company? DupayCorp? How did that happen?"

46

"After a few close shaves he was smart enough to go straight. Or rather, he appeared to go straight. He set up a financial services outfit in Aix, starting with insurance – personal and property – before branching out with a small investment fund. Property development at first – commercial and residential – before moving in to the financial markets and trading stocks and shares."

"Where did the start-up money come from?"

"All above board, but who can say? Sometimes it's not easy telling the difference between clean and dirty money. And he certainly had the contacts. All his running mates from Toulon days."

"How old was he?" Jacquot leaned forward, and butted out his cigarette.

Lefèbre took one last pull, and did the same. "Late thirties, by then."

"So how come you still know about him?"

"I read the newspapers, Chief Inspector. And his name is always cropping up. Photos, too. Business and gossip pages. A performer in both arenas. And business was booming. Head office here in Marseilles, and associated offices in Aix, Montpellier, Toulon, Fréjus... Slick-suited, always the prettiest girl on his arm."

"And Madame Dupay?"

"Like I said, he got her company to clean his offices. Here in Marseilles to start, and then all of them. Helped her branch out, too. Office design and refurbishment."

"And arranged her investments?"

Lefèbre shook his head. "Maybe she took his advice, but she did it all herself. Hands off. My business, my profits. She was no fool."

"But she married him."

"Like I said, not so foolish. And they've cut a path, the pair of them. A power couple here in Marseilles. Every big party – first nights, gallery openings, you name it. And he put in a lot of funding. Anything she liked, any good cause, he stepped up to the mark. Her name, his money. It worked."

"Did she know he was dodgy?"

Lefébre sighed. "By the time they got together it wouldn't have been too easy to tell. A *mec* he might have been but, like I said, he was smart; nothing ever stuck. Maybe he really has gone straight. It's just... I can't quite see it."

Taking the lift back to the third floor, Jacquot decided that the time he'd spent with Sergeant Lefèbre had provided more insight than any computer. It would be a sad day for all of them when Lefèbre handed in his stripes and limped away.

Sometimes the old ways were best.

15

Luc Dutoit was waiting for him when Jacquot returned to the squad room.

"We got a lead on Loum."

"And?"

"Woman who lives on Daumier, across the road from Loum. She works shifts as a croupier at Club Trente-Six over Noailles. Called an hour ago to say she'd seen two men leaving Loum's place around midnight, just as she left for work."

"Around the time of death."

"Near enough, yes."

"She took her time calling it in."

"Shift work. Back home before we found him, and out for the count. Got in touch as soon as she heard about it."

"Description?"

"She said she couldn't see their faces, but she reckoned they were late twenties, early thirties. The way they walked, she said, was like a kind of swaggering lope. Not quite a run, but in a hurry. One was tall, and one short. Drove off in a blue Renault. No registration, before you ask, but here's something you'll like."

"You have my undivided attention."

"One of them was carrying a briefcase."

Jacquot whistled. "Good one, Luc. Now what we need..."

"Already done."

Jacquot shot him a questioning look.

"Soon as we got the news, we put out some calls. Claude and me. Lorry driver first of all. Was he sure about the briefcase? He was. The guy was carrying a briefcase, no question. Then we worked the names we got on Daumier, door to door. Called them up. Did Loum ever carry a briefcase? No one we spoke to had ever seen him with one. Couple of them just laughed. A backpack now and again, slung over his shoulder, but never a briefcase."

"Which means he must have got it from Madame Dupay. Must have done. Part of the haul."

"Can't see it any other way."

"Anything in the address books? Loum's and Dupay's."

Claude and Al are still working on Dupay. If, like you said, she was coming back from a meeting in L'Estaque, there's no one they've spoken to so far who's said they saw her Thursday. But they're still checking. As for

Loum, there's a few names come up on file. Small timers, tappers like him; couple of dealers."

"Good place to start." Jacquot looked round the squad room. It was the usual scene. A thin layer of bluey-grey smoke hovering below the ceiling panels, telephones shouldered, ties unknotted, a low muttering of voices. "Why don't you get Charlie and Etienne and start knocking on doors. Knocking them down, if needs be."

"Sounds good to me. Oh, by the way, you got a call while you were out. The new Examining Magistrate, Madame Solange Bonnefoy. Boulard's replacement. She'd like a word."

"I'll call her Monday. When we've got something to give her."

Luc shook his head. "Not an option, boss. Lunch, today, she said. She'll be at Bistrot Savarin, one o'clock. Rue Montgrand, near the Palais de Justice."

16

The fish-scale sky that had filled the gaps between Le Panier's rooftops on Jacquot's early morning walk to rue de l'Évêché had turned to a soft spring blue as he set off from police headquarters for rue Montgrand and the Bistrot Savarin. An hour with Lefèbre in the basement Records Office, and the rest of the morning in his squad room, had been enough to see off the day's uncertain start without Jacquot noticing. He still had to keep his collar up, but there was warmth and promise in the air. If only the Dupay case could boast the same credentials. A woman murdered, her killer murdered. They might be progressing with the investigation, but what they'd learned so far would be nothing more than an appetising starter for the newly-appointed Examining Magistrate.

Jacquot had never met, never even seen, *Maître* Bonnefoy, but he knew all about her. A deadly prosecutor, and a stickler for detail. In the four months since taking up her post, she had proved herself not only an adroit administrator and convincing counsel but she had also been the bane of his predecessor's life. Whenever Guderoi came back to the squad room after a meeting with Bonnefoy, his face would be as red as a boiled beetroot, and his temper as short as an eyelash. For an hour or more afterwards, he would have a handkerchief in his hand to wipe away the spittle that would gather on his thick red lips whenever he spoke, in a voice squeezed tight with fury. Which was one of the reasons Jacquot was looking forward to his lunch with Madame Bonnefoy. Anyone who could wind up Guderoi like that was worth knowing. And if his own encounter turned out to be a bruising one, which he had every reason to believe it might, thanks to the lack of any real progress in the murders of Madame Dupay and Adam Loum, then at least there was the prospect of a very fine lunch to ease the pain, at one of the law profession's favourite watering holes.

From Monday to Friday most of Bistrot Savarin's clientele might have shrugged off their gowns, but few would have bothered to remove their white-collared *rabats*. And there would be a lot of them, too, huddled at their tables in what was little more than the Palais de Justice canteen. Those who didn't sport this signature neckwear were either high-end plaintiffs or defendants, or solicitors, or senior-ranking clerks and other officials of the court invited *à table* by those same advocates. To discuss a case, plan strategies, explore avenues.

But never cops. Not at Bistrot Savarin. No matter how high up the greasy pole an officer managed to rise, or how crucial their role in a pending case. Why waste public money on the running dogs when the lawyers of Bistrot Savarin knew they could get whatever they wanted through official channels? A summons to appear in an advocate's chambers was as much as a *flic* could hope for or, in most cases, fear. Which meant that an invitation to Bistrot Savarin was certainly a point in Madame Bonnefoy's favour, even if, on a Saturday, the corridors of the Palais de Justice were as empty as a picked pocket.

It was a brisk twenty-minute walk to rue Montgrand, enough to work up an appetite, and when he pushed open the door Jacquot knew he wouldn't be disappointed. The warming scent of garlic and sweet onions in the air, twists of rosemary, and the sharper hint of fennel; red gingham tablecloths, bentwood chairs, and ancient coat racks; blackened, twisted beams to walls and ceiling, and a worn wooden floor that creaked underfoot. The ceiling was low, and the Bistrot's interior suitably dark and confidential. A dining room used to secrets, Jacquot could tell, with a dozen tables set judicially apart so that those secrets might not be too easily shared.

Even on a Saturday, with its most regular clientele out of the city for the weekend, the place was still busy. Only two tables remained empty, in the window recesses either side of the door. The Savarin's Siberia, Jacquot decided. Too visible, and too drafty. As he closed the door behind him and stepped between these tables, he saw the Bistrot's balding patron look up from behind a hammered zinc bar and frown. The man was large and big-boned, with a beefy neck and solid shoulders, his ears oddly crumpled and swollen. A boxer maybe, but more likely a rugby player, Jacquot decided, the damaged cartilege a testament to his years in the scrum. He was also a man who knew a cop when he saw one, and was equally surprised that one should walk through his door, even on a Saturday.

"Chief Inspector Jacquot, for Madame Bonnefoy," said Jacquot, pausing at the *zinc* and looking around. He couldn't see the examining magistrate anywhere, nor anyone who came close to the description he had of her, but when he turned back to the bar the patron's expression had changed from suspicion to a kind of wide-eyed disbelief. And it wasn't Jacquot's casual acknowledgement that, yes, he was, indeed, a policeman, and that he was looking for Madame Bonnefoy that had caused this shift. It was something else, something that Jacquot had grown used to over the years. That sudden recognition. Not just a policeman, not just a Chief Inspector, but the man. The man himself. Daniel Jacquot. Number Six. The pony-tailed wing-forward who had come on as substitute in the closing minutes of a rain-swept Five Nations final, who'd snatched the ball from an English scrum-half and set off down the length of the Twickenham pitch to score the winning try. 'You'll never buy a drink again,' one of his team-mates had told him, and he was right. Sixteen seconds, that was all it took to make that mud-clogged run, and all these years later he was still remembered, and recognised, for that mighty effort. For beating *les Rosbifs* on their own turf. A nod, a smile... Or that look of dawning, delighted disbelief now working its way across the patron's face.

"If I'm not mistaken, monsieur, aren't you–?" the man began.

"It was a long time ago," said Jacquot, falling back on the familiar disclaimer, with a dismissive wave of the fingers. "Just a lucky break. One of those things."

"Lucky break? I saw it. I was there. In the stands. It was... magic. A wonderful... miracle."

"You look like you played yourself?" Jacquot countered, in a further attempt to redirect the conversation, tipping his head to nod at the man's ears.

"*Bouf*, small time. A couple of seasons as tight-head prop with the B team, RC Toulonnais," he said, coming from behind the bar, and reaching for Jacquot's hand. A hearty shake, a clap on the shoulder. "Grégoire

Malherbe's the name, though you won't have heard of it. An honour to meet you, monsieur, and to have you here at Bistrot Savarin."

And then the man's shoulders slumped, as though suddenly pained, as though he could have stood there all afternoon chatting with Jacquot, the man who'd made that run. "But I mustn't detain you. Madame Bonnefoy, you said? Let me show you to her table."

17

Jacquot wouldn't have spotted Solange Bonnefoy, even if he'd known what she looked like, because her table was in the furthest reaches of the room behind a thick stone column. When Malherbe reached it, he stood aside and extended his hand. *Voilà.* The lady herself. She looked up from an open file, gave Jacquot a smile of welcome, and waved him to a chair.

"Thank you, Grégoire. How kind," she said, her voice an odd mix of soft and sharp.

"*Maître* Bonnefoy," Jacquot began, settling into his chair and nodding at the file. "I hope I haven't kept you waiting?"

"The police have always had an irritating habit of keeping me waiting. Me, and every other examining magistrate. I can only trust that, given your attempt at punctuality, it is your intention to set matters straight." She gave him another smile; questioning, quietly amused.

"I shall do my very best, *Maître.*"

"And doubtless time will tell if that is sufficient to the task. Please, take a look at the menu. Grégoire knows my tastes and will deliver accordingly. Which would be a good habit to take up, Chief Inspector." Another quiet smile. "And my congratulations on your promotion, by the

54

way. Relieved congratulations, I'd like to think. As you may know, I was not a fan of your predecessor."

"Nor he of you, madame."

"Which is enormously satisfying to hear." She smiled again, as if at a fond memory. But then the smile faded, and she gave a tiny shudder. "To have to work with such a man, it was a torment; a true test of my patience. How he lasted so long…"

"Not an easy or pleasant introduction to the office of examining magistrate. You have my sympathies, and my congratulations, of course. New kids on the block, the pair of us."

Without waiting for a response Jacquot picked up his menu, flipped it open, and glanced at the two pages. *Table d'hôte* on the left, *À la carte* on the right. Three starters, four main courses, and three desserts for the *table d'hôte*, and a longer list of Savarin classics for the *à la carte*, priced accordingly. He knew immediately what he would have, but pondered a few moments more, as though still undecided, to take in his companion.

She may have been sitting, but it was clear that *Maître* Bonnefoy was a tall woman, with a cap of wavy grey hair, a long face and hollowed cheeks. Somewhere in her early forties, Jacquot decided. In addition to this, he noted her hands were thin and delicate, fingers too, nails short and unvarnished, her eyes a bright twinkling brown. She wore no make-up that Jacquot could detect, and no jewellery either, beyond a man's watch strapped tightly under her cuff. Since she hadn't stood up to greet him, he could only guess that the cream jacket she wore would be part of a trouser suit, and that the blue topcoat and black scarf that hung from a brass hook on the stone column beside their table were hers.

It was also abundantly clear, even after such a brief initial exchange, that his companion was as sharp as a winter's morning, the possessor of a sparkling intelligence. The way she used the language, chose her words, gave them heft and weight – exactly what every good advocate should do, but few managed quite so well. And though her conversation may have been clipped, and direct, Jacquot sensed that beneath the surface there was humour there, and understanding, though he knew those qualities would forever be in limited supply for those who tested her. Little wonder that Guderoi, in their short time together, had loathed her so enthusiastically. It was almost his duty, Jacquot decided, to make up for his predecessor's failings. But then, did he have any other choice? Only time would tell, as she herself had said.

While Jacquot idled over the menu, he watched his companion finish her reading, close the file and slide it into a large tote beside her chair, straighten herself and reach for her napkin. As she arranged it over her lap, he put aside the menu and smiled.

"I have always heard good things of the Bistrot Savarin, but I have never been here."

"Named after a lawyer, did you know?"

"Jean Anthelme Brillat-Savarin. A politican, too. Deputy for the Estates-General at the start of the Revolution. But, happily for you and I, a noted gastronome and *bon viveur*. A writer, too."

For a moment, *Maître* Bonnefoy looked surprised, though her expression of that surprise was just the flickering of a raised eyebrow.

"'*The Physiology of Taste*'," she began, after a pause. "Such a demanding read, I'm sure you'll agree. But what I do so love about Brillat-Savarin is how he doesn't bother with telling us how to cook the food, but how to think about it. So important. Such a... wise man." Her grey eyes fixed firmly on Jacquot. "'Tell me what you eat; and I will tell you what you are,'" she said.

"I trust I won't give too much away," Jacquot managed.

"I certainly hope you do," she said, with a light chuckle that was warm and genuine. "I'm rather relying on it."

At that moment, Malherbe re-appeared bearing a silver salver with two flutes of champagne. With a flourishing serve, he stood back, nodded at the champagne and wished them enjoyment of it.

Once again, *Maître* Bonnefoy looked taken aback. After Malherbe had retreated, she said, "Extraordinary. In all the time I have come here I have never known Monsieur Malherbe to be quite so... generous." She picked up her flute, swirled the wine, watched the lines of bubbles sway. "A judge, on occasion, might be offered a *digestif*, at the conclusion of a celebrated case, say, but an examining magistrate?" She shook her head. And then, "Ah, but I think I understand. Our patron is a rugby man, is he not? And so, too, I believe, are you?"

So she'd done her homework, thought Jacquot. And he wondered what else she might have found out about him.

"A long time ago, *Maître*. In the mists of time. And best left there. For me, the past is a room with the lights off. It seems safer that way."

"Only if you have things you wish to forget, surely? Or hide?"

"Too many to list. The bad... and the good."

"I always rather like men with a past."

"Chief Inspector Guderoi had a past."

"Ah, say no more."

Once again, Malherbe was back at their table.

"Madame *Maître, à vot' plaisir*," he said, with a smile and a tip of the head.

"My usual, Grégoire. And the Bandol."

"And for you, Chief Inspector?"

57

Jacquot knew his companion would be watching him, waiting.

"The special, *s'il vous plaît*. The sardine *beignets*, and the grilled *Dorade*. Green salad, new potatoes."

"*Bien sûr*, monsieur," said Malherbe, and hurried off.

"So, what have I managed to give away?" Jacquot asked, turning back to Bonnefoy.

"I'm sure we'll find out," she countered, and then, in the blink of an eye, the niceties were put aside and business took their place.

"So, the Dupays. Where are we?"

"Two days in, and some developments."

"Which are?"

"The man who robbed Madame Dupay–"

"Shot her to death."

" –is Adam Loum. Gambian. And he, too, is dead."

Maître Bonnefoy cocked her head.

"He was found yesterday. We were following up a prints match on a shell casing and on Madame Dupay's car."

"Murdered?"

"A beating, and a cut throat."

"Where?"

"In his home. Not long after his 'tap' on Madame Dupay."

"Could there be a connection, any kind of link? His murder, her murder."

Jacquot shrugged. "None that I can see. He was just a tapper, and a user, looking for a few thousand to see him through. Madame Dupay was just a chance encounter. For her, wrong time, wrong place. For him, just a job. Do it and run, though I doubt he meant to shoot her; there must have been some kind of struggle, the lady not wishing to give up her valuables.

And then, a few hours later, it's his turn. Someone comes round to collect a debt, or drop off the next wrap, sees the haul and decides to take it. In this instance there were two assailants, which would match a drug delivery or debt collection. One to hold him for the beating, the other to weigh in."

Monsieur Malherbe returned with their wine. A white Bandol, Jacquot observed. The cork was pulled, the wine poured, tasted, and approved with a clipped nod and equally clipped smile.

"And this haul, Madame Dupay's jewellery?" asked Madame Bonnefoy, when Malherbe had gone. "What this Loum character stole."

"No sign of it. Just an earring, which Monsieur Dupay has identified."

"And what did you make of Monsieur Dupay?"

"Not a man who could be a friend."

Another cock of the head.

Jacquot spread his hands. "Not a man I would trust."

"Does he know that this Loum, his wife's killer, is dead?"

"Yes, he does."

"His response?"

"I had the feeling he wished the man was still alive. So he could see him pay for his crime, and provide some kind of resolution. He struck me as an-eye-for-an-eye kind of man."

"So, what next?"

"With Loum's death, the murder of Madame Dupay is now case closed. But his own murder remains an ongoing investigation. And I'd like to find the jewellery, if I can. Monsieur Dupay has sent a list of items with descriptions and photos. Right now we're working through Loum's contacts to see if we can find something."

"So, we seem to have a sense of direction. And the investigation appears to be moving forward. Good," said Madame Bonnefoy, and then, glancing over his shoulder. "But here comes our lunch, Chief Inspector."

The next instant Malherbe was back at their table.

Serving two dishes of the sardine *beignets*.

The same starters.

Madame Bonnefoy caught Jacquot's eye, and smiled.

"And for my entrée," she said, picking up one of her crisply floured *beignets* and biting off its head, "Monsieur Malherbe will bring me my *Dorade*. And you, yours. Let us hope that this... agreement, this... pleasing synchronicity, bodes well, Chief Inspector."

18

The pistachios were never shelled. Just a glint of green flesh and purple husk through the parted lips of the shell. Roasted. And lightly salted. Only from Kerman Province, in Iran; nowhere else. Purchased by Burak Imports in sealed twelve-kilo bags, from the merchant, Qasem Nafisi, in Tehran's Sadzé Grand Bazaar; a day's supply kept in a silver box on Burak's desk.

Sometimes Burak would take a handful, breaking open the nuts and tossing them back in quick succession from a closed fist.

Bitten into, quickly chewed, swallowed.

And another, and another.

Until his fat red lips were tight and sticky with the salt.

Other times, when something weighed on his mind, the old Turk would reach for the silver box, finger his way through its contents and select just a single nut, prise its shell apart with the hardened tips of his thumbnails, and pop the soft green kernel into his mouth. A contemplative swirl of the tongue, removing any trace of husk, and then a long pleasurable chew. This was what Burak was doing, sprawled back on a tapestried divan in the corner of his office on Châteauredon, when his assistant, Javad Dalan, knocked on the door and entered.

"*Effendi*," he said, with a short bow. The man was thin and wiry, hands clasped behind his back, head lowered and tipped to one side. He wore jeans, leather slippers, and a woolly red jumper a size too big for him.

"I've decided I want the boy here."

"He's safe where he is, Osman says." Their Turkish was formal. Dalan deferential, Burak bored.

"No matter what Osman says. It's what I say. And I want the boy here."

Dalan recognised the tone. A decision had been made. There was no room for manoeuvre. When Burak wanted something, Burak got it.

"Shall I call and let him know?"

"I think you should. The young one will be happier, more comfortable, here."

But not for long, thought Dalan. Once here, he'd see and hear too much; could never be released – to identify, to testify. But Dalan kept his counsel. "Shall I prepare somewhere for him, *effendi*?"

"The room beneath your office? Is it suitable?"

"I can have it made so."

"Then see to it."

"When should I have him here?"

"Without delay. Tonight would be good."

Dalan bowed again, just a nod of the head this time. "I shall see that it is done, *effendi*."

19

They worked well together, no question. After his first few days as Cap or *Capitaine*, or, as likely, Dan, Danny, or *patron*, Jacquot was pleased to note that the homicide team on rue de l'Évêché treated him no differently from Guderoi's time, when he'd been one of them. If he asked for something, it was done. With an agreeing nod, no argument; as though the request made sense, or they hadn't thought of it themselves. And that's all there was to it. More comradely, than an order given and followed.

Jacquot wasn't the oldest or the youngest on the squad. Old Grenier took the former slot, and Charlie Serre, somewhere in his early thirties, took the latter. And every one of them had worked enough cases on the Marseilles Homicide Division – not to mention time in other departments and in various postings in other *judiciaires* – to know the game and play it. A team. What Jacquot loved about life as a cop. One of a team.

Which was why, at first sight, the new boy looked like he might be a liability, wouldn't fit in.

According to the file on Jacquot's desk his name was Michel Rully, a computer sciences graduate from the University of Montpellier and Les Quilliers police academy who had spent three years with Montpellier's Serious Crime unit before requesting a transfer to Marseilles. He would have worn a gun, Jacquot knew, an old Beretta drawn from Armaments, but as chief coffee-getter, ashtray emptier, and dry-cleaning runner, he wouldn't have had much opportunity to use it save a few sessions on the range. As far as Jacquot could remember, not a single one of his team had been near a range since the last obligatory Test Session. But then they didn't need to. They used their guns enough to know how to shoot, and hit, and bring down an opponent. A kill shot if they had to, if they could – to the head, to the heart; but usually just a crippler into the arms or legs. Incapacitated, but still able to talk.

But Michel Rully was still only a couple of levels up from rookie. And looked it. Lace-up black shoes buffed to a shine, pressed grey trousers, blue jacket, and a dark blue tie on a clean white shirt that showed its cuffs. A mop of black hair, a healthy tan, and wide, enthusiastic brown eyes. He was nearly as tall as Laganne, and as sturdy in build as Dutoit, but he looked stiff and wary that Tuesday morning, like a new teacher taking on a class of north-suburb trouble-makers at École Severin; standing there in the squad room door, trying to get someone's attention to ask where he could find Chief Inspector Jacquot.

Jacquot watched him from his office door; raised a hand, waved him over.

"Rully?"

"*Oui, Capitaine.*"

"Come on in, sit down, make yourself at home."

The new boy looked surprised at the informality, but did as he was told.

"Guimpier says you're going to be my assistant. Guderoi never had one, and nor have I, so I give you fair warning I might not be much good at it."

"Then I'll try to make allowances, *Capitaine*," he said, and smiled.

And that was the moment, with that first smile, that Jacquot knew the two of them would get on. The Chief had been right. The previous afternoon Guimpier had handed him Rully's file, and told him to take him under his wing, teach him a thing or two. And when Jacquot had tried to remonstrate, the old boy had patted his arm and said, "You'll like him."

63

And Jacquot did. Despite initial appearances, the young man looked like he could handle himself; on the outside, and with the squad. Tough if he had to be, self-reliant, but there was a gentleness there, too, and honesty. If he had to have an assistant, it might as well be this one.

"I'm sure you'll manage. We all do, somehow."

20

It had been a long day. Chasing up Loum's contacts, now that the Dupay case had been closed, and circulating copies of the jewellery photos that Alain Dupay had sent in following the robbery, and death, of his wife. A watch, necklace, earrings, bracelet, rings. Photos for the city's jewellers, pawn-brokers, and known fences. A reward for information promised to this last group, the most likely recipients. As encouragement.

By now, Rully had removed his jacket, his tie, had a coffee brought to him by Dutoit, and was working through a list of names from Loum's notebook. Contacts that couldn't be found on a first trawl, for any number or reasons: phone numbers disconnected, apartments abandoned, whereabouts currently unknown. Pure grunt work. Telephone never back in its cradle. Just press down the pips, and dial another number, one number after another. So far, he'd drawn a blank with nine of the twenty-odd names on his list; going through previous form sheets looking for any leads – old phone numbers, addresses, known associates – but the options were wearing thin.

"You got someone called Marcel Boultier on your list? Or Marc?" asked Jacquot, stopping at Rully's desk.

Rully didn't need to look. "On him now. Last known address at Marroniers, but moved a couple of years ago. Whereabouts currently–"

"Known," Jacquot interrupted, "so let's get moving."

"Where to?" asked Rully, five minutes later, as he swooped down the ramp out of police headquarters, spun the wheel to the right, and turned into rue de l'Évêché.

"Faranese, the Alfa dealership off Plombières," Jacquot replied, then wondered if Rully would know it, would know how to get there? "You know where it is?"

"Out past St-Charles?"

"That's the one."

"How come a car dealership? Does Boultier work there?"

"He's a customer. Which is what makes it interesting," Jacquot replied, and then he fell silent, turning away from his companion to watch the sidewalks, the shops and shoppers pass, the thin reflection of traffic in store windows, the piled garbage, wondering once again at the small world of Marseilles that he lived in, and thinking of the man they were about to visit.

Gino Faranese was standing in the forecourt when they drove in, the sun glinting off the showroom window behind him. A father and daughter were walking around an old red Citroën in a line of used cars. Faranese had clearly gone through his sales pitch and was standing back while the father gave the car a personal once over, opening the driver's door to point out a scar of rust on the door sill to his daughter, shaking his head. Faranese was wearing his usual working kit: an open-collared white shirt, a lightweight blue jacket whose weave shone in the sunlight, a pair of cream chinos and signature Italian loafers. He was a tall man, deeply tanned, with a hairline that started on the crown of his head; a half-dome of sleek, dyed wavy black hair that curled around his ears and swept down over the back of his collar as though to compensate for the thinness up front.

When Faranese spotted Jacquot he waved, held up a finger. Give me five.

Rully parked by the service-bay doors and Jacquot climbed out, leaned against the squad car, and watched the dealer approach his customer.

Their exchange took two minutes. The words might have been lost beneath the drone of traffic from Plombières, but the nature of the conversation was clear. The father nodded to the open driver's door and rusty sill, pointed to some other failing towards the rear of the car, rubbed his chin, then made an offer. Faranese looked as if he'd received news of a loved one's death. He took a step back, spread his arms and cocked his head to one side. Jacquot could hear that oily Marseillais drawl, punctuated with the sharper, more dramatic Italian flourishes that three generations in the city had never quite diluted. Disbelief, incredulity... Oh, monsieur, please, you must be joking. And so it went, until the father shook his head, the daughter tried hard to swallow her disppointment, and the pair of them walked off.

"He knows his cars, that man," said Faranese, striding over to Jacquot and Rully and shaking their hands. "Knew right off the Citroën was a crock. So, Danny, good to see you again. It's been a long time. How's that rogue, Salette?"

"Said you still owe him a drink, for the race at Borély. And told me you wanted a word."

Faranese looked around, as though checking to make sure that no one was watching them, or within earshot. Just to be sure, he took Jacquot's elbow and led him into the cool darkness of the service bay. A radio was playing, the air smelled of hot oil, and two mechanics were rolled up under a jacked-up Alfa saloon, just boots and work trousers showing.

"Something you might be interested in, nothing more," Faranese began, as though apologising in advance for wasting Jacquot's time.

"Yesterday, this *mec* by the name of Boultier called by, asked to see some of the showroom models we got. New, not used, he tell me. Like he had that kind of money, you know what I'm saying here? Anyway, I take him in, show him what we got, and he goes for the Spider. Like he's already made up his mind. So, look, the Spider's the top model we got. A beauty. Just in off the loader from Turin. The latest Series 3, a two-door soft-top, fuel-injection, 2-litre engine. And she goes like a rocket, like the shit off your shovel, you don't mind me saying. But she cost more money than he'll see all year. I think he's joking, you know? Pulling a fast one. But he wants it. Brings out a wad from one pocket and a wad from the other and just drops them on the bonnet. 500s. No chat, no haggle, just wrap it and I'm off, kind of thing?"

"You know him?"

"Know of him, sure. Back in the day."

One of the mechanics rolled himself out from under the Alfa, got to his feet and walked over to a work bench, started sorting through a selection of wrenches.

Faranese glanced at the mechanic, and lowered his voice. "Ran with a rough crowd, you remember?"

Jacquot did remember. Not Boultier, but the reference. When Jacquot was working his way up to Inspector with the Marseilles *Judiciaire*, Faranese's son, Freddi, had got into trouble. During a routine stop, a kilo of hash had been discovered under the saddle of his Vespa. Jacquot was the one who had found it, but knowing that Freddi's father, Gino, was a friend of Salette, he'd managed to persuade his boss to drop possession and dealing charges for Freddi in return for inside information. Freddi had helped out, and a few months down the line a bigger ring of bad boys had been hauled off to Baumettes. Freddi might have moved on, running his own air-conditioning firm up in Aix, according to Salette, but Gino wasn't the kind of man to forget a favour; knew a debt was a debt. For as long as it took. So, every now and then, he'd call Salette, mention something, see if it might be of interest. For Salette to pass on to Jacquot. The cop who'd saved his son. Mostly it was nothing, but sometimes…

"How did Boultier get here, Gino?"

"An old Renault."

Jacquot frowned. "Was it blue?"

Faranese looked over Jacquot's shoulder, nodded. "Blue, yes. That one."

Jacquot turned. Beyond the jacked-up Alfa stood a blue Renault 5, with a clean arc of wipers on a dusty windscreen, dented bodywork, and Marseilles plates.

"You give him a good price?"

Faranese raised his arms, stooped his shoulders. "As good a price as I could. For such a rust-bucket." He straightened, smiled. He'd got a good price.

"And Boultier took what you offered?"

"On the button. Like he didn't care. No problem."

"Well, the problem you do have, Gino, is that I don't want anyone near that Renault. Right now, it's out of bounds." He turned to Rully. "Call up Peluze, and get him to send a forensics team round here. No delay."

"Anything else strike you?" asked Jacquot, turning back to Faranese.

"You come to mention it, his hands."

"Hands?"

"Left-hand bandaged, right hand some nasty red swelling on the knuckles." Gino gave Jacquot a look. "And he's left-handed, which made it tricky signing the papers. Big hands, too. You wouldn't get up too swift after a punch from that one."

No, you wouldn't, thought Jacquot.

Adam Loum certainly hadn't.

21

Jacquot had Rully park fifty metres from the address Gino Faranese had given them, a hardware shop on rue Sainte-Cécile with two floors above it, a graffiti-daubed side-door, and a tangle of TV aerials sprouting from a flat roof. The sun was low enough now for the street to be cast into shadow, its last blast of light branding the upper floors of the buildings opposite. Parked outside the hardware shop was a bright red Alfa Romeo Spider.

"You mind?" asked Jacquot, pulling out a pack of cigarettes.

Rully looked astonished; that a Chief Inspector should ask an assistant if he could smoke in the car. It was the same kind of stunned expression that had slid over Rully's face when Dutoit had brought him that cup of Hamid's coffee earlier in the day. Working for the *Judiciaire* was proving to be a great deal more agreeable than he had anticipated, and a definite improvement on Montpellier.

"Not at all, boss. Feel free. So, what's the plan?"

"Wait here and see what happens. An hour, maybe."

"So, you think this Boultier's tied in with Loum's murder?"

"Seems likely. We'll know more when the forensic team have gone over the Renault."

"Why don't we just pull him in? Have a chat?"

Jacquot smiled. "Best be prepared before we try that, don't you think? I mean, he's not going anywhere, is he?"

But he was.

Twenty minutes later, a tall young man in a green quilted windcheater, black polo-neck and blue jeans came out of the shop's side door and trotted down a short flight of steps to the pavement. He carried a briefcase in his right-hand, and a rucksack over his shoulder.

"That's him. That's Boultier," said Rully, who'd seen his mug shot in the file.

Jacquot didn't recognise the man, but noted the bandaged left hand. And the briefcase.

As if to confirm it, Boultier went to the Alfa, affectionately trailing the bandaged knuckles of his left hand along its flanks, opened the boot and dropped briefcase and rucksack into it. Closing the boot and locking it, he went to the driver's door, opened it and slid in behind the wheel. A moment later, the brake lights showed a deep red, and the offside rear-indicator, a vibrant orange, blinked on. With a spinning grip of the rear wheels, the Spider pulled out into the evening traffic.

"So, let's see where our friend is headed," said Jacquot, tipping an unfinished cigarette out of the window. "Just keep him in sight, no closer."

Rully did as he was told, staying a couple of cars back as the Alfa headed down Sainte-Cécile, turned into Boulevard Baille and accelerated away to Place Castellane. At the *rondpoint*, Boultier slung an elbow out of the window, spun round the fountain and took the Boulevard du Prado turning.

They followed the Alfa for a couple of kilometres along the tree-lined avenue, enough rush-hour traffic left to keep a rein on Boultier, and traffic lights to do the rest. At one set of lights, they were close enough to hear the dull beat of music from the Alfa, and for Jacquot to see Boultier's bandaged left hand reach down and beat a gentle finger tattoo on the door panel.

And then they were off again, crossing Rabata and passing the Velodrome on their left, its spotlit flanks hung with a line of L'Olympique Marseilles' blue and white club streamers that shifted weakly in a breeze. By now, heading east, the sky was darkening fast, street-lights blinking on in orange sodium flares, and stars starting to show above the approaching foothills of Mont Redon. When they passed Mazargues and saw a line of tail-lights rising up Tassigny to La Gineste, Jacquot told Rully to take the next right.

"You know a shortcut?"

Jacquot chuckled. "No, I'm hungry."

"But Boultier...?"

"We know where he's going."

"We do?"

"Cassis, Sanary, Toulon. Within a hundred kilometres is my guess. And when the time's right he won't be difficult to find. Not with that Alfa." As they came off Tassigny, Jacquot turned in his seat and looked at Rully. "How about you?"

"Me?"

"You hungry, too?"

22

Jacquot lifted the spoon to his mouth, blew lightly across the broth's steaming rust red surface and tipped the ocean over his tongue.

"Best *soupe de poissons* you'll find," he said, putting down his spoon, wiping his lips with a paper napkin. He reached for the bread, broke off a crust, smeared it with *rouille*, dipped it into pile of grated cheese, and dunked it into his bowl.

They were a block back from the harbour at Pointe Rouge, with the lights of Marseilles twinkling across the bay, in a small fisherman's bar called La Marmite Criée that smelled of seaweed and drying fish nets; the kind of sharp sinuous smell you get on a rocky foreshore before the tide returns. There was sand underfoot and every surface had a salt-sticky feel to it. Two steps in from the half-curtained glass door stood a small zinc bar with three rush-seated stools, its dimpled surface furnished with an old water spigot, an empty metal egg rack, and two pump handles for a draft beer and lager. The harder spirits stood on a low shelf between a Gaggia coffee machine and the cash register, no more than a dozen bottles – Pastis, Whiskey, Vodka, Calvados, Cognac, and a selection of Marcs. Two of the stools were taken, both occupants in their sixties, with grey stubble, hunched shoulders under thick-knit black jumpers, and workman's boots; elbows on the bar, cupping their beers in hands that looked big enough to crush a chicken. There were four tables at the back of the room, where Jacquot and Rully sat, and both restaurant and bar were manned by old Madame Criée, and her younger brother, Albert.

"Didn't look much from the outside," said Rully, reaching for the tureen to ladle in some more of the broth.

"That's often how the best ones are. They don't blow trumpets or sing hallelujahs. They just… deliver. Old Madame Criée starts with the ugliest fish she can find in the market, and by lunchtime she's turned them into something… well, sublime." He swallowed his wad of bread and picked up his spoon. "Just this soup, some bread, maybe a grilled sardine if you're lucky, or some clams. But that's it. No menu here. You eat what Madame puts in front of you. Like it, or leave it. Your choice. And the wine. Just one red and one white, from a small vineyard back in the hills."

"So how did you find it?"

"I didn't. My father brought me here. He and Madame's husband fished together. Out of the old port. Two days, three days at sea, or until the holds were full. One day they didn't come back. So I try to make it out here every once in a while. For my father, for the memories, for Madame Criée… and for the soup, of course."

"And your mother?"

"She died shortly after my father. In an anarchist attack," said Jacquot, in a distancing, business-like tone. "She was painting backdrops for the shop windows of a department store on Le Canebière when a bomb went off at a bus stop. Seven people killed, and many injured."

"I'm so sorry," said Rully, clearly relieved to have Madame appear at that very moment to scoop up their bowls and spoons, the tureen and bread basket, and what was left of the *rouille* and grated cheese.

"*Ça suffit*, Monsieur Daniel?" Madame Criée's voice was as rusty as the broth, with a rasping southern twang.

He looked at Rully. Coffee? More wine? A *digestif*?

A smile, a shake of the head.

"Just a coffee, and Calva, if you please," said Jacquot.

Madame Criée nodded, as though she approved of the order, and then set off for the bar and the kitchen door beside it.

"So why the transfer? Why Marseilles?" asked Jacquot, reaching for his cigarettes, wanting to move the conversation on.

"Call it a clash of personalities."

"Don't tell me, Verdier."

Rully looked surprised. "He was not an easy man to work for."

"He's a *con*. Everyone knows that." And just like Guderoi, thought Jacquot. Two of a kind. Greedy, bent, self-interested, and always ready to shift the blame, or step into the spotlight whenever it beckoned. Or empty a wallet, if the opportunity arose, or pocket a baggie or two to sell on.

"The long and short of it is," Rully continued, "he didn't like me, and I didn't like him. From the first day."

"A point in your favour, believe me. But why Marseilles? Are you local? You seem to know your way around."

"My mother grew up here, over in Fausse Monnaie. She moved to Montpellier when she married my father, but we came back quite often. Friends, family, you know?"

Madame Criée returned with Jacquot's coffee and Calva. "You're not careful you'll end up with a throat like mine, you carry on smoking those things," she said, nodding at the cigarette he had lit. But then she leaned forward, tipped back her head and breathed in the smoke. "Ah, but there's nothing like it, is there? A good smoke is a fine thing, and that's God's truth. I still have one, every now and again, you know? Easter, Christmas. High days and holidays. But don't tell Albert, eh?"

"So how was your first day on the squad?" asked Jacquot, as Madame shuffled back to the bar.

"Very different. I feel at home."

"They're good boys, every one of them. Watch what they do, and how they do it, and you'll be fine. So, what do you make of the Loum case?"

"Gang related? Drugs? He owed money? A settling of accounts. Could be anything."

"But why kill, when you can just take what you want, when you want? A slap or two to keep him in line, but nothing more. Loum was killed for something else."

"Which is?"

Jacquot spread his hands. "Just a feeling. When he shot Madame Dupay he was seen running off with a briefcase. Since tappers don't carry briefcases, let's assume it was hers. Part of the haul. And after Boultier and his chum left Loum's apartment, one of them was carrying a briefcase. Maybe the same briefcase in the Alfa's boot. I'd just like to know what was in it."

"Why don't we ask her husband? He'd know."

"I did, but he didn't."

"Seems strange. So, what now?"

"We wait for our friends in Forensics to find something in the Renault, and for you to draw up a list of known Boultier associates. Who else he might have been with on Thursday night. But right now," said Jacquot, tossing back the last of his Calva and pulling out his wallet, "it's home time. A good night's sleep, and everything else will follow."

23

Nasrullah, the *tellak*, naked save a knotted loincloth, was perfect for his chosen profession. His palms were smooth, his fingertips inquisitively, almost sensually probing, but his knuckles and his elbows were nothing less than offensive weapons. After the cold room and warm room of the Haseki Hammam on rue Cordon, Nakim Burak waddled into the last of the rooms, the hottest of all, and with Nasrullah's help hauled his considerable bulk onto the marble slab beneath the hammam's central dome, settling his shoulders as comfortably as he could and resting the side of his face on his folded arms. The air here was dry and scorching, and Burak knew that too deep a breath would earn him a scalding burn in the back of his throat. But sometimes a deep breath was unavoidable once Nasrullah had completed his initial

75

calming strokes with palms and fingers, and started on Burak's hair-slicked back with the points of his elbows, pressing down into the folds of flesh around Burak's spine.

The real grunting and groaning began with the knuckles. Short, regular grunts from Nasrullah, followed by longer, pained groans from Burak as the bones in his back bent and shifted under the *tellak*'s considerable weight. It was at this particular moment, when imminent injury seemed a very real possibility, that Burak had learned to divert his thoughts from the merciless pummeling to more pleasurable pursuits.

Like the little boy.

Well, not so little.

Burak had felt the weight of him when the boy clambered onto this lap. Not that he was fat, just… chubby. Like a naughty little boy too fond of baklava. And such odd eyes, clear blue and strangely piercing given that they seemed never quite to connect with what he was looking at. But his laugh was a wonder, the deep, chortling delight of it, laughter just bubbling out of him… over nothing. A raised eyebrow, a tongue poked out, a tickling finger to the ribs. So easy to please, so easy to… and his skin was such a marvel. Smooth, startlingly white, with the very tiniest blonde hairs on his arms and at the back of his neck. Burak had tried to remember skin like it. Maybe Samir's? If there was any contender, his dear Samir came close. But that little boy with the strange eyes and funny voice was the clear winner. Soft to the touch, soft to the lips.

And then it had all gone wrong.

Slowly, at first, with no warning.

But frighteningly fast at the end.

And just a shared bowl of pistachio ice cream to blame for it, mixed by the merchant Tekdimir, delivered weekly and kept in a freezer in Dalan's office. It was as though the child had never seen ice cream before, never tasted it, tilting his head to get it properly into view, and watching with a kind of disbelieving awe as Burak lifted a spoonful to his mouth, offered it.

At first the boy had tried to shake his head, shy away, but curiosity had drawn him back. He'd peered at the scoop of ice cream, dipped his finger into it, and then taken a tentative lick.

The smile was immediate and magical, and the very next moment he'd grabbed the spoon from Burak and swallowed the lot, his little round face wincing at the sweet coldness.

By now Nasrullah was closing on his shoulders and Burak knew the masseur was only a few small centimetres from the worst of the onslaught. For a moment he was tempted to bear the pain rather than live again through the horrible moments that followed that first spoonful. But revisit it he did; anything to avoid the next few minutes.

The bowl slipping from the boy's fingers. A puzzled frown creasing his little forehead. And then the first of the rasping, shortening breaths. Desperate, wheezing gasps to find some air, head flung back, mouth wide open, every choking heave jerking his body like an electric charge. Writhing away from Burak's grasp, falling from his lap to the carpet, eyes blinking wildly, the backs of his heels drumming the floor, tiny hands scrabbling at his throat in a frantic, breathless panic. On and on it went, until, with one last frenzied, strangled gasp, it was over – his eyes closed and his body stilled. Fingers loosening around the throat, tongue sliding between the lips, and the lightest blue tint starting to shadow the cheeks.

A slap on the shoulder from Nasrullah, and Burak realised the session was over. It was time to shower, and dress, and return home.

He slept well after his visit to the hammam, as he always did, and in the morning he settled himself on his office divan with just a pleasureable ache to remind him of Nasrullah's attentions.

"Is it done?" was the first thing Burak asked when Dalan knocked and entered with a tray of coffee and sweetmeats.

His assistant nodded.

"When?"

"While you were sleeping, *effendi*. As you requested."

"When will he be found?"

"Soon."

"Today?"

Dalan raised his shoulders, spread his hands, but said nothing. Whatever might happen, who could say? It was the will of the Prophet.

Burak considered this, then rubbed a hand over the bristled dome of his head. It was strange how sometimes things worked out. After all, the boy could never have gone back, could never have been released.

"And the money?"

"I am told on its way, *effendi*."

"Good."

24

The call came in the following morning.

Luc picked up the phone, listened, then put it down. He went over to Rully's desk, had a few words, then made his way to Jacquot's office.

"One of the units just called in a homicide. Male. Moroccan. Over in Belle de Mai. Name of Hakimi, Youssef Hakimi. Rully's already tagged him on that list of Boultier associates you asked for. Shall I tell him to get a car?"

"You don't want to come?"

"If you want, sure. But why not take Rully? He's been working that list of his since he got in. First here, by the way."

"So, you think he needs a breath of air?"

"I'd say so, boss."

Thirty minutes later, Jacquot and Rully pulled up between an ambulance and two squad cars on rue Autran. On the way there Rully had told Jacquot what he needed to know. Hakimi was a school drop-out turned street kid who'd been pulled in on a number of occasions for various petty offences from pick-pocketing to shop-lifting. He'd spent six months in youth custody for beating his sister's boyfriend to a pulp, and had come out harder than when he'd gone in. He'd picked up work where he could find it, as a club bouncer, debt collector, and enforcer; work that suited his size, just another heavy for hire. But he'd never been brought in for anything until, four years after his stint in youth custody, he'd had been stopped for speeding – in a stolen car with a fifty-gram bag of cocaine wraps under his seat. A guilty plea had earned him a two-year term at Baumettes Prison on the outskirts of the city, but numerous fights and bad attitude had extended his stay by a further six months. Since his release five years earlier, nothing had been heard of him. And now, nothing would be heard from him ever again.

"Top floor, Chief," said one of the uniformed cops, when Jacquot showed his badge. Not that he had to; everyone recognised the ponytail, the green eyes and slightly broken nose; the boots in winter, the sockless espadrilles in summer. Everyone on the beat knew who Jacquot was. But he always reached for his badge, as though he needed to. As though it somehow denied the recognition.

"When was he found?"

79

"This morning. By his girlfriend. She's up there, too."

The girlfriend was sitting on the top step of the final flight of stairs. Her forehead rested on her knuckles, her elbows on her knees, and a frizzy mess of dyed blonde hair hid her face. She wore patterned Lycra leggings, trainers and a sweat shirt. She looked as if she'd been for a run. As Jacquot and Rully came closer, they could hear the sobbing, and when they paused to step past her she looked up at them with cheeks stained with mascara and eyes red from rubbing. Despite the smeared cheeks and bruised eyes, she was young and pretty. Nineteen or twenty, Jacquot guessed, and he smiled gently, put a comforting hand to her shoulder.

"I wasn't gone more than an hour," she began, without prompting. Her voice was cracked, brittle with disbelieving shock. "Down to the port and back. Like most mornings. And when I get here..."

"Has anyone given you something to drink?" Jacquot asked.

She shook her head, reached down beside her and pulled out a water-bottle, shook it. There was still some left.

"You smoke?" Jacquot reached to his pocket for his cigarettes.

"I run," she said, and tried a smile. "But I'll have one all the same, thanks."

She took a cigarette and Jacquot lit it for her.

"What's your name?"

"Selmina."

"Do you want us to call anyone for you, Selmina?"

She took a drag of the cigarette, and shook her head. "They told me I was to wait; there'd be some questions, they said."

"Do you live here? In the apartment?"

"Now and again." She gave a rueful smile, tight and sad.

"Last night?"

80

She nodded. "Three nights in a row. A record."

Jacquot reached for the banister, and she shifted over for him. "Well, anything you need, just come and ask, okay?"

"Okay," she replied.

The door to Hakimi's apartment, one of two on either side of the top floor, was open. As they crossed the landing, a paramedic in a luminescent hi-viz green jacket bustled out, hefting his Medikit bag over his shoulders, pushing arms through the straps. Jacquot couldn't remember his name, but he'd seen the man around.

"Male, early thirties at a guess, North African," he said, not waiting for the questions. "Three gunshot wounds. Heavy calibre. Two just for fun, the last between the eyes. Asking questions, my guess. No sign of the weapon. Dead two hours max. I had to move the body, otherwise he's like I found him. On his back, between the bed and wardrobe. There's a couple of your boys in there. I gave them gloves, just in case." And with a nod, he shouldered his way past them, steered around the girl, and trotted down the stairs. His job was done; another call to answer.

Inside the apartment, the two cops were standing at a set of terrace doors in the salon. The room had been turned over. A table, a couple of easy chairs, a sofa with its foam guts spilling out, magazines, glasses, mugs, takeaway cartons and beer cans scattered over the floor. Both cops wore the paramedic's dusted latex gloves. One was an old timer, the other a spotty twenty-something who'd never tan.

"Body's in the bedroom, Chief," the older of the pair said, with a quick salute, more because it was Jacquot rather than any consideration of rank; like everyone else on the force the old man knew who he was. The latex gloves made the salute rather comical, Jacquot decided. "Down the hall, last door on the left. Forensics are on their way. Here within the hour, they said. But you never can tell."

"Thanks, Sergeant. Why don't you get your chum there to get some coffee for us, one for the girl, too." He glanced at the younger man, pulled somes notes from his wallet and handed them over. "White, one," he said, and looked at Rully.

"Sure. The same, thanks."

"On it, boss," the young man said, and hurried from the room.

As his boots clattered across the landing's stone floor, Jacquot and Rully made their way to the bedroom along a corridor that smelled of incense, dope, and curry spices, a dark interior space lit by a single glass-bowl ceiling fixture. The bedroom at the end, on the other hand, was filled with light, sun streaming through another set of terrace windows, the walls painted a soft beige, the drapes printed with blue and white vertical stripes, Marseilles' L'Olympique team colours. A football fan. And not just the curtains, but the shirt Hakimi was wearing, lying there on a sheepskin rug between bed and wardrobe. Home strip, white with blue chevrons on sleeves and collar. And not a spot of blood to be seen beyond a single scarlet tear-track trickle down the side of his head, from a small blackened hole just above and between his thick, dark eyebrows. Jacquot knelt down, keeping clear of the blood that had soaked into the rug and carpet, and reached for Hakimi's far shoulder, drew it towards him until the head lolled and the curls fell across his greying face.

If there was no blood on the front of his shirt, there was plenty on the back, the blue number Seven and the name CANTONA only partly visible under a darkening spill of blood that had come from what was left of the back of Hakimi's head, a jagged creamy red crater clotted with hair and bone. The killing shot.

Jacquot laid the shoulder back to the floor and sat back on his heels. And found the other two wounds. The ones for fun, the paramedic had said. The ones, Jacquot knew, that had accompanied the killer's questions. The gunshot wound in the side of the right knee, and the other one in the left ankle. For encouragement. He couldn't say which had come first, but it would have been enough to get anyone to talk. Either Hakimi had given the right answer, or he hadn't. The only thing that was certain, was he'd seen his last club game.

"Two killings. Five days apart," mused Jacquot.

"You think this is linked to Loum, and Boultier?"

"Fair guess," said Jacquot. "Two men leaving Loum's place and driving off in a blue Renault. A blue Renault that turns up in Faranese's garage, and the owner, Boultier, driving away in a brand new Alfa, paid for in cash. But if it was Boultier who killed Loum, he didn't kill this one. Not his style, and the timing's way off. So who did? And how did the killer track him down?"

Jacquot got to his feet, looked around the room. Moving past Rully he went to an armchair in the corner of the room, by the terrace window. It was piled with clothes: crumpled jeans, t-shirts… and a leather jacket, warm in the morning sun. He picked it up, went through the pockets and pulled out a small black address book. Flicked through it. Nothing under A, but he found what he was looking for under L. The name, Loum, written in pencil, and the telephone number, followed by a line of crossed-out numbers in pencil, biro and felt-tip. Threes and fours and fives. The last number was five and had not been crossed out. Five what? Jacquot wondered. Hash, maybe, or wraps most likely, given Loum's tracking. So it looked like Hakimi was the money man, as much as the muscle, with Boultier riding shotgun. He closed the book, slipped it into his own pocket, and glanced at Rully.

"You reckon that lad's back with the coffee yet?"

25

Sipping his coffee, Jacquot sat on the stairs a couple of steps down from Selmina. Rully leaned against the wall further down.

"Where do you work, Selmina?"

"Club Zouzana, off Lieutaud."

"Waitress?"

She gave him a look. "You could say."

"Is that where you met Hakimi?"

"He was the bouncer for a while. And looked after us girls."

"How long have you been together?"

"On and off, about six months. I know I'm not the only one, but…" she shrugged. It didn't matter. Not now.

"So, you have your own place?"

"Off Paradis. Me and three other girls. It's a bit of a squeeze but it's central and good for work."

"Are you Marseillaise? A local?"

"Born and bred. Sainte Severin, up in the 15th."

"So you know your way around?"

She gave a Jacquot another look, as though he should know better than to ask. "Projects, you have to. You're a cop, you know that. But doesn't mean you join the club, do what they all do up there. There's other ways out. That's what I did. Outta there."

Jacquot took this in. Life in the Projects, places like Sainte Severin and La Castellane in Marseilles' northern suburbs, was tough. Keep you head down, and keep walking. Anyone who managed to find their way out and keep it straight was worth a nod. She might have been young, and pretty, but it didn't take much to see the hard edge to Selmina. And she'd have earned it, for her own survival. The wary eyes, the tight lips. Any sense of threat, he knew, any challenge, and her expression would change, the edge show through. Soon enough, she'd look old before her time.

"When you went for your run this morning, how was Hakimi?"

"Still asleep."

"He always sleep late?"

"You work the clubs, it goes with the territory."

"You came back here together last night?"

"Got off at two. A slow night so they closed early."

"And?"

"You know… Hung out. Smoked. Had a drink."

"And went to bed."

"And?" Selmina gave Jacquot a quick, sharp glance over the tops of her knuckles.

"About three?"

"Round there."

"So how come you're up and out running so early?"

"Light sleeper. And Youssie snores. Plus, we were going off someplace. Have some fun."

"Today?"

She nodded.

"Did he say where?"

"A surprise, he said. A treat. I'd see soon enough."

"He often give you treats?"

Selmina shrugged.

"And did you notice anything, anyone, suspicious out in the street? When you left for your run, or when you came back?"

Selmina shook her head. "Just a normal morning."

"Tell me, did you see Hakimi last Thursday?"

She thought about it, shook her head again. "One of the girls I share with had a birthday. We were out partying."

"And the last few days, how was Hakimi?"

She smiled, almost wistfully. "In a real good place. Just... up, you know?"

Jacquot frowned. Selmina saw it.

"I mean, he can be a bit dark sometimes, difficult, work and all. But suddenly he was just full of it. Plans. Let's do this, let's go here, let's go there. Even took me shopping. First time ever."

"Did you know any of his friends?"

"Not really. There's a few guys come round, listen to music, smoke some dope."

"Do you know someone called Marc Boultier?"

Her face hardened at the name. "Marc, sure. Who doesn't? He and Youssie were tight."

"When did you last see Marc?"

"Not for a while. A month maybe."

"Not in the last week?"

"No."

"Did Hakimi talk about him, say anything?"

"Nothing."

"Do you know what Marc did, his job?"

Selmina gave a deep, disapproving sigh. "I know he worked some of the clubs, like Hakimi. On the door, and inside. Like Security kind of thing.

But for Marc, it was more than just a job. He liked it, liked being the hard man. Not the kind of guy you'd want to get on the wrong side of. Not a guy you'd want to hassle. I mean, stay out of his way if you want to keep your teeth. A Castellane boy, you know?"

"He have a girlfriend?"

"Never saw him with anyone in particular. Most of the girls I know are frightened of him. He has this way of looking at you… like you're meat." Selmina shook her head.

Jacquot tipped back the last of his coffee and got to his feet. "You happen to know if Hakimi ever carried a knife? As part of the job? For protection?"

"Never. Not his style."

"What about Boultier?"

"If he did, I didn't know. But it wouldn't surprise me."

"Did either of them have a briefcase? Did you ever see one around?"

"A briefcase?" She shook her head, chuckled.

Jacquot pulled out his wallet, found his card, and handed it to her. "If you think of anything, or remember something, that's where you can find me. Any time. And leave your contact details with the Sergeant inside, okay? In case we need to speak to you." He put his hand on her shoulder, gave it a gentle squeeze. "And I'm sorry about your friend."

Selmina nodded, smiled a grim, tight-lipped smile. "Me too."

Out in the street, a black Citroën van had pulled into the space where the ambulance had parked, and the Scene-of-Crime boys were unloading their gear, pulling on their blue Nyrex fatigues. Three of them; just another day, just another house call

"You think Selmina knows more than she's saying?" asked Rully, as they buckled up their seat belts.

87

"What I think is, she's lucky she went for a run."

26

"Traces of blood on the Renault's foot pedals. Same blood type as Loum," said Charlie Serre, when Jacquot and Rully got back to headquarters. "Valéry's assistant, Teri, called an hour back with initial findings. Wants to know if you need anything more?"

"What about prints?"

"Forensics still on it. Door handles, steering wheel, sun visors, gear stick, ashtray, brake. The obvious ones," said Serre, and handed Jacquot a scribbled sheet of paper. "What you asked for, from one of our boys in Sanary," he said, then headed back to his desk.

"So we've got him. Boultier," said Rully.

"It'll be worth a word," said Jacquot, glancing at the paper Serre had given him.

Rully frowned. "A word? Nothing more? And his pal, Hakimi, taken out?"

"Somewhere to start. Who knows? Too early to leap to conclusions."

"But the blood."

"Could be Loum, Boultier, and Hakimi have the same blood group. And if it's just the blood, there's not much to pin on him. All he'd have to say is he and Hakimi found the body, maybe trod in the blood, but didn't want to get involved. Or, just as likely, Boultier will tell us they weren't there, at Loum's place; must be someone else's blood on his shoe, in the car. From a fight, he'll tell us; some argument outside a club. Maybe just a nosebleed."

"And the Alfa? The cash?"

88

"Well, that's where it gets interesting. Just everything starting to build up. Boultier and Hakimi calling in on Loum – delivering some dope, picking up some money, who knows? And either they find him dead, which I doubt given the time frame, or one of them kills him. But why? Like I said, a slap or two if he was getting behind with his payments, but not a slit throat. My guess is, whoever killed Loum wanted to keep him quiet. Probably because of the briefcase, the one he'd stolen from Madame Dupay earlier in the evening, down on Joliette, the one that Boultier and Hakimi were seen with a little later that night on rue Daumier. So, either Boultier and Hakimi used it to carry off Loum's haul, or they took it because there was something more valuable inside. Which makes sense if you remember that there hasn't been much time to sell on any jewellery, and whatever price they got for it, split between the two of them, wouldn't have covered the price of an Alfa."

"So, what's the next move?"

Jacquot raised the piece of paper that Serre had given him, flicked it with his fingers. "We get back in the car and go to La Résidence des Cyprès in the hills above Sanary. There's someone we need to talk to."

27

It was no more than fifty kilometres as the crow flies, from police headquarters on rue de l'Évêché to the garrigue slopes and chalky bluffs above Sanary-sur-Mer. But the road out of the city was as busy as it had been the previous evening when Jacquot and Rully had been trailing the Alfa, and once they hit the rising heights of La Gineste their speed was further reduced by a series of hairpin bends going up on one side and dropping down on the other. One cautious driver on either stretch, and the traffic started to build up, one car after another joining the queue with little chance to overtake.

With no tape deck in the car Jacquot found Radio Nostalgie, tuning in half-way through J.J. Cale's *Travellin' Light*, which perfectly matched their increasing speed as they passed above Cassis, followed by Canned Heat's *On The Road Again*. As appropriate soundtracks went, Jacquot couldn't have been happier. The sky was a light promising blue, there were occasional glittering flashes of the sea on their right, and the hillsides above them were still a strong spring green. It felt good to be alive, even if they had started their day with a dead body on a blood-soaked sheepskin rug.

"When you get to Ceyreste follow the Garrigues road, and signs for Signes. It's not far now."

Rully nodded and pulled out to overtake a lorry, only to find himself caught behind another one not two kilometres further on.

"Enjoy the ride, there's no rush," said Jacquot. "Our boy's not going anywhere."

"Our boy?"

"Boultier. One of our lads spotted the Alfa."

Ten minutes later, Rully pulled off the Signes road and after a few hundred metres they came to a set of pillars. On one of these was a brass plate and the words *La Résidence des Cyprès* in an elegant scrolling script, with a suitably cypress-lined driveway leading to an old bastide with creamy limestone walls, pale blue shutters, and a low pantile roof.

"*Relais et Châteaux*, no less," said Rully, pulling up in the gravelled courtyard beside an open-top Bentley. The red Alfa was there too, also with the roof down, and a gleaming blue BMW with its black hood up was reversing out of a space. "Not bad for a Marseilles *mec*."

"He should have taken a taxi," said Jacquot, as they walked past the Alfa. "We'd never have found him here."

At the front desk, a slab of polished veined marble resting on a fluted stone plinth, Jacquot asked the Receptionist if she could tell him where they might find Monsieur Boultier? The girl was in her early twenties, dressed in a cream blouse with knotted bow and blue pencil skirt. She was pretty, fresh-faced, with a fall of brown hair kept in place with a blue velvet Alice band.

It was clear that hotel staff were not in the habit of providing visitors with information about guests, particularly a visitor with a ponytail who arrived in a dusty, dented Renault. The helpful but questioning frown on the girl's face was enough for Jacquot to reach for his badge, and show it with a smile. "If you would be so kind."

The frown disappeared in an instant. "I believe he is down at the pool, monsieur."

"Does he have company?"

"His wife, I believe."

"His wife, of course," said Jacquot. "And the pool is…"

"Through the archway there, monsieur. Just follow the colonnade to the gardens and you'll find the pool on your right, on the lower terrace. Or, of course, you could go through the restaurant if you prefer."

Jacquot took the colonnade route, an arched open-sided passage lined with ferns in terracotta urns and its marble tiles ringing with the sound of Jacquot's boots. Blooms of early lilac drooped from the arches and filled the air with a soft beguiling scent. At the end of the colonnade they followed a sloping gravel path towards a screen of red-barked twisting cypress, and stepped out onto a neatly-striped lawn that surrounded the pool. Two dozen sunbeds under tilting parasols were drawn up along its sides, but only three of them were occupied. An elderly couple, both in bathrobes, and a young woman, lying on her back, a leg raised, the bikini she wore as red as the Alfa. But no sign of Boultier.

Back at Reception, Jacquot asked for Boultier's room number. They had been unable to find him at the pool.

"I'm so sorry, monsieur. Of course. Suite 204. You can take the lift, or the stairs."

"Is there any other way to Monsieur Boultier's suite?"

"From the Terrace Bar and restaurant, there is an outside staircase."

"Do you have a key for the room?"

"Of course, monsieur," she replied and, opening a drawer, selected a plain metal key, handed it over.

With a nod of thanks Jacquot and Rully took the stairs, a sweep of white marble with a blue runner held in place with shining brass rods, and followed the room signs to the right. Suite 204 was at the end of the corridor. When they reached it, Jacquot gave Rully a *you-ready*? look, and knocked on the door.

There was no answer.

Jacquot knocked again, a little harder this time. "Monsieur Boultier, it is the concierge here. A package has arrived for you."

Still no answer.

Reaching for his gun, Jacquot tried the door handle, turned it slowly and eased the door open. No need for a key.

The room was bright with sunlight, and muslin drapes at the open terrace windows billowed in a lilac-scented draft as the door opened.

"Monsieur Boultier? Monsieur…" Jacquot stopped dead.

"*Merde*," said Rully, coming in behind him.

Marc Boultier was dressed in a white towelling robe and sat on a plumply cushioned sofa, his arms by his sides, his legs apart. The robe was open and showed a pair of blue striped swimming shorts and a tanned well-muscled torso, his head flung back over the top of the sofa. He could have been sleeping. It was only as they drew closer that they saw the bullet wound, in the centre of his forehead, the blood still dripping onto the carpet from the back of his shattered skull.

Holstering his gun Jacquot nodded to the bedroom and bathroom, and Rully left him to check them out.

Stepping past the body Jacquot went to the french windows. They opened onto a wide stretch of terrace, with a stone staircase at either end. Beyond the balustrade lay ribbed slopes of bunched grey lavendar still to bloom, a distant line of blue hills, and a glimpse of glittering sea between their lowest pitches.

Turning back to the room, Jacquot took in the plumped-up cushions on the sofas and armchairs, the fresh flowers, magazines and newspapers arranged in tidily stacked lines on the glass coffee-table, the carpet still showing the brushed passage of a vacuum cleaner. But no sign of a struggle. Nothing out of place. Just Boultier, answering a knock at his door, or the killer coming through from the terrace, pointing a gun at Boultier's head; telling him to take a seat.

But no need here for any encouraging shots.

The visitor got what he wanted, and no argument.

"No one, boss, the place is clear," said Rully, coming back into the room. "Two cases in the wardrobe. Boultier's rucksack, and a Vuitton leather weekender. But no briefcase. And the safe door is open and empty." He leaned forward, touched the man's cheek, lifted his left hand. There was no bandage but the knuckles were red and slightly swollen. "He can't have been dead long. Still warm. The killer's probably still here."

Jacquot shook his head. "If I had to put money on it, I think he may have left in that blue BMW."

28

Leaving Rully in Boultier's suite to report their find and call up a Scene-of-Crime team, Jacquot went down to Reception.

"The owner of the blue BMW who drove off just before we arrived?" he asked. "Is he a guest?"

The girl in the velvet Alice band shook her head. "Not a guest, no. A Monsieur Petroux. He's booked a table for lunch."

"And he's left before having it?"

The receptionist looked surprised, as though she hadn't thought of that, then frowned.

"Perhaps he had to leave suddenly? Or possibly, maybe he'd forgotten something?"

"How many guests was he expecting?"

She checked a reservations book. "A table for eight, on the restaurant terrace. So, seven."

"Are any of them here?"

"I... don't believe so." She picked up a phone and tapped out a number. "Has the Petroux party arrived? Okay... Sure... Thank you." Putting down the phone, she said, "No one is here yet, monsieur."

Jacquot looked at his watch. A little after one o'clock. "Wouldn't you have seen them, when they arrived?"

"Not necessarily, monsieur. For the restaurant, guests can take the path from the car park. They do not need to come through the hotel."

"Did Monsieur Petroux do that, or did he come through here?" asked Jacquot.

"When he arrived? Through here, yes. He just walked in, crossed the hall to the restaurant. He looked as though he knew where he was going."

"And what time was this?"

"About an hour ago. Maybe less?"

"Could you describe him, please?"

The girl spread her hands. "It was just the briefest look, you understand. I was on the phone. But I would say a little taller than you, monsieur, maybe a few years older too, with curling grey hair, and a moustache I think…" She pursed her lips, frowned, "… but that is all."

"And what was he wearing?"

"A linen jacket; blue or grey, I can't remember exactly which. Cream cotton trousers, a white open-neck shirt. Casual, you know, but well-dressed."

And driving a smart BMW. So he wouldn't have been approached by staff, wanting to know his business, thought Jacquot. The kind of man at home in a place like La Résidence des Cyprès. Unlike he and Rully, in their creased workaday jackets, with their dusty old Renault.

"Has Monsieur Petroux been here for lunch or dinner before? Or has he stayed here?"

"Not that I am aware of."

"And you didn't see him leave?"

She shook her head. "Just his car reversing, as you were arriving."

So there was no point asking if she had seen him carrying a briefcase, thought Jacquot. Not that it mattered. He knew he'd have been carrying one. Instead, he asked, "And Monsieur Boultier? Is he a regular guest? Has he been here before?"

"I don't think so, monsieur."

"And when did he book in?"

"Monsieur Boultier? For the room?"

Jacquot nodded.

"He called to make the reservation yesterday morning."

"And how long is he staying?"

The receptionist turned to her monitor, tapped some keys. "For a week," she replied.

"Did he pay by card or cash?"

She checked her screen. "Cash, monsieur."

"The full amount?"

"The full amount, with a deposit, of course, to cover extras. It is the same for anyone paying cash."

"And his wife? Madame Boultier. Did they check in together?"

"Separately, I think. She arrived about two hours after Monsieur Boultier."

"She came by taxi?"

"I think so, yes."

Jacquot took this in. "And Monsieur Petroux? Do you happen to know when he made his reservation for lunch?"

"This morning."

"You took the call?"

"Yes, I did."

"And did he leave a contact number?"

"I seem to remember he hung up before I could ask for one."

Jacquot thought about this. It all made sense. A professional, no question. And someone who knew La Résidence, knew the kind of place it was, knew he'd need a reason just to drop by. A convincing cover. And no contact number to follow up. A little less than an hour, and the job he'd come for was done.

But how did he find out that Boultier was here? Had Hakimi told the killer? It seemed a reasonable assumption. Maybe this was where he was going to take Selmina for that treat? Meeting up with Boultier to split the cash?

"I wonder if I might have a word with the Manager?" Jacquot asked.

"Monsieur *Le Directeur*? Of course, monsieur," and the receptionist reached for the phone again.

"But not right now, mademoiselle. In, say, thirty minutes?"

"Of course, monsieur. Not a problem."

Monsieur *Le Directeur*, thought Jacquot, as he left Reception and headed for the colonnade. That sounded about right. La Résidence des Cyprès was not the kind of place to have just a manager.

29

"Madame Boultier?" asked Jacquot.

It was a good bet. The woman in the red bikini stretched out on the sunbed was the only person around the pool, or in the terrace bar that he had strolled through, who was under thirty.

She raised herself on an elbow and lowered her sunglasses, took him in.

"Yes?" It was an uncertain affirmative.

Jacquot pulled over the sunbed beside hers and sat down. "I wonder if I could have a few words?" he asked, reaching for his badge and flipping it open.

The change in her was immediate. A stiffening of the body, legs tensing as though preparing for a quick sprint, and a tongue tip slipped across her lips. But she said nothing.

"So, let us cut to the chase, mademoiselle," said Jacquot, with a gentle smile. "Exactly how long have you known your husband, Monsieur Boultier?"

The sigh was long. The game was up. She tightened her lips, looked away, shook her head. "Yesterday. I met him yesterday, here at the hotel, in the evening."

"And you are staying for how long?"

She turned back to Jacquot. "As long as he wants me to stay."

"And how do you feel about that?"

'Madame Boultier' shrugged, as though it was no business of hers. "A job's a job. The pay is good, and the surroundings are… *génial.*"

"But…?"

She gave him a rueful smile. "There's always a 'but', monsieur."

"Do you know where your husband is right now?"

"He went to our suite. Maybe…" she glanced at her watch, steadying it on her wrist. "An hour, maybe fifty minutes ago?"

"Did he say why?"

"It was a call from the manager, I think. They brought out a phone. It was something to do with an upgrade. A better suite was available, and would he like to see it? He told me he wouldn't be long."

"Who brought him the phone?"

"One of the barmen."

Jacquot nodded. He knew what had happened. The killer had found Boultier at the pool, but needed him alone. So he'd used one of the house phones that Jacquot had noticed at the entrance to the colonnade, called for Monsieur Boultier, and was put through. At which point the killer, Monsieur Petroux, becomes *Monsieur Le Directeur*, apologising in honeyed tones for the intrusion, and requesting a moment of his guest's time to discuss an upgrade. An irresistable summons.

"So he went to his room to see the manager?"

"I guess." She took off her sunglasses and levelled a pair of almond-shaped brown eyes on his. She might have been young but those eyes had seen it all. There was nothing this girl couldn't handle. And right now, Jacquot knew, with all the attention focused on Boultier, she was clearly feeling on safer ground. A cop, looking for Boultier…? Best stay out of this one, be as helpful as I can. And he hasn't even asked for my real name. That's what was going through her head, thought Jacquot. She was in the clear. "But what's all this about anyway? What's going on?"

"I hope you have your money, mademoiselle. Because there won't be any more."

She raised an eyebrow. "He's been arrested?"

"There was no time to arrest him. My condolences."

It took a moment for his meaning to sink in, and then, eyes wide, "Shit, you're joking? He's dead?" She swung her legs off the bed, clasped her arms round her shoulders as though she was cold, then reached for her bathrobe, shrugged it over herself. "When? How?"

"In your room. Murdered. So, mademoiselle, I'm afraid your stay with Monsieur Boultier has come to an end. Given these unfortunate circumstances I will arrange for another room to be made available for you, and for your belongings to be brought to you. In the meantime, just a couple more questions?"

"Of course, no problem."

"Your real name? Your address?"

"Madeleine Sabrine. I live in Toulon. 52 Passage Delors off Zola. Top floor."

"And you work for an agency?"

"That's right." She reached for a pack of cigarettes on the table beside her. Jacquot took up the book matches beside the packet, tore off a match, struck it and lit her cigarette.

"Its name?" he asked, pocketing the matches.

"*Siffle.* They're based in Cannes."

Just Whistle. Jacquot smiled.

"So your agency, *Siffle,* set you up for this?"

She nodded. "I got the call yesterday, after lunch. Are you free? Sure. So pack a bag, go to La Résidence, and ask for Monsieur Marc Boultier. You're his wife."

"You hadn't met him before?"

"No."

"And the agency? Was he a regular? A known client?"

"I don't think so. If he had been, they would have said. Given me the low-down."

"Low-down?"

"Likes, dislikes. Any preferences I should know about. Best to be prepared."

Jacquot nodded. "So how was he, when you met?"

"In charge. Full of it. So, I knew straight off it was going to be tricky. He was just… he made me feel uncomfortable. Like I was bought and paid for, so he could behave however he wanted. No class."

Jacquot nodded, remembered what Selmina had said to him the previous day. *Most of the girls I know are frightened of him. He has this way of looking at you… like you're meat.*

"Tell me, did your companion have a briefcase?"

"In the wardrobe. On a shelf. Leather."

100

"Did you happen to see what was in it?"

"Nothing. It was empty."

Jacquot tipped his head.

Madeleine Sabrine was caught, knew it, shrugged. "I looked. He was in the bathroom."

"Did you have any belongings in the safe?"

"No, nothing."

"Did Monsieur Boultier?"

"I don't know. It was locked by the time I arrived, so maybe he did."

"You have been most helpful, mademoiselle," said Jacquot. "Thank you. And since I have your contact details, please feel free to leave whenever you choose. I understand, however, that your late husband booked your suite for a week. And paid in advance." He looked around, at the pool, at the shaded terrace restaurant, then turned back to her. "So, might I suggest that you take advantage of his generosity…?"

She gave Jacquot a smile, shrugged off the bathrobe, and stretched back on the sunbed.

"What a good idea, Chief Inspector," she said, handing him her cigarette to stub out. "Maybe you'd like to join me for lunch?"

30

"I regret to inform you, monsieur, that one of your guests, a Monsieur Marc Boultier, has been murdered. In his room."

Monsieur *Le Directeur* Edouard Veyras sat behind his desk, a blue paisley tie knotted as tightly as a rosebud in a starched white collar. When Jacquot's words finally settled, he blinked, opened his mouth, but the words didn't come. And then, in a panicking rush, "Murdered? Here? At La Résidence?" As if such a thing could not possibly be imagined.

"In Suite 204. In the last hour or so."

"Do any of our guests know? The staff?" He reached for his tie knot as though to loosen it.

"Apart from his wife, Madame Boultier, you are the first, monsieur."

The relief was obvious. The fingers released the tie knot, the shoulders slumped as though a weight had been taken off them, and a breath whispered between his lick-spittle lips. But how to keep such a thing quiet? Jacquot could see the man's brain spinning. So many things to consider: his remaining guests, the hotel's reputation, future bookings, the possibility of unpleasant press coverage.

"Poor Madame Boultier," he managed. Best not forget the wife.

"I left her by the pool," said Jacquot. "She was going to swim and then have some lunch."

"A swim? Some lunch? But she must be devastated."

"Not that much, monsieur. *En effet*, they were not married; she is not his wife. I'm sure you understand."

He was certain the man would not. Or rather, he would imagine that Madame Boultier was another man's wife, or maybe Boultier's mistress, just a little *cinq à sept*. Nothing more. Had he known that Madeleine Sabrine was a high-class call girl working for the *Siffle* agency he'd have had her off the premises in the blink of a sanctimonious eye. The very least she deserved, thought Jacquot, was a week at La Résidence, if she chose to stay on, and grieve. There seemed no good reason why she shouldn't take some advantage of the situation.

"I understand Monsieur Boultier paid for a week's stay, in cash?"

Veyras spread his hands. "If you say so, monsieur. Without checking…" he gestured to the computer on his desk.

"Do many of your guests pay cash?"

Veyras looked suddenly uncomfortable. "That is purely at our guests' discretion. If they wish to pay cash, then of course they can."

"And there is a deposit, too, I believe, when a credit card is not used?"

"Just a small amount, you understand. An additional payment to cover any… unforeseen expenses."

Jacquot smiled, recognised the man's discomfort, and liked it. Paying cash meant no records, no paper trails. Which meant that both guest and host would profit from their encounter. The guest certain of anonymity, the hotel's management able to save on their tax bill. Jacquot wondered how Monsieur *Le Directeur* dealt with such an obvious temptation, and whether he declared such income. He doubted it very much. The man, for all his shiny-cheeked bonhomie, had a sly, calculating look.

With a soft clearing of the throat, he asked, "What now, Chief Inspector?"

"Our Scene-of-Crime team will be here within the hour; an ambulance, of course."

Veyras' face fell, his shoulders slumped a second later. *Catastrophe.*

"But I will ask the boys not to advertise their presence. Maybe there's a room near Suite 204 where they could suit up, without drawing any attention? And a room for Madame Boultier, where her luggage can be sent. I understand she will be staying on."

"Yes, of course. We are not full. I'm sure…" Veyras had swiftly recovered.

"And for the purposes of our investigation, I really see no reason why I need to speak to any of your guests. We have all we need."

"I'm most grateful for your... understanding, Chief Inspector. Most grateful."

31

Much as he might have enjoyed it, Jacquot did not have lunch with Madeleine Sabrine. Instead, after speaking to the barman who had taken Petroux's call – "a cultured voice, monsieur, softly-spoken, but friendly" – he and Rully checked out the Alfa. The sun had warmed its shiny red leather seats, and the cockpit had that characteristic scent of engine oil and newness. Just as Jacquot had expected there was no briefcase in the boot, and nothing of interest in the car.

As they finished their inspection the SOC team arrived and, asking them to keep a low profile, Jacquot had Rully show them to Boultier's suite. He might not have liked Monsieur *Le Directeur*, but Jacquot saw no reason to spoil his guests' holidays. And when the ambulance crew arrived from Sanary shortly afterwards, Jacquot told them that a heart attack seemed the best explanation if they should be asked.

Low key, all the way.

They understood.

The drive back to Marseilles was as enjoyable as the drive out. The sun still shone, the sky was a deeper richer blue, and the breeze shuffling through their open windows brought a soft resinous scent from the hillsides on their right. But these scents of the countryside lasted only until Jacquot and Rully reached the high pass of La Gineste and began their downward path into the chalky sprawl of the city. Here, the lightly perfumed air from the sun-drenched slopes was swiftly replaced by a thick stewing stench of spilled rubbish and rotting vegetation that had them wind up their windows.

Now in its second week, the City Services strike had taken hold. Every corner, every sidewalk they passed had its slumped pyramid of shiny black and green bin liners and, increasingly, the foul odours that slid from loosely knotted necks and split seams.

"*Merde*," said Jacquot, as they drove around the Vieux Port, its pavements piled high with refuse, the seagulls pecking for scraps, squalling and scrapping overhead. "A body in one of those piles, it could rot to bones and you'd never notice it."

He didn't know how right he was.

32

The refuse workers' strike lasted another four days during which time the homicide squad on rue de l'Évêché tried, without any real success, to make progress in their investigation into the murders of Adam Loum, Youssef Hakimi, and Marc Boultier.

Jacquot wasn't surprised. Sometimes an investigation just slowed right down. But it never stopped altogether. And it had all started with Loum, tapping on the window of Madame Dupay's Mercedes with the muzzle of his Makarov 9mm, taking a briefcase along with the woman's jewellery, and ending up just a few hours later with his throat cut.

A throat cut to keep the Gambian grifter quiet.

A throat cut either by Hakimi or Boultier, though Jacquot, without any real evidence, favoured Boultier as the killer. That was the kind of man he was, Jacquot had decided. Based solely on Selmina's and Madeleine Sabrine's description. And his own gut instinct, of course. Just a nasty, merciless *mec* who wouldn't be too worried about blood on his hands. The kind of man who might easily have killed Hakimi as well, if someone hadn't beaten him to it. Because, sooner or later, Hakimi would have met up with Boultier at La Résidence or some other rendezvous to share out their ill-gotten gains and, somewhere along the line, Boultier would have put him down. Why share, when a knife got rid of the problem? He'd cut Loum's throat; why not Hakimi's? And Selmina's, too, if she'd been with him. Or maybe he'd have used Loum's Makarov which the SOC boys had found under the bed in Boultier's suite. Except someone else had done the deed, a third party who, thanks to Hakimi, had followed Boultier to La Résidence des Cyprès, shot him, and taken the briefcase. With whatever it contained.

Money, of course. And given that a briefcase was needed to carry this money, not a small amount, Jacquot reasoned.

The question was, what was Madame Dupay doing with a briefcase filled with cash?

Avoidance of tax, as practiced by the estimable Edouard Veyras, La Résidence's Monsieur *Le Directeur*, was not a convincing option. Neither Monsieur nor Madame Dupay had any reasonable cause to stuff a briefcase with cash and drive off to the docklands of Joliette in order to ease their tax burden. Dupay was a financier after all, and having met him Jacquot was in no doubt that he could have come up with more ingenious schemes for hiding money.

The only reason to account for that briefcase filled with cash was blackmail.

Someone was being paid off.

By Camille Dupay, for some past indiscretion? Or on her husband's behalf? For something he might have done?

But paid off for what?

Financial secrets? For services rendered? The threat of exposure? The return of something stolen? There weren't too many other options, and

106

without giving it much further thought, Jacquot had settled for the return of something taken. Except, the money to pay for this transaction had been intercepted. Stolen, quite by chance, by Adam Loum, just moments before Madame Dupay was about to make the drop-off. And then stolen again by Hakimi and Boultier who, again by chance, happened to call by while Loum was busy counting it. And who, in turn, were shot by someone who must have known about the cash being taken. Someone getting his money back? Or hiring a third party to do it for him? Given the clean and efficient nature of Boultier's and Hakimi's dispatch – no sounds of gunshots from Hakimi's apartment or Boultier's suite, suggesting the use of a silencer, and no shell casings at either scene – it seemed likely that a contract killer had been hired for the job, so someone more important wouldn't end up with blood on their hands.

And that same killer was still out there. Job done, money returned to rightful owner, with a hefty fee for settling the matter. Right now Monsieur Petroux, or whatever his name was, could be anywhere, leaving no clue to his identity beyond a brief description from the receptionist at La Résidence – in his forties, tall, with grey hair, possibly a moustache too. And his car – a blue BMW. No registration, no model, no distinguishing features beyond the black hood.

But how had he found Boultier and Hakimi in the first place? How had he tracked them down so swiftly?

So many unanswered questions. Which was why the investigation had slowed. Two murders, four including Madame Dupay and Loum, and nothing to go on. Not a single lead.

Which, Jacquot decided, walking home that Monday evening, was something that *Maître* Solange Bonnefoy would not be happy about. But what else could he do? What else could she expect? When an investigation stalled like this, when every means at the *Judiciaire*'s considerable disposal failed to provide any kind of momentum, they both knew there wasn't a lot they could do about it; they'd have to sit it out until something else came into play. Something unconnected. Something unforeseen. And it would, it would.

Police work, Jacquot had long ago decided, was like a game of rugby; the game he loved, the game that had changed his life. The back and forth of advance and retreat. Ground gained, ground lost. Ball passed, ball fumbled, ball kicked. Possession disputed. Scrums, line-outs, rucks and mauls. And then, from nowhere, without warning, that sudden, wonderful, breathtaking passage of play. A lucky, well-aimed pass. And then another. And another. The players suddenly aligned, until that final perfect pass from one pair of muddy hands to the last. An unseen opening, an unexpected chance. A feint, a dummy, a strategic change of direction. And the way was clear. The ball cradled, legs pumping. And with a final, lung-tugging charge, amid the rising roar of a crowd, the line finally, gloriously crossed and the ball touched down.

And Jacquot knew all about that.

So it was that a housewife on rue Berthelot, fed up with the cats and dogs of the neighbourhood scavenging away at the mounds of rubbish piled high outside her apartment block, the rank stench that hovered over it, and the clouds of flies that settled and fed off it, took up a broom and a shovel and set to work on the stinking refuse. One broken bag after another, scooping up the spill, rebagging it, knotting the tie handles, and arranging the sacks in a more orderly manner. She wore a blue polka-dot handkerchief tied over her nose and mouth like a Wild West bandit, only pausing while she swept and shovelled to swat away the buzzing clouds of flies, so busy in her endeavours that she failed to notice what her efforts had unearthed.

It was her six-year-old daughter, standing by her side, who saw the arm fall free from its black plastic cocoon, stretching out a tiny clenched fist. A grey, mottled arm, with a bluish thumbnail.

And what looked like writing.

On the arm. A word.

"*Maman*," she whispered, tugging her mother's skirts with one hand and pointing with the other. "Look. Look."

33

Her skin was as smooth as glass. Warm glass. And softer than the silken sheet they lay on. Skin lightly tanned, with a sprinkle of pin-prick freckles on her shoulders that would darken in the summer's sun, freckles gathering at the nape of her neck and beneath the fall of blonde hair, in the small of her back, and on the very tops of her tightening thighs. Skin that smelled of fresh apples, ripe and warm, but firm and muscled too, as she moved against him. Whispering what she wanted; surprised, surrendering sounds on a breath drawn in, words on a breath released, in a rush. Instructions, imperatives, insistence... With the softest sighs and groans, rising in speed and volume, until they grew louder and urgent and real...

A single, repeated sound. A knocking. Someone knocking at a door. Their door. His door. Now, at this most crucial of moments.

And as Jacquot came to, still scrabbling for the warmth and comfort of the dream, he knew where he was, and knew he had to let it go. No choice; it was gone.

Pulling a towel round his waist, knotting it – "*Oui, oui, j'arrive*" – he hurried through his apartment under the eaves of Place des Moulins, reached the door, and swung it open.

Rully.

It took a moment for Jacquot to gather himself. Glanced at his watch. A few minutes before seven.

"What's going on? What are you…?"

"We tried to call, but there was no answer. Engaged. You must have knocked the phone off the hook."

No, he hadn't. He'd disconnected it. Just a few hours earlier, after coming home from Sydné and César's place. One of their many soirées. Always the best parties; the best people, the best music, the best food. Out on their rooftop terrace above the Vieux Port. Sometimes he'd stay the night in their spare room, or somewhere else depending on the company, but last night he'd come home late. Alone. Weary, needing his bed.

"Your concierge let me in."

"*Merde*," said Jacquot, knowing he'd be in for it now. Knowing it would cost him a pack of Madame Foraque's favourite cigars from Delormes, or a bottle of Charentais pineau, to sweeten the old girl's mood. "So, what's happening? What's it all about?"

He gestured for Rully to come in, closed the door and headed back to his bedroom. "Help yourself to coffee," he called through the door, pulling on jeans, a white t-shirt, a blue Levi shirt over it, sitting back on the bed to tug on socks, his boots from where he'd left them. In the bathroom he cleaned his teeth, cupped hands and splashed water over his face; brushed his wet hair, held a length of it between a circling thumb and forefinger and snapped on a rubber band. Pulled too tight, it pinched. He loosened it, shook it into place, straightened his shoulders. Wondering all the time about the dream, the girl, and why Rully had come round so early?

He found out in the kitchen, taking a coffee from his assistant and giving him a questioning look.

110

"A body," said Rully. "Found last evening in a pile of rubbish on Berthelot. Male, around ten years old. I tried to get hold of you last night, but…"

"I was out. A party. And?"

"Teri, at Pathology, called just as I was leaving. A name had been written on the arm, in felt-tip marker. Lucien."

Jacquot frowned. The name seemed familiar.

"He had Down syndrome."

And then the name registered.

"Dupay? Lucien Dupay?"

34

Teri Manon, the State Patholgist's assistant examiner, was dressed in green theatre scrubs. She wore white plimsolls that squeaked on the lino floor and her brown hair was tucked up and clipped into a blue paper cap. She was in her late thirties, with a tired, care-worn face bare of make-up. But her eyes were a clear bright blue and Jacquot knew, from a chance meeting with her and her husband in a restaurant off rue d'Endoume, that away from her work Teri looked altogether different, so much so that he hadn't even recognised her until she reached out for his arm as he passed their table.

"Cause of death is asphyxia, brought on by anaphylactic shock," she said, drawing back the sheet covering the body, standing aside for Jacquot and Rully to see.

The boy was naked, short and tubby, with fine straight blonde hair that fell away from his broad puffy face. The eyes were closed to curving slits, the bluish lips still swollen, the tip of a grey tongue peeping between them. A raised and sutured Y-shaped scar ran from the points of his rounded shoulders to his sternum and down to his pudgy abdomen.

"Judging by the contents of his stomach – what looked like the remains of pistachio ice cream and other nuts – I'd say the anaphylaxis was brought on by an allergic reaction." She turned to Jacquot. "In Down syndrome cases – like this one, particularly – the abnormally large tongue and low palate would have dramatically increased the fatal consequences of such a reaction. In short, eating those nuts or ice cream in any quantity was a sure-fire killer. He simply choked to death."

"You said there was a name written on the body?"

Teri reached for the boy's left arm, raised and turned it. The letters, L to N in faded black capitals, reached from the inside of the elbow to the wrist. "It's as if whoever did this wanted the body identified." She shrugged. "I can see no other reason."

"Time of death?" asked Rully. He was rubbing his chin, almost contemplatively, but Jacquot knew he was trying to cover the smell coming off the body. He was also breathing through his mouth. Sure signs. Not even the strong astringent scent of chemicals could quite cover the smell of death and decay that hung around certain corpses.

"Seven, eight days." Teri pursed her lips, and closed her eyes.

Jacquot knew it wouldn't have been an easy post-mortem examination. A young boy with Down syndrome, bloated like a grey balloon before the scalpel cut, but now deflated. He watched her reach for the corner of the sheet and draw it back over the body.

"Any signs of violence, any bruising?" asked Jacquot.

"Just a few bite marks. On his feet and toes. Rats."

"Any… interference? Abuse?"

"Nothing obvious."

"Clothes? Belongings?"

"Not a thing. Just dumped, naked."

There was silence for a moment, only the slow tap-tapping of water dripping onto stainless steel somewhere across the room.

"It's the Dupay boy, isn't it?" she asked.

Jacquot nodded. "That's how it looks, even if he hasn't been reported missing by his stepfather. Has anyone been in touch with him? Monsieur Dupay?"

Teri shook her head. "I just called you. Spoke to your colleague. *C'est tout.*"

"Thanks, Teri. We'll take it from here."

"Oh, by the way," said Teri, as Jacquot and Rully turned from the table. "Your Loum man? The one you asked about, with the cut throat?"

Jacquot paused, turned.

"You were right. It was a left-handed cut, from behind. No question."

35

Alain Dupay was at his office on rue Vacon, an elegant nineteenth-century building on a Haussmann-style block with a brand-name boutique at pavement level and DupayCorp offices above, its stern façade decorated with neatly shuttered windows and ornately scrolled wrought-iron balconies.

Jacquot and Rully had called first at the Dupay residence in Malmousque, and been told by the maid where they could find him. At DupayCorp, a receptionist directed them to a lift and the fourth floor. When they reached it, a middle-aged woman in a pleated plaid skirt and bow-fronted blouse was waiting for them, introduced herself as Monsieur Dupay's PA, Delphine, and asked them to follow her. Monsieur Dupay was in a meeting with one of his investment team, she told them, over her shoulder, as they passed through an open-plan space filled with shirt-sleeved brokers cradling phones and scanning computer screens, but he would be free sometime in the next few minutes. If they would be so kind as to take a seat, and wait?

They did as they were told, in a panelled, thickly-carpeted room furnished with a pair of black leather couches, and a glass-topped coffee table neatly set with daily newspapers at one end and business and financial magazines at the other. A pair of spreading ferns in burnished brass urns stood either side of Dupay's office door, and on the wall behind Delphine's desk was a collection of gold-framed black-and-white photos of old Marseilles – a Vieux Port crowded with tall masts and tethered sails, pipe-smoking rope-makers at Vallon des Auffes, a gaff-rigged topsail schooner passing the Fort de St Jean, and a scrum of horse-drawn carriages on what looked like La Canebière – the room lightly perfumed with a fresh citrus scent, and a soothing atmosphere of monied calm. Delphine offered them coffee, which they declined, and then went back to her desk and her typing, offering them a conciliatory smile every few minutes, assuring them that Monsieur Dupay would not be long.

Not quite ten minutes later, there came the sound of voices approaching the other side of the doors, a man's voice and a woman's. The meeting was clearly over.

Rully put down his newspaper and shot a look at Jacquot, who smiled back at him.

And then the door was opening, and there was Dupay in neatly pressed grey slacks, and a white shirt, its sleeves rolled back to the elbows in a down-to-business style, standing aside to thank his departing visitor, a willowy blonde called Simone, for some report she'd prepared, that he'd look at as soon as he could. In the meantime, his thanks again.

It was Simone who recognised Jacquot, before he recognised her. He saw her stop dead, look at him, place him, and then smile uncertainly, with what looked like a blush.

And a second or two later he knew who she was. A photo on a fridge, in an apartment on avenue Sadi, his first day as Chief Inspector, the morning after the night before, suffering from a monstrous hangover. The woman he'd spoken to on the phone, the woman he'd been dreaming about just a few hours earlier.

But there was no time for anything beyond her surprised smile of recognition, as Dupay gestured to them to follow him into his office, closed the door behind them, and Simone was gone.

"Monsieur Dupay," Jacquot began, gathering himself for the matter at hand. "It is very good of you to see us at such short notice."

"You have anything to report?" Dupay had gone to a pair of windows behind his desk and stood looking down at the street, hands plunged into his pockets. He gave no indication that they should sit, but Jacquot did, nodding that Rully should do the same. When Dupay turned he seemed surprised that they should have done so without an invitation. He looked at them for a moment, then sat at his glass-topped desk, in a high-backed, black leather chair which he swung to and fro with the tips of his shoes.

Jacquot was not going to make it easy. "I just have a few questions about your stepson, Lucien?"

"Which are?"

"He's at home, I assume? At Malmousque, with his nanny?"

"And?"

"Does Lucien have any allergies? Nuts, for example?"

115

"Yes, he does."

"So there will be a supply of Epinephrine in case of emergencies?"

"An epipen, that's correct. A number of them. At the house, in the cars, on the boat. Wherever we happen to be. Without them…" He spread his hands.

"And Lucien knows about this allergy? Knows to be careful?"

"Of course."

Jacquot nodded, made a show of taking this in, but watched Dupay's expression. The man gave nothing away.

"But why do you ask? What has that to do with my wife's stolen jewellery? That's why you're here, isn't it?"

"Not exactly, monsieur. You see, we have a body in the morgue. Found in a rubbish heap not far from here. A young boy, with Down syndrome. No means of identification, save the name Lucien written in marker-pen on his forearm."

Dupay stiffened, stopped his chair-twisting.

"But, of course, it cannot be your Lucien, can it?" Jacquot continued, lightly. "When he is at home in Malmousque, with his nanny, Trudi."

36

At Jacquot's request, the body of Lucien Dupay had been moved from the pathology department's basement to a viewing room on the floor above. Jacquot drew back the sheet from the boy's face, and turned to Dupay.

On the drive from rue Vacon to the mortuary, Dupay hadn't said a word. And he didn't say a word now. Just clenched his jaw, swallowed once, and nodded.

It was up to Jacquot to make the running.

"Police headquarters is just a short walk, monsieur," he said, as he and Rully followed Dupay from the viewing room into a lino-floored corridor that smelled of polish and shone beneath the overhead light panels. "An explanation would be useful. If you wouldn't mind?"

Outside in the street, a crew of refuse workers in orange hi-viz jackets were tossing bin-liners into a refuse truck, and shovelling up the spilled mess from the split ones. The air was warm and stale and foetid, and Jacquot wondered if Dupay was thinking about his stepson being found, naked, in a pile such as this? If he was, it didn't show.

At police headquarters they took the lift to the third floor and, with Jacquot leading the way, they crossed the squad room to his office. Faces looked up from desks, and phones, and screens, watching their progress, and Grenier caught Jacquot's eye. There was no need to smile. The old boy's look was enough. *Good luck*, mon brave, *rather you than me*. But then Grenier didn't know what Jacquot knew.

"So, let's begin with your wife's briefcase," said Jacquot, as he pulled off his jacket, draped it over his chair back, and sat at his desk. "The briefcase stolen from her car. The briefcase you don't know about." He gestured to the chair in front of him, and Dupay took it, crossing one leg over the other and straightening the crease in his trousers. Making himself comfortable. Rully took the second chair, putting it by the window, a metre or so behind Dupay and just beyond his eyeline. He knew his stuff, thought Jacquot. The perfect way to rattle someone. So long as that someone wasn't Alain Dupay. Jacquot suspected he could have brought in the entire team, ranged them around the room, and the man wouldn't have batted an eyelid.

"Whatever you need to know, Chief Inspector." The voice was steady, but no less chill.

"What was in it?"

117

"A large amount of money," he replied.

"A ransom, I assume."

It wasn't a question, but Dupay nodded.

By the window, Rully frowned. He hadn't been expecting that. But for Jacquot it had been the only possible explanation.

Money. A briefcase full of it.

Money to steal, money to die for. Madame Dupay, Loum, Hakimi, and Boultier. Four of them.

And now Lucien, too, for the lack of it.

"So I take it that your wife was not visiting friends in L'Estaque the night she was shot?"

"No, she was not."

"She was making a drop?"

"Correct."

"How much money?"

"Ten million francs."

"And the instructions?"

"The briefcase to be placed in a bin with a yellow top, twenty metres past the access gate for Bassin Quatre. Out past Joliette."

Jacquot frowned. "So what was your wife doing, heading back to town and the money still with her?"

"Knowing my wife she took the wrong road. Got mixed up. She was nervous. And frightened. And worried sick about Lucien."

"You were there when she left the house?"

"Of course."

"You didn't think to deliver the briefcase yourself?"

"It was made clear that my wife should do it. Frankly she wasn't fit to drive, but we had no choice. We had to do what we were told."

"Man or woman? The person who gave you these instructions?"

"A man. No accent. The voice was a little muffled. The sound of traffic in the background. I'd guess a pay-phone."

"How many times did he call?"

"Three times. On the Wednesday, and twice on the Thursday. The first time he called, he spoke to Camille, told her that he had Lucien, that the boy was safe, and would be returned in exchange for the money. He told her how much, and said he'd call back the following day, at the same time, around five, with further instructions."

"When did you realise Lucien was missing?"

"We didn't, until that phone call. But just a few minutes later Trudi came racing into the house, and told Camille what had happened."

"Which was?"

"She had taken Lucien to the playground at Prado. It was a special treat. Every Wednesday. The swings, the carousels. He loved the lights and the music. He had been on the carousel, whirling around, with Trudi watching from the side. When the carousel came to a halt, there was suddenly no sign of him. Thinking he must have jumped off by himself, she ran around the playground searching for him, calling his name. There was no sign of him, and no one she spoke to had seen him. So she went back to the house."

"You were in your office when that first call was made?"

"The first I heard of it was Camille phoning me. In a panic. I went straight home."

"How would someone have your home telephone number?"

"It's listed. We are not ex-directory."

Jacquot nodded, and then, "What were your thoughts when I told you that the man who shot your wife had been seen carrying a briefcase?"

"Either she'd tipped the money into the bin from the briefcase…"

"Not really likely at the present time. With bins overflowing."

"…Or she hadn't delivered it," continued Dupay, paying no heed to Jacquot's observation. "Because she'd taken the wrong road, as I suggested."

"But there was no way of knowing?"

"Exactly. I just had to wait for the next call. Either they'd want to know where the money was or, if they'd got it, where to pick up Lucien. I didn't know which it would be, or how long I would have to wait, but telling you about it seemed a bad idea."

"I assume that the person you spoke to had said there should be no police involvement?"

Throughout this conversation, Dupay had kept his eyes on the clasped hands in his lap, or raised his head to look through the window. Now he turned them on Jacquot, a cold icy blue, as though in reprimand for such a stupid question. Of course, he'd been told no police involvement. Didn't every ransom demand come with the same proviso?

"And I intended to keep it that way," he said, at last, coolly, matter of fact, running a finger down his bearded cheek. "What could the police possibly have done?"

"For a starter, they could have followed your wife, watched the drop-off. Or maybe intervened when her assailant, the tapper, tried to rob her. Before he had a chance to shoot her."

Dupay shrugged. 'Maybe' was clearly not a word he put much store in. Instead he said, "What would be interesting to know is if she tried to conceal the briefcase, or fight for it, or whether she simply handed it over."

Jacquot tipped his head, frowned. Which earned him another icy glance.

"Because," Dupay sighed, "if she gave it up freely, there would have been no money in it. The ransom would have been paid. Isn't it obvious?"

"I have no doubt that she fought for it, monsieur, which is why she was shot. Probably by accident, in a struggle. Because the money was there. All of it. And four murders later, there is still no sign of it."

For the first time, Dupay looked taken aback.

"Four murders?"

"The man who robbed your wife, and killed her, Adam Loum. And later that night the two men who called on Loum, found the money, killed him for it and took off. Both of whom are now dead. Shot. By a person unknown. You don't by any chance own a blue BMW do you?"

Dupay frowned, shook his head.

"So, you are out of the frame, monsieur," said Jacquot, with a chill smile. "And we will carry on looking. For the killer, and the money." Jacquot reached back, into his jacket pocket, and pulled out his cigarettes, offered one to Dupay, who declined with a terse shake of the head, then lit one for himself. He blew a plume of smoke towards the ceiling fan, watched it spill round the still blades.

"So tell me about the second phone call."

"It was just before the hospital called to tell me about Camille. The same voice, the same man, telling me the drop had not been made."

"What did you say?"

"That the money was being delivered. Right then. My wife had left an hour or so earlier and must have got lost; she would be there any moment. The caller told me he would give me another hour."

"Or what?"

"He didn't say."

"And what happened then? After the call from the hospital."

"I left Trudi at the house, to field any calls, while I went to the hospital."

"And were there any?"

"An hour later, just as he'd said."

"And Trudi took the call, you say?"

"Yes. I'd told her to agree to whatever was asked, and then call me at the hospital."

"And the new demand?"

"The same amount again, with a twenty-five per cent penalty charge added."

"To be delivered where?"

"Another yellow-topped bin. On rue Honnorat, behind St-Charles station."

"And when?"

"The same time the following evening. Eight-thirty."

"Your meeting in town? When I came to see you with the earring?"

"Correct."

"He didn't give you much time to find the money. Another ten million plus."

"I'm in the business," Dupay replied, with a shrug. "He must have known that."

"And you made the drop?"

"Yes, I did."

"And then you came back home and waited?"

"What else could I do?"

Jacquot nodded. He might not like the man, but he could imagine how nerve wracking that wait must have been. But for someone who could accept the death of a wife and a stepson with such little reaction, maybe it hadn't been so bad. Just a business transaction gone wrong.

"Do you have any enemies?"

"Every time I lose someone's money."

"Does that happen often?"

"It's a racetrack out there. You win some, you lose some. The name of the game. But we make every effort to ensure that doesn't happen. That our investors have the very best advice, that we make sound and appropriate investments on their behalf."

"What about someone from your past? An old score to settle? Or someone who might be jealous of your success?"

"You ask me," he replied, sidestepping the question, but levelling a sharp look at Jacquot, "it's just someone out to make money. To take it from those who have it. Any way they can."

Jacquot wasn't convinced. A man like Dupay would have made himself an army of enemies. Growing up in Toulon. In Aix. Here in Marseilles. All it took was one.

"If you don't mind," said Jacquot, leaning forward to stub out his cigarette, "I would like to speak to Lucien's nanny."

37

When Jacquot, Dupay, and Rully arrived at the house in Malmousque, Jacquot asked Rully to stay with Dupay while he interviewed Mademoiselle Trudi Oberstock. On the drive to Malmousque Dupay had told them that Trudi was single, Swiss, and thirty-two, and had been working for the Dupays for the last four years. Jacquot found her in the main salon, sitting on a sofa, facing the windows. A cloud-shrouded spring sun caught her features and gave them a soft glow. The lightly tanned skin, the anxious blue eyes, the strong angled jaw line, and pale lips. Her blonde hair was bound back in a tight little French pleat and she was dressed in a pair of cream slacks and jumper-cardigan combination. She wore gold studs, a plastic Swatch that hung loose on her wrist, and an Eidelweiss broach that pinned together the rounded collar on her cardigan. She looked sweet, demure, but there was beauty there too, and a knowing look beneath the innocence. Not the kind of nanny a wife might comfortably choose to share the marital home, thought Jacquot, unless she was sure of herself, and her husband.

"Mademoiselle Oberstock, my name is Chief Inspector Jacquot of the Marseilles *Judiciaire*," he began, sitting on the sofa opposite her, leaning forward, elbows on knees. "I am afraid I have bad news about Lucien."

The nanny lowered her head, shook it, and a tear dropped. "I knew it. I just…" The voice was soft, educated. Just those few words were enough, the French only lightly accented. Then she raised her head, wiped at the tear track with the back of a hand, and looked imploringly at Jacquot, as though hoping he'd tell her something she might want to hear. That Lucien was hurt. In hospital, maybe. But not dead.

"He was found yesterday. I'm so sorry."

With a desperate sigh, Mademoiselle Oberstock rose from the sofa and crossed to the windows, stared out at the shifting grey sea. She was tall, and slim, and stood there with an air of strained elegance, the fingertips of one hand spread on the glass, the other held to her heart. Down in the city, there was just a breeze coursing through the streets, but here, on the heights of Malmousque, that same breeze had a buffeting bluster, slapping in gusts against the glass and making it creak. It could have been a photo-shoot for a fashion magazine, a young woman, fragile, wistful, looking out to sea. A cover shot. Everything about her just…

"And Monsieur Dupay knows?" she asked, turning from the window.

"He identified the body earlier today. He is here, now, with one of my team. But first, if you wouldn't mind, mademoiselle, I would like to ask you some questions. About the fairground at Prado."

She came back to the sofa, settled herself, straightened her back, hands in her lap. "Please, whatever you need," she said.

"I understand that your visits to the fairground were a weekly event?"

"Yes, they were. Every Wednesday. Lucien…" she lost her voice, cleared her throat, and continued. "For Lucien it was the highlight of his week. He so looked forward to it."

"What time did you leave the house?"

"Always the same time. After lunch. In the morning some of the rides don't operate, so Lucien preferred the afternoon."

"And you went there by car?"

She nodded, smoothed fingertips over the palm of a hand. She had beautiful nails, lacquered a pale shiny pink.

"Did you notice anything out of the ordinary? On the drive to Prado, or while you were there?"

"Nothing. It was no different to any Wednesday."

"You weren't aware of a car trailing you, or being followed around the fairground?"

She shook her head. "If I was, I didn't notice. Anyway, I had to keep an eye – and a firm grip – on Lucien. One minute he'd be tugging my hand, and then he'd let go and be off. Sometimes it was hard to keep up. He'd get so excited."

"What was he wearing?"

"A pair of red corduroy shorts, his favourite, a white polo shirt, white socks and blue trainers."

125

"You didn't ride on the carousel with him?"

"No. He liked to do it on his own. I just stood and watched as he whirled around. It was always so lovely to see him have so much fun. Waving each time he passed me, laughing. He was always laughing, always a smile; dear, darling Lucien."

"And when the carousel came to a stop?"

"Most times it seemed to stop where he got on, where it started, where I was waiting for him. And he never liked to get off until it came to a complete halt. For Lucien, every second counted. But on this occasion, as the ride slowed down, he passed me and went on for another half circle until he was on the other side from me. And that's where the carousel stopped. Which meant he was out of sight. Just for a moment. The time it took me to push through parents who were waiting for their children to get off, or people waiting to put their children on. There is always a crowd there for the carousel. But when I reached the other side, there was no sign of him. He'd got off, and just wandered away without waiting for me. So, I called his name and started looking for him. There's another ride he loves, the bumper cars, so I went there next. But still there was no sign of him. By now I'm getting worried, and I start asking people if they'd seen him. They couldn't miss him. A little boy, ten years old, red trousers, with Down syndrome. But no one had, no one had seen him. I asked everyone, running all over the place. But he wasn't there. I couldn't find him."

"So you came back here."

"There was nothing else I could do. I had to tell Madame."

"And she phoned Monsieur Dupay?"

"She was reaching for the phone to call him when it rang. And we found out that Lucien had been kidnapped. After that…" She slumped back into the sofa, spread her hands. "I just can't believe it. Little Lucien,

Lucien… how could anyone, possibly, want to do that lovely little boy any harm?"

38

A mid-afternoon sun had broken clear of its earlier clouds and was shining brightly, but all the lights of the Prado funfair were blazing when Jacquot and Rully pulled up in the car park. Coloured lights, flashing lights. The clamouring, confusing jangle of pop songs and barrel organs, whistles and shrieks, a pop-popping and tin-tapping from the shooting gallery. Balloons and bunting and teddy bear prizes. The sweet and savoury smells of popcorn and toffee apples, candy floss and hot dogs. Swings and rides and carousels… Jacquot's mother had brought him here many times, catching the bus from the Vieux Port, always as excited as he was, always jumping on the rides with him, her laughter filling the air. Two kids together. It all seemed somehow so close, yet so distant.

"It's either one or the other," Jacquot explained to Rully as they made their way through the crowds. "Either the nanny was followed, maybe not for the first time, and Lucien was simply snatched when an opportunity arose, or the operators of the carousel were involved."

"How?"

"Someone paid them to stop the ride with Lucien as far away from the nanny as possible. If they'd been followed before, whoever took Lucien would have known it was his favourite ride, and made arrangements. We just have to find out which."

The carousel was an old one, maybe even the same that Jacquot had ridden all those years ago with his mother. And big. Three concentric lines of prancing animals: tigers, lions, antelopes, zebras, even unicorns; all prancing legs, rolling eyes, and garish lolling tongues, all saddled up and ready to go. By the time they reached it, the carousel was racing round in a golden, light-filled blur with a strange tinny soundtrack that blared out over the hunched riders, rising and falling as they spun around. When it finally came to a halt, Jacquot and Rully worked their way through the dismounting riders to the centre of the carousel where a man in a greasy singlet, shorts, and leather sandals stood at the controls, its levers and switches and buttons housed in a panel of the central column. He eyed them suspiciously, two grown men who clearly had no intention of riding the carousel.

He was about to wave them away when Jacquot pulled out his badge and held it up. The man in the shorts didn't need to look. He knew who they were.

"Monsieur, a word?"

The carousel operator looked over their shoulders as the new riders chose their mounts and settled themselves onto their saddles.

"Come closer," he said, pointing to the platform he stood on, "or you'll be talking to yourselves."

Jacquot and Rully did as they were told, crowding onto a narrow strip of wooden decking, as the man leaned down into the central column and, with a final look around to see that everyone was ready, made to release the brake and start the ride. But Jacquot reached out a hand to stop him. The message was clear; until his questions were answered the riders weren't going anywhere.

He pulled out the photo of Lucien that he had taken from Dupay and showed it to the man.

"You recognise this boy?"

The man took the photo, turned it in the lights, squinted. "Yeah, I seen him," he said, handing it back. "Funny little fellow. Always laughing, he is.

And always goes for the unicorn. His mum don't ride though, she just watches."

There was something certain, yet uncertain, in the man's response. Too much detail, thought Jacquot. As though he'd been preparing for this encounter, and knew more than he was saying.

"You remember the last time you saw him?"

"Comes every week, he does, but haven't seen him ten days or more."

"Last time he was here, he went missing. From your carousel. You know anything about that?"

"Ain't my job to go babysitting. I sees 'em on, gives 'em a ride, then I sees 'em off. That's it. Talk to his mum, why don't you?"

"I have, and she told me the ride always stops where she put him on, so she's there when he gets off. Only the last time you did it differently, and he got off on the other side from her. How's that then?"

"Look, mister, I start it up, give it fifteen circuits, and then slow it down, stop it. And ain't no saying where that stop is."

"And that's where we have a problem, because I've heard different."

"Well, you heard wrong, is all. And right now I got a ride to run here, and you're holding things up."

"So start telling me what I want to hear, or you won't have any ride to run. I'll stop this carousel right now, close it down, and have my boys drop by, seal it off, and go over every centimetre." Jacquot looked around, and shook his head. "And something this kind of size, could take them a week, maybe more, before you could open it again." He turned, smiled at the man. Your choice, his look said. How do you want to play it?

The man gritted his teeth, shook his head as though he knew the game was up.

"It was the dad, right. Comes up to me a couple of rides before the kid

129

gets here, the kid in your photo, and says his wife's giving him a hard time, won't let him see the boy. Just wanted a few minutes with him, give him a hug, buy him an ice cream."

"He make it worth your while?"

The carousel operator spread his hands, then wiped one of them across his mouth.

"I said, did he make it worth your while?"

"Couple hundred. Felt sorry for him, tell the truth. All he wanted was to see his boy."

"What did he look like?"

"Darkie. You know, kind of Turkish, Middle-Eastern looking."

"A darkie?" Jacquot repeated, tapping the photo of the blonde Lucien. "His dad?"

"Hey, man. What do I know? Who's to say?"

"What else?"

"Good-looking, you know. Maybe late thirties, early forties. Well-dressed. Nice watch. Like he had money. And like I said, I felt sorry for him, you know."

"So when you slowed the ride down, you stopped it with the boy near his dad?"

"That's what he wanted."

"Did the boy recognise his dad?"

"Shit, man. You think I'm looking? I got a ride to run. Kids getting off, getting on… I ain't got no time to see nothing but the next load."

"You know what happened to him? After you set him down with his dad?"

"Not my business, man. Just doing the guy a favour."

"Well, let me tell you about that favour. A couple of days ago we pulled his naked body out of a pile of rubbish. Dead. Ten years old. How does that make you feel?"

The man swallowed hard, his face paled. "Aw, *merde...*"

"So, you got anyone to handle the ride? While you spend the next few hours at police headquarters going through some mug shots."

39

The sun had gone and the sky was darkening fast over the distant slopes of Mont Redon when Jacquot finally left police headquarters. It had been a long trawl of a day since Rully had banged on his door on Moulins, dragging him from his bed and his dream. The trip to the mortuary and Teri, to Malmousque and back to the city for Dupay, then off to the pathology department's viewing room, out to Malmousque again for the nanny, and then down to the Prado funfair. He felt drained, wiped out, with little to show for the day's work save Dupay's grudging acknowledgement of the ransom demand, and the carousel operator's admission that Lucien and his nanny had been set up, by a man who might or might not feature in the mug files that the operator was still wading through. And, finally, his call to *Maître* Bonnefoy to bring her up to speed on developments, a call that, thankfully, had been taken by her answering machine. As Jacquot headed down to the Vieux Port, he realised he wasn't just tired, he was hungry. Very hungry. Just a pitta fill from Hamid's at his desk, and a length of sugared *churros* that Rully had bought from a street stall. Thirsty, too.

But an empty stomach and dry throat would have to wait a while longer. There was one final call he needed to make before dinner, a drink or two, and his bed on Moulins.

131

Ten minutes after leaving headquarters Jacquot finally located the apartment block he was looking for, and rang the bell for M. Fontaine/S. Laronde.

"Yes?" The voice on the Entryphone was the voice he remembered from that early morning phone call.

"Chief Inspector Jacquot. I'd like to speak to…" But before he could finish, the door buzzed and the lock disengaged.

He took the lift, pressed for the third floor. When he got there he pulled open the lift's cage doors, turned to the right, and saw that the door to Simone Laronde's apartment was open.

"I'm in the kitchen," she called out, as he knocked and stepped into the apartment's hallway. "Wine? Or something stronger? I make a mean Martini."

He followed the voice, and found its owner by the fridge in the kitchen. The pinstripe skirt, high heels and cream blouse she'd worn earlier that day had been replaced by an oversize light blue sweater that hung low over a bare shoulder, darker blue slacks, and trainers. When she turned from the fridge and kicked the door shut, a bottle of Tanqueray and Noilly clenched in one hand and two frosted Martini glasses in the other, he saw that the make-up had gone too, wiped away to leave just the freshest, loveliest face. Lightly tanned beneath the white-blonde hair, and prettily freckled, she looked extravagantly healthy, vibrant. Sparkling blue eyes couched with the finest feathery lines when she smiled. And that smile.

"What if I'd wanted wine?" asked Jacquot, nodding at the two cocktail glasses.

"Then I'd have been wrong about you. And I'm very rarely wrong." She splashed a good few measures of gin into a shaker, followed it with a single handful of crushed ice, and handed it to Jacquot. "A gentle shake, please. Count to thirty. Not a second longer."

While he did as he was told, Simone Laronde twisted the cap off the Vermouth, blocked the top of the bottle with her thumb, and tipped it upside down.

Jacquot watched, frowned, got to fifteen seconds.

Picking up one of the glasses, she rubbed her thumb around the inside of the rim, then repeated the operation for the second glass. Twenty-two seconds. Next came the lemon, a mandolin, and the thinnest slice of peel. Cut in two, one curling sliver in each glass. As Jacquot hit the count of thirty, Simone pushed the two glasses across the kitchen table. "*Et voilà...*"

Jacquot worked the top off the shaker and poured out the contents. An equal measure in each frosted glass, just a centimetre from each rim. And not a drop left in the shaker. The perfect amount, expertly judged.

Simone reached for her glass, and then pulled out a chair, settled herself at the table. Waved to Jacquot to do the same.

"It was quite a surprise to see you this morning." She sipped her Martini and worked her lips on the icy taste.

"You and me, both," he replied, and did the same.

"So, is it Chief Inspector Jacquot, or Daniel, who's come calling?"

"You have a good memory."

"Names and numbers. My party trick."

"Well, I'm afraid it's Chief Inspector. But still..."

"But still... what?"

"But still... it's good to see you again."

She gave him a long cool look, took another sip of her drink, and put down the glass. "Well, let's start with the official stuff, Chief Inspector. And see how it goes from there."

"It's about your boss, Alain Dupay."

She said nothing, waited.

"Just a few questions."

Again, no response.

So he began, "How long have you worked for him?"

"Three years at the office in Aix, four years down here. In July."

"And your work is…"

"I'm an investment researcher. An analyst. I find interesting investment avenues for our customers, work out whether to play them long or short or somewhere in the middle, assess any possible threats, and pass on my findings and recommendations to Alain. Like I said, names and numbers; nothing to it."

"Alain?"

"It's Christian names at DupayCorp. Everyone. From mail room to board room."

"Well, as you know, Monsieur Dupay's wife, Camille, was killed a couple of weeks ago."

Simone nodded. "And you're surprised that he should be back at work, and in control, so soon?"

Jacquot tipped his head, gave the slightest shrug as though such surprise was understandable. "Did he return to the office this afternoon, after our visit?"

"Yes, about four."

"And how did he seem?"

"The same. Friendly, but business-like."

"Would it surprise you to learn that when he left with us this morning we went to a viewing room at the pathology department's mortuary to identify the body of his stepson, Lucien?"

Simone's eyes widened, her hand flew to her mouth. "Lucien's dead? How?"

"He was kidnapped two weeks ago. The ransom hand-over went wrong, and that was that. He was found yesterday afternoon. And you had no idea?"

She took a breath, shook her head. "No. None at all. How… awful."

"You didn't notice any change in Monsieur Dupay during that time?"

"Nothing."

"Business as usual."

Simone nodded.

"And how long did Monsieur Dupay stay at the office this afternoon?"

"He was still there when I left. He had a business dinner scheduled. A new investor."

"And he's keeping the appointment?"

"I believe so."

"Are you surprised, given what I've just told you?"

"Yes, and no. Alain's a very private person, the kind of man a lot of people might call cold. He doesn't give much away. On a professional level, he's absolutely focused, absolutely committed. Never lets his emotions come into play. But to lose his wife, and then Lucien…"

"Did you know his wife?"

"I met her a couple of times. Charity things tied in with work. She was a lovely lady, warm and generous, and very striking. Very upright, too. Very… classy, but…"

"But?"

"Kind of damaged, you know? As though she'd been through a lot of bad stuff and still couldn't quite believe that she was out of it, that she was safe. As if someone was going to snatch it away at any moment."

135

"And Lucien?"

"He came by the office sometimes, with Madame Dupay, or the nanny. The sweetest little boy. Just the biggest smile." And then Simone frowned. "But why all these questions about Alain? Is he in trouble?"

Jacquot waved a hand. "Just background stuff, really. He's not the easiest man to deal with."

"That's Alain."

"Tell me, does he have enemies? People who might want to see him hurt."

"There'd be a queue round the block. No different to any financial adviser. But there'd be just as many who worshipped the ground he walked on, people he'd made rich. It works both ways."

"Anyone you can think of, in particular, who might bear a grudge?"

She gave it some thought, then shook her head.

"What about you? Do you like him?"

"I like working for him. Because I like clever people. And I admire what he's done. The way he thinks."

"Has he ever made a pass?"

She tipped back the last of her drink, and Jacquot followed suit; let the question settle.

"Never. That's not his way. Not the kind of man he is."

And then, without any warning, Simone looked at her watch, and pushed away from the table. She picked up her empty glass, reached for Jacquot's, and went to the sink, rinsed the glasses, and racked them. The bottles of gin and Vermouth were stowed away in a cupboard and as she turned back to the table, drying her hands on a dishtowel, there was the sound of a key in a lock, the front door opening and closing, and a rough, southern voice calling out, "I'm home, honey."

40

"Monique, this is Chief Inspector Jacquot of the Marseilles *Judiciaire*," said Simone, making the introductions.

Monique stood in the kitchen doorway, brought up short, and looked at Jacquot suspiciously. She was shorter, darker, and a few years younger than Simone, with a wiry spread of copper-coloured hair. She was dressed in a blue nurse's uniform, with a name tag on the collar, and a leather tote over her shoulder. Jacquot got to his feet, held out his hand, and she stepped forward to shake it.

"Mademoiselle, a pleasure."

"My papers are in order, you know?" The hand was dry and hard, the voice too, with a sly, goading challenge in the words. He remembered the books on the salon coffee table. He knew which ones were hers.

"I am sure they are," replied Jacquot, with a friendly smile. "But I am not here to check papers. It is another, more serious matter that Mademoiselle Laronde is helping us with."

"The murder of Camille Dupay," said Simone, wrapping an arm round Monique's shoulder and leaning down to kiss her cheek. "So, I have to go to police headquarters to look at some mug shots. They think the man who killed her might have come to the office. I waited till you got back rather than leave a message." She turned to Jacquot. "Will it take long, Chief Inspector?"

Jacquot, taken by surprise, spread his hands. "An hour, maybe a little longer, if you could spare the time?"

"Go ahead," said Monique, swinging her tote onto the kitchen table which, Jacquot noticed, still showed wet rings from the Martini glasses.

"After the day I've had, it's a hot bath and a cold drink for me. Taken together. Doctor's orders." Brushing past Jacquot, she went to the fridge and reached in for a beer, pulled off the tab, and raised the can towards him. "Here's to crime, Chief Inspector, but I hope you get your man." She took a swig, wiped her mouth. "Still, don't keep her too long, you hear? We girls need our beauty sleep." And with that, she tipped her head to Simone, slid an arched look at Jacquot, and loped off to the bathroom.

"So," said Simone, with a conspiratorial smile, pulling on a coat and opening the apartment door. "Let's get going, Chief Inspector."

Out on the landing, they took the lift that Monique had come up in. She hadn't properly latched the cage doors behind her. "She's always doing that," said Simone. "When she gets home before me, it's a good bet I'll have to walk up three flights."

"Good exercise," said Jacquot.

"I can think of better. So where are you taking me?"

"Are we still official?"

As the oiled wheels and cables whined above their heads, Simone Laronde leaned back against the wall of the lift, folded her arms and narrowed her eyes. "Well, now, that depends, doesn't it?"

Out in the street, she pulled up the collar of her coat and looked around. "You have a car?"

"I walked."

"You remembered the way?"

"Just."

They started walking, back towards République, keeping a professional distance between them. But when they turned the corner, she slid her arm through his, like an old friend.

"She's very jealous. You got off lightly. The last straight guy in our apartment got very short shrift."

"I'm a cop. She was behaving."

"Cop, President of the Republic, King of Siam… Makes no difference to little Monique. She's a terrier; just doesn't care."

As they walked, Simone kept looking back over her shoulder, as though making sure they weren't being followed, but then she stepped out from the kerb and waved down a cab.

"Best to put some distance between us," she explained, as they settled into the back. "You have anywhere in mind?"

Jacquot leaned forward over the front seat. "You know Maman?"

The driver nodded. "Off Breteuil, right?"

"That's the one."

41

Chez Maman was bustling with an after-work crowd; a buzz of chatter, a low cloud of cigarette smoke over the *zinc*, and not a table to be found.

"Don't worry, I'm not hungry," said Simone, looking around.

"But I am," said Jacquot with a smile. "Same again?"

"Will their Martinis be as good as mine?"

"Maybe not."

"So why risk it? Get a bottle of red, and I'll find a table."

"Good luck with that," said Jacquot.

Five minutes later, he found her in a booth at the back of the wine bar.

"How did you manage that?"

"I knew the guy who was sitting here. He works for Borse. I did him a favour, so he owes me."

"Favour?" said Jacquot, dropping into his seat and pouring the wine.

"He's a coker. Who isn't, at Borse? I just pointed you out, said you were Drug Squad, casing the place. Worth a punt, as we analysts say, and it paid off. He and his chums were outta here. And now we have their table." She gave Jacquot the smile, eyes crinkling into feathery lines. "So, if we've finished with my boss, Chief Inspector," she continued, "don't you want to know how you ended up in my bed?"

"I hope I asked nicely." He picked up his glass, and tipped it gently against hers.

She gave him another of her probing looks, then reached for her glass and tipped him back, cocked an eyebrow. "I didn't think you'd remember."

Jacquot winced. "It was my birthday…"

"And you'd just made Chief Inspector, I know."

"All I remember is waking up and not knowing where I was, or how I'd got there."

"And, by implication, who you'd slept with. You certainly know how to make a girl feel special."

"I wish I did remember."

She gave him a fond smile. "Not many honest men in my line of work. It makes a change."

"So how, exactly…?"

She shook her head, frowned. "Tell the truth, I can't really remember either…" Then she laughed. "But of course I can. It was a bar on Dumas, back from the port. Late. And you weren't the only one celebrating. I'd just got a real big bonus, and was starting to spend it. I went out onto the terrace for a breath of air, and the view, and you came out after me. We just got talking."

Jacquot shook his head. "I should remember."

"You were celebrating. You're forgiven."

"You were, too."

"Maybe I hold it better than you."

"Maybe you hadn't drunk as much as me."

"It wasn't me smoking that joint."

"Ah."

"Some Chief Inspector."

A waitress came to their table, delivered a platter of cheese and *charcuterie*, a basket of warm bread.

"But you had lovely eyes, and a lovely voice." Simone continued, when the waitress had left. "And you didn't come on to me. Just chatted away. Light and easy. No angle. No... agenda. And then we went back inside. Later, I saw you on the corner of rue d'Abbesse, looking for a cab, so I pulled mine over and offered you a lift. You got in, were half-way through telling me where you lived, and you literally... passed out. Just..." She tipped her hand from up to down. "Out like a light."

"So you took me back to your place?" Jacquot pushed the platter towards her and she took a slice of Finocchiona.

"All I knew was Place des Moulins, but I couldn't very well dump you unconscious on the pavement, or deliver you to police headquarters. And you were a cop, after all, so the odds were in my favour. Mmmh, nice salami."

"But you got me up to your apartment?"

"Eventually."

"You undressed me? Put me to bed?"

"I was going to put you on the sofa," she said, reaching for the bread. She broke some off, wrapped another slice of salami around it, and bit into it. "This is so good…"

"But you changed your mind."

"You changed it for me. A moment of weakness."

"And Monique?"

Simone swallowed, sighed. Took a sip of wine.

"We're an item, Daniel. She's special to me. But sometimes… sometimes I go walkabout. If you can live with that, fine. If you can't…" She shrugged. "In my life Monique, or someone like her, will always come first. That's the kind of girl I am."

"How long have you been together?"

"Two years, now. I cut my hand on a paring knife, badly." She held up her left hand, and he saw a thin white line traced across the ball of her thumb. "Couldn't stop the bleeding, so I wrapped it up in a dishcloth, went to *Urgences* at La Timone, and she cleaned it up. Just watching her fingers work the wound, her soft, calming voice, the way her eyes twinkled. That's all it took."

"She's a lucky girl. And so are you. I wish you both well."

Simone smiled, uncertainly. "Is that a sign-off?"

"That's for you to decide. I mean, I understand what you're telling me. The ground rules. And that's fine by me. But the next time you want to go walkabout, I'd love to keep you company."

"And I know where to find you."

"Yes, you do."

Later, in his bed in Moulins, Jacquot went to sleep thinking about Simone Laronde. Their taxi dropping her back outside her apartment building, her kiss, her smile. The touch of her hand on his cheek. The promise she'd call.

But he didn't dream about her.

42

Burak was happy. Not that anyone would know, because his hard, brutal face and cold black eyes gave nothing away, and the poor state of his teeth had long ago persuaded the Turk that smiling was something best avoided. Unless he wanted to frighten someone. Too many nuts, and too much salt, had done their damage, not to mention the sugar in his favourite eighty-layer Gaziantep *baklava*, topped with a generous dollop of *kaymak*. It was just such a dish that his assistant, Dalan, now placed on the ottoman in front of Burak's divan. A gift from one of his many suppliers.

"From Yilmat, you say?" said Burak, waving away a fly as a spill of brown Turkish honey oozed onto the plate.

"With his very best wishes for all your enterprises, *effendi*. May the Prophet bless and guide you." Dalan gave a little bow. It was a wise man, he knew, who observed the formalities in any dealings with his boss.

Burak leaned forward, picked up the fork and dug it into the sweet dessert. The pastry layers crackled lightly and bent beneath the fork's pressure. "A little dry, don't you think?" He lifted the sticky slice of cake, examined the portion with a tip of his head to left and right, then slid it between his lips. He chewed a moment. "Mmh, maybe not as dry as I thought. But nowhere near so good as Tekdimir's. He still has work to do, this Yilmat. But thank him, anyway."

Dalan stepped back, bowed again, but did not leave. Nor did he speak until Burak had finished eating, licking his lips before wiping them on the embroidered cuff of his *jubba*.

"There is something else?"

"Just the man you wanted to see."

143

"The mechanic?"

"He is the one, *effendi*. Feghouli is his name."

"Is he pretty?"

"I would say he is not, but you will be the best judge of that."

Burak waved his hand. "Send him in. Is his gift prepared?"

"On your desk. As you requested."

Burak nodded, and watched Dalan back away, turn and head for the door. A good man, thought Barak. A trusted retainer, for some years now. But then they were always the ones to watch most carefully, was that not what his father had told him all those years ago? He took another slice of the *baklava*, not because he particularly liked it, but because he was hungry. Always hungry. But then, as his mother had liked to say, after talking and drinking what else was a mouth for? Poor woman. No imagination, he thought.

There was a knock at the door, and Dalan came back, stood to one side and waved in a young man dressed in a light grey suit, tightly buttoned. The knot of his blue tie was a little low so Burak could see that the top button of his white shirt was missing.

"Eren Feghouli, *effendi*," said Dalan. Another bow, and the door closed behind him, leaving the mechanic from Faranese's garage to clasp his hands in front of him and then reclasp them behind his back. He didn't know what to do, or what to say. Which was good, Burak decided, because the boy was frightened. What he wasn't, was pretty. A mop of greasy hair trained low over his forehead, rather large red ears, and darting fearful eyes under thick black eyebrows. And the hands! Big and gnarled, the fingernails and wrinkles darkened with grime.

"Come closer," said Burak, waving a hand at him.

His visitor shuffled forward, uncertain, as though he didn't want to get too near.

"You are married?" Burak began, smelling the sharpness of some cheap cologne.

"Yes, *effendi*."

"You have children?"

"Yes, *effendi*."

"How old?"

"Three years and five, *effendi*."

"Boys or girls?"

"We are blessed with boys, *effendi*."

"Blessed, indeed. Their names?"

"Tarik, and Yunus, *effendi*."

Barak nodded. Which one, he wondered, had his father's ears? And which, the hands? Or did they have both? Poor boys, what future would there be for them with such handicaps? But at least their father was clever, so all was not lost. He had seen that *mec*, Boultier, with the wad of cash, and had called it in. To Torkmaz, who'd passed it on to Gereç, who'd passed it on to Aysal. And from there to Dalan. Something of interest.

"Loyalty is a great thing, Eren. And you are as blessed with it, as you are blessed with boys. You have done me a great service, for which I am very grateful."

"I… I…" the mechanic could say no more, relief flooding through him. He had been summoned that morning to meet with *Effendi* Burak, and his heart had almost stopped beating. But now…

Burak held up his hand, and the stammering stopped. But Burak could see that there was still fear in the man's eyes. Which was how it should be.

He nodded towards the desk. "There is a package there for you, my friend Eren. For your help. For your sharp eyes. Take it, and spend it wisely.

Maybe, too, a gift for your young sons, from their uncle Nakim."

"It will be as you wish," the mechanic managed. With a series of quick, jerky bows, he went to the desk, and picked up the package. He knew what it was, the weight of it, the shape of it, the riffling feel of the notes shifting against his fingertips as he slipped it into his jacket pocket. And backed away, bowing as he went, heading for the door.

The great Burak. The feared Burak.

And he had been rewarded. Received money from the man himself.

Such a thing was surely not possible. And yet it was.

As he ran for the bus for Plombières, Eren Feghouli realised he had never been happier. Nor more relieved.

43

Jacquot had been expecting it. A summons from the newly-appointed examining magistrate, Solange Bonnefoy. But this time the meeting was held, not at Bistrot Savarin, but in her chambers at the Palais de Justice. A high-ceilinged, book-lined room on the Palais' second floor, with a honey-coloured herringbone parquet floor, an oak desk tidily stacked with ribboned documents, and a set of terraced French windows that overlooked an inner courtyard. The room was cool, had a soft flowery smell, and the pitter-pattering of a fountain could be heard splashing merrily below.

This morning, a little before lunch, *Maître* Bonnefoy was dressed in her formal advocate rig of black gown and long white cravat, her cap of grey hair almost boy-like, and her features even more drawn and severe than he remembered them. But an advocate's robes would make any face look grave, and the rimless rectangular spectacles she wore, which had not been present at Bistrot Savarin, added to that impression. Sharp and business-like, thought Jacquot as he took the seat she indicated, and not to be underestimated.

Putting aside the file she'd been reading and taking off her spectacles, *Maître* Bonnefoy gave Jacquot what seemed like a sympathetic look.

"Thank you for your message," she began. "It would appear that someone's been busy since we last met. Four murders now, and the Dupay boy, Lucien, found dead in a pile of rubbish." She frowned. "Poisoned, apparently, but was it deliberate?"

"Hard to say, *Maître*. It could have been an accident – whoever had taken Lucien did not know of his allergy. Or maybe they did, and used the allergic reaction to cover their crime. We will only know for sure when we have those concerned in custody."

"And how long do you suppose that might be, Daniel, before you have 'those concerned' in custody?" she asked, tapping the spectacles against her knuckles.

The use of his Christian name eased Jacquot's initial concern, but he knew not to take advantage of it. The examining magistrate was not the kind of woman who'd think too highly of any liberties being taken. Best to play it straight.

"I cannot tell you that with any certainty, *Maître*. As you know, Madame Dupay's killer, the tapper, Loum, died from a right-to-left cut to the throat which we have now established puts the left-handed Boultier in the frame for his murder. But both Boultier and his accomplice Hakimi have also been murdered. Youssef Hakimi was the first to die, shot in the ankle and knee to encourage co-operation, followed by a killing shot to the head once the killer had what he wanted – presumably the whereabouts of Boultier and the ransom money. As for Boultier, we have a cleaner kill. A single shot to the head, using the same kind of weapon. With a silencer, in both cases, since no gunshots were heard. So, unquestionably a professional. Once we have him, we will be close to whoever took Lucien."

"But how, exactly, did this professional find Boultier and Hakimi so swiftly?"

Jacquot spread his hands. "I cannot say, *Maître*."

"And the man is still at large. And could be anywhere by now."

"As you say, *Maître*. Still at large." Jacquot cleared his throat. "And to be honest, unless we are very fortunate, he will probably remain so. Professional killers are professional for a reason. They are rarely apprehended, once they have left a crime scene, and they are expert at covering their tracks. Which means we have no useful description, no fingerprints… nothing to go on. Just an assumed name, and a blue BMW." Jacquot spread his hands. "I wish I could give you more."

"So, we have a single killer out there somewhere. And no way to find him. Or, rather, two killers, since it's unlikely that your shooter killed Lucien?"

"Quite so, Madame. But I do believe there's a link. Loum stole the money Dupay had raised for the ransom demand, and Boultier and Hakimi stole it from him. Whoever took it from them was hired for the job. Retrieve the money, put the offenders down, and leave no trace."

"Hired by whoever had taken Lucien?"

"Maybe…"

The examining magistrate tipped her head, frowned. "Maybe?"

"As I see it there are two possible options. One, the kidnapper found out about Boultier and Hakimi taking the money, and put someone on their trail."

"Or?"

"Or it was Dupay."

"Dupay? How do you figure that?"

Jacquot shrugged. "Dupay might have had someone follow his wife for the hand-over. Someone to see who picked up the ransom money, to follow them, track them down. Get the boy, and keep the money. Dupay has a history. I wouldn't put it past him."

"But if his wife was followed, as you suggest, surely whoever it was could have stopped Loum robbing her and shooting her in the first place?"

"Perhaps the tail lost her in traffic, or she did something he wasn't expecting... like taking the wrong road. Which is what she must have done, to be heading back to town, away from the drop at Bassin Quatre with the money still in her possession. By the time anyone following her got back on her trail, Loum had the briefcase and was gone."

"You think the man following her might have seen him, given chase?"

"It's possible. Of course, he'd have had to leave his car and follow on foot. There's no way he could have crossed lanes on that stretch of road. He'd have had to park up somewhere first. It wouldn't have been easy."

The examining magistrate gave Jacquot a long, shrewd look. "Are you sure that your feelings about Dupay, on a personal level, are not clouding your judgement?"

"I like to keep all my options open, *Maître*. Sometimes such instincts pay off."

"Have you asked Dupay about this?" There was a gleam of amusement in her grey eyes; but it was just a brief gleam.

"No, I haven't. Not yet."

"It might be a good idea, don't you think? Narrow the field down."

"Whatever he might say, can I be sure to believe him?"

Bonnefoy sighed. "Well, he's certainly keen to get to the bottom of all this. Quite insistent, in fact. He's been on to the Procurator General, which I'm sure won't surprise you. Suggested a more experienced officer be appointed to head the investigation into his stepson's death." She paused, smiled. "It would appear that he has no confidence in your ability, and wanted the PG to know that."

"And?"

"I told the PG that, in my opinion, you were the officer best qualified to handle the case. That I had every confidence in you."

"Thank you, Madame."

"But you'd better make that confidence pay off, and bring me something, Daniel. There's momentum building here for a resolution, and I need to provide it."

"You have my assurance that I will do everything that I can."

44

It was a week of funerals, and Jacquot attended each of them. Five in all, held at the St-Pierre Cemetery in Marseilles' fifth *arrondissement*.

The first, a delayed Muslim ceremony for Adam Loum, was held on a Tuesday afternoon, the washed and shrouded body lowered into its final resting place and laid on its right side facing east. It was raining softly and Jacquot stood in a line of trees separating this Muslim area from its Christian neighbour, close enough to watch the proceedings, but too far away to hear the whispered funeral prayers – "*Bismilllah wa ala millati rasulillah*". Apart from two clerics from the Bilal Mosque and the burial party, there was no one to bid the man farewell – no family, no friends. And for Jacquot, more importantly, no possible leads in terms of Loum's associates; no one to identify, no one new to question, no way to advance the investigation any further through Adam Loum. Literally, a dead end.

The following morning, it was Youssef Hakimi's turn. This time more than a dozen people turned up. His father, three uncles, and a group of younger men who had worked with Hakimi at one time or another, or been friends, their names and contact details found in his address book. Formally attired in dark suits and wearing traditional *taqiyah* skullcaps, each of these men had already been questioned by the *Judiciaire* in the course of the investigation. And, once again, standing in the same spot as the previous afternoon, the same soft rain drifting down from a leaden sky, Jacquot saw no new faces.

As the funerary prayers came to an end, Jacquot turned and walked away, hands in his pockets, collar up and head down. How he hated funerals, he was thinking. Such grey and sombre occasions. When his time came, he'd long ago decided he wanted music and laughter and colour. And food and wine in abundance, and a light breeze in blue sunshine to carry his ashes from the ramparts of Fort St Jean across the entrance of the Vieux Port. So absorbed was he in these reflections that if she hadn't spoken he would have passed her by without a glance.

"I wasn't allowed to be there. Just the men."

Jacquot was just a few strides from the squad car he'd used, parked on a side road off the cemetery's Grande Allée, when the young woman stepped out from the cover of a plane tree. At first he didn't recognise her; a dark blue shawl drawn up around her head and face, her slim figure in a belted black coat, her hands tucked tightly in its pockets. He frowned. And then… Selmina, the girl on the stairs outside Hakimi's apartment.

"I'm so sorry," Jacquot replied. "It seems so unfair. But Youssef will know you're here, and he will be pleased that you came."

She took a deep breath. "I miss him, you know? I mean, I know we weren't together all that long, and maybe he wasn't the best kind of man in the world, but he was good, you know. In his heart." She looked so sad, so sorrowful, that Jacquot found himself opening his arms and, after a moment's hesitation, she was hugging him tight, sobbing into his collar.

"It's never easy," he said, patting her shoulder. "But you will be fine, young lady. You have what it takes. Today you are sad, but soon you will be stronger. And you will always remember him. That is enough."

There was some more snuffling, but then she gathered herself, stepped away from him. She wiped her nose, and tried a smile.

"Thank you."

"Can I offer you a lift, wherever you need to go?"

Selmina looked at the car, its blue stripe, its rack of lights, and the uniformed driver. "I don't think that would be a good idea, do you?" And with a wan smile she walked away, back to the cemetery's entrance, sparing him just a final glance over her shoulder before turning through the gates and disappearing.

Yes, thought Jacquot, you'll be fine.

Marc Boultier's funeral took place two hours later in the Christian section of St-Pierre. The thin, shawling drizzle had returned after a brief lunchtime break and the hearse had its wipers on as it led the cortège to the far end of the cemetery, turned along the northern wall and drew up at a line of small headstones. At the far end of this line a humped pile of earth covered in a sheet of Astroturf marked Boultier's final resting place, and a small group of mourners watched with bowed heads as the the coffin was lowered into the grave beside it.

As with Hakimi, there were no new faces, no one the *Judiciaire* had not interviewed. His mother, a widow, three younger brothers, an older sister, and assorted family members. Only the mother and sister wore black, the rest of them in a mix of jeans and dark quilt *gilets*, the graveside gathering huddled under shared black umbrellas while the priest hurried through his prayers for the dearly departed. Sitting in his own car this time, on a slight rise two avenues away, Jacquot stubbed out his cigarette, started up the engine and drove away. He wasn't surprised that the three burials he'd attended so far had provided no new leads, but he had no doubt that the last two funerals that week would be far more interesting.

45

The Dupay funeral service was held at the Ste-Marie-Majeure Cathedral and, unsurprisingly, thought Jacquot, the sun shone for the great and the good of Marseilles with a blue spring-like abandon. Just two feathery white wisps of cloud above the distant Pharo Palace, the air fresh and warm and promising, the dome and turrets and striped flanks of the cathedral patrolled by swooping, cawing seagulls.

Standing at the window of his third-floor office at police headquarters, Jacquot watched the two hearses draw into the square and stop at the cathedral steps. Two hearses and two caskets. One for Camille Dupay and the other for her son, Lucien, the longer casket borne on the shoulders of six pallbearers, the smaller carried by just four, the white lacquered wood flashing in the sunlight, the gleaming brass handles tied with coiled ribbons of spring flowers, bevelled lids loaded with dyed-black Cana lillies.

An hour later, alerted by a slow toll from the cathedral's bells, Jacquot went to the window again in time to see the two caskets brought out, noting that while Alain Dupay had been one of his wife's pallbearers on the way in, he had changed position and was now one of the four men carrying his stepson's casket on the way out. A neat trick, thought Jacquot, uncharitably, chiding himself the very next moment. He might not like the man, but such thoughts were inappropriate, both unkind and unwarranted.

By the time the caskets had been loaded into the hearses, with the congregation gathered on the cathedral steps to see them off, Jacquot and Rully were turning out of rue de l'Évêché onto the Vieux Port, and heading for the cemetery to take up position ahead of the cortège. Three of the squad – Charlie Serre, Peluze and Grenier – had attended the service at the cathedral, tasked to keep an eye out for anyone who might, in any way, be significant, while he and Rully would do the same at St-Pierre.

Given that only close friends and family would be attending the burial, Jacquot was still surprised at the number of limousines that came down the cemetery's Grande Allée, pulling up behind the two hearses at the Guichot-Navarre family mausoleum where Camille and Lucien Dupay were to be interred, chauffeurs jumping out to open doors for the funeral party. From their observation point, behind a line of trees at the far end of the Allée, Jacquot watched through a pair of binoculars as the mourners gathered around the mausoleum's gates, while Rully shot off frame after frame with a camera and telephoto lens. Which was just as well. Of the thirty or so mourners watching the caskets carried into the mausoleum one after the other, Alain Dupay in a sharply-tailored dark suit, and the nanny, Trudi Oberstock, in veiled hat and demure black dress, hands clasping a small black bag, were the only faces he recognised.

He was scanning the crowd with his glasses, face after face, when he noticed, beyond the funeral party, the blurred shape of a slim, wiry man leaning against one of the Allée's plane trees. He was watching the proceedings as any visitor to the cemetery might do – the line of limousines, the formally dressed mourners, an ancient mausoleum on the Grande Allée itself – but there seemed something unsettling, even suspicious about the man's presence there. Jacquot adjusted the focus and the blurred shape sharpened. Short, curly black hair, dark skin, a stubbly beard and hawkish nose. A red wool cardigan, grubby jeans.

Jacquot nudged Rully. "That one. At the back there, by the tree. You see him?"

46

When the cemetery pictures were developed Rully offered to go through them and make the various identifications, but Jacquot had a better idea.

Down in the Records Office Sergeant Lefèbre shuffled through the prints. There was no hesitation. The man was a walking, or rather limping, encyclopaedia.

"There on the far left, that's Madame Thiers who heads the Opéra Committee and her husband, Arnaud; the man with the cane is Georges Olivier, head of the DupayCorp Children's Fund; then there's Régine and Henri Chappe from the *Mairie*; and Marc Gilhaud from the Cantini Gallery on Grignan; next to him is…" And on it went. One after another. A quick glance, a name, and the next shot, the stack of photos played like a pack of cards.

The last print showed the man by the tree. Lefèbre squinted, brought the picture closer. "Now there's a face from the dim and distant."

"You know him?"

Lefèbre tapped the picture against the edge of his desk, looked at the ceiling. "D… D… Name begins with a D… Diman, Daman, Dagan… Dalan! J… J… Javad. Javad Dalan. That's him. But what's he doing at St-Pierre?"

"Your guess is as good as mine. Could have been visiting, but he seemed very interested in the Dupay party. Like he'd come for it."

"You think to follow him?"

"Leaning against that tree one minute, gone the next. Like he'd never been there."

"Memory serves, he used to hang round Capucins. Market boy, smart as a buttonhole, and slippery as seaweed. Now you see him, now you don't."

"Has he got a sheet?"

"Not him. Too smart, that one."

"Any ideas where we might find him?"

The old Sergeant shook his head. "If he worked Capucins, the market traders might know what he's up to."

"An address?"

Lefèbre gave him a look.

47

The blow-up photograph of Javad Dalan at the St-Pierre cemetery was blurred and indistinct, an out-of-focus head and shoulders shot that could have belonged to anyone with dark curly hair and a swarthy complexion. There were no particular features – no shape to the nose, no angle to the stubbly jaw, no real detail for the mouth or eyes – and given the necessary cropping no sense of height or weight; just a distance-smeared close-up, like someone seen through frosted glass. But now, thanks to Lefèbre, they had a name, something to accompany the photo; something to focus the attention, jolt the memory.

"Don't bother with the kids," said Jacquot, as he and Rully strolled past the Noailles metro into the early morning bustle of the Capucins market square. The air smelled of salted fish and sliced watermelon, the sea and the land, sharp and fresh, and he took a long, deep breath of it. "Just speak to the old guys," he continued, "the ones who've been around the longest," and prodding Rully's arm, he nodded to a small café on the sunny side of the *place*. "But coffee first, and Calva to stiffen the sinews."

They took a pavement table by the café's door, close enough to the market stalls to feel the brush of passing coats and bags, and the warmth of an early sun just rising across the rooftops. When the coffees arrived and the Calvas were dealt with, Jacquot lit up a cigarette, settled back in his chair and blew out a lazy plume of smoke.

"So why not the young ones?" asked Rully, leaning forward, elbows on the table and hands clasped round his coffee cup.

"A matter of pride. You're a cop, they won't tell you a thing. But the older ones, their dads and their uncles, are past all that. A quiet word, a smile, respect – man to man – and they'll help if they can. If not, well things have a way of getting around. Something will come of it."

"So why tell them? That we're cops, I mean?"

Jacquot gave Rully the same kind of look that Lefèbre had given him in the Records Office. *Are-you-kidding?*

An hour later they sat at the same table and compared notes.

"Couple of the stall holders knew the name," said Rully, "but they hadn't seen him for a while. Moved on, and up, one of them said, but he didn't know where."

"That's more than me. All I got was a shrug, or a spread of hands. Oh, and a bag of..." Jacquot reached into his pocket, drew out a brown paper wrap and opened it up. "Probably the best dates you'll ever eat." He pushed the bag across the table and Rully peeled one away from the gluey, wrinkled pile. "Malouf's *Deglet Nours*. From Algeria," he said, drawing the bag back

157

and taking one for himself, turning the honey-coloured date in the sunlight with a thoughtful anticipation. He popped it into his mouth, licked his fingers, and chewed appreciatively.

"So, what next?" asked Rully.

"Regrettably our options are limited. For now, another cigarette, another coffee, and some more of Malouf's irresistible dates." Jacquot shrugged, reached for the bag. "But something is sure to turn up. It usually does."

48

It was just one word. 'Walkabout?' Written on a piece of headed cream vellum DupayCorp stationery, slipped into an envelope with DupayCorp's logo printed in its top left-hand corner and his name scrawled across the front in black ink.

"Such a well-spoken young lady. Not like some's I could mention," said Madame Foraque, looking to the hallway's tiled floor and sniffing dismissively.

For Jacquot it had been a long and tiresome day, with the Dupay case now on hold so the squad could catch up with other investigations. But at least there'd been no further enquiries from *Maître* Bonnefoy, for which he was grateful. That Alain Dupay had expressed his dissatisfaction with Jacquot's handling of the case to *Maître* Bonnefoy's superior, the Procurator General, requesting his removal as lead investigator, had come as no surprise. What had surprised, and heartened him, was Bonnefoy's vote of confidence. He knew, however, that such confidence and support would come at a price. For all his assurances, he would have to bring her something. And sooner, rather than later.

"Opened the door on the poor girl, just as she was trying to push the letter through the box," his concierge continued, nodding at the envelope, and flicking a finger at its contents.

Of course, he could have slipped the letter in his pocket and opened it in his room, but when Madame Foraque handed it to him, she'd held it a beat longer than she might have. The message was clear. Putting it in his pocket had not been an option.

"Lunchtime it was. Caught her by surprise, I can tell you. The look on her poor face, and so apologetic; worried she might have given me a start, standing there like she was. As if…"

"Just a friend, nothing more," lied Jacquot.

"Then more's the pity is all I'll say. Not many around like that one," she continued, trying to catch a glimpse of the message. "The manners on her."

For a moment Jacquot wondered what Madame Foraque would have to say if she knew of Simone Laronde's leaning and lifestyle choices, but there was no point enlightening her. Instead, he gave her a nod and a smile, and trotted up the stairs to his apartment where he picked up the phone and made the call.

They met an hour later at La Marine, Jacquot shaved and showered, in black jeans, deck shoes and his favourite leather jacket. Simone was there ahead of him, sitting at an outside table with a *demi-pression* and leafing through a day-old copy of *Les Échos*.

"Checking your investments?" asked Jacquot, pulling out a chair and signalling to a waiter; there was no need for him to order here.

"Light reading," Simone replied, folding the paper and tossing it onto the empty table beside them. "Every little helps."

"Don't you ever leave it all at the office?" asked Jacquot.

159

"Do you?"

He spread his hands. "I guess not," he replied, as his *jaune* arrived. He poured a dash of water over the pastis and stirred the ice, tipped the glass against her beer, and took a sip.

"Then we're in the right businesses, you and I. Like my father used to say, if you go to bed on a Sunday night and you don't want to go to work the next day then you're in the wrong job."

"Sunday, Monday, it's all the same when you sign up with the *Judiciaire*."

"Markets, too. Once you're in, that's it – you're caught. There's always someone trading somewhere. Always a deal to do."

They settled back in their seats, took each other in. She was wearing a light blue sweat shirt the colour of her eyes, Lycra leggings, and trainers. There was a gym bag on the chair beside her.

"So how did you find me?" asked Jacquot. "I know I said Moulins the night we first met, but that's a lot of houses."

"Well, it wasn't past midnight for starters, so it was easier. I just knocked on a door and asked. Isn't that what the cops do?"

He smiled. "And you met my concierge."

"It was a little embarrassing. I couldn't get the flap on the letterbox to work, and suddenly the door opened and there she was. Like a little red sprite."

Jacquot nodded. "That's her."

"And so lovely, so sweet."

"I've been working on her." Jacquot pulled out his cigarettes, offered her one and lit it, then lit his own. She tipped back her head and blew out the first of the smoke, the line of her jaw tight and firm, the lips puckered, the white blonde hair falling back past her shoulders. She was, thought Jacquot,

160

a stunningly attractive young woman. Relaxed, carefree, confident, and utterly beguiling. He only hoped that he'd be offered another opportunity to get to know her better. "So, what's the plan? How come the walkabout? Monique?"

"It's her mother's birthday, so she's away for the weekend."

"You didn't go with her?"

Simone sighed. "Her parents don't know about her. About us, I mean. How she is."

"I'm sorry. It must be difficult. How about your parents?"

"No parents. A car crash. I was nineteen, just starting an economics course at Aix. They were taking my little sister to the cinema. On their way home they got hit by a drunk driver jumping a set of lights." She gave a small, wistful smile, then shrugged, waved away the memory with her cigarette. "And you?"

Jacquot told her, and she smiled again. "Two little orphans," she said, lifting her beer. "So, what do you say we drown our sorrows, and get this show on the road?"

49

Simone took charge from the start.

"You did Maman, so now it's my turn," she told him as they left La Marine, and after dropping her gym bag at her apartment and changing her Lycra leggings for jeans, she led him to a line of lock-ups behind the avenue Sadi service station. "Time to meet my baby," she said, and unlocking a metal garage door she rolled it up and went inside. "You better stay outside. It's a bit of a squeeze in here."

A moment later, Jacquot heard a low growl in the shadows, a set of brake lights came on, and then the reversing lights. He stepped to one side, and she backed an open-top red and cream sportster out of the garage.

"An Austin-Healy 100-6. Came off the line in 1959," she told him as he settled into his seat and looked for a seat belt. There wasn't one. "One of the last before they started in on the 3000 series. The only trouble is the right-hand drive, but you get used to it."

At first Jacquot wasn't so sure that he would get used to it. Sitting in the left-hand seat as a passenger seemed altogether more nerve-wracking than being behind the wheel. It was seeing the headlights coming towards him, with no real control over steering or traffic breaks or judgement. But Simone was clearly a confident and proficient driver, working the gears and accelerator with impressive skill, leaning across him to check the road ahead before pulling out. He quite liked that, for the closeness as much as the caution, and he settled back to enjoy the ride as best he could, swinging around the Vieux Port and onto the Catalans road, the wind in his hair, and the roar of the engine filling his head.

Once on the Corniche carriageway Simone let rip, her blonde hair streaming out behind and her jaw set tight. Then, as the slipstream wind grew in pitch to match the roar of the engine, she indicated left and with a sharp brake turned left, up into the slopes of Malmousque. Jacquot leaned back in his bucket seat and looked up at a star-studded sky, a half moon sliding over the heights of Mont Redon, the air filled with an enticing mix of hot engine oil and the sea. It was the perfect night, and he felt a confirming sense of exhilaration, and anticipation. And then, wherever they were, there was another squeal of brakes, a spin of the wheel, and an "*Eh bien, nous sommes ici.*"

Paula's exterior was exactly the kind of place that Jacquot would have gone for had he chanced upon it, the kind of place that promised nothing but gave you a meal to remember. It was just a doorway, woodplanked, with a lopsided pink neon scrawl of letters above it spelling the name, and an interior that was dark and close. A driving enthusiast's haunt with framed black-and-white photos behind the bar of chequered flags and laurel-wreathed Grand Prix winners from a distant past. He'd never heard of it, never been there, but he loved it before the door closed behind him.

"The pasta's always good, but mussels take the prize," Simone advised, settling herself at a table at the back. "If there are any left. An old fellow from Sormiou brings them in from his ropes out on Riou. For his family, and for Paula. No-one else. Every day, fresh. You won't get anything like them anywhere else in town."

They turned out to be even better than Simone had said, served in a thick white china tureen to share, with a basket of toasted sourdough bread. "Way tastier than *frites*, don't you think?" she asked, dipping a crust into the creamy broth, not really expecting an answer. Jacquot reached for his napkin and wiped his chin; he knew it would be glistening, just as he knew that these mussels were probably the best he had ever eaten. Soft, plump and steaming hot, a vibrant, almost neon orange.

It was Simone, wiping up the last of the broth with a wad of bread, who first brought up the Dupay investigation.

"I didn't see you at the funeral. I thought that's the kind of thing cops did. To see if anyone interesting turns up."

"Yes, we do, and some of the squad were there. But I went to the burial at St-Pierre."

"Any results?"

"A lead or two, maybe, but nothing more. Sometimes an investigation stalls. You just have to be patient. Something usually breaks."

She shook her head. "I hate waiting. I want everything yesterday."

"In a perfect world," said Jacquot, leaning back and reaching for his cigarettes. "But then we wouldn't need cops. Whether we like it or not, our world isn't perfect."

A waitress cleared the table in a single sweep, and with the dishes balanced to the crook of her elbow, she took their order for coffees.

"Oh, and two Cointreaus, on the rocks," said Simone, looking at Jacquot who nodded. "After Martinis, my absolute favourite." When the waitress had gone she took the cigarette he offered, and they lit them from the candle on the table. "So, are you still suspicious about Alain?"

"Did I say I was suspicious?"

She gave him a look, blowing the smoke sideways. "Not exactly, maybe. But all those questions when you came round to Sadi."

"A cop has to cover the bases. And in any murder investigation you start with the nearest and dearest. From there…"

"But Camille was shot in a hold-up. It had absolutely nothing to do with Alain."

Jacquot smiled. "Who's to say? He could have set it up."

"Hardly," she replied, as though such a thing was quite ridiculous. "Anyway, the newspapers said the shooting was random. Wrong time, wrong place."

"Then we should all be thankful that the newspapers and their reporters don't run the *Judiciaire,* or investigate homicides."

The Cointreaus arrived in large *balons* and they tipped glasses, the ice chinking. He took a sip of the cloudy mix… sweet and sharp and strong. Almost medicinal. The kind of drink that cleared the passages. He put down the glass, but didn't say anything. He had a sense that the conversation about Dupay wasn't over, but if questions were going to be asked, it should be Simone who did the asking.

"Did you know he doesn't like you? Alain, I mean."

Jacquot raised an eyebrow.

"Well, he didn't actually say anything to me, you understand, but according to Delphine, his PA, he'd been held up at police headquarters, the day after his wife's death, when he should have been at a meeting. And he'd had some choice words about the man responsible, the man handling the case, which I'm guessing is you. I can only assume that your first impression was not favourable?"

Jacquot spread his hands. "People react badly in situations like that. They don't understand the way we work. What surprises me is that he held any meetings at all. I'd have thought he'd have cancelled everything."

"I told you, that's not the way he is, not the way he thinks. And there's an argument that maybe that's better than moping around at home. But then, you're not like him."

"I'm not?"

"Please. He's a different kind of creature."

"Is that good?"

"If you work for DupayCorp, it is. Otherwise, I'm not so sure."

Jacquot took this in, and then changed tack. "The Dupays have a very attractive nanny."

Simone shot him a look, shook her head. "No. Not Alain."

"You seem very certain."

"It takes one to know one."

Jacquot frowned. "You've lost me."

"Are you joking?" Her smile made her eyes twinkle in the candlelight. "You didn't know?"

"Know what?"

"Alain is gay. A player." She tipped back her head and chuckled. "You really didn't know, did you? Oh, my darling man, you really are too trusting. And a cop to boot. You ought to know by now that sometimes people are not who, or how, they seem."

Jacquot was stunned. The possibility of Dupay's particular preference had never crossed his mind. But then... the crisp tailoring, the red socks; the finely-worked fingernails, and the beard so fastidiously trimmed; the... attention to personal detail. And the self-awareness, that... posing. There was no other way to describe it: standing at the window in Jacquot's office that first morning; the way he settled himself in his chair, his fingers just so as he lifted the crease in his trousers after crossing his legs; and on the terrace of his home in Malmousque, no more than a kilometre or two from where they now sat, with his elbow cupped in the palm of his hand as he took a call, leaning against the railing with a casual but studied grace; in a house with no evidence of a child in residence. Everything almost ascetically tidy.

"You didn't guess?"

"But Camille? Their marriage..." And as he said the words, he realised how naive he must sound.

"Daniel," said Simone, reprovingly. "Really?" She swirled the melting ice and Cointreau, and tipped it back. "Call it marriage as camouflage – it happens all the time. And good camouflage by the sound of it."

"The best. I had no idea," and he wondered what Sergeant Lefèbre would make of it.

166

"Let's just say it's a useful tool for people like Alain. People with something to lose. Sometimes their particular leanings are best kept out of play, if you know what I mean? Public perception, let's say... The Press. And investor confidence, of course. That's the top priority. Serious punters aren't going to want a faggot with his hand in their pocket... and I mean that in the nicest possible way, of course." Her eyes twinkled again, and her voice softened. "Which thought leads us to the next subject on the agenda."

"Which is?"

"Oh, Daniel. You can be so slow sometimes. But I love it." She reached for his hand and gave him a frank, unmistakeable look.

And he knew.

She didn't have to say anything.

But she did: "What I mean is: Your place or mine?"

50

Jacquot woke to an empty bed, and the smell of coffee. He sat up and looked around. No sign of Simone, but from the bathroom came the muted sound of a shower. Then the water was turned off and, a moment later, he saw her reflection in the bedroom mirror as she stepped out into the hallway wrapped in his dressing gown. The gown swirled around her ankles and he watched as she walked to the kitchen, bare feet on the varnished floorboards, head tipped, brushing back damp hair with her fingertips.

"Breakfast on the terrace," she called over her shoulder. "It's a lovely morning. You've got ten minutes."

With no dressing gown to wear, Jacquot pulled on jeans and a white t-shirt, and barefoot, too, he followed her out onto the salon terrace hidden from the *place* below by the topmost branches of a plane tree. The table was

167

covered in a white cloth and ladened with breakfast offerings. Croissants, jams, bacon, scrambled eggs, a peeled, stoned and quartered mango, orange juice and coffee… more food than he remembered in his fridge.

"You didn't have much in the way of breakfast, so I popped out earlier to re-stock. And yes, I went quietly so that Madame Foraque wasn't disturbed."

"You could be invisible, and she'd know," said Jacquot, starting in on the eggs and bacon. He was unaccountably hungry.

She watched him, and smiled. "We had fun."

"Yes, we did. I like walkabouts."

"Well, I'm afraid this one is about to finish. Monique will be back soon, and I have work to get done for tomorrow."

"Another day in the office, for both of us."

"Will last night's indiscretion at Paula's help or hinder your investigation?"

"Let's say, it provides some background we didn't have, and will maybe give us something to work with. Tell me, does Alain have a partner, someone who…?"

Simone sipped her coffee, shook her head. "Who can say? If he does he'll be very discreet." She put down her cup. "Do you suppose this could have something to do with Camille and Lucien?"

"Not directly, but maybe he made himself vulnerable, and someone took advantage. Would Camille have known about his tastes?"

"If she did, she didn't show it. And it was good for them, the marriage. They both knew it. Her name, their money. And even if she did know, or find out, it would have been in her best interests, as much as his, to maintain the cover."

"How so?"

"It would have been so messy. The people they were. Their...
position. Their visibility. Not something either could afford to jeopardise."

"You like him, don't you?"

Simone put her cup on the table, and spread her hands. "In a kind of way, yes, I do. He is an operator. He makes things happen, and I admire that."

Simone left an hour later, with a kiss on Jacquot's lips, and her hand on his cheek. Jacquot stood at his door and listened to her footsteps going down the three flights. And the door of the *conciergerie* opening as she reached the hallway – as he had known it would. Madame Foraque might have missed Simone's first outing, but she'd never miss a second. He could hear muffled voices, Simone's laughter, and Madame Foraque's rough sing-song murmur. It sounded like an agreeable encounter. The front door opened and closed, and Jacquot went back into his apartment, and out onto the terrace. But he couldn't see her, just a shape flickering through the branches, and a moment later, the low growl of her car. He followed its progress in his mind's eye, turning the corner out of Moulins and onto rue des Muettes, the sound of its engine amplified in the narrow street, but slowly diminishing as it sped away.

Like any Sunday, there were chores that needed doing, things left over from a busy week, and after clearing the breakfast table Jacquot put on some music and set about his tasks. The dishwasher emptied and re-filled, a pile of clothes in the washing machine, a quick patrol with the Hoover. And as he worked he tried to see how this fresh picture of Alain Dupay might throw some new light on the case.

The most obvious possibility was blackmail; someone, maybe a spurned lover, threatening to reveal Dupay. As Simone had said, that would be a secret worth protecting, no matter what the cost.

169

But why kidnap Lucien?

To encourage payment? To underline the seriousness of the threat?

No, no, thought Jacquot. It made no sense. Dupay's preferences, Jacquot was sure, had nothing to do with the kidnap and murder of his stepson.

And right now whoever had arranged that kidnap, for whatever reason, and whoever had murdered the boy, they were still on the loose, the case still unsolved.

51

Alain Dupay stepped from the shower, reached for a towel and dried himself vigourously. Tossing the towel aside he pulled on a gown, cleaned his teeth, brushed his hair, and then set about trimming his beard. An electric razor to its edges – cheeks first, then neck, and finally a careful buzz between nostrils and moustache and around his lips. Putting aside the razor he turned his head from one side to the other, tipped it back, checking his reflection. It was a good beard, he decided. Thick enough to cover the deep, irregular lines around his mouth and the pitted scars of teenage acne, its Dutch burgher's point concealing what he had always considered a weak chin, with any whitening patches carefully dyed away the moment they showed. Camille had hated it, but he'd always refused to shave it off. It gave him a certain gravitas, and he was not prepared to sacrifice that for anyone.

With Camille and the boy gone, and the nanny dispensed with, the house was quiet that Monday morning, still early enough for stars to show in the dawn sky over Prado. It would be an hour or more before the maid, Jasmine, arrived so Dupay headed for the kitchen and set about preparing his breakfast. A soft-boiled egg – two and a half minutes for the boil – a slice of butterless toast with honey, and two cups of strong black coffee. Only then did he return to his bedroom and dress. Black silk socks and black suede loafers, a lightweight grey suit, white shirt and black tie. He would wear the black tie for another three days and then put it aside.

Time to get on with his life, and leave the past behind him.

Driving down to the Corniche carriageway he went through the day's schedule: his regular Monday morning briefing session with Simone, Philippe and the various team heads, a lunch meeting with Serge Garot, DupayCorp's chief financial officer, to sort out a series of recent poor showings on some of DupayCorp's older accounts, and the usual slew of prospective customer meetings set for the afternoon. He'd also make another call to Louis Jobert, his squash partner and the Procurator General, to see if there had been any developments regarding the cop, Jacquot. There was something he didn't like about the man, an irritating persistence, not to mention a grating lack of respect, that set his nerves on edge. Just who the hell did this jumped-up *flic* think he was? Nothing more than some newly-minted Chief Inspector out to make a name for himself.

But not at Dupay's expense, not a chance in hell.

The man had to go.

52

There was no particular reason why Jacquot took the long route to police headquarters that Monday morning. It had just seemed a good idea at the time, a spur of the moment decision as he closed the front door behind him and stepped onto place des Moulins. But he was glad that he did. The sky was a light blue, the breeze was fresh and invigorating, and there was a jauntiness in his step as he made his way down rue du Poirier and then turned up the slope of Montées des Accoules. By the time he'd settled at an outside table at Café du Théâtre on place de Lenche, his cheeks were blooming and his heart moving along at a pleasingly steady clip. Café-calva ordered, a cigarette tapped out on the table, Jacquot was about to light up when he spotted a familiar figure making his way up the side of the *place*.

Albert Moineau, 'The Sparrow', lived up to his name. Short and oddly stout-chested, he had thin, bandy legs, and arms to match, a set of limbs that never seemed to be still, swinging and jerking to their own mismatched beat, in a stop-start, darting-everywhere-at-once kind of movement. Even when seated 'The Sparrow' was never quite still, head flicking left and right, squinty black eyes flitting here and there, shoulders ruffling, hands fidgeting. What was he like when he slept, thought Jacquot? Or maybe he didn't?

Moineau was on the shaded side of the *place*, heading for Cathédrale, when he spotted Jacquot. With a squaring of his shoulders, a jerky flap of his arms, and a glance around the square, he changed directions and flitted between the café tables to where Jacquot had sunk back his Calva and was taking the first sip of his coffee. He was dressed in an oversized army coat that flapped around his knees, a pair of unlaced working boots, and what looked like faded blue dungarees, its grubby bib showing between the turned collars of the coat.

"A fine morning," he chirruped, taking the table beside Jacquot and reaching into his coat pocket. He produced a handful of coins and sorted through them with a stiff grimy finger as though looking for a gem. There wasn't one. With a careless shrug of the shoulders he shovelled the coins back in his pocket, and Jacquot took the hint. He called over the waiter and ordered the same again, a coffee and Calva, indicating the man at the next table.

Anyone seeing the two of them, sitting at their separate tables, side by side, both men looking out over the square, would not have thought anything of it. Just two customers taking their ease, one in the sun, one in shade, far enough apart to be unremarkable, yet close enough to speak and be heard without looking at one another. Which was how Albert Moineau liked it.

"You well, Albert?" Jacquot began.

"Better with a Calva inside me," the old boy replied, taking his drink from the waiter's tray, swirling its coppery contents in the *balon*, before taking a gulp. "Whoo-hoo," he gasped. "Such a grand invention."

For a minute or two there was no further talk. Jacquot finished his cigarette, stubbed it out and reached for the last of his coffee. He put the cup back in its saucer, reached into his pocket and peeled through a fold of francs to cover his bill. He was sliding the notes under the ashtray when Moineau broke the silence.

"Heard you was looking for someone."

"Always looking for someone. Anyone in mind?"

"Your darkie. I don't mean your black darkie, you understand, but Eastern-like. One of them Turks, you ask me, like over in La Stampe." Even the manner in which Moineau spoke was a hop and a swing, as jittery and chirrupy as birdsong. "You know the one I mean. Dalan. Used to work on the fruit and veg. Old Perdue's stall, over Capucins way."

"His name came up. We just wanted a word."

"Like that other *mec*? The one you was after a few weeks back, on Sainte-Cécile? The one in the red car, the one you followed. The one got done in that hotel out Ceyreste way."

"And what of him?" asked Jacquot, wondering how Moineau could possibly know about Sainte-Cécile and Boultier's red Alfa, but feeling a warmth spread through him. Not just information on Dalan, but a likely lead or connection with Boultier.

"Not the kind you'd want as a friend, that's for certain. Not the kind you'd even want to know. Not that you're likely to now."

"You knew him?"

"You needed something done, he was your man. Take the *sou* from a *soupion* he would. Fists, forehead, boot. Whatever it took. But always handier with a blade. Nasty piece of work. Got what was coming, you ask me. We're all better off without the likes of him."

So he'd been right, thought Jacquot. Another compelling indication that it had been Boultier who'd cut Loum's throat, though they had failed to find the knife – in his car, in his apartment, in his hotel suite. No sign of any kind of blade. "And Dalan?"

"Now there's a man. Sharp as a tailor's shears. Maybe doesn't say much but that don't mean his brain's gone to sleep."

"You know where he lives?"

Moineau shook his head, scratched the side of his chin. "No, can't help you there," he said, with a sad look on his face. The old boy tipped back the last of his Calva, gave a deep sigh of contentment and then, after a moment's reflection, the sad look brightened. "But I know where he works."

53

Javad Dalan crossed rue d'Aubagne and turned up Châteauredon. It was early still, and the low spring sun would not reach this narrow passageway until midday. From the front seat of his unmarked car Jacquot watched Dalan pass into shadow, shoulders hunched, hands in pockets, stopping after about twenty metres to open a door on his left and disappear inside.

According to Moineau, there were two entrances to Burak Imports. This single door on Châteauredon, and the gated yard on rue d'Académie where the company's vans were kept. Between these two entrances were a covered warehouse, offices, and Burak's own quarters overlooking a small courtyard on Châteauredon. Jacquot and Rully had walked both streets the previous afternoon, watching the gates and door, but there had been no sign of Dalan. They had returned an hour before the morning's rush hour and parked on Aubagne, watching the entrances to both streets. Of course, Dalan could easily have come from the other end, from Lieutaud, and they would likely have missed him. But luck was on their side.

"What now?" asked Rully.

"Let him settle," said Jacquot, lighting up a cigarette, "and then we'll have a word."

Jacquot had spent the previous day sourcing information on Dalan, and Burak Imports, but had nothing of any real significance to show for his efforts. Not even Sergeant Lefèbre in Records had come up with anything of interest. All he had been able to establish was that Javad Dalan was forty-seven years old, the only child of Turkish immigrants, and that he had worked Capucins market for the Perdue family, as Moineau had said, before moving to Burak Imports eleven years earlier.

As for Burak Imports, company records showed that the business was owned and run by a man called Nakim Burak, that it had been started by Burak's father shortly after the war, and specialised in middle-eastern imports – dates, nuts, fruit, spices, pulses, even tobacco. Following the father's death the business and the company's premises, both residential and commercial, had been left to Burak. The company currently employed a staff of fifty-two, and its tax affairs were in good order. Everything above board.

And yet... why would one of Burak's employees, Javad Dalan, choose to visit the St-Pierre cemetery and watch, from a distance, the interment of Camille and Lucien Dupay? It was this question that Jacquot intended asking the Burak employee. Maybe something, maybe nothing.

Ten minutes later, Jacquot flicked away his cigarette into the shadows of Châteauredon and pressed the bell at the door that Dalan had used. When a voice on the intercom asked the nature of his business, Jacquot gave his name, his *Judiciaire* rank, and said that he wanted to speak to Javad Dalan. A moment later the door lock buzzed open and Jacquot and Rully stepped off the street into an arched passageway that led into a gravelled courtyard open to the sky. After the morning's rush-hour bustle on rue d'Aubagne the courtyard was a place of unexpected peace and tranquillity, just the chirruping of sparrows flitting about its first-floor balcony, or perching on its stone balustrade to inspect the new arrivals, the life of the city no more than a distant hum beyond the rooftops. There was the softest hint of scented woodsmoke in the still air, lacy drapes of vine looped down from the upper floor, and set beneath it a number of arched recesses fitted with filigreed wood panels, each with a pair of delicately-framed windows and one of them with a single wood-panelled door left ajar. It felt, thought Jacquot, looking around, like some ancient Persian caravanserai, both a place to rest and to do business.

From somewhere beyond the open door a friendly voice called out, "The door is open, monsieur. Please to come in, come in."

Jacquot and Rully did as they were told, ducking under the low-framed door to find themselves in a long stone-walled passage that, at its far end, opened onto what looked like a second courtyard. But this one, Jacquot could see, had wrought-iron gates at the rue d'Académie entrance for Burak Imports, with a couple of forklifts manoeuvring between Burak delivery vans and stacks of palleted sacks and boxes. Quite a business, thought Jacquot, as Javad Dalan came out of a side office. The photo Jacquot had of him at St-Pierre was blurred with distance, but there was no mistaking the curl of hair, the narrow face and hooked nose, and the thin wiry body. He gave them a small bow and smiled helpfully. "Messieurs," he said, standing to one side of the door. "Please to come through into office, and make yourself comfortable."

Which Jacquot and Rully did, taking a pair of chairs with tapestried arms, while Dalan settled behind his desk. "So, messieurs, how can I be of assist to *Judiciaire*?" he asked, his French a little fractured, clearly not his first language.

"I wanted to know if the name Alain Dupay seemed familiar to you? Either socially, or through your business?"

Dalan frowned, pushed out his lower lip, and started to shake his head. "No, monsieur, that is not name I know."

"I see," Jacquot replied. "You're absolutely certain?"

"Of course. Absolute certain."

"It's just, you were seen at the funeral of Monsieur Dupay's wife and stepson at the St-Pierre cemetery. Last week. On Thursday."

Again the head began to shake. "No, I so sorry, the name still mean nothing. But I am often there, at cemetery. It is peaceful place to be after the rush and bustle we have here in city. A place of contemplation. And often there are funerals, of course. But thanks be to God, no one I know." The shaking head was replaced with a tilt of the head and an accommodating smile.

"What about DupayCorp?" asked Rully. "A financial trading company here in the city."

Another slower shake of the head, another regretful smile.

Jacquot glanced round the low-ceilinged office, its panelled walls set with filing cabinets, its stone floor spread with faded rugs. "May I ask, how long you have worked here?"

"Ten, maybe eleven year now. I start as trader on Capucins, but when Monsieur Burak ask me to come work for him, well…"

"It was an offer you couldn't refuse?"

"Hah! As they say in film; yes, you are right. And it is honour, too, to be asked to work for such a man. A big step up for me."

"And why would that be? Why would Monsieur Burak select you, from all the traders on Capucins?" asked Jacquot.

"On Capucins I was best. I have name. And Burak stock was my special skill."

"And Burak stock is…?" asked Jacquot, knowing all to well.

"The best, of course. Our dates, our nuts, spices from the east, fruit…" Dalan shrugged, spread his hands. The list was too long to detail further, and clearly incomparable. The business spoke for itself.

I wonder," said Jacquot, "if we could have a moment with your boss, Monsieur Burak? To ask a few questions."

Dalan straightened. "I afraid Monsieur Burak very busy man. If this concern your enquiries about this Monsieur Dupay, I can assure you my employer–"

"–Will see us at his earliest convenience," Jacquot interrupted; no room for manoeuvre. "Today, or tomorrow at the latest. I trust I make myself clear." He pushed back his chair and got to his feet, felt for his wallet, drew out a card and laid it on Dalan's desk. "My number is there. I'll be expecting your call."

54

There was a spring in Jacquot's step, as he and Rully walked down Châteauredon.

"He's a liar," said Jacquot, waiting for a break in the traffic on Aubagne before crossing to their car. "And I love liars. Liars have something to hide."

"You think he knows Dupay?"

"He might not actually know him, as he said, but he was there at the cemetery for a reason, and it wasn't contemplation. He had come for that funeral. To see it. The only question is, why?"

Back at police headquarters, Jacquot picked up his phone and dialled a number, asked to be put through to the relevant extension.

"You said you were good with names and numbers," he said when Simone answered.

"So, I'm guessing this would be a business call?"

"And to say again how much I enjoyed our walkabout."

"But business all the same?"

"A bit of both."

"So, try me. With the names and numbers, I mean."

"Nakim Burak. 27 Châteauredon, 35 rue d'Académie."

There was a silence on the other end of the line. And then, "Burak Imports?"

"You know the firm?"

"I've heard of it."

"Professionally?"

"Not here. In Aix."

"While you were with DupayCorp?"

"Correct."

"And the nature of the business?"

"The usual."

"Investments?"

"It's what we do."

"And is there any business connection now?"

"Not that I know of."

"Any reason?"

Another silence from the end of the line.

And then, "Daniel, this is confidential information. I could lose my job."

"But it's years ago. Back in Aix, you said."

"That doesn't make it any less privileged. There are rules. Contractual obligations."

"This is an enquiry from the *Judiciaire*. An official enquiry. In a murder investigation."

Jacquot heard her sigh down the line. He knew what was coming next.

"Then you must address your questions to a higher authority," she said at last. "I have said more than I should have."

"I am grateful for your assistance. It really will help."

"And I am glad to hear that, but I also want to make it clear that this phone call never happened."

Jacquot smiled. "What phone call?"

55

Javad Dalan called police headquarters the following morning. His boss, Nakim Burak, would be free to see Chief Inspector Jacquot at four o'clock that afternoon. Rully passed on the message.

"Then we have time for Monsieur Dupay," said Jacquot, pulling on a leather jacket and heading for the lift. "An opportunity to see if the name Burak Imports rings any bells."

When they arrived at DupayCorp they were shown straight up to Dupay's office. He was at his desk, working through a stack of papers – a tick here, a cross there, a scribble of his pen. He didn't look up when they came in, took chairs and made themselves comfortable.

Finally, Dupay turned his attention to his two visitors.

"The name is not familiar," he said curtly, when Jacquot asked about Burak Imports. "Should it be?"

He shot Jacquot a challenging look – cold, and sharp – then returned to the sheaf of papers. Another tick, another scribbled note.

"Just following up on our investigation, monsieur."

"And what investigation might that be?"

"The murder of your stepson." As if there could be any other, thought Jacquot.

"And what could this Burak thing have to do with Lucien's death?"

"The name came up, in the course of our enquiries. Probably nothing but we need to follow it up. You never know."

"And how, exactly, did the name 'come up'?" More ticks, another cross.

"Someone at your wife's funeral. Someone watching. As I said, it may be nothing, but..."

"I will have someone check it," said Dupay, reaching for his phone. He pressed a number, and asked for any information on a company called... He looked at Jacquot questioningly.

"Burak Imports."

"Burak Imports," Dupay repeated. "That's right. Thanks Philippe, and as quick as you can. Like yesterday." He gave a grunt of a laugh and put down the phone. The laugh did not extend to Jacquot. Just another brief, chill look, and back to his papers.

"I understand your company had some dealings with this firm. In your Aix office, I believe? A few years back?"

"And how would you know something like that, Chief Inspector?"

"Police investigations can turn up the most surprising things, monsieur."

Without looking up Dupay said, "I'm sure they do, save the most important."

"Leads are there to be followed. It is our job. The way we operate. Nothing goes unnoticed."

"And I am more than happy to hear it, and to co-operate in whatever way I can," he said. Now he did look up, settling cold, hard eyes on Jacquot. "But do you have any idea how many clients we have, Chief Inspector? How many clients we have represented, advised, over the years? And how many companies and interests each of those clients controls? I can hardly be expected to remember every single name. Which is why we keep files," he continued, reaching out for just such a file, brought in by a young man in jeans and cuff-linked shirt, and handed across the desk. "Thanks, Philippe." He took the file, flipped it open and scanned the contents. "Any news on the Deutsche thing by the way?"

"Nothing yet," Philippe replied.

"Okay, let me know."

"Sure thing, Alain."

Dupay skimmed through the Burak file, and with a nod he closed it.

"Burak Imports. A trade and distribution company, based here in Marseilles. Fruit and vegetable importer. Wholesale operation. Restaurants, hotels, bars… here, in Toulon, Aix. It appears we carried out some short-term capital investments on their behalf… A few months' work, back in the eighties. Then nothing more."

"Just a few months? Is that usual?"

"Whatever the client wants. It is always the client's call."

"And how did their investments go?"

"According to the file their trades did well in the beginning," said Dupay, twisting his pen between thumb and forefinger. "Some significant gains."

"And then?"

"Not so well. The name of the game."

"They lost money?"

"Yes."

"A lot?"

Dupay shrugged. "For some it might be a lot, for others…"

"And the sum involved?"

"Substantial."

"How much?"

"As I said, substantial. Though it needn't have been."

"You're saying Burak Imports should have pulled out while they were ahead?"

"When you sit at a roulette wheel and win, do you put all your winnings back on the table?" Dupay shook his head. "No, you don't. You take a view. Pocket the profit and walk away. Or maybe re-invest a part of that profit. As I said, the choice is always the client's. And the spinning wheel can be a friend again – or not. As this company of yours discovered to its cost."

Jacquot nodded. It was clear that Dupay was not prepared to say more. He tried another tack: "Strange that Burak Imports should use your Aix office, when your two companies are only a few blocks' distant, right here in Marseilles?"

Dupay shrugged. "Again, that would be the client's decision. At his or her discretion. Here, Aix, Toulon. It makes no difference."

"Did you ever meet Monsieur Burak?"

Dupay shook his head. "Not that I recall."

"Or maybe his assistant, Javad Dalan?"

Another shake of the head. An impatient sigh.

"Well, we won't take up any more of your time, monsieur," said Jacquot, getting to his feet. "And, as always, we are most grateful for your assistance in this matter."

56

Nakim Burak, sprawled on a tapestry-covered divan, waved Jacquot and Rully to a pair of chairs when Javad Dalan ushered them into his office. Like Dalan's on the floor below, the room was stone flagged and spread with overlapping Persian carpets, but its ceiling was higher, its line of windows – opening onto the balcony and overlooking the courtyard – screened with filigreed purdah shutters, and the air richly scented with a mix of sandalwood and tuberose.

As for Burak, reaching for a silver bowl on the low table beside him and scooping out a palmful of pistachios, he was dressed in a striped red and green robe that did little to disguise the man's vast size. Indeed, so large was he that Jacquot wondered if he had to be helped to his feet whenever he got up from the divan. But it was his head that drew the attention: a perfectly round skull with a black bristle-cut scalp white-lined with a tilting scar that started somewhere behind his left ear and wound around the front of his head. It looked, thought Jacquot, as though the top of his skull had once been lifted off – for an operation, or as the result of some kind of wound he couldn't say. Beneath this scar was a bulbous wrinkled forehead, and thick black brows hooding eyes as dark as squid ink. The nose was hooked and fleshy, the cheeks plumply unlined, and the lips fat and shiny.

With a casual wave of his hand, Dalan was dismissed.

His assistant gave a short bow, and closed the door behind him.

"So, Chief Inspector, how can I be of assistance to the *Police Judiciaire*?" Given Burak's size, Jacquot had expected a deep, rumbling voice but his words were sharp and high-pitched, as though they had been squeezed out of him.

"We are investigating a series of recent murders in and around the city. Might I ask if the name Adam Loum is familiar?"

"Loum, you say? No, I do not believe so."

"Or Marc Boultier? Or Youssef Hakimi?"

Burak pushed out his bottom lip, as smooth and shiny as a pink slug, and shook his head. "Neither of these gentlemen, I regret. But why would I?"

"We are chasing up a number of possible leads, and believe they may be involved in the deaths of Camille and Lucien Dupay," Jacquot replied.

Burak nodded, cracked open a pistachio shell and popped the nut into his mouth. "I did not know these poor people either, you understand, the mother and the son, but I did once have dealings with the good lady's husband."

"Which is why we are here, monsieur," said Jacquot, noting that Burak remembered Dupay's name but Dupay had not recognised his. "It was a business relationship, I understand?"

"An unfortunate business relationship. One I would not wish to repeat."

"Would you mind explaining why?"

Burak waved a hand, small pudgy fingers. "I lost a considerable amount of money. Not something that makes me happy."

"And how exactly did you lose it?"

"Bad advice. Which I took. The investments recommended proved to be, how to say it, inadvisable."

"And when was this?"

Burak took another pistachio, split the shell and licked out the nut. "A long time ago. Six, seven years, maybe. But I do not forget such a thing. It makes me unhappy." He leaned forward and dropped the shell halves into a bowl on the ottoman.

"How much was involved?"

"A very large amount. Millions. And gone like that! I should never · have been persuaded."

"Persuaded?"

"The company, DupayCorp, was so enthusiastic, so confident. And I took the bait. Greed. It all comes down to greed." Another pistachio selected, dispatched. "My greed, and I am not afraid to admit it. Like the dog with the bone. So, perhaps, my fault. I should not have been so careless, so easily seduced."

"And this was in Marseilles?"

"No, in Aix."

"Why not here in Marseilles? Where DupayCorp have their head office."

Burak picked a sliver of nut skin from the tip of his tongue and flicked it away with his thumbnail. "All my accounting is handled in Aix. That is where I bank. That is where such transactions would be arranged and managed. Here, Marseilles," he waved his fingers around the room, "this is where we concern ourselves with everything we import – the storage, the packaging, organising distribution, serving our many customers. The sharp end of the business."

"And the nature of the business?" asked Jacquot, as though he didn't know.

"Produce, from Turkey, Lebanon, Syria – the Levant. Foodstuffs: dates, grains, fruits, vegetables, spices; sausage like *sucuk*, and other smoked meats; cheeses, honey, sweetmeats, and tinned goods, too, like anchovies from Black Sea – what we call *hamsi*. All of it, food from home, to make us feel at home. Like these nuts," he said. "Pistachios, as you will know. But the very best pistachios. From Kerman Province, in Iran. Without equal. Please, do try. You will not be disappointed." He picked up the silver bowl and held it out to Jacquot.

Jacquot took advantage of the invitation – he loved pistachios – and reached for a handful. He prised the first shell apart and picked out the nut, popped it into his mouth. An explosion of taste. Salty, meaty, rich; unlike any other pistachio he had ever tasted.

"You are right, monsieur. Really, very, very good." He dropped the empty shells in the bowl on the ottoman, already filled with cast-offs. "Now I know what a pistachio should taste like."

Burak tipped his head, and gave a sharp little chuckle. "I am delighted to hear it. It was what we try to do. Only the very best."

"Quite an operation, finding the best and providing it like this."

"Is good business. Is honest business. We have reputation."

"Of course, my brother might not agree," Jacquot continued. "He is allergic to any kind of nut. His lips and tongue would swell and he would be very sick. We always had to carry Epinephrine in case of emergencies." The lie came easily and he watched Burak for any tell-tale nervousness. There was none.

"What a worry for your parents. Such a terrible weight to bear."

Jacquot nodded, and then, "Coming back to your dealings with DupayCorp, do you recall how you became involved in their operation?"

"As I said, it was a long time ago."

"Did you contact them, or did they contact you?"

"I cannot remember exactly. I think they make first approach. I think that is what they do."

"Do you recall any names?"

"No name, but she was young. And pretty."

"Simone Laronde?"

Burak shrugged. "It was a long time ago…" he said again.

"Did you feel that you had been misled? In terms of the investments recommended?"

"I took a risk, and paid the price. There was no room for remonstration. But it was a lesson. Nothing is for free, save the love of the Prophet."

188

Jacquot nodded, and then rose from his chair. Rully did the same. Behind them Burak's door opened and Javad Dalan appeared. He must have been listening at the keyhole, thought Jacquot, to time it so perfectly.

"Well, thank you for your time, monsieur, and for your help," he said to Burak, who moved his head from side to side, and up and down, neither a shake nor a nod.

"A pleasure to be of assistance, Chief Inspector. And do be assured that I am at your service, if there is anything more you might need." A hand was raised, then lowered to brush away a scatter of shells from his lap, as though he had only just noticed them.

And with that, Dalan ushered them out of Burak's office and led them down a flight of wide wooden stairs to the courtyard below. By the entrance to Châteauredon Jacquot saw a delicately filigreed table inset with mother-of-pearl that had not been there when they arrived. Two ribboned boxes had been placed on it.

"A small gift from Burak Imports," said Dalan, passing the boxes to Jacquot and Rully. "The finest *lokum* from Kastamonu. What you call Turkish Delight."

"How kind," said Jacquot, taking one of the boxes, and Rully, taking the other, nodded his thanks.

With a bow from Dalan, they stepped through the gate and he closed it behind them.

"Do you suppose these count as bribes?" Rully asked, as they walked back to their car.

"If they do, they're not going to work."

"So what did you make of Burak, boss?"

"Plausible. Butter wouldn't melt. But sly as a snake."

"Some scar, too. Looks like someone lifted off the top of his head. And those nuts. He must have eaten a dozen or more."

"Makes you wonder, doesn't it?" replied Jacquot, pulling on his seat belt and starting the car.

"You think there's a link?"

"A lot of people eat nuts," said Jacquot, pulling into traffic and heading for the port. "But worth noting, all the same."

57

Back at police headquarters Jacquot told Rully to call it a day, and made his way to the basement Records Office where Sergeant Lefèbre was sitting at his desk surrounded by packing cases.

"They've given me a month," the old man said, waving his stick at the filing cabinets and shelves. "Everything to be boxed up and sent to Central Records in Aix for, get this, 'digitalisation'. And you know what else? They're going to turn this place into a new canteen."

"You're joking?"

"Nope. Word came down first thing Monday. I'm doing everything alphabetically." He thumbed to the shelves behind him. "They've given me some kid to help out. So far we've got to 'C'. We stack the files by the lift and off they go, a dozen at a time. There's a van comes twice a day." Lefèbre shook his head. "I'm not the sentimental sort, Chief, but I like to think of this place, and everything in it, as mine. And now it's being taken away." He pursed his lips. "Looks like the end of the road for me, too. Box me up, and pack me off."

"You want to stay on?"

"Not much for me now, not with this," he said, tapping the calliper on his leg. "Not much good on the beat."

"We could do with a good man on the third floor. Someone who knows his way round. Helping out with enquiries."

Lefèbre smiled. "And hold the fort while you lot go gallivanting? You're kind to offer, Chief, but you know when your number's up. It's time. Plain and simple. Guess I was lucky I had it as long as I did."

Jacquot sat at the old boy's desk and pulled out his cigarettes, offered one. They both lit up.

"If you change your mind, you know where to come. I mean it."

And he did. Old boys like Lefèbre deserved more than this – ten years in a neon-lit basement with dusty air and dog-eared files for company. His choice, but still. And now discarded. Surplus to requirements.

"I'll give it some thought, Chief. And I'm grateful for the offer. But you're not down here to pass the time of day. You're after something. So, what do you need? What can I do for you? While I still can."

"Burak Imports. Nakim Burak."

"The Turk." It hadn't taken more than five seconds' thought. As quick as any computer.

"That's the one."

Lefèbre looked at the ceiling. "Been around a good while, he has. Big deal trader up around rue Aubagne. Foodstuffs mostly, and wholesale only. Not a bowl of nuts in town that doesn't come through Burak Imports."

"Any form?"

"Nothing official, but there's always been whispers."

Jacquot cocked an eye. Lefèbre saw it.

"He's a trader, got a good cover. Ships coming in from Turkey, Lebanon. Roads, rail… You know the kind of thing."

"Drugs."

"I'd say it's more than likely. But he keeps the wheels well oiled. Lot of boys down in the port take their *vacances* courtesy of the Turk."

"They turn a blind eye," said Jacquot, thinking of the box of Turkish Delight sitting in his car and bound for Madame Foraque.

"Both eyes more like."

"He's a dealer?"

The Sergeant snorted. "No, no. Not Burak, no chance. Dealing's way down the food chain – not his line of work at all. But I'd bet my pension he imports and supplies – or someone does it for him. And with distribution already in place, he's pretty much got it sewn up. Real arm's length, and nothing to stick."

"Do the names Mark Boultier or Youssef Hakimi mean anything?"

Lefèbre gave it some thought. "Nothing. Can't check under Boultier, now the 'B's have gone, but you want me to check out the 'H's?"

"No need; we already checked them. Just wondered if maybe you could see any link between them and someone like Burak?"

"Dealers, probably. Selling Burak imports. But there'd be no link. Buy in bulk from the source, sell on for the profit. And they'd be small-time boys. Deliveries and enforcement. So how did Burak's name crop up?"

"We got to him through Dalan. That's where he works now, after Capucins. Burak's right-hand man by the look of it."

"He's done alright for himself. Place to be…" Lefèbre frowned, trying to remember. "Did he tell you why he was at the funeral?"

"Just chance. Likes the quiet, he said, and St-Pierre was a good place to be."

The old man snorted, bent down to rub the side of his knee. "And I'm training for the next Olympics. Hundred metres."

192

Jacquot laughed. "You and me both."

"Hey, you're young."

Jacquot pointed to his ankle. "Snapped tendon, remember. My last game. It's never really been the same after that."

"Aches in the winter?"

"Not my favourite time of the year."

"Tell me about it. So, what's your next move? How come Burak's in your sights?"

Jacquot leaned forward and stubbed out his cigarette. "Tell the truth, I don't know. Just… following the thread."

"Like any cop worth his badge. And if you're lucky, or smart, that thread'll turn to rope. Enough to pull 'em in, and land 'em. Is this something to do with the Dupays?"

Jacquot stretched back in his chair, spread his hands.

"The two men have had dealings. Six, seven years ago. Some investment deal in Aix that went bad. Burak certainly knew Dupay's name, but Dupay couldn't recall Burak's. Not surprising, with millions down the pan according to Burak. Something Dupay preferred to forget. But not Burak. No chance. And Burak doesn't strike me as the kind of man you'd want to get on the wrong side of."

"He still got that scar, or has he grown his hair? Or wearing that fez of his?"

"Still there. Pretty much the whole way round."

"You want to know how he got it?"

Jacquot gestured that he could think of nothing he'd like more.

"Years back some market trader Burak had crossed took a machete to him. Just the one swipe, but he was holding it wrong – hit Burak with the blunt edge. Sharp side, he'd have cut right through, but the blunt edge just cracked the skull pretty much right the way round. He was off sick a while after that. Got some kind of metal plate in there now."

"How would he feel about Dupay losing his money?"

"Same as he felt about the man with the machete."

"What happened to him?"

Lefèbre chuckled. "No one knows. He just didn't open his stall one morning. Still down as 'Missing', either under 'machete' or his name, whatever it was." He nodded back to the emptying shelves behind him.

"Six years is a long time to wait, to get your own back."

"For a man like Burak, time is just a waiting game. A trader looking for the right price, and the right moment. That kind of operator, you don't get mad, you plan. So, you're saying Burak might have something to do with the Dupay murders?"

"Not the wife. That was just bad luck. But I can see there'd be a motive for taking the boy for ransom. A ransom she was delivering when she got hit."

"Leaving Burak with the boy, but no money. Some chancer's nicked it. He wouldn't have liked that."

"If it's him, he didn't. Dupay had to pay another stack, and a few days later the boy ends up in a pile of rubbish."

"So this time round it's Burak who's smiling, and Dupay who's pissed."

"You have a way of looking at things, Sergeant. And you don't get that from a computer," said Jacquot, with a grin. "By the way, did you know he was gay? Dupay, I mean."

Lefèbre jerked back in his chair. "Gay? You serious? Dupay?"

"A very reliable source."

Lefèbre rubbed his chin, thumb and forefinger deepening the cleft. "I'd never have guessed. Not in a million. And never a whisper." He shook his head, as though to clear it. "*Merde*. Mind you, that makes two of them. Everyone knows about the Turk. I wonder if he knew about Dupay?"

"Burak's gay?"

"As a parrot's plumage," said Lefèbre, "though I can't see them dating, or hanging out in the same places. Thing is, it would have been far easier for Burak to squeeze Dupay with exposure – now that he's doing so well – rather than snatching the son. I know what I'd have done."

Jacquot remembered what Simone had said, about investors not wanting the hand of a faggot in their trouser pockets. There was no question about it, any disclosures on that score would cause Dupay real problems. So, as Lefèbre had pointed out, why would Burak bother to take the son? If, indeed, he had. There was only one reason. Because Burak couldn't have known Dupay was gay.

"Of course," continued Lefèbre, "that would mean Burak knew about Dupay. If he didn't, then the son was the only option."

Jacquot smiled, both men on the same wavelength.

"The boy died from a nut allergy reaction," he said. "Which a kidnapper might easily not have known about…"

"And Burak imports nuts by the ton." Lefèbre gave Jacquot a look. "I'll give you the thread, Chief, but it looks to me like you're still a long way from turning it into rope."

58

Jacquot left his car at police headquarters and walked home, swinging the box of Turkish Delight and going over his time with Lefèbre. It wasn't so much the information he'd provided, as the way he made you think. The old boy was right; computers had a way to go, and he was still a long way off pulling in any rope. If it even existed. But there was, Jacquot felt, a sense of movement, a feeling of progress.

Madame Foraque was waiting for him, or rather, watering the small tubs of basil and thyme she kept outside the window of her *conciergerie*. It amounted to much the same thing.

"Your friend called by again," she said, putting down the can, and taking Burak's box. She untied the ribbons and cracked open the lid, parted the tissue paper, sniffed the contents, and a smile, or as close to one as she could manage, creased her cheeks. "How did you know I liked Turkish Delight?"

"I didn't," Jacquot replied; he had quickly learned that it was never a good idea to soft-soap his concierge. Tell the truth, and hope for the best. "It was a guess. But I'm glad you do." He paused. "So, what did my friend have to say?" he asked, wondering why Simone hadn't phoned. She had his number at home, and at police headquarters.

"Oh, she wanted to see you, asked if you'd call her. And not too happy, you ask me. Hope you're not playing any of your little games with that nice young lady." Madame Foraque poked a hand into the box and came out with sugared fingertips and a cube of pink dusted delight. "*Ooh là là*, would you look at that," she said and popped it into her mouth.

With her most effective weapon thus employed, Jacquot made his escape and hurried up to his flat.

"I've just been fired. Given my marching orders," was the first thing Simone said when she heard Jacquot's voice. "Or rather, I've been transferred to Aix to supervise some back-office re-shuffle. Which, for me, is pretty much the same thing. I mean... everything I've built up here. The job, my home, Monique. That's it." There was a pause, and then, angrily, "What have you been doing, Daniel? What have you been saying?"

"Nothing that would implicate you in any way, I can assure you," Jacquot replied, going over his conversation with Dupay in his head. Her name had not been mentioned, though the Aix reference might have pointed in her direction. But then, Dupay would not have known that he and Simone were close. It could have been anyone.

"Really? So you call on Alain this morning, and after lunch I get handed the good news."

"From Dupay?"

"The personnel people. They phoned, told me what was happening and said how pleased they were for me. More money, more responsibility... yadda, yadda, yadda..."

"So you haven't exactly been fired. It's a promotion."

"It's Aix, Daniel! Back where I started. And either I commute, or I have to relocate. Neither of which I want to do."

"So what are you going to do?"

"Right now... I just don't know."

"Why don't we meet? A drink, something to eat? I could get to you in twenty. Just say where."

"I can't. We've got friends coming for supper."

"Tomorrow, then?"

"Tomorrow I'm in Aix. Getting briefed. Don't know when I'll be back. But right now, there's someone ringing the doorbell so I've got to..."

"Before you do, just tell me one thing."

"What?"

"Were you the one who persuaded Nakim Burak to invest with DupayCorp?"

There was a sudden cold silence.

Jacquot knew he had crossed the line, but hoped for some measure of understanding.

He wasn't going to get it.

There was just a quiet, measured, "Fuck you, Daniel," and the line went dead.

59

When Dupay arrived at his office the following morning, Delphine had laid out his correspondence on the glass top of his desk. It was a smaller pile than normal but Dupay would have spotted the envelope no matter how high the stack. Exactly square, a pristine white, the high-grain bonded paper stiff and weighty. Dupay slit open the top and withdrew the gilt-edged invitation it contained. From Hospices-Med, the charity of which Camille had been patron. A new production of Puccini's *La Bohème* to be performed at the Marseilles Opera House at the end of July to celebrate the Charity's tenth anniversary. Their names handwritten in a slanting black copperplate.

Dupay grunted. Did the organisers not know that his wife was dead? How inefficient. With two firm strokes of his pen, he put a cross in the top right corner and pushed it aside. Without Camille to force his hand, it was an easy decision to make. Declined.

Dupay had always hated... no, had always loathed opera. The ridiculous gesturing flamboyance of it, the screeching, booming voices, the whole overblown falsity of it. Three, often four hours of backside-numbing boredom, when there were so many other useful things he could be doing. Who on earth had ever come up with this pompous charade as a credible form of entertainment? And he was certain he wasn't the only one in

Marseilles' opera house audience who felt the same, other husbands and wives whose partners had corralled them into an evening of aural torture. But Camille had loved it, teasingly called him a philistine when he complained at the prospect of yet another first night, which always irritated him, as if his Toulon market background had somehow deadened his ability to appreciate such high artistic endeavour. All he could really say about it was that he enjoyed the attention it brought: the press coverage on a first night, the flash of cameras as they stepped from their limousine, and the other opera-goers whose contacts frequently bore profitable fruit for DupayCorp.

Yet it was on one such first night that he had met someone very special. It was the intermission break in a new production of Mozart's *Don Giovanni*, and Camille was busy working the crowd, seeking pledges and donations for something or another, just as she always did. For Dupay it was the perfect opportunity to slip out for a breath of fresh air in the opera house's forecourt. And there he was, sitting on a step in the shadow of a pillar, a cigarette being lit, the flare of the match on his face. Another opera-goer, dressed in a beautifully-cut evening jacket and tight, satin-piped trousers, the patent leather pumps actually tasselled. Early twenties, Dupay guessed, and utterly beguiling – a fall of auburn hair framing a face of startling beauty: smooth, dark skin, taut young cheeks that hollowed as he pulled on his cigarette, and, when he turned to look at Dupay, eyes the soft slanting shape of almonds.

"On stage it is such a wonder, but in the bar now," the young man nodded behind him, "it is such a boring old crush. So I always come out here to breathe some fresh air." He got up, walked towards Dupay, tall and careless, pushing back the fall of hair with his cigarette hand and reaching out the other for Dupay to take and shake. A warm, smooth palm and strong, squeezing fingers.

"My name is Samir," he said, the voice enticingly accented, the smile a flash of white teeth. Then he'd looked curiously at Dupay, tipping his head, still holding his hand. "And if I am not mistaken, monsieur, I would say we share the same feelings, that we are maybe members of the same club, *n'est-ce pas?*"

It was the start of a long and satisfying relationship, even if the boy had loved opera. And smoked.

Only Camille and her son, and his own reputation, had stood in his way.

Until it didn't matter anymore.

60

Laganne, a cigarette hanging from his lips and a glint in his eyes, was waiting for Jacquot when he got into headquarters the following morning. He came straight to the point.

"A jeweller on rue Paradis phoned in. He says a friend in Aix called him a few days ago about some gemstones a customer had brought in for valuation and sale. The guy in Aix said the stones were high quality and thought our jeweller might be interested in having a look. When the jeweller here asked for details, he remembered the notice we put out following the Dupay robbery and got in touch."

"And?"

"I have the jeweller's address in Aix. I thought, maybe, you should pay him a call."

Jacquot gave Laganne a look. "Why is it I have this feeling there's something you're not telling me?"

"The stones, boss. Diamonds and sapphires... and a single pearl."

Joaillerie Cahn was a small jewellery shop on rue Fabrot off Cours Mirabeau in the centre of Aix. Squeezed between a L'Occitane outlet and a designer shoe shop, the jewellers might have been smaller and more discrete than its neighbours but it was no less exclusive, with two velvet-lined cabinet windows either side of a brass-handled plate-glass door. In one of the cabinets was a single pair of pendant diamond earrings, and in the other a gold and diamond necklace, both items of jewellery displayed on a plump square of deep blue velvet, glittering in the beams of hidden spotlights. But there was little opportunity to admire the display. A thin, intermittent rain had started on their drive out of Marseilles, and by the time Jacquot and Rully reached Aix the windscreen wipers were working overtime. Rully parked as close to the shop as he could, but they still had to brush the rain from their jackets and slick back their hair when they pushed through the heavy glass door.

Inside the shop there were three glass-topped display cases on three sides of the room; high-end Swiss watches on the left, a selection of glittering engagement rings in the middle, and on the right, brooches, bracelets, and earrings, everything displayed on angled black or white velvet trays. And not a price tag to be seen. The floor was thickly carpeted, the walls finely panelled, and high in the corners of the room Jacquot could see four small security cameras. Two women, dressed in matching blue silk blouses and darker blue skirts, comprised the shop's staff. The elder of the two was showing an elegantly-dressed woman in her fifties a selection of bracelets, pointing with a hushed whisper at this setting and that design, while her younger colleague behind the middle counter, greeted Jacquot and Rully with a nod and a smile, and a smoothly delivered "*Messieurs*?"

"I wonder if I could have a word with Monsieur Cahn?" said Jacquot, showing his badge.

"Of course, monsieur. He is downstairs in the workroom. If you would care to wait a moment." She went to the cash register, picked up a phone and dialled a number. When the call was over, she turned to Jacquot and Rully with another smile, and asked them to follow her.

Which they did, stepping between the display cabinets and following the young woman to the back of the premises. At the bottom of a flight of stairs was a sturdy metal door. Pressing a bell, she spoke into a metal grille announcing her visitors, and a moment later three separate locks turned and the door swung open.

The basement was stone walled with a vaulted stone ceiling, but its medieval origins were little more than a backdrop for the scene that greeted Jacquot and Rully as they stepped past the young woman and the door closed behind them. There were no windows here, but the space was brightly lit with four neon strips suspended from the ceiling, and a line of desk lamps set above two long workbenches. There were four men at work, two per bench, each intent on their various tasks: one was working on an antique carriage clock, another was examining various gemstones through a microscope, a third using tweezers to place a tear-shaped diamond into a platinum setting, and a fourth fixing the clasp on an extravagant necklace. All four men wore satin-backed waistcoats and black yarmulkes, and each of them looked up briefly from their work to see who had come in. One of them, the man working on the clasp, put down the necklace, got to his feet, and came over to them. He was in his late fifties, dressed in baggy black trousers, an open-necked white shirt with the sleeves rolled back, and wide blue braces. His face was lined and drawn and looked like it didn't get much sun, his eyes were dark and sad, and his lips tight and thin above a receding chin. He wore his hair in orthodox *payot* sidecurls that swung forward when he reached out to shake their hands.

"Monsieur Cahn, it is good of you to see us," Jacquot began, showing his badge once again.

"And how can I be of assistance, Chief Inspector?"

"I understand you have some gemstones for sale. Some diamonds, sapphires and a single pearl?"

Cahn nodded. "That is so. And are you in the market to buy Chief Inspector?" There was something approaching a grin on Cahn's face, as though he knew full well that Jacquot was certainly not there to buy.

"Not exactly," Jacquot smiled, and reaching into his jacket pocket he drew out a plastic bag containing the single pearl earring he had found on the floor of Adam Loum's kitchen.

Cahn took the bag and turned it to the light. "May I?" he asked, indicating that he wanted to open the Zip-Lok bag.

"Of course," replied Jacquot.

Cahn slid the seal open, tipped the earring into the palm of his left hand, returned the bag to Jacquot, and then picked up the pearl between the thumb and forefinger of his right hand. His nails, Jacquot noticed, were beautifully manicured.

"A natural pearl," Cahn began. "Saltwater. From the Persian Gulf, I'd suggest. Quite large, and perfectly spherical, with an excellent luster. Weight somewhere between fifty and sixty grains; approximately fifteen carats. A very fine example, indeed." He brought a loupe from his waistcoat pocket, twisted it into his eye and examined the setting, a tiny gold and enamel bowl securing the spike. "Cartier, at a guess. And beautifully done. Late nineteenth century." He removed the loupe, and handed the earring back to Jacquot.

"I understand you might have a pearl that matches this one?"

"I am sure that you haven't come all this way on a whim, Chief Inspector. So I assume that you already know that, yes, I do have such an item in my possession. But loose, no setting." He gave them a smile, and his lips tightened.

Jacquot turned to Rully. "Do you have the photographs?"

Rully reached into his jacket pocket and handed Jacquot the insurance photos that Alain Dupay had provided. His wife's necklace, watch, bracelet, rings.

Cahn looked at the photos. "Very nice, very nice indeed. Modern and antique settings. And beautiful workmanship. Really lovely." He went through the photos again, looked more closely, seemed to be counting the stones. "In my opinion, there can be little doubt. The size, the variety, the numbers. Except for the Ebel watch which I do not have, a very fine Châtelaine '54 if I'm not mistaken, the stones in my possession clearly come from these pieces of jewellery. And the matching pearl earring would appear to confirm it."

He shuffled the photos into a tidy stack and handed them back to Jacquot.

"Do people often take gems out of their settings for valuations and sale?" asked Jacquot.

"Not if they want the best price, Chief Inspector. But for many people it is the way they prefer to operate. No settings, no provenance. Nothing to identify the stones. Just the market price for loose gems." Cahn spread his hands as though he was not responsible for such reckless behaviour. "So would I be right in thinking that the stones in my possession are stolen? Hot, as you say?"

"Yes, you would."

Cahn sighed. The way of the world. Let down again.

"And your customer's name?"

"A Madame Luca."

"A regular?"

Cahn shook his head.

"Any contact details?"

Another shake of the head.

"Description?"

"Maybe mid- to late-thirties. Not particularly tall. Maybe so high." He held a hand to just below his shoulder. "Elegant, well-dressed, well-educated, possibly not French by birth. There was a certain accent." Cahn frowned, thought about it. "Lebanese, Syrian, Turkish perhaps?" It sounded a lot like Cahn's description of the pearl, Jacquot thought. Precise, knowledgeable, confident.

"Colour of hair? Eyes?"

"Black hair. So black it looked dyed. As for the colour of her eyes," he spread his hands, "I have no idea; she wore large dark glasses"

"Anything else you can remember about her?"

Cahn shook his head.

"Tell me," said Jacquot. "Did this Madame Luca give any reason why the stones were loose?"

"Yes, she did. And I have to say it was very convincing. Very plausible. And I don't say that just to excuse my possession of stolen gems." Cahn gave another of his tight-lipped smiles. "She said her mother had done it. The lady was old, suffering from dementia, and shortly before her death she had set to on her jewels, removed all the stones. It was tragic, Madame Luca said, such beautiful pieces."

"But she didn't bring in the various vandalised settings along with the stones for repair?"

"No, she did not."

"Was there anything that struck you as strange, out of the ordinary, about the stones she brought in?"

"It is interesting that you should ask that," said Cahn. "Normally, such vandalised gems would show the marks of the settings. A rim of dirt indicating a metal clasp. Dirt, dust... that sort of thing. Years of accumulated bits and pieces. You would be surprised to learn how infrequently people clean their jewellery. But these stones had no such markings. It was as if they had been washed, you know? Almost scrubbed? The stones were as pure and clean as a wrap from an Antwerp diamond dealer."

"And what would have happened to the settings? The gold, the silver, and platinum?"

"Small fry. A few thousand francs." He shrugged.

Jacquot considered this. "And she was happy to leave the stones with you?"

"If she wanted a serious valuation I told her she had no choice. I could not possibly give her a figure there and then, and that for stones of such quality – even without their settings – a proper estimation was the more sensible and professional approach, that the pearl itself would need an expert eye and more informed appraisal. I have found in all my dealings that honesty is always the best approach."

"So, you didn't make an offer yourself?"

"I did not, though I did volunteer to seek a valuation on her behalf, at a small consideration, if that was what she chose to do."

"Which she did?"

"Yes, she did. She asked me to get the best price I could, and said she would phone me in a few days to see how things were going."

"And has she called?"

"No, she hasn't. But I'd expect to hear from her by the end of the week."

"How so?"

"Because I told her I would need four or five days for the valuation. She came here on a Saturday, so…" Cahn spread his hands.

"What value would you put on the stones?"

"At least three hundred thousand. Possibly a great deal more."

"When she calls, I would be grateful if you could tell her that you have a firm offer from someone willing to buy, with a price that she will find hard to resist. Say, four hundred thousand?"

"And?"

"Contact me immediately so that we can make arrangements."

"Arrangements?"

"Call it a welcoming committee."

"And the money? You want me to pay her?"

"Tell her that you'll have a cheque for her."

"And if the lady wants cash?"

"Then tell her that will not be a problem."

61

Jacquot should have felt a real sense of gratification on the drive back to Marseilles. The Dupay jewels had been found, and the woman, this Madame Luca, who had brought them to *Joaillerie* Cahn for appraisal, was now a person of considerable interest. Who was she? And how had the jewels come to be in her possession? Out of the blue, a new and very promising lead had suddenly opened up. Progress, at last. And something positive for *Maître* Bonnefoy.

But any such gratification was mitigated by what had happened to Simone, how she'd been 're-assigned' at DupayCorp, and how she had reacted so violently when he'd asked about the Burak deal, slamming the phone down on him. No, not slamming it down, he decided. That suggested passion. What she had done was simply replace the receiver in its cradle. Just that. Gently, carefully… finally. So much more damning. Of course, he had tried to call back but each attempt had gone straight to her '*Please-leave-a-message*' recording; he could almost see her standing there, listening to his apologies. Pushing back that loop of blonde hair over her ear, lips tight with fury. Or maybe not. He no longer existed.

But he did. And he wanted to see her, face to face, to explain, to apologise. So, when they reached Marseilles, Jacquot asked Rully to drop him on the corner of République, and with a brief wave to his assistant he set off for avenue Sadi. If phoning hadn't worked, maybe a personal visit might be a little more successful, he'd decided. Five minutes later, Jacquot stood outside her apartment block and rang the buzzer, for a third time. He was about to give up, remembering how she was supposed to have been in Aix that day and maybe hadn't returned yet, when a man carrying a loaded shopping bag came up beside him, unlocked the door and went in. Jacquot didn't hesitate, following the resident inside and joining him at the lift. He looked at Jacquot suspiciously.

"Don't worry. I'm here to see Simone Laronde," he said, adding, to sound more convincing, "We're work colleagues." It seemed to do the trick. The man nodded, gave a brief smile, and the lift arrived, its cage doors opened from the inside by a middle-aged woman in jeans, sneakers, a loose blue sweater and dark glasses. She had curling auburn hair, and a leather tote over her shoulder. Both men stepped aside, and she slipped between them with a curt nod and a passing swirl of scent. In the lift Jacquot pressed for Three and the resident for Four, and, as the lift jerked upwards, he tried to remember where he had smelled that perfume before. Such a familiar smell. But so familiar that he couldn't quite place it. When they reached his floor, Jacquot stepped out with a nod and '*M'sieur*', and noticed immediately that the door to Simone's apartment was open. Just as it had been the first time he had visited. Only this time she wouldn't have been expecting him. Perhaps Monique had just come home and left it open?

"Mademoiselle Laronde?" he called through the open door. If Monique was there, he didn't want to cause any further problems for Simone by using her Christian name. "Mademoiselle?" he called out again, tipping his head round the door. And then, as he drew breath to call once more, he became aware of the perfume. The perfume from the woman stepping out of the lift. And he remembered in an instant whose perfume it was.

Without bothering to call again, Jacquot pushed the door open and hurried down the hallway, passing through one room after another.

Kitchen, empty; bathroom, empty; salon empty; bedroom empty.

On a second, more careful round of the apartment, he found Simone in the kitchen.

62

On the far side of the kitchen table one of the upper cupboard doors beside the fridge was open, a length of what looked like a silk scarf knotted around its handle. Stepping round the table Jacquot saw what he'd missed the first time. For a moment he couldn't believe what he was looking at. Simone Laronde, wearing a white flower-print dress with short puffed sleeves and a buttoned front, appeared to be sitting on the floor, with her legs out in front of her, arms at her sides, and bare feet under the table. But it was clear at once that just her heels and fingertips touched the floor. The rest of her body was held above it by the silk scarf. Stretched tight, tied around her neck, it tilted her head to one side; her eyes open, the tip of her tongue showing between her lips.

Without a moment's hesitation, Jacquot hauled her up to her feet, reached past her for a knife from the rack and, supporting her weight against the counter top, sliced through the scarf. He was braced for the weight, and lowered her gently to the floor, felt for a pulse, and bent his cheek to her open mouth for any whisper of a breath. There was neither pulse, nor sign of breath. Simone Laronde might still have been warm to the touch, but she was definitely dead.

The next few minutes were a blur of anger and disbelief. He called headquarters to report the death and ordered up a Scene-of-Crime unit. Then he went through the apartment, checking each room thoroughly, touching as little as possible. It was just as it had been when he'd woken up in her bed that first morning. No sign of a struggle, nothing out of the ordinary save her bottle of perfume in the bathroom, out of line from the rest of the toiletries, its top off. He could smell it. Just used. The same scent he'd noticed in the hallway when the lift doors opened.

In the salon Jacquot went to the phone. Just three messages. Using the knuckle of his little finger he pressed the 'Play' button. The first message was from him, earlier that day, and the second from Monique who'd called to say her shift was finishing early and that she would be home by six. Jacquot glanced at his watch; sometime in the next thirty minutes. The third and final message, recorded a little more than an hour earlier, made Jacquot start. Dupay's voice. Honeyed, charming. "Hey, Simone. Great news about your promotion. You deserve it. Don't hesitate to call if you need anything. Proud of you." Jacquot wondered what Simone would have made of that message, if she'd heard it. It was clear from the blinking light that she had listened to none of them.

Back in the kitchen, Jacquot sat at the table and laid the back of his fingers against a mug of half-drunk coffee. It was lukewarm, could have been made no more than an hour earlier, just before Rully dropped him off at République. But who makes themselves a cup of coffee if they're about to kill themselves, wondered Jacquot? Which seemed to suggest that someone might have set it up to look like a suicide. Like the woman who'd stepped out of the lift just a few moments earlier, cool and calm enough to have sprayed spray herself with Simone's scent before leaving the apartment. A woman, this time. Not a man, like Boultier's killer, whom he and Rully had seen driving away from La Résidence des Cyprès. This time it had been a woman.

But why?

Why would someone want to kill Simone Laronde?

Because this was certainly a murder, not the suicide it had been made to look like.

63

Twenty minutes after calling headquarters, Jacquot heard the lift doors rattle open and the first of the SOC response team came into the apartment.

"Down here," Jacquot called out, and got up from the table as they bustled into the kitchen. He pointed to the body and a paramedic knelt beside it, went through the motions. It didn't take long. He looked up at Jacquot, shook his head.

Without needing any instructions from Jacquot, the team had gone to work, a half-dozen men in blue Nyrex suits moving through the apartment, room by room, the snap of cases opening, the murmur of voices, the flashes of a camera.

Rully was the next to arrive, breathless from the stairs. "Someone didn't close the lift doors properly," he said, coming into the kitchen as the paramedic was leaving. He went over to the body, peered at it a moment and then turned to Jacquot, frowning.

"I've seen her before," he said. "We've seen her before. Remember? DupayCorp."

"Her name is Simone Laronde. An investment analyst."

"You… know her?"

Jacquot nodded. "I was calling by, after you dropped me. I was the one who found her."

Rully frowned, looked from Jacquot to Simone, and back again. And then, putting two and two together, "I'm so sorry," he said. "I didn't realise you…" He paused. "Do you have any idea why she might have killed herself?"

"I don't think she did," he replied. But there was no time to explain. From behind them came a sudden cry of shock. Both men turned, to see Monique standing in the kitchen doorway, a hand to her mouth, her eyes wide.

"What? What?" was all she could manage, the words muffled by her hand. And then her bag was flung on the table and she was pushing past them, down on her knees, lifting Simone's head, and cradling it in her arms. "No, no, it can't be… What have you done, *chérie*? What have you done?"

212

Jacquot and Rully watched, waited till the sobbing subsided, waited until she turned and looked up at them.

"I'm so sorry, mademoiselle," said Jacquot, reaching out a hand to her, coaxing her off the floor, Rully pulling out a chair for her to sit on. "Can I get something for you? Can I call someone?"

Monique was clearly in shock, shivering, head shaking, tears spilling down her cheeks. No words, just gasps of horror, disbelief.

Jacquot went to the cupboard where Simone kept her gin and vermouth, found a bottle of brandy, a glass, and poured out a measure. He took Monique's hand, put the glass into it, held it there until the shaking had eased sufficiently for her to raise it to her mouth and drink.

"Just toss it back," he said, gently. "It will help."

She did as she was told, tipping it back in one gulp, some of the liquor missing her mouth and dripping onto her nurse's uniform. She put the glass down, coughed and gasped, wiped her mouth with the back of her wrist.

"I should have known something was wrong. I should have known," she said, in a quiet, fractured voice. "She was so upset."

"How, upset?" asked Jacquot, knowing the answer.

"Work. They'd given her some new job, in Aix." Monique drew in a lungful of air, blew it out, and then took another longer breath. "More money, but it wasn't what she wanted. Said she was being sidelined. Like it was a demotion."

"And when was this?" Once again, Jacquot knew the answer to the question he was asking.

"Last night when I came home from work, she was just so upset. So angry. But we had friends coming for supper, and she seemed to perk up."

"And this morning?" Over Monique's shoulder, Jacquot saw one of the response team come into the kitchen, unfurling a black zip-up body bag. He shook his head, and the man retreated.

"She seemed okay. Quiet, you know? Said she was going to Aix, to sort it all out, but would be home early."

"You left together?"

"She went before me. Maybe an hour." She started to shake her head again, reached for her bag, fumbled out a pack of cigarettes and lighter, pulled one out and lit it with trembling fingers. "I can't believe she would do such a thing," she said, blowing out a stream of smoke.

Nor could Jacquot, but he didn't say anything. Instead, he asked again if there was someone they could call for her, someone she could stay with. "This is maybe not the best place for you to be," he said, gently.

She sighed. "My friend, Adèle. She lives nearby. I can stay with her."

"Just get anything you need, and I'll have someone drive you there." He looked at Rully, who nodded. "And once again, mademoiselle, I am so, so sorry for your loss."

"Me, too," she said. "Me, too."

64

"When they first moved in we were nervous, of course," said Madame Dolmas, the wife of the man with whom Jacquot had shared the lift. "Parties, loud music that sort of thing. Drugs, you know?" She cast down her eyes, raised her eyebrows disapprovingly. "They were the youngest in our block, by far, and I think most residents felt the same. A little... concerned."

Her husband, Giles, a retired accountant, nodded in agreement. Jacquot decided he did a lot of that. In his sixties, thin and stoop-shouldered, there was something mute and resigned about him.

"But they turned out to be such a lovely, charming couple," his wife continued, pudgy ringed fingers playing with the bow of her blouse. "No bother at all. Always ready to help with any bags I might be carrying. From the supermarket, you know? And now," she spread her hands, "…this. Such a terrible thing. Poor, poor girl."

Jacquot nodded. He'd knocked on their door ten minutes earlier, while the response team worked in the apartment below and Rully drove Monique to her friend's home. He didn't expect to hear anything of interest from the couple, but it took him out of Simone's apartment. Something to fill the time before Rully came back for him. Just a few questions, he'd explained, after telling the Dolmas what had happened, to find out if Madame had heard anything during her husband's absence, or noticed anything out of the ordinary.

"But to answer your question, no, I heard nothing."

"And you, monsieur? When you went out shopping. How long were you away, before we met at the lift?"

"Maybe forty minutes," he replied, looking to his wife for confirmation.

"I think a little longer, *chéri*," she said. "There's a small supermarket across République. I had run out of a few things. Giles said he would go and get them for me."

"And did you notice anything, anyone, while you were out? Someone or something that caught your eye?"

Giles Dolmas gave it some thought. "That woman who got out of the lift... The one with the leather bag over her shoulder? On my way to the shop, I'm sure I saw her sitting in a car."

"Is she a resident?"

Dolmas shook his head. "But maybe she has a friend who lives here."

"Have you ever seen her here before?"

"No, I don't think so."

"And how far from the entrance had she parked?"

"Oh, quite close. Maybe ten, fifteen metres."

"And what was she doing in the car?"

"Putting on lipstick. Using the mirror on the back of the sun visor to see what she was doing. I remember she was leaning forward, head tilted, and I seem to recall there was a... how do you say? A mole? Or maybe a birth mark? A slight discolouration on her throat..."

"Do you remember what kind of car?"

"Blue. With a black roof. A soft top, I think. A BMW?"

65

"A blue BMW," said Jacquot, as he and Rully turned the corner onto République and joined a line of stop-start rush-hour traffic. "That's what the neighbour said. With a black soft top. No registration, of course, but quite a coincidence wouldn't you say?"

"You mean the BMW at La Résidence?"

"But this time with a woman behind the wheel."

"You think there could be two killers?"

Jacquot shrugged. "Who knows? But it might be worth considering."

"And you're sure it wasn't suicide? Mademoiselle Laronde."

"Not her style. Simple as that. It's all just too... perfect. Too... convenient."

"But why would someone want to kill her?"

"I think she might have worked on the Burak account in Aix. Maybe she knew things."

"You think she's involved somehow?"

Jacquot shook his head. "No, I don't. But maybe she'd begun to suspect something. Started checking things out. And someone realised they needed to keep her quiet."

"Dupay?"

"It seems a reasonable place to start. Which is why you should take a left up ahead. Rue Vacon. A courtesy call on Monsieur Dupay. To break the sad news."

Rully did as instructed, taking a left and at the next set of lights turning right for Vacon. "You don't like him, do you?"

"It's not a question of liking the man, or not liking him. Although you're right; I don't like him. It's more than that. It's just... I don't trust him. I don't... believe him. There's something not right about the man."

"You think he's got something to hide?"

"I've never met a rich man who didn't. We just have to find out what."

At rue Vacon, at a little after six in the evening, the offices of DupayCorp were still busy. Phones ringing, men in shirtsleeves hurrying here and there. On the fourth floor they went straight to Dupay's office and Jacquot told Delphine that he would like to see Monsieur Dupay.

"I'm afraid he's in a meeting at the moment..."

"Then call him, please, and tell him to conclude the meeting without delay."

Delphine picked up the phone and passed on Jacquot's request. A moment later Dupay's office door opened and four men came out; young, bright-eyed, but tired, too, maybe relieved the meeting had been interrupted. Time for home.

"This had better be good," said Dupay, leaning back against the front of his desk. Ankles crossed, arms crossed. Confrontational. A mess-with-me-at-your-peril look. Which gave Jacquot some considerable pleasure. No, he really didn't like this man.

"I thought you should be the first to know, monsieur," he began, pulling out a chair and settling himself without being invited to do so. Behind him, Rully remained standing.

Dupay glared at him. "First to know what?"

"That we have located your wife's stolen jewellery."

Dupay's eyes widened. His response did not surprise Jacquot. "You break up an important meeting to tell me that? You could have phoned. Left a message."

"I thought I could kill two birds with one stone."

"There's something else you'd like to tell me? Something equally important? Maybe even more important?"

"Oh, certainly more important, monsieur. But before I continue, might I ask if the name Luca is familiar to you? Madame Luca? I'm afraid I do not have a Christian name."

"No. Not familiar. Not at all. Is this the woman who has my wife's jewellery?"

"Not any more," Jacquot replied. "But rest assured we will be talking to her about how it came to be in her possession."

"And your other 'bird'?" asked Dupay.

"The death of one of your employees."

218

Dupay frowned, shifted. Uncrossed his arms and dug his hands into his pockets.

"And who, exactly...?" Dupay began, when Jacquot failed to elaborate.

"One of your investment analysts. Mademoiselle Simone Laronde."

Dupay looked startled, shook his head as though he had misheard. "But that's... It can't be. I saw her only yesterday. She was in great form."

Jacquot spread his hands.

"Where? How?"

"Here in Marseilles. At her apartment. Just a couple of hours ago, in fact. She hanged herself. Or, at least, that's how it appears. Of course, we will know more later, when our Scene-of-Crime boys have finished their work, and when we have the state pathologist's autopsy report."

"What exactly do you mean? It 'appears'."

"Precisely that, monsieur. I would say that the circumstances of her death are, let us say, suspicious. Things not quite how they seem."

"Are you saying that she has been killed? Murdered?"

"A distinct possibility, monsieur. But for now, I'd just like to ask you a few questions about Mademoiselle Laronde's work here."

"Are you suggesting that someone here, at DupayCorp...?"

"I am suggesting nothing, monsieur. Just trying to put together some background, you understand."

Dupay gathered himself, drawing on some last shred of patience. "Well, Simone has been with us a long time. In Aix, to start with, and then she transferred down here. She is... I mean, she was a first-class analyst. One of our best."

"Strange, then, that you should have such a valued analyst sent back to Aix?"

"How do you know that?"

"The message you left on her phone, earlier today."

"Ah, I see."

"Which wasn't a surprise."

"I'm afraid I don't follow," said Dupay, with a puzzled frown.

"I knew about the move last night. Simone told me herself. She was a friend, you see. A very close friend."

Dupay removed his hands from his pockets and went round his desk, sat in his chair. Said nothing.

"She was very upset about the move to Aix," Jacquot continued. "Felt it was a demotion."

"Well, if you've heard my phone message you'll know it wasn't."

"I'm sure it wasn't. But that's what Simone thought. She said she was being sent back to Aix to organise some back-office re-shuffle."

"Well, if it has anything to do with her suicide…"

"If it was a suicide, monsieur. As I said, she was very upset, but not enough, in my opinion, to take her own life. Simone was definitely not that kind of girl."

Dupay caught and held Jacquot's eye. "You have known Simone a long time, Chief Inspector?"

"Long enough."

Dupay nodded. "Well, you're right. She was not that kind of girl. But sometimes, given the pressures of this job, people react in ways that surprise us. They keep things hidden, and then they just snap."

"So, Aix wasn't a demotion?"

"No, certainly not. Not at all. In fact, I've been planning to expand the Aix operation for some time, and Simone was really the only sensible choice to carry those plans forward in the most effective manner."

220

"Because she had worked there before?"

"Yes, of course. But, also, because she was the right fit. A first-class analyst, but a leader, too. Someone who could make things happen. A very strong, focused individual. As I'm sure you will have noticed, knowing her as you did."

Jacquot nodded. "Tell me, monsieur, when Mademoiselle Laronde first worked in Aix, was she involved in your firm's dealings with Burak Imports?"

"Burak? That again?"

"Yes. That again."

"I really don't see…"

"Then let me explain. As you said the last time we met, a large amount of money was lost by Burak Imports about six years ago, money that Nakim Burak, the company's owner, was invited to lodge with DupayCorp in Aix for certain investment possibilities. It would, I am sure, be no surprise for you to learn that Monsieur Burak was not happy to have lost such a large amount…"

"And you think he may have had something to do with Simone's death?"

"If Simone was involved in that account when she was working in Aix, if she had initiated the introduction, or recommended an investment strategy that failed to produce the promised returns, then it would certainly bear…"

"No returns are ever 'promised', Chief Inspector," Dupay interrupted. It was clear his patience was running thin. Which pleased Jacquot. "In this business, you cannot guarantee anything," he continued. "You can win, but you can lose, too, as I told you before. Risk always has a downside. And that is made very clear to prospective clients, if they did not already know it. We do our very best for them, at every level, but nothing is ever 'promised'. And any broker who makes such a promise would be lying, and any client who believes such a promise, well… they probably deserve to come unstuck."

"And in this case someone did come unstuck. A one-time DupayCorp client who was not happy with the advice he was given, the way his investments were handled, and the losses sustained. And someone who might have been involved in that account is now dead. I'm sure you can see that this is an avenue any policeman would be obliged to explore. So, let me ask you again. What role did Simone Laronde play in DupayCorp's handling of Burak Imports' investment?"

"And let me ask again, are you telling me that this Nakim Burak is responsible for Simone's death?"

"Well, someone is. Either she committed suicide because she was devastated by what she saw as a demotion in DupayCorp after several years of loyal service – which seems highly unlikely – or she was killed for something she was held to be responsible for. Or knew about," Jacquot added.

"If I remember correctly, this account was wound up… what? Five, six, seven years ago? Rather a long time to wait, wouldn't you say?"

The reply came easily, Lefèbre's words. "For some people time is just a waiting game, monsieur. A trader looking for the right price, the right moment. You don't get mad, you plan."

The telephone on Dupay's desk gave a soft bleat. He snatched it up, covered the mouthpiece.

"I will have someone put together all the information we have on this Burak business and pass it on to you. And now," he said, gesturing to the door, "if you'll excuse me. I have some work to attend to."

"As do we, monsieur," said Jacquot, getting to his feet. "As do we."

66

"I think that's what's called 'rattling a cage'," said Rully, as they came out on to rue Vacon and the glass doors of DupayCorp swung closed behind them.

"And a good cage to rattle," Jacquot replied.

"At least he'll provide the records."

"Whatever he chooses to give us. But what interests me more is what he might do, now that he thinks Burak is in our sights, that Burak may be behind the kidnapping of his stepson, and the loss of many millions of francs. His francs. The cat amongst the pigeons, wouldn't you say?"

Back in their car, Jacquot took the wheel and drove down to the old port.

"So what do you think?" asked Rully.

"I think Burak kidnapped, and probably killed the boy," replied Jacquot. "Deliberately, or accidentally, given his medical condition, I can't say. I also think Dupay and Burak may have some kind of past, a shared history that we don't know about yet. It's also possible that Dupay may have had something to do with Simone's death. Right now, I don't have a shred of proof beyond Burak selling nuts, and Dupay selling dodgy investment packages that may or may not have resulted in her death. But it's not enough. What I need is proof." Jacquot pulled out of Canebière, and drove along the quai de Rive Neuve, parking just a few metres from Bar de la Marine. "But right now, I'd say it's time for some refreshment," he said. "Unless you've got something planned?"

"A drink would be good," said Rully.

They had only just taken a table on the pavement outside the bar, and ordered their *jaunes*, when a familiar figure approached.

"You haven't got any work to do? You have time to sit around and drink?" The old harbour master, Salette, drew up a chair and joined them.

"And good evening to you, old man," said Jacquot. "But haven't you got a harbour to run?"

"It's there," said Salette, pointing to the port across the road. "And I am keeping an eye on it. Which is a sight more than you appear to be doing."

"Rully, meet Jean-Pierre Salette. A cantankerous old fellow who managed to finangle himself a cosy desk job where he can read the paper and ease his aching bones. Jean-Pierre, this is Michel Rully, my new assistant."

The two men shook hands, Rully rising a little off his seat in deference to the older man.

"Don't worry about good manners," said Jacquot, signing to the waiter for another *jaune*. "They're wasted on him. All he'll be interested in is a free drink."

Jacquot and Salette looked at one another, and started to chuckle. The usual banter. Rully looked perplexed.

"It may seem that we don't think much of each other," said Salette, watching the waiter set down the pastis and water jug in front of him, "but we love each other really. It's just that your friend here hates the idea that he can't get through a day without my help. *Santé*," he added, splashing some water into his glass and tipping it against theirs. He took a healthy swig; it might have been water. "So, have you heard the news?"

"News?"

"*Eh voilà*, what did I tell you?" He gave Rully a wink, and turned back to Jacquot. "The *Lucien*. The gin palace over there." He waved across the port to a sleek white super-yacht berthed on the opposite quay. "Up for sale, would you believe? As of this morning. And at the price Monsieur Dupay is asking it'll probably be gone by the time I finish this drink."

Jacquot sat up. "He's selling it?"

"Barnacles and all," Salette replied. "Twenty million."

"I wouldn't have thought he needed the money," said Rully.

"He clearly doesn't," said Salette. "He's splitting the proceeds between his late wife's two favourite charities. Hospices-Med, and the Down Syndrome Trust. It'll be front page news tomorrow, so you can read all about it then. I'm just here to give you a heads-up. As usual."

Jacquot said nothing, absorbing this astonishing news. This would put Dupay in an almost impregnable position was his first thought. And the pressure he could exert didn't bear thinking about. He would be the last person a cop would want to tangle with, and *Maître* Bonnefoy would be hard pressed to offer any substantive support.

"You'll tell me next he's thinking of running for mayor," he said, at last.

"That's what they're saying. Those who know."

"*Merde*, that's all we need."

"A year to go to the next elections. It could be a done deal."

"Has Dupay made any comment?"

"I'd say twenty million is all he needs to say, wouldn't you?" Salette made to raise his glass. It was empty. "So, what does a man need to do to get a drink round here?"

67

"You've got a visitor," said Rully, when Jacquot arrived at headquarters the following morning. He had slept badly, unable to shake the image of Simone lying on the kitchen floor: the staring eyes, the tip of her tongue between her lips, the odd, tilting angle of her neck. He might not have known her long, and her particular tastes may not have left much room for him save occasional walkabouts, but he was still shaken by her death. "I took her through to your office," Rully continued. "I hope that's okay?"

Jacquot looked across the squad room, but his office blinds had been lowered.

"And the visitor is?"

"Lucien Dupay's nanny, Mademoiselle Oberstock."

The young woman waiting for him in his office was seated in front of his desk and turned when he entered. Jacquot was startled by her appearance. The last time they had spoken was after the discovery of Lucien's body, and the last time he had seen her, at some distance, was at the St-Pierre cemetery. He remembered an elegant and attractive young woman in cream slacks standing by the window in the Malmousque salon, her hand against the glass, and in a veiled hat and demure black dress at the Guichot-Navarre family mausoleum. But now she was just a shadow of the woman he remembered. The clothes were still smart and stylish – clean white plimsols, pressed blue jeans, black jumper showing white collar points – but the hair, once bound in an immaculate French pleat, looked greasy and unbrushed, tied back in a ponytail, her face pale and drawn, and her eyes bruised with tiredness and sorrow. When he shook her hand he could feel the bones, a lightness, and the slightest trembling.

"Mademoiselle Oberstock, it is a pleasure to see you again," he said, sitting in the chair beside her rather than taking the one behind his desk.

She tried a smile, and it hovered on her lips for a moment. "And you, too, Chief Inspector," she replied. And then, wistfully, "It seems such a long time."

"So how are you? How is everything in Malmousque?" he asked, gently fishing.

She looked a little surprised. "But I am not in Malmousque. I thought you would know."

Jacquot frowned, shook his head. "Know what?"

"I am no longer there. The day after the funeral Monsieur Dupay said that maybe it was time that I returned to Switzerland..." She took a deep breath. "Since there were no real duties for me anymore. That's what he said. So, I did as I was told and moved out."

"You went back to Switzerland?"

She shook her head. "No, no. I am staying with a friend off Cours Julien."

"I am sorry to hear that, about your being let go. It sounds... a little heartless. After all, four years is a long time."

"It is something Monsieur Dupay is good at," she replied, quietly.

"I suppose he has to be; running the kind of business he does," Jacquot began. Feeling oddly ill-at-ease for seeming to defend a man he really did not like. "But still..."

There was a moment's silence, and Jacquot wondered again what this visit was all about, why this young woman should come to police headquarters and ask to see him? He didn't have long to wait.

"My friend said I should come. He said it would make me feel better, to get everything off my chest."

"And what exactly...?"

"I know it sounds silly, but it's all that money... The money Monsieur Dupay is giving away. I read it in the paper this morning. Selling his yacht and giving the proceeds to these charities." She started to shake her head,

227

and clasped her hands till the knuckles whitened. "It just made me so… cross. No, no, actually, it made me furious."

"For giving money to charity? Really? I would have thought…"

"But it makes him look so good, doesn't it? So kind, so generous… such a wonderful man. When he is no such thing." These last words were spoken with a controlled but icy edge. And then, the next moment, "Oh, this is so hard," she said, unclasping her hands, working the fingers. "Saying things like this. But it is true. I have to say it, like my friend said." She raised her head, looked at him, her eyes now blazing with anger, her lips tight. "But I know you will think I am just trying to get my own back for being sacked."

"I don't think that at all. And I'm happy to hear whatever you have to say." And, thought Jacquot, I don't think I have ever been more honest. Whatever she wanted to say about Dupay was fine by him.

She cleared her throat, composed herself. "They were not happy, you know that? Monsieur and Madame Dupay. Not the perfect couple. It was a bad atmosphere there in Malmousque. She wanted this; he wanted that. Never any kind of agreement. Always arguments, or silences."

"In front of you?" asked Jacquot, wondering if Trudi Oberstock knew of her boss's particular tastes.

"Never, no. But you can hear raised voices a long way in a house, and you can…" She cast around, as though trying to find the right words. "You can… sense ill-feeling in a room. Between people. But they always put on a good show. Always. When I was there with Lucien, they were like nothing had happened."

"Tell me about Monsieur Dupay and Lucien. How did they get on?"

"Monsieur did not like him. In front of Madame, of course, he seemed caring, attentive, but when she wasn't around he would just ignore the boy, as though he wasn't there. And if Lucien bothered Monsieur in any way, he would look at me with an expression that didn't need words – *Get-this-child-away-from-me*, kind of thing. And that is why I am here. To tell you these things. So you know the kind of man he is."

She paused a moment, but Jacquot said nothing.

"The thing is, Lucien was such a lovely little boy, so innocent, always smiling. But also, you know, so, so vulnerable. And when Monsieur was cold or dismissive you could see him... You could see him... almost shrink; so hurt, so puzzled. One minute his stepfather is kind, the next he is cruel. Lucien just didn't understand it, this change. Which always made me want to hug him, to let him know that someone cared, that someone understood. Often, after being... spurned, or ignored, we would go up to his room and he would be quiet, for a long time, trying to make sense of it. But Monsieur never knew that, or if he did he didn't care."

"Why are you telling me all this?" asked Jacquot.

"Because there is something wrong with this kidnapping thing. If you ask me, Monsieur was more concerned with the loss of his money – having to pay a ransom for Lucien – rather than any threat to the boy. Lucien was... secondary. No, not even that. Just... baggage. Part of a deal."

"Maybe if the boy had been his..."

She shook her head. "Believe me, he is a cold man. There is no heart there. No sense of compassion, or caring. It's just as well he has no children. His life is just money, and power, and appearances. Nothing else matters."

"You may not like that, but he has done nothing wrong. And he did pay that ransom. Twice over. A very large amount."

She took a deep breath, as though she had reached the point where she needed to explain herself.

"I know he paid the first time, Chief Inspector. I saw the money, in the briefcase. I saw Madame Dupay carry it to the car and put it under the

229

driver's seat. But… But I do not believe that he paid the second time. After Madame Dupay's death."

Jacquot took this in. It was something he hadn't expected.

"And what makes you think that?"

"Because I know him. I know the man he is."

Jacquot nodded.

"You took the call from the kidnapper, didn't you? When Monsieur Dupay was at the hospital."

"Yes."

"And you called Dupay there to tell him about the new demand?"

"Yes, I did."

"And when you told him about it, how did he respond?"

"There was just a silence on the line. And then he said he'd be home later. Just that."

"But he made the payment. The following evening. He told me that himself. Dropping the ransom money in a waste bin on rue Honnorat."

"That's what he said to me, as well." She paused, held Jacquot's eye, and her expression seemed to harden. "But I don't believe him. With his wife dead, why should he bother? Let whoever kidnapped Lucien do whatever they wanted. He didn't care. For him it was a way out, a way to get rid of something unwanted, uncared for. And someone to do it for him. No strings. Which is what makes me so angry now. He wouldn't pay the ransom to get Lucien back, but he would sell his precious yacht and give the money to charity. This big, extravagant gesture. So that everyone thinks how wonderful he is. When he is no such thing. As far as I am concerned, he was the one who killed Lucien. By not paying."

"There is no law that says you must pay a ransom. Maybe he should have contacted the police, explained the situation and asked for help. But he didn't break the law. And there is no proof, mademoiselle, that he didn't pay the money. It is just your opinion. A suspicion."

"Proof? Maybe not. Just this," she said, and pressed her hand to her heart. "And something has to be done about it, Chief Inspector. For Lucien. And for his mother. If Monsieur had paid that money Lucien would still be alive. Instead that beautiful boy is dead, and he let it happen. For me, he might as well have killed the boy with his own hands. And he cannot be allowed to get away with that. He cannot–"

There was a knock on the door, and Rully entered, almost at a run.

"Boss, sorry to interrupt, but something's come up."

68

"We've just had a call from Lev Cahn, the jeweller in Aix," Rully explained, after Jacquot had seen Trudi Oberstock to the lift, taking her telephone number and address before the lift doors closed, and assuring her that he would be in touch. "Madame Luca phoned him a few minutes ago, accepted the offer he gave her, and told him she would drop by the store at two o'clock this afternoon to pick up the money in cash."

Within an hour of the call, most of the homicide squad were on their way to Aix. While Al Grenier headed for the town's police headquarters to brief their colleagues there, the rest of the boys took up their positions. Since rue Fabrot was closed to traffic Laganne and Chevin loitered at one end on the corner of Place St Honoré, Charlie Serre and Bernie Muzon manned the other at Fabrot's junction with Cours Mirabeau, Peluze and Rully took a table at a terraced bistro on rue Madeleine, while Jacquot waited in the shop. When Madame Luca arrived he would appear to be a customer looking for a gift for his wife.

The rain that had fallen the previous day had given way to a bright blue sky and rue Fabrot was as busy as it ever was at this time of year, a few tourists exploring the old city, workers heading back to their offices after a well-earned lunch break, mothers with prams, and idle shoppers moving from one shop window to the next. In *Joaillerie* Cahn, Jacquot had given Cahn a briefcase of counterfeit 100- and 200-franc notes he had requisitioned from the Marseilles *Judiciaire*'s Property Office, had briefed the two women shop assistants, and had asked for a selection of necklaces and bracelets to be laid out for him on the counter. All he had to do was wait.

Two o'clock came and went, and radio reports from his squad in their various positions offered no sightings of a woman matching Cahn's description. At two-forty-five, as Jacquot began to wonder if one or more of his men had been spotted, the door buzzer sounded and a young boy no more than twelve or thirteen, in baggy shorts and an Asterix t-shirt, pushed into the shop. He came up right beside Jacquot and handed a note to the younger of the two assistants.

"For Monsieur Cahn," he said, in a croaky, just-broken voice. "I'm to pick something up."

The assistant did what she'd done when Jacquot first came to the store. She went to the cash register, picked up the phone and called down to the basement. A couple of minutes later Cahn appeared carrying a briefcase. He put it on the counter, took the note, read it with a frown, and looked at the boy.

"You are to take this?" he asked, indicating the briefcase.

"That's what she said."

"Madame Luca?"

"I don't know. This woman just told me to bring you the note, pick up a bag, and take it to her."

Cahn glanced at Jacquot. What should he do, the sad, panicking eyes asked?

"Where do you have to take it?" asked Jacquot.

The boy gave him a look. "What's it got to do with you?"

Jacquot reached for his pocket, to show his badge, but the boy grabbed the briefcase and was out of the door before Jacquot had a chance to stop him.

"Young kid, coming out now with the briefcase," he shouted into his radio. "Follow him."

But there was no chance of that. Through the plate glass door, Jacquot saw the boy leap on a bike and pedal away at speed, the briefcase banging against his pumping leg.

"*Merde alors*," said Jacquot, coming out onto rue Fabrot in time to see the boy swerve past Charlie and Bernie at the Cours Mirabeau corner and race away.

It was Rully who saved the day. As he stood outside the shop, Jacquot was aware of a blur as Rully sped past him, crouched over the handlebars of a bike, and heading after the boy.

He watched him hurtle down the street in pursuit and swing round the corner onto Cours Mirabeau.

"That Rully was off like a rocket," said Peluze, lumbering over. "When he saw that kid go, he just grabbed someone's bike and was right after him." He shook his head, smiled. "'Course, he beat me to it, is all. Otherwise…"

"Well, let's hope he comes back with something more than a yellow jersey," said Jacquot, gritting his teeth.

Ten minutes later, a breathless Rully swung round the corner and pedalled up to Jacquot and the rest of the boys gathered outside Cahn's jewellery shop. He dismounted, rested the bike against a lamppost, and took a breath.

"It was all set up," he began. "Up past the fountain, the kid threw the case into the back of a parked car. And the car was off, gone; the boy, too. No way to catch either of them."

Jacquot winced with annoyance. So close.

"The car?" he asked, hopefully. "You get anything?"

"A blue BMW convertible. Looked like a woman driving." Rully shook his head, shrugged, as though to say that was the best he could offer, and was sorry not to have more.

And then, like a cheeky choirboy, he grinned. "But I did get the registration, if that's any use?"

69

It didn't take long to chase up the BMW's registration number, thanks to Al Grenier at the offices of the Aix *Judiciaire*. In less than an hour, passing the time over beers and coffees at Les Deux Garçons on the corner of Fabrot and Cours Mirabeau, Jacquot and his squad had a name and an address. It was all they needed.

Edmond Duhamil. Mas des Pins, Chemin Carré, in the hills south of the city near Montaiguet. And with a name and an address, Jacquot had no problem securing a search warrant from *Maître* Bonnefoy, the relevant paperwork faxed through to the Aix *Judiciaire* and brought to Les Deux Garçons by Grenier.

For the first time, on his first case as Chief Inspector, Jacquot felt a whisper of excitement, a sense that at last they were moving in the right direction. And not just moving, but catching up. The start, maybe, of an ultimately satisfying passage of play. Monsieur Duhamil, if that was his real name, could be the key to the murders of Boultier and Hakimi. And if he'd had Madame Dupay's jewellery, then he must surely have her briefcase and the ransom money, too.

But who was Madame Luca, the woman who had brought the gems to Lev Cahn for valuation and sale? Possibly the woman Rully had seen driving off in the BMW just a couple of hours earlier? An accomplice?

It was late in the afternoon before Jacquot and his team left the café on Cours Mirabeau and headed south in four cars, passing beneath the autoroute and taking the road for Meyreuil up into wooded hills above Trois Sautets. The sign for Montaiguet was easy to miss, almost covered by a spread of ivy and pointing to a narrow single-lane road to the right. Four hundred metres further on the turning for Chemin Carré was equally missable, a tilting blue marker partly obscured by low branches.

In the lead car, Jacquot cautioned Rully to slow right down, second gear, windows open, tyres crunching over the stony road surface. The sun was low now, winking through the trees, a mix of pine and scrubby holm oak, flashing against the windscreen. The first house they came to, on the left, had no gates, just a pair of low stone walls set between the trees, opening onto a rutted sloping driveway leading to what was clearly a weekend or summer home, its shutters closed, no cars, no sign of life. The second property they passed, on the right, with stone pillared wrought-iron gates, bore the name Les Arbres Verts, but no house was visible. Up ahead the lane turned to the left, dipped down and ended fifty metres on at a final set of pillared, wooden gates, the name Mas des Pins carved into a square of lichen-scabbed limestone. The gates were open, the planked wood a blanched silvery grey, and at the end of a stony driveway stood an old, bastide-style house.

235

While they'd been waiting at Les Deux Garçons for the examining magistrate's search warrant to come through, Jacquot had seriously considered the possibility of posting a team near the house to keep Duhamil under surveillance, to see where he went, to see who might visit. But now he realised that such a measure would have been unworkable. Chemin Carré was the perfect hideaway; there would have been no way to monitor the man's movements, no way to follow him without being spotted. Reaching for the dashboard mike, Jacquot radioed his squad to stay back and wait while he and Rully went ahead, passing through the gates and starting down the driveway. At the end of the slope the drive opened up into a gravelled turning circle bordered with a line of pines that grew taller than the house. Parked in shadow to one side of the front door was a dark blue BMW M3 soft-top. As they walked to the front door, Jacquot noted the matching registration number and trailed his hand across the bonnet – still warm.

The front door, greyed by the weather like the gates and studded with black nailheads, opened within moments of Rully knocking. A man in his mid forties stood there, lean and broad-shouldered with a narrow, tanned face and warm brown eyes. He was dressed in scrubby denim jeans, with a black V-necked wool jumper over a white t-shirt. A man who could handle himself, Jacquot decided, but there was no Petroux moustache and the hair was cut short to the scalp. He looked from Jacquot to Rully, and back again, offered them a polite questioning look.

"Monsieur Duhamil?"

"In person. How can I help?" the voice was friendly, helpful, with just the slightest accent.

"My name is Chief Inspector Jacquot of the Marseilles *Judiciaire*. I wonder if we could have a word."

"The police?" Duhamil frowned, seemed surprised. "Why, of course," he said, and stood aside to let them pass, closed the door after them.

The house was warm, and the salon he led them into stone floored and spread with rugs, its ceiling set with twisted limewashed timbers. Chiselled into a high stone fireplace was the year 1746, its hearth furnished with a log-filled fire basket and brass-handled fire irons. A set of windows looked south-west over wooded slopes and distant hills, and a setting sun spilled blood-red light over the landscape. A hunting lodge, Jacquot decided, for shooting parties from Aix after boar and deer, a fine old house, comfortably appointed, and meticulously tidy; everything in its place, like a hotel suite after a Room Service make-over.

"I'd like to begin by asking if you have used your car this afternoon?" Jacquot began, as he and Rully took the seats that Duhamil had indicated.

Duhamil stood by the fireplace, pulled a pack of cigarettes from his pocket and lit up. "Just after lunch. I went to the *tabac* in Gardanne." He waved the cigarette, to illustrate.

"But not Aix? Even though it is closer."

"Aix is a nightmare. The traffic is terrible, and it's impossible to park. From here, Gardanne is so much easier. And quieter, less busy."

"Then maybe you can explain how your car was seen in Aix shortly after 2:30? And its registration number noted."

Duhamil grunted. "I can't explain it. Because it wasn't there, and nor was I. As for the registration, there must be some mistake."

"The driver was a woman."

"Then it certainly couldn't have been me, could it?"

"Your wife, perhaps?"

Duhamil held up his left hand, wiggled his ring finger. No ring, no tan mark. "One wife was enough. I don't intend to make the same mistake again."

"You live here alone?"

"Very happily."

"And your profession?"

"I don't have one."

"You don't work?"

"I am fortunate. There is no need." It was a convincing show of bored entitlement, but it didn't work for Jacquot. Duhamil was lying, but was not about to be caught out. A real professional.

"I understand that you were in Marseilles last week. Rue Autran, in Belle de Mai. Early Wednesday morning?"

"Once again, Chief Inspector, you are misinformed. I haven't been to Marseilles in months."

"Or what about La Résidence des Cyprès? On the road to Signes."

"Again, I'm afraid you're mistaken. I've never heard of the place."

"Does the name Petroux ring any bells?"

"Petrus? Like the wine? None at all. Should it?" He smiled, took a last drag of his cigarette and tossed it into the fire basket.

"It was the name you used at La Résidence, to book a table for lunch. The receptionist there, remembers you. Gave us a description." Though the short hair and missing moustache might throw her, thought Jacquot. He certainly couldn't rely on her for a solid identification.

For the first time, Duhamil looked uncomfortable.

"And your car was in the hotel car park. I saw it myself. Maybe you remember us arriving just as you were leaving? After you had killed Marc Boultier."

Duhamil started laughing. He was certainly a smooth operator, appeared to have every angle covered, but Jacquot suspected it was all a show. He just had to break down the man's defences. He reached into his pocket and drew out the search warrant, stood up and handed it to Duhamil.

"A search warrant, monsieur. I'm sure, as you say, you have nothing to hide but, if you don't mind, we would like to make certain." He turned to Rully. "Get the boys."

It didn't take long for Jacquot's squad to complete their search of the house. Every room, every drawer, every shelf, every cupboard. But there wasn't much to find. A single man, living by himself; nothing to tie Duhamil into the murders of Hakimi and Boultier.

"I trust you're quite satisfied," said Duhamil, sitting out on the terrace, when Jacquot came to find him. His voice was hard, his expression tight and disapproving. He had right on his side, and he knew it.

"Yes, I am," replied Jacquot. "More satisfied than I had imagined." He reached into his pocket, and handed something to Duhamil. The man took it, examined it, and frowned. "Perhaps, monsieur, you would be so kind as to explain how we found this in one of your jacket pockets," Jacquot continued. "Book matches, from La Résidence des Cyprès. When you said earlier that you had never heard of the place."

70

"Book matches? Really?" The examining magistrate's voice was soft, but doubtful.

Jacquot cradled the phone between head and shoulder, swung his legs onto the corner of his desk, and crossed his ankles. "From an hotel Duhamil claimed not to know, had never visited. With his finger prints all over it."

"It's thin, Daniel. He could have picked up those matches anywhere."

"And his car, seen in Aix by a police officer; a woman driving away with the *Judiciaire*'s briefcase?"

"But no other witnesses. And it's easy to misread a registration number. At speed. In traffic. From a bike, wasn't it?"

"A coincidence too far, *Maître*."

"You should know that Duhamil has retained Bernard Mendy. Mendy Frères, Paris. A formidable defence counsel. He's been here in my chambers this morning demanding his client's immediate release on bail."

"Duhamil would be a flight risk, *Maître*. Best he stays in Baumettes," replied Jacquot, surprised to hear Mendy's name. Before Duhamil was locked away that first night in custody in a holding cell on rue de l'Évêché, he had been content with the duty counsel provided for him by the State. Now, just three days later, he had one of the best-known, and most feared, criminal defence lawyers in the country. How would he know such a man, wondered Jacquot, and why did he think he might need him?

"Which is what I told Monsieur Mendy. Pending further enquiries, of course. Which are?"

"Ongoing. Paperwork mostly. Building a file. Bank accounts, phone records, holdings. But there's very little on him. Suspiciously little."

"Which is the way some people like to live, Daniel. Tidy, unremarkable lives. What about the hotel receptionist? Could she identify him?"

"We brought her in on Saturday, but she wasn't sure."

"No help there then."

"Maybe, but out of seven in the line-up, Duhamil was one of two. We are also bringing in the carousel worker from Prado. Whoever took Lucien, paid him to make it happen. If it's Duhamil…" But he got no further.

"You should know that Mendy says you planted the book matches on his client." The information came with a hint of a question in her tone.

"Well, he would, wouldn't he?"

"And the woman? The one your colleague saw driving away in the car?"

"No sign of her. No women's clothing or toiletries in Duhamil's house."

"A mystery woman."

"For the time being."

"You think you'll find her?"

Jacquot paused. "Yes," he said.

"You sound very sure."

"Because I am."

"Where will you start?"

"I'm going back to the house this morning. Another thorough search. She was driving his car just a few hours before we tracked him down. And the car was at his house."

"Have forensics had an opportunity to look it over yet?"

"We brought it in on Friday. But they haven't given us anything yet."

"What about the briefcase with your counterfeit money?"

"No sign of it."

"And the jewels?"

"They were returned to Monsieur Dupay this morning. There were no settings, just loose stones, but he identified them, and signed for them."

"Is he still a person of interest for you?"

Jacquot thought about what Trudi Oberstock had told him about Dupay. The kind of man he was.

"Yes, he is."

71

Yes, of course he had planted the evidence, and when *Maître* Bonnefoy told him of Mendy's suspicions Jacquot had felt a twist of discomfort. It was just the kind of trick that his predecessor, Guderoi, would have played. Madeleine Sabrine's book matches from La Résidence wouldn't be enough to convict Edmond Duhamil, as *Maître* Bonnefoy had intimated, nor the BMW's registration, but it gave Jacquot an opportunity to unsettle a man he was convinced had been hired to find and kill Boultier and Hakimi, and retrieve the briefcase and its contents. There was something cold and disconnected about him, not unlike Alain Dupay. Something arrogantly superior, as though both men considered themselves somehow above the law, not party to the usual processes of justice. Untouchable. Two of a kind. And Jacquot had not the least shred of doubt that both men were involved in the ongoing investigation.

But how, exactly? Had Dupay hired Duhamil to follow his wife and chase the briefcase? For someone whose business was money, Dupay certainly wasn't the kind of man to let twenty million francs slip away from him without a fight, even if Trudi Oberstock believed the second payment had not been made. And for all his rough Toulon past, Dupay probably wasn't the kind of man who could actually kill. He might be lethal in his business dealings and at a boardroom table, but Jacquot suspected he lacked the similar steel with a weapon in his hand. As Trudi Oberstock had said – no strings. So, he would need someone like Duhamil to get his money back.

Which was one possibility.

The only other option that Jacquot could see was that Duhamil had been hired by someone else, and the most likely person was the one who had taken Lucien, demanded a ransom, and when that ransom wasn't paid, had killed the boy and dumped the body in a pile of stinking garbage. Like Dupay, this individual would not like to lose his money, and would probably go to excessive lengths to get it back. Someone with ties to Hakimi and Boultier?

But which option was it? That's what Jacquot needed to find out.

If it had been Jacquot's intention to unsettle Duhamil by planting the book matches, arresting him on the strength of it, and driving him back to Marseilles in handcuffs, his actions had failed to produce any result. On Friday evening, in an interview room at police headquarters, with a tape recorder running, Duhamil had remained calm, unflustered, and wearily patient for more than two hours, listening to the questions put to him by Jacquot, but refusing to answer a single one of them. Which further persuaded Jacquot that they had the right man.

It began with the preliminaries. His full name, his address? How long had he lived at Mas des Pins? Did he have any other homes? What did he do for a living? Did he own a blue BMW? Had he driven it that day? Had he let anyone else drive it? No response beyond a request for a lawyer to be summoned. Which was done. And while they waited Jacquot pressed on, matching Duhamil's studied sang-froid as though he was equally sure of his ground, when of course he wasn't. He knew this was little more than a fishing trip, but there was always the chance that it might furnish some possible leads, that something might slip.

Duhamil's whereabouts on the day that Lucien Dupay had been kidnapped?

A simple shake of the head.

His whereabouts on the night Adam Loum had had his throat cut?

A shake of the head.

His whereabouts when Hakimi and Boultier had been shot?

A shake of the head.

Had he heard of a company called DupayCorp?

Another shake of the head – not to imply that he didn't know the name, but that he had no intention of answering.

Did he know a woman called Madame Luca?

A smile this time, a spread of the hands.

And on it had gone until the duty counsel arrived and asked for a moment alone with his client. Through the one-way glass, Jacquot, Rully, and Peluze watched Duhamil lean in close to the lawyer and whisper something in his ear. When they were summoned back into the interview room, Jacquot, as the lead investigating officer, was asked by the lawyer to make a formal charge against his client, or release him forthwith. So Jacquot did as he was asked, charging Edmond Duhamil with the murder of Marc Boultier at La Résidence des Cyprès, and his possible involvement in the murders of Youssef Hakimi and Adam Loum. There was always the possibility that Hakimi and Boultier had simply beaten the Gambian tapper to a pulp and left him bleeding at the kitchen table, until Duhamil turned up, asked his questions, got what he wanted, and then cut the man's throat – even if, as Jacquot had noticed, Duhamil was right-handed.

So, Edmond Duhamil was held overnight in a basement cell at police headquarters, and the following afternoon joined six other men in an identity line-up. Standing behind a one-way glass panel, with La Résidence des Cyprès receptionist, Nicole Favère, beside him, Jacquot watched the men straggle in and line up – shuffling into position, with a number card in their hands, as instructed – and turned as Mademoiselle Favère leaned towards the glass, her eyes moving from one man to the next, left to right and back again. And he'd felt a quiver of excitement as her gaze lingered on Duhamil, even without his moustache and long hair, before moving to the man beside him, another lingering gaze, and back again to Duhamil. It was then that she'd sighed, turned to Jacquot. "I'm so sorry, I just can't be sure. Those two, at the end, on the left, maybe, but I couldn't swear to it. The man I saw at the hotel, Monsieur Petroux, was taller than both of them, with longer hair, and he had a moustache. Otherwise..." she'd shrugged, shaken her head. "I'm so sorry, Chief Inspector."

It was equally inconclusive when the carousel operator was brought in for another line-up.

He'd also shrugged, shaken his head. "I cannot say, monsieur. Maybe, I don't know. It was so quick. I wasn't really paying much attention."

72

The house was quiet and still, an empty, settling sense of dampness in the air. Jacquot and Rully let themselves in with Duhamil's keys, and stood in the hallway, looking around. The flagstone floor, the steps into the salon, and at the end of the room the long window with a view over treetops to distant blue hills.

"Very tidy, don't you think?" asked Jacquot.

"A single man, living alone? I'd be surprised if it wasn't."

"You should see my place at the end of a week."

Rully frowned, thought about it. "Mine too, I suppose."

Jacquot started forward. "You take upstairs, I'll nose around down here."

"What are we looking for?"

"Anything that catches your eye. Something... Anything..."

"My kind of search," Rully replied, and headed over to the stairs, started up them.

"And don't forget," said Jacquot. "A single man, living alone."

Forty minutes later, they met up in the salon.

"And?"

Rully shook his head. "Nothing… particular."

"Try me," said Jacquot, dropping down into the sofa, leaning back and clasping his hands behind his head.

"Just little things. Not many clothes. Two or three outfits: four shirts, four t-shirts, two pairs of jeans, some sweaters, socks, underclothes. Just the basics, really. No old clothes."

"Linen?"

"Enough for the bedrooms, I suppose."

"Laundry basket?

"A t-shirt, and a towel."

"Bathroom?"

"The usual."

"Toothpaste? Shampoo?"

"Of course."

"Full?"

Rully frowned, trying to remember. Jacquot wondered whether he'd thought to look. If he hadn't, Jacquot knew he'd admit it, not try to cover.

"Both full, hardly used. Same with the soap, nearly new."

"Like a hotel," said Jacquot. "It's the same down here. Four of everything – cups, plates, glasses, cutlery. Weird; and everything matching, nothing… arbitrary: an odd knife, or china, or glass; something he might have picked up in the market – some antique kitchen implement: a pepper-grinder, an old bread board, that sort of thing. Like a rental property someone's just moved into." Jacquot unclasped his hands, leaned to one side and rummaged a pack of cigarettes out of his pocket, lit up. "Lot of tinned stuff, too, in the cupboards. Fridge, just a block of unopened butter and half-a-dozen beer bottles. Nothing perishable. Dish-washer empty. Rubbish bin much the same – a couple of cans, some stale bread, a take-away carton. No old newspapers or magazines lying around, no books, no mail except for flyers, nothing with a name and address, and no photographs either – parents, friends, children if there are any. Nothing."

Rully had started to nod. He knew what Jacquot was getting it. "You're saying he doesn't live here."

Jacquot blew a plume of smoke into the still air.

"Exactly what I'm saying. It's just not... real."

73

There were two other houses on Chemin Carré. Leaving their car in Duhamil's driveway Jacquot and Rully set off on foot, walking the few hundred metres to Les Arbres Verts, the nearest of the two properties. The air was sharp and resinous, and the first *cigales* were calling drowsily as the two men passed through the open wrought-iron gates and started down the driveway. The house had not been visible from the road, but as they rounded a bend it showed itself through the trees. Stone built, two floors under a pantiled roof, a faux-château tower on one corner and a built-on garage complex on the other side with two sets of doors. One of the sets was open, the space empty, but as they approached they could see beyond it, in the closed section, the sloping hood of a sleek black Porsche 928. The house was not as old as Duhamil's place, no date incised above the hearth here, but it was still a desirable and well-kept property. The window frames and shutter paintwork were new, the stucco a gleaming white that showed no weathering, and the door's thick shiny varnish had still to dull, or peel and flake.

The woman who answered the door was clearly not the owner of Les Arbres Verts. She was small, stooped, and in her sixties, with a worn housecoat belted below a heavy bosom. Her face was free of make-up, plain and flat, her grey hair bound in a headscarf, and her hands short and stubby. "*Oui, messieurs?*" she said in a voice as rough as her hands. A cleaner, she could be nothing else.

Jacquot showed his badge, Rully too, and asked if the owner was at home?

"*Oui, moment,*" the old girl replied, and with a bob of the head hurried away into the house, leaving them at the door. What they could see from there was a wide panelled hallway with a red-tiled floor, a worn pale blue flowered strip of oriental carpet, and a vacuum cleaner with a coiled hose laid across its body. Work in progress. The house was clearly kept in good order. On one side of the hallway there was a highly polished buffet with a foxed, gold-framed mirror above it, and on the other side a row of coat hooks. There were Barbours, mackintoshes and woollen scarves in country greens and browns, all hung in lumpy piles, and beneath them a line of tidily ranked Wellington boots. In an old brass shell-casing were a number of bone-handled crooks. Whoever lived in Les Arbres Verts clearly liked to walk.

Two minutes later a woman appeared at the end of the hallway and walked towards them; in her early fifties, slim and elegant in baggy blue dungarees and a woolly black jumper. Her ash-blonde hair was caught up in a ragged bun and the sleeves of her jumper were pushed up to the elbows. Like her cleaner, she wore no make-up that Jacquot could see, but unlike the older woman she was clear-skinned, high-cheekboned and delightfully, gracefully petite. She was also barefoot, moving as if on tip-toe, almost floating towards them. An ex-dancer, Jacquot wondered? Ballet? Choreography? As she drew nearer, she tilted her head and said, "Messieurs, *bonjour*, how may I help you?"

After introductions had been made, and 'a moment of your time, *s'il vous plaît*' requested and agreed to, Madame Fuchet led them to the kitchen where she set about making them coffee. A ballet dancer, Jacquot decided, the elegant fall of a hand, her tiny, blunted feet set effortlessly heel to instep as she spooned the coffee into the percolator.

"Of course, I saw all your cars out there on Friday," she was telling them. "What was going on? It looked like some kind of raid. And here, on Chemin Carré? Whatever next?" Madame Fuchet chuckled at the absurdity of it. A light, entrancing chuckle, to match the soft and lilting voice.

"One of your neighbours, Monsieur Duhamil, is helping us with some enquiries," said Jacquot.

"The man at the end of the road?"

"You don't know him?"

Madame Fuchet gave them an apologetic shrug. "Oh, I have seen him, of course. Coming and going. Passing in the car. A smile, a nod, a wave, you know? But my husband and I are not the sociable types. We like to keep ourselves to ourselves."

"And your husband is…?"

"Bertrand, Bertie, like the English say. He's chairman of the Aixoise music festival. For the last eight years. And soon to retire, thank God. This is his last season. More time for one another. I can't wait." She gave them both a bright hopeful smile, then brought the pot of coffee to the kitchen table, poured the coffee into china mugs with tiny violins for handles.

"My own work," she said, when Rully commented on them. She sat across the table from them, back straight, shoulders gently sloped. "I have a studio in the garden. A kiln. All the trimmings. Something to keep me out of mischief, Bertie says. But you were saying, the man at the end of the road. Monsieur Duhamil, was that it?"

"You didn't know his name?"

"It must sound strange, I know. But we've only been here a couple of years, and I'm afraid we haven't really made much of an effort with our neighbours. We're not the sugar-borrowing types."

Jacquot sipped his coffee. It tasted as good as it smelled. Very good coffee, very well made.

"Well, there's Monsieur Duhamil," he began, "and... and... what's the name again?" he turned to Rully, who looked blank. "The house on the corner?"

"The lady with the short hair?" volunteered Madame Fuchet. "Oh, I see her, too, when I'm out in the garden. Walking past, you know? Quite small, but very pretty all the same. Coming and going, like Monsieur Duhamil. Here one day, and then not a sign of them. Weeks, sometimes months apart. Bertie says they're away more often than they're here. Sometimes it's like we're the only people on Chemin Carré. Which suits us fine." Another of her chuckles, as she lifted her mug to sip at her coffee, fingers as thin and delicate as spider legs. The lips tightened, and tiny radiating lines appeared for an instant before they disappeared behind the rim of her mug. Older than she looks, thought Jacquot.

Madame Fuchet put down her mug. "Of course, I did call round to say hello, to introduce ourselves, at first, but there never seemed to be anyone in. And to be honest, you know... well, they are younger than us... and we're quite happy how things have turned out. As I said, we like our privacy. But if they ever need us, we are here, of course. And I have no doubt the same applies to them. If we ever needed anything, you understand?"

"So Monsieur Duhamil, and this Madame…Madame…?"

"Oh, what is her name, now? I should remember, I really should." Madame Fuchet put on a suitable 'racking-her-brains' look, frowning, shaking her head. Altogether overstated. Theatrical. Which, Jacquot supposed, was to be expected; her background, the kind of woman she was. "That's right. We bumped into each other in Gardanne, at the petrol station. Introduced ourselves. Of course. Now I have it. Madame L… L… Lucalle."

74

"It's just too close, don't you think? I mean, Lucalle. Luca."

That was what Rully said, after taking their leave of Madame Fuchet, thanking her for the coffee, and managing quite easily to avoid answering any of her questions about what she called 'the raid'.

"Way too close," said Jacquot. "I just wonder how Madame Fuchet managed to see Madame Lucalle walking past, when the road is an *impasse* and there is nowhere else to go except Duhamil's place?"

"Maybe she was borrowing sugar?"

Turning left after leaving the Fuchet house, Jacquot and Rully crossed the road and walked on another hundred or so metres to the first house on Chemin Carré. When they'd passed it on Friday, Jacquot had seen the shuttered windows and assumed a weekend home, or summer rental, and given it no more thought. And there was no more reason to think any differently now, as they passed between the gateless knee-high stone walls. The windows were still shuttered, the driveway strewn with weeds, and there was not the least sign of life.

Except for that name.

Lucalle. Luca.

Unsuprisingly, there was no response to their door-knocking.

"Let's take a look around," said Jacquot. "You take that side. Meet you round the back."

It took no more than five minutes for the pair of them to make a circuit of the house. On Jacquot's route he followed a cement path past three small windows at the side of the house – a pantry, a cloakroom, a utilities room, perhaps? – but they were too high to see through. There was also a side-door with a glass panel – a kitchen door – and he peered through, carefully. An open-plan kitchen-dining room, with dishes in the sink, an apron over the back of a chair, and a saucepan on the range with a wooden spoon in it. A working kitchen, but an untidy one. He tried the handle. The door was locked.

There was a large wheeled dustbin a few metres on. He raised the lid. Two knotted pedal-bin liners with room for a dozen more. He moved on, coming round the back of the house to find a flagstoned terrace, a conservatory, and Rully on his knees, trying to look beneath the line of conservatory blinds, drawn as low as they could go. He got to his feet, dusted off his hands.

"Looks empty."

"But lived in." Jacquot glanced up at the back of the house, a set of five tall windows in a weathered *crépi*, two of them with small balconies, all with closed grey shutters. He turned to the grounds, a slope of clumpy grass rising to a border of scruffy holm oak and pine that shielded this corner property from the Montaiguet road.

"Is there a garage?"

"Locked tight, no windows, but it's been used," said Rully. "The tyre tracks look recent."

"There's a kitchen door, too. With a broken pane. I'll show you."

When they got there, Rully shot Jacquot a look. "There's no broken pane."

Jacquot turned his back to the kitchen door and jabbed his elbow against the pane above the handle. There was the screeching, tinkling sound of breaking glass. "There is now," he said, putting a hand through the opening and reaching for the lock. "Looks like a break-in. We'd better investigate."

After the damp chill of Duhamil's house, this one was warm, its rooms generously furnished and clearly lived in, though darkened by the closed shutters. The sofa cushions in the salon were flattened out of shape and the sofa's springs sagged, there was a red woollen jumper draped over the back of an armchair, and a lighter and pack of Gitanes on the mantelpiece. The pack was on its side, open, a half-dozen white filters showing. Jacquot could smell tobacco, the blackened remains of a log in the hearth, and the thick, musky hint of a woman's perfume. Like Duhamil's house, there were no photos to be seen, but the walls had a series of daubed reproductions, one or two pictures per wall: sunset over the half-dome of a mosque, a tiled fountain, the stepped rows of an amphitheatre, a gowned man smoking a hookah. Scenes from the Middle East. Syria, Turkey, Iran, Iraq, Jacquot wondered?

Upstairs they found four bedrooms, one with its own bathroom, the others sharing a family bathroom at the end of the corridor, over the kitchen. Two of the bedrooms had been used; beds made, but slept in; a man's clothes in one of the bedroom wardrobes, a woman's in the other.

"Mother and son," said Rully.

253

"The clothes are too big for a son. Grown-up brother and sister? A husband and wife who sleep apart?" Jacquot picked up a paperback from the bedside table in the woman's room, a thriller, judging by the cover, and written in Turkish.

It was then, standing together in the woman's bedroom, that they heard a car turn into the drive, and brake to a stop. There was the whine of the garage door being raised, and the sound of an engine revving, moving forward.

By the time they heard a car door slam, followed by another whine as the garage door closed, they were back on the ground floor.

"Kitchen?" asked Rully, looking anxious.

"Front door," Jacquot replied. "We should introduce ourselves."

75

When Jacquot opened the front door and stepped out on to the porch with Rully, a woman was striding towards them, pulling off a pair of driving gloves. She was slim and petite with wavy auburn hair cut short to her shoulders. She wore blue jeans tucked into leather boots, a zip-front cream blouson with a fluffy rabbit-fur collar, and she carried a leather tote in the crook of an elbow. As she pushed the gloves into the bag, she looked up and saw Jacquot and Rully standing at her open front door. It stopped her in her tracks. Like an animal caught in a beam of light. Tensed, alert.

"Who are you? What are you doing here?" Her voice was sharp, proprietorial. Challenging. She was not afraid.

"Madame, *bonjour*. My name is Jacquot. Chief Inspector with the Police *Judiciaire*–" It was as far as he got.

With a swift, fluid grace the woman ducked to one side, reached into her bag, and in an instant had a gun levelled on Jacquot and Rully, shooting off two rounds that whined past their heads and splintered the edges of the door jamb. Another three rounds followed as they tumbled back inside the house, scuttling for cover, Rully behind the still open front door, Jacquot crouching beside a hallway table. They drew their own guns, Jacquot from his belt, Rully from his shoulder holster. Another three rounds raked the doorway, smashing a picture and splintering a vase of flowers. But the sound of gunfire was muted, more pop than blast. A silencer, thought Jacquot, here on Chemin Carrée?

"It's her," said Rully. "The woman in the BMW. I recognise her. The hair, the fur collar."

"Looks like she recognised you, too," replied Jacquot, wondering if this could be the same woman who'd stepped past him while he waited for the lift with Monsieur Dolmas. Maybe she'd recognised him as well? Peeping around the edge of the door frame to see if he could get another look at her, he pulled back as another two shots, fired wildly, slammed into the hallway. Then they heard the garage door whining up, a car engine firing, and as they got to their feet, double-handing their Berettas and ready to return fire, they came around the door in time to see a blue BMW reverse out of the garage, swing round in a half circle and, with another wild spin of the wheel from the driver, accelerate away up the drive, dust and grit billowing, its rear end snaking for a grip.

In a built-up city street, Jacquot and Rully would have been more circumspect in their shooting, but here in the country, firing uphill, surrounded by wooded slopes, with little or no passing traffic, and only two other houses some distance away, they loosed off a volley of fire, maybe a dozen shots, some of which peppered the BMW's boot and tore through the raised hood and plastic rear window, with the rest going wild.

But to no avail. The car was gone, swerving out onto the road and heading off towards Gardanne.

"Get the car," said Jacquot, tossing Rully the car keys. "I'll call it in from here, and meet you at the top of the drive."

Back in the house, Jacquot called police headquarters in Aix, gave a description of the car, its driver and possible direction, put in a request for an SOC unit to visit the house, and by the time he reached the top of the drive, Rully was waiting for him.

"Which way?"

"Right. To Meyreuil," said Jacquot, struggling with his seat belt as Rully accelerated away, hoping she hadn't turned left for Aix. If she had, the city police had better keep their eyes open. "You okay?"

"First time anyone's taken a shot at me."

"Doesn't quite feel real, does it? Until afterwards."

"When it happened, no. I couldn't believe it. Now..."

It didn't take long before the road started to drop down from the heights of Montaiguet to Gardanne and Meyreuil, but Jacquot knew that their chances of catching Madame Lucalle's BMW were slim. Her five- or six-minute start would have given her easily enough time to put some distance between them, with three possible routes to choose from at the bottom of the hill. Keeping on her tail would be guesswork, a one in three chance they'd get it right.

But then, coming round the final bend before the long descent, there was the BMW, slewed across the road, broadside on, with a white Citroën van crumpled against it, bonnet to front wing.

Pulling up ten metres short, Jacquot and Rully leapt from the car and reached for their guns, approaching warily. Steam rose from the BMW's radiator and wisps of rubber-scented smoke curled from a shredded rear tyre that clung to the wheel rim like a badly-fixed toupée. The driver of the Citroën van was tugging at the BMW's driver's door when they arrived, calling out to them for help, but when he saw them draw their guns he backed away.

"I didn't do anything, okay. I didn't see anything."

"Police," Rully called out, reaching for his badge. "It's okay. Just stay back."

"Go and call it in," said Jacquot, wrenching the driver's door open to find Madame Lucalle slumped across the passenger seat, the gun she had used lying in the passenger footwell. A line of blood had trickled across her cheek from a head wound, and more blood had soaked through the torn right sleeve and shoulder of her cream blouson, slicking the fur of its collar into spiky red tips. But she was alive, and as far as Jacquot could see there were no other wounds beyond a large reddening lump in the centre of her forehead where she must have struck it against the steering wheel. Just a couple of lucky shots, and driving too fast, had brought her to this.

The van driver confirmed it. "She just came round the corner, boss, right over on my side, sparks coming off her back wheel. Didn't have no control, she didn't; just swerved away when she saw me, but left it too late. Nothing I could do."

"You need 'cuffs?" asked Rully, back from their car with a set in his hands.

Jacquot shook his head. "She's not going anywhere."

"We've got an ambulance on the way. Shouldn't be long," said Rully.

But Jacquot wasn't listening. Something had caught his eye. He went round to the passenger door and pulled it open, leaned in and eased Madame Lucalle's left hand away from her body.

A shaft of sunlight coming over his shoulder glinted off the gold bezel of an Ebel Châtelaine '54 wrist watch.

76

Dupay was not a sentimental man, never had been, never would be. Sentiment was just a weakness, something to be avoided. But he would have been the first to admit that had he suffered such a weakness it would have been for his yacht, *Lucien*. Sixty metres of streamlined elegance designed and built in 1983 by Dutch boatbuilders Van der Glissen, commissioned by an Arab prince who'd grown bored with it after a couple of years, and sold to him for a song.

Lucien was everything the boy she was named after was not. Sleek, not chubby, with perfect unmarred features. And this would be his last time aboard, watching the forts of St Jean and Saint Nicholas slide by as his skipper held his course between various smaller craft, feeling the warm sun on his face, the wind in his hair, and the salty taste of the ocean on his bearded lips. Ahead the low, rocky outcrops of the Frioul Islands rose out of the sea. There was still five hundred kilometres of fuel in Lucien's tanks and Dupay was intent on using up every last drop before the new owner took possession at the end of the week.

"Take me to Sanary," Dupay had told his skipper when he came aboard, and an hour later he watched the bow swing to port, crossing between incoming and outgoing ferries and slicing through their wake swells with a surgical precision.

Samir had always loved *Lucien*. The first time the boy had come aboard Dupay could see the breath catch in his throat, though he did well to disguise his wonder. It was a weekend, Camille was visiting friends in Paris, the nanny was looking after Lucien, and the two of them had sailed this same route, to anchor off Sanary and take the tender to a quayside restaurant that Dupay particularly loved. Samir had loved it, too, and had shown his appreciation when they returned to *Lucien* later that night.

By the time they berthed in the Vieux Port the following day, Dupay realised that he had never met anyone quite like Samir.

The young man had stolen his heart.

77

"So, what have we got?" Jacquot scanned the faces in the squad room, friends every one of them, a band of brothers, a team. It was a good feeling. He caught Chevin's eye. "Pierre?"

"L-L-Latest from the hospital, Madame Lucalle is recovering from her wounds. A single gunshot to the t-t-top of her right arm and shoulder, a second that grazed the side of her head, and a c-c-concussion sustained in the crash."

"When can she be interviewed?"

"Maybe tomorrow, her d-d-doctor says."

"She'll tell us nothing," growled Grenier, shifting his bulk in his chair and making the wood creak. "Like her friend, not a word."

"Friend?" asked Luc, who'd returned to Marseilles that very morning from Perpignan. His mother had broken her wrist in a fall and he'd taken a short leave of absence. He had looked drawn and tired when he arrived in the squad room, but it didn't take him long to get back in the rhythm. The catch-up was as much for him as the rest of the squad.

"Forensics have matched Lucalle with a man called Edmond Duhamil, currently in custody," the ex-legionnaire Peluze explained. "Starting with his BMW. A lipstick under the seat. New, hardly used."

"He could have just offered her a lift?" This from Charlie Serre, playing cat's cradle with a long rubber band. His eyes were focused on his fingers as he worked the elastic, but his attention was on the briefing. "Good neighbour kind of thing? And she dropped it?"

"Where did they find the lipstick? Which seat?" asked Luc, shuffling a cigarette from its packet, and lighting up.

"Driver's," said Peluze. "So he wasn't being neighbourly. She drove the thing."

"And it's definitely her lipstick?" asked Luc.

"A pretty good chance. SOC boys found an old lipstick – same brand, same colour – in a kitchen bin-liner."

"And thrown away since the snatch at the jewellers," said Jacquot. "Rubbish on Chemin Carrée is picked up every Thursday."

Grenier grunted. "They don't get strikes in Aix?"

There were snorts of laughter around the room. Even though the refuse strike had ended the scent of rot remained, weakening by the day but still noticeable.

"But not a single print of hers in the car," said Jacquot, remembering how she'd pulled off driving gloves before reaching for her gun. "Just that lipstick, and a few strands of hair."

"She have her own car?" asked Luc.

"Another BMW," said Peluze.

"Anything of his, in hers?" Luc tipped some ash into an empty coffee mug.

Peluze shook his head. "No, but they shared the same house. Her house. His, further down the road, was just a front, an address."

"They an item? Sleep together?"

"Separate bedrooms, so no," said Jacquot. "More likely, given their passports, they're brother and sister."

"Passports?" asked Charlie. It was the first he'd heard about it.

"SOC have found four in Lucalle's house. Two for each of them: French and Lebanese. Duhamil's name in the Lebanese passport is Osman Muhtar. In Madame Lucalle's, it's Fighen Muhtar. Dates of birth in the Lebanese passports put them six years apart, with the same birthplace – Bhamdoune, Lebanon. We've put in for more information from Beirut, but I'm not holding my breath."

"So how come the different French names? Duhamil, Lucalle. Adopted, maybe?" asked Laganne.

"Adopted? Did you really say that?" This, from Grenier. There were chuckles around the room. Charlie unwrapped the rubber band from his fingers and flicked it at Laganne.

"French passports first issued fourteen years ago," said Jacquot, "with separate dates and places of birth, so no, not adopted. Looks like false documentation, but we'll have to check."

"Any exit or entry visas in the passports?" asked Grenier.

"Nothing after the death of Adam Loum, but in the months before that they both travelled extensively. Between the beginning of January and the end of March they visited Frankfurt, Istanbul, Beirut, and Tel Aviv, at pretty much the same time."

"Passports like that? Different names?" Luc shook his head. "They have to be pros, the pair of them. And two houses, on the same road?" He thought of something. "Rented or owned, the houses?"

"Rented, but owned by a company called Koza Han Holdings," said Charlie. "Based in Zurich, so a dead end there. Except Koza Han happens to be the name of some market or bazaar in Turkey. That, from the new boy." Charlie tipped his head in Rully's direction, and gave him a smile.

Rully reddened a little, and Luc nodded. "Good one. So what *do* we know about them? The houses, I mean."

"Koza Han bought them five years ago," Charlie continued. "And Aix Registry has Marie Lucalle and Edmond Duhamil, under their French passport names, as residents from that time."

"Do we know where they lived before that?" asked Jacquot.

Charlie shook his head. "Still checking, but nothing so far."

"Were the two houses bought at the same time?"

"A week apart at completion. Both properties previously owned by a local businessman, Jean Calonne, until he went bust."

"Anyone spoken to him?" asked Luc.

"Dead. Committed suicide a few months before the sale."

Which made Jacquot think. Suicide. Such a convenient cover for murder if you knew how to do it.

"Did he have a wife? Kids?" asked Luc. He took a last drag of his cigarette and dropped it into the mug.

Charlie shook his head.

"Any bank records for Lucalle or Duhamil? Do they have jobs?"

"Neither seems to work," Charlie replied. "And movement of funds in their separate current accounts is limited to monthly deposits from the same Koza Han Holdings, enough to cover basic living costs but not much more. Looks like they probably get their real money somewhere else, but right now we don't know how much, or from whom, and we don't know where it's kept."

"What about the two cars? The BMWs?" asked Jacquot.

"Bought eight months ago," said Peluze. "Identical, save the colour of the hoods. Dark blue, and black. Duhamil's from a showroom here in Marseilles, and Lucalle's in Aix. Paperwork has them resident in Chemin Carré, French driving licences. Payment for both cars in cash."

"There is also the question of the guns we have found." Jacquot looked around, smiled at the startled expressions. No one in the squad had heard about the guns. Jacquot had received the information just an hour earlier from the SOC officer in charge of the search, still ongoing at Madame Lucalle's house. "Not just Lucalle's unregistered Beretta 92 – which Ballistics has confirmed was not the gun used on Boultier and Hakimi – but a number of high-powered rifles and shotguns found in a gun safe in a bedroom cupboard, with enough ammunition to stock a small army. They're checking for licensing and prints as we speak."

"Well, that's it then," said Grenier. "Sure beats book matches, wouldn't you say?" He cocked a look at Jacquot; a sly, knowing look.

"It's not just book matches," said Jacquot. "As well as her gun, Lucalle was wearing an Ebel Châtelaine watch. I've checked the model number. It matches Dupay's insurance details."

"So she's banged to rights."

"Let's see what she has to say for herself."

"So, what's next?" asked Luc.

"Baumettes," said Jacquot. "Time to tell Monsieur Duhamil that his sister is in hospital following a car accident, and under arrest for shooting at cops."

78

Baumettes Prison was at the southern edge of Marseilles in the city's ninth *arrondissement*, a good way along Chemin de Morgiou and across the road from a nursery and a primary school. That Thursday afternoon a group of parents waited outside the shared playground for their children, while another crowd gathered around the main entrance to the prison, waiting to visit the inmates. Set between flat-faced stone pillars and flanked by two Sartori bas reliefs, the prison gate's green metal doors were scuffed and chipped, and the smaller Judas door screeched on its hinges when it was opened for Jacquot and Rully, clanging like a cracked church bell when it slammed shut behind them.

"That's got to be one of the saddest sounds in the world," said Rully.

"Unless you're coming out," replied Jacquot, as the two men showed their badges to a guard behind wired glass and handed over their guns.

Once past the guard, they stepped into an open courtyard and followed a barbed-wire corridor to the prison's administrative block. The sky was low and grey and a trapped breeze stirred up dust on the empty exercise yards either side of them, whisking it this way and that as though daunted by the wire.

"You know what I always think when I come here?" asked Jacquot, looking up at the buildings ahead. He didn't wait for an answer. "No curtains. So many windows, but no curtains. I wouldn't want to live in a house without curtains. Or blinds. Something."

Since Duhamil was not yet a convicted felon, but held on remand, on *garde de vue*, he had been accommodated in Baumettes' 'A' Wing, a smaller holding block to the left of the main prison where cells were not shared. He was wearing fresh clothes, not prison issue, he was shaved, and when he came into the interview room he had a supremely confident air, almost a swagger. He knew they had nothing on him, had been assured of that by his esteemed counsel, Jacquot assumed, and was intent on playing the game to his advantage. He would be hearing that Judas door clang shut as he stepped out onto Chemin de Morgiou within a matter of hours. No book of matches could keep him there a moment longer. That was what Mendy would have told him. But Mendy didn't know about his client's sister, because the shoot-out three days earlier on Chemin Carré had not yet made the papers or evening news, and at police headquarters there had been a complete lockdown. No one knew anything, save Jacquot and the officers of the *Judiciaire*. Not even the hospital staff at La Timone had any idea who their patient was, beyond the presence of an armed guard outside her room on the third floor.

"Monsieur," said Jacquot, by way of greeting, but staying in his chair, waving at the seat across the table. "Please, make yourself comfortable."

Duhamil settled himself, glanced at Rully standing by the barred window, arms folded, ankles crossed; he could have been waiting for a bus. Then he turned back to Jacquot. "Do you have a cigarette?"

Jacquot fished the packet from his pocket, added a lighter, and pushed it across the table. Duhamil slipped out a cigarette, fixed it between his lips, and flicked the lighter's wheel. Jacquot watched the flame drawn into the tip of the cigarette. Duhamil put down the lighter, inhaled deeply and leaned back in the chair. He took the cigarette from between his lips and exhaled gently, the diluted smoke drifting from his lips, his nostrils.

"So, tell me, Chief Inspector, when is this pitiful charade coming to an end?"

"Don't you want Monsieur Mendy present?"

"Why should I? He has assured me there is no case to answer, and he will be back here this evening with the release papers he has petitioned for."

"Release papers, of course." Jacquot sighed. "If only it were that simple, monsieur."

Duhamil cocked his head, smiled, took another pull on his cigarette and tipped some ash onto the floor.

"By now your lawyer will have discovered that these release papers he has requested will not be forthcoming. Because you are not going anywhere, monsieur. For a very long time." Jacquot smiled. "So why don't we start at the beginning, Monsieur Duhamil? Or should that be Monsieur Muhtar? Osman Muhtar."

Despite the man's studied composure, Jacquot could see a flash of surprise in his eyes. The only way the police could have known this name was because they had found, and searched, his sister's house, and discovered their passports. But how? And why? That, Jacquot knew, was what he'd be thinking.

"I see the name is familiar to you."

Duhamil tried hard, covering any discomfort by leaning forward to stub out his half-smoked cigarette, using the crumpled remains to thoroughly extinguish a few glowing embers. When he was satisfied, he sat back in his chair and scratched his chin contemplatively. "Call me whatever name you chose, Chief Inspector. Whatever makes you happy."

"So, you will know now that we have found your sister's house – so conveniently close to yours – and that not only did we find your various passports but a surprisingly comprehensive cache of guns which, I have no doubt, will bear both your fingerprints."

"And every single gun registered and fully licenced, Chief Inspector," replied Duhamil, without correcting Jacquot's reference to his 'sister'. "And we have them because we enjoy hunting. The rifles for boar and deer, the shotguns for birds. If you need to verify my interest I suggest you contact Jules Maran, the butcher in Gardanne. He makes a very fine *saucisson sanglier* from the boar we bring him, and the meat makes a fine winter's stew."

"And that is most heartening to hear, monsieur. But what you won't know is that when we visited your sister's house, she opened fire on us and drove off. In the ensuing chase she was shot in the arm and crashed her car. She is currently in hospital and, when her doctor allows it, she will be charged with murder, conspiracy to murder, and the attempted murder of police officers in the line of duty. A weighty list that will undoubtedly carry a very substantial sentence. A sentence the pair of you will share."

Without asking, Duhamil reached for Jacquot's cigarettes, tipped another one out and lit it. "I can only hope that you were not threatening, Chief Inspector. My sister is, as they say, of a nervous disposition. Sometimes, she's been known to react in a quite unexpected way. Not that she is unaware of it. She has, in the past, sought professional help. You should speak to her doctor, Renée Duprix at the Prieuré Clinic in Marseilles. I have no doubt she will confirm it."

Jacquot felt a stir of unease. The man seemed so certain, so sure of himself. As if everything was covered. Nothing that Jacquot could come up with that wouldn't be knocked out of the park.

Jacquot shrugged. "For now, monsieur, we have all we need."

"And you're sure of that? Really?"

Jacquot studied the man for a moment, then got to his feet, reached for his cigarettes and lighter and slipped them into his pocket. "As I said, I have no doubt that our investigations will provide everything we need. And more." He nodded to Duhamil. "Monsieur, I thank you for your assistance, and I wish you a pleasant stay. For however long it may be."

Turning his back on Duhamil, Jacquot went to the door and rang for the guard to unlock it.

As the door opened, Duhamil said, "It's still just book matches, Chief Inspector. A few guns, all registered, maybe some possibly questionable documentation, and my sister no doubt defending herself in her own home against two men she believed to be intruders. I cannot believe that Monsieur Mendy will encounter too many obstacles having these spurious charges laughed out of court. At the very worst, a year or two behind bars. And somewhere comfortable, I have no doubt."

He settled himself back in his chair, blew out a stream of smoke and chuckled lightly.

<h1 style="text-align:center">79</h1>

"One cool customer," said Rully, as the prison gate clanged behind them. "He seems so... relaxed."

"But worried, too. Under all that front, his mind will be racing. Thinking ahead, trying to cover all the angles."

"Worried?"

"Worried that whoever hired him might find out where he is right now, in police custody. And he'll know that that person may have to take a view. Should Duhamil, knowing what he knows, be left in prison to be interrogated by the police whenever they feel like it, and take the risk of him making some kind of deal? Or should he be removed from the picture? No loose ends. It would be easy enough in there for something like that to be taken care of. If he isn't already, he'll soon be looking over his shoulder. In the meantime, all we have to do is keep on digging. Finding the gun he used to kill Hakimi and Boultier would be a useful start."

Back in the car, Rully took the wheel and they drove back to police headquarters. Jacquot was silent, staring ahead, and Rully made no attempt at conversation. As he turned into rue de l'Évêché, Jacquot finally broke the silence.

"I have something I want you to do for me."

"Of course. Anything, boss."

"There's someone I want you to meet."

At police headquarters Jacquot crossed the reception area and pressed for the lift. When it arrived he stepped in with Rully behind him, then pushed the button for the basement.

"Sergeant Lefèbre, this is my assistant Michel Rully," said Jacquot, when they reached what was left of the Records Office. "He is a graduate in computer sciences from Montpellier, but for some obscure reason he chose to join the *Judiciaire*. He will help you with that machine there." Jacquot pointed to the large grey computer terminal that stood on Lefébre's desk. "I think the pair of you should see this as a period of mutual instruction," he continued, looking pointedly at Rully, "and I have no doubt that you will both benefit from the experience."

"What exactly do you want?" asked Rully.

"Everything the two of you can find on Burak Imports and DupayCorp, on Loum, Hakimi and Boultier. On Duhamil and Lucalle, and Simone Laronde. Not a stone left unturned. From start to finish. And I mean everything."

"I'm down to 'P'," said Lefèbre, thumbing to the emptying shelves behind him. "There's not much left."

"As I said, I'm talking about that," Jacquot replied, nodding at the computer on Lefèbre's desk.

The old sergeant looked a little bemused at the prospect, and Rully a little uncertain.

"So, young man," said Lefèbre, taking a breath, breaking an uncomfortable silence. "Why don't you show me what you've got?"

Rully glanced at Jacquot, then looked at the computer cable coiled like a black snake below Lefèbre's desk.

"Well, maybe we should start by plugging your computer in."

80

Up in his office Jacquot found the state pathologist's autopsy report on Simone Laronde waiting for him on his desk. He settled down to read it, glancing at his watch to make sure he had enough time. He would miss Simone's funeral service at St-Agathe in La Treille in Marseilles' eleventh *arrondissement* but he had no intention of missing her burial in the village's tiny cemetery.

Ten minutes later he filed the report away, pulled on his jacket, and left headquarters.

Thanks to the traffic, it was a thirty-minute journey up into the hills, and would have been nearer forty minutes if he hadn't turned on the squad car's blue lights and sounded the siren at a couple of intersections. When he finally arrived in La Treille he could find no directions for the cemetery and was looking for someone to ask the way when he spotted Simone's open-top red and cream Austin-Healey parked on a side street beside a high stone wall. Finding the nearest space to park his own car, he walked back to the sportster, remembering the last time he had seen it, with Simone behind the wheel and the wind whipping through their hair, and felt a stab of sadness. How she had loved that car. Her 'baby' she called it. And how lovely that it should be here to see her off, driven here, he was in no doubt, by Monique.

It didn't take Jacquot long to find the burial party, a knot of black-suited mourners grouped around a small plot in a corner of the cemetery. He was the last to arrive and though he could see only the backs of heads and shoulders, he was able to make out Monique's spread of copper-coloured hair glinting in the sunshine. And beside her, the clipped grey hair of Alain Dupay. He couldn't see the coffin but was close enough to hear the sound of dirt falling on it and the last murmured blessing of the Curé.

And then the mourners were turning away, stepping past him with lowered heads or sad smiles if they caught his eye. Most of them were young, many of whom Jacquot recognised as Simone's co-workers from the office on rue Vacon, and there, Delphine, Dupay's secretary, nodding bleakly as she passed him. Dupay, a few steps behind her, gave Jacquot a grim look but walked on without a word.

Monique, with a single red rose in her hand, stood alone by the open grave, gazing into it as though she wanted to follow. Couldn't bear to leave.

"You brought the car," said Jacquot, quietly.

She turned. Her eyes were red with spilled tears and sadness. At first she seemed not to recognise Jacquot, but then she placed him. "It's what she would have wanted. I'd have carried the coffin in it, if there had been enough room."

Jacquot nodded, and Monique looked up at the sky.

"No one should die in the spring. It's not fair," she said.

"Dying's not fair, at any time."

"Me, I'd wait till autumn. That's when I'd want to go."

She looked back at the grave, and then, after a couple of false throws, she tossed the rose into it, turned at last and started to walk away.

Jacquot fell into step beside her. "I'm so sorry for your loss," he began. "I know how hard it must be."

But Monique wasn't listening, something else on her mind. "Tell me, Chief Inspector. Did you sleep with Simone?" There was an icy edge to her voice.

"No," said Jacquot, firmly.

"You wouldn't have been the first."

"I asked, she said no."

"That's what they all say."

Jacquot remembered what Simone had once told him about Monique. *'She's a terrier; just doesn't care.'* But a terrier who would survive.

They reached the cemetery gates, and started up the slope towards their cars.

"So, what are your plans?" he asked, wondering whether she'd stay at La Timone or move on. Another city, another hospital. He doubted she'd be able to afford the rent on the apartment on avenue Sadi.

Monique stopped at the sportster and dug into her bag for the key. When she found it she brandished it at Jacquot.

"I'm going to take her for one last little spin," she said.

Jacquot smiled. "What I meant was…"

But Monique wasn't listening, wasn't interested.

She settled behind the wheel, started up the sportster, and with a growl from the engine and a squeal of tyres, she swung the car out of its space and headed away, up the hill and into the trees.

81

Bernard Mendy, the lawyer representing Edmond Duhamil, was short, fat, and bug-eyed. He had a bald, shining head with just the thinnest horseshoe rim of dyed black hair that curled over his ears and turned into the kind of bushy sideburns that had gone out of fashion in the seventies. He sat at ease at *Maître* Bonnefoy's desk, and when Jacquot entered Mendy turned his head, raised a shiny, bloated chin from a too-tight collar, and gave Jacquot a once-over nod.

"Ah, Monsieur Book Matches," he began, but didn't get out of his chair, just held out a pudgy-fingered hand for Jacquot to shake. It felt warm and spongy, and a large garnet signet ring sparkled on his not-so-little finger. He reminded Jacquot of a large pink toad; watching, blinking, gulping.

Jacquot ignored the book-matches jibe and took the chair beside Mendy, wishing *Maître* Bonnefoy a gentle '*bonjour, madame*'.

"Thank you for dropping by, Chief Inspector." She made it sound as though he had just called in on a whim, rather than being summoned by phone not a minute after arriving in his office that morning. "It seems we have something of a problem."

"Problem?" Jacquot smiled, looked from *Maître* Bonnefoy to Bernard Mendy, wondering whether the bulbous rolls of the lawyer's chin would simply drain away into his chest if he loosened his collar.

"To be precise," Mendy began, "you have no case, *cher monsieur*. My client is innocent, is being held unlawfully, and should be released forthwith. You may have charged him with various crimes, but you have no credible evidence to support such charges. No witnesses, no forensic support... nothing beyond your very own book matches."

"Are you suggesting the book matches are mine?"

Mendy shrugged, smiled, spread his hands. As though that were the only reasonable deduction. But he didn't reply.

Jacquot turned to *Maître* Bonnefoy. "I visited Duhamil at Baumettes. For a man with no case to answer he seemed very keen to strike a deal." The lie came easily.

Beside him, Mendy gave a croak of indignation. "What rubbish? A deal? Why would my client do such a thing? It's absurd."

"A deal?" asked Bonnefoy.

"He seemed very keen to discuss such an outcome when I informed him that his sister was in hospital suffering from a gunshot wound and a car-crash concussion following a shoot-out in which my colleague and I narrowly escaped serious injury. It also seemed strange to us that both brother and sister should have four passports between them, in different names, not to mention a considerable stash of guns and ammunition. Furthermore, there is increasing evidence that in addition to her role as Duhamil's accomplice in the Dupay case, she may well be involved in the murder of Mademoiselle Simone Laronde, a data analyst at DupayCorp."

"Simone Laronde? A murder?" Solange Bonnefoy leaned forward on her desk.

"I received the state pathologist's autopsy report yesterday morning," Jacquot continued. "It appears that a part of the lower larynx, the cricoid cartilage at the top of the trachea to be precise, had been damaged, a possibly fatal – and easily missed – injury that, in the opinion of the state pathologist, could not be associated with the victim's apparent suicide by hanging. In other words, Simone Laronde had been put out of action with a blow to the throat before the scarf used in the hanging had been tied around her neck, to make her death look like a suicide. And Duhamil's sister, Madame Marie Lucalle, is in the frame."

"That's ridiculous," said Mendy, bristling as much as a fat man can.

"I saw her coming out of the apartment block myself," said Jacquot, "less than five minutes before finding the body."

"The word of a policeman, with his ever so handy book matches? Hah!"

"And I have a witness."

Mendy raised a doubtful eyebrow, but said nothing.

"And your witness is?" asked *Maître* Bonnefoy.

"Monsieur Giles Dolmas, a retired accountant who lives in the apartment above Mademoiselle Laronde. He went out shopping and noticed Madame Lucalle in a car parked quite close to the apartment building. When he came back from his shopping expedition there was no one in the car. When he and I met in the foyer, the same woman got out of the lift and passed between us. Dolmas recognised her from the car. She had been putting on lipstick, he told me, and he'd noticed a mark – a mole, probably – on her neck. Our shooter, currently in hospital, has the same mark."

"And he is prepared to swear to that?" she asked.

"Yes, he is," said Jacquot, hoping that Dolmas would.

Solange Bonnefoy turned to Mendy. "For now, *Maître* Mendy, given this latest development, I will allow Chief Inspector Jacquot's request for Duhamil to be kept at Baumettes pending further enquiries, and for his sister to remain under arrest for murder and attempted murder. I assume you have no objections?"

Mendy cleared his throat, waved a hand dismissively. What the local authorities wished to do was of no significance, caused him no problems. His time would come.

"If that is what you wish…" he said lightly.

82

With Rully holed up in the *Judiciaire*'s basement with Lefèbre, Jacquot drove himself to La Timone hospital where Duhamil's sister, Marie Lucalle, had been given a private room with police guard on the building's third floor. When he reached her door, he showed his badge to the officer on duty and, with a brief salute, was allowed in. Closing the door behind him he looked around. A typical private hospital room – a little under five metres square, with a window overlooking nearby rooftops, a built-in cupboard, and two plastic-seated armchairs either side of the bed. On the wall facing the bed was a TV monitor but, like Lefèbre's computer, it had been unplugged. Nor was there any chance that Madame Lucalle could get out of bed and reconnect it. Her left wrist had been handcuffed to the bed rail.

"*Bonjour, madame,*" Jacquot began, drawing one of the chairs to the bedside and making himself comfortable. She turned her head and watched him. Jacquot returned the look with a smile, noting the two squares of bandage taped to the side of her head and forehead, a yellowing bruise on her cheekbone, and her right shoulder heavily bandaged, the arm in a plaster cast and sling. The head of the bed was tilted, so that having taken his seat Jacquot's eyes were on a level with hers. "We meet again," he continued, "but without the gunplay–"

"I have nothing to say," she interrupted him. "I am under no obligation to speak to you without my lawyer present." She made a pained effort to move her head from side to side, as though looking around the room for her lawyer. "And as far as I can see he is not here. So next time, make sure you arrange any meeting with Monsieur…"

"Mendy? Of Mendy Frères, Paris? We have met and spoken. He is representing your brother, too. Quite a challenge for him, I would say."

Marie Lucalle kept watching him but did not respond.

"Even he seems awed by the state's case against you, and your brother."

"Awed? Or bewildered?" she asked, with a smile, before turning her head and looking at the ceiling as if the conversation was of no further interest to her. Like Duhamil, she had not corrected Jacquot about their relationship.

"I think you will find, madame, that the charges against you will provide both you and your brother with quite enough time to see the error of your ways."

She said nothing. Closed her eyes.

"But I am not here to ask any questions. The *Judiciaire* has all the evidence it requires to prosecute this case with the utmost confidence, and a certainty that it will obtain the penalties such crimes command. No, nothing like that. My reason for calling by is to let you know that I saw your brother yesterday, at Baumettes Prison, just a few kilometres from here. And I'm sure you will be interested to learn that he was very enthusiastic about the possibility of a deal."

Jacquot paused, but Madame Lucalle's eyes remained closed.

"In return for some form of personal immunity – a lesser sentence in other words – he was prepared to give us the name of the person who hired him to find and retrieve, by whatever means deemed necessary, the ransom money paid by Monsieur Alain Dupay for the return of his stepson, Lucien." He hoped that the suggestion of immunity, or at the very least the promise of a shorter sentence, might trigger some reaction if only to protect herself. But it was not to be.

"I cannot for the life of me imagine," she began, her eyes still closed, "what crimes you have charged my brother with, nor can I believe, for an instant, that he would wish to engage in horse-trading when he is so patently innocent of any criminal activity that you might have dreamed up for him. As for me, and my so-called crime," she continued, opening her eyes and settling them on Jacquot, "you should know that I grew up in Beirut. When I see two men I don't know coming out of my house, neither of them in uniform, one of them reaching into his pocket, ostensibly to offer identification, my instinct is to protect myself – immediately, without hesitation – and face whatever consequences arise from such a response. I can understand a slap on the wrist for such an overreaction, but not much more. And do remember, Chief Inspector, that I am the one in this hospital bed, that I am the one with a shattered arm and shoulder, and various other wounds. Not you."

"If it was only that single incident, madame, I might agree with you," said Jacquot, sitting back in his chair. "Not a great case to argue. A slap on the wrist might indeed be the best we could hope for. But you are also in possession of a watch owned by Madame Camille Dupay, stolen from her during a robbery in which she was murdered, which ties you in with the charges brought against your brother."

"My watch?"

"The Ebel Châtelaine '54. A very fine timepiece."

"And bought by me not a week ago in a street market in Avignon. A bric-a-brac stall whose owner clearly didn't know what he was selling. But I did. I spotted it immediately. A steal at five hundred francs." She permitted herself a brief smile to accompany the word 'steal'."

"And that's a possibility we will have to check out. You have the name of the stall-holder, of course."

She shook her head, smiled again.

Jacquot nodded, smiled back. He was enjoying himself. "Of course, we still have to discuss the murder of Mademoiselle Simone Laronde."

The name brought no change in Madame Lucalle's expression, as though she hadn't even heard it.

"According to the state pathologist's autopsy report," Jacquot continued, "Simone Laronde was seriously injured by a blow to the lower throat which so incapacitated her that you were able to make her death look like suicide. Apart from myself – you may recall passing me in the foyer of Madame Laronde's apartment block – the *Judiciaire* also has another witness, who saw you waiting in a car outside that apartment block, looking in the sun-visor mirror to put on lipstick, as though you were about to visit a friend and wanted to look your best. Which means you were seen just minutes before the murder, in your car, and then stepping out of the lift only minutes after Mademoiselle Laronde's death. Which is unfortunate for you, madame. Because you are not going anywhere." He nodded at the handcuffs. "Anytime soon."

83

Jacquot was not a happy man. Or rather, not as confident coming out of the hospital as he had been going in. He knew he had failed to unsettle the woman and, back in his car in La Timone's parking lot, he pulled out his cigarettes and lit one up, opening the window for the smoke to escape.

Everything and nothing. An absolute certainty that he had the right people in custody, but nothing really to pin on them with any degree of conviction. Instead, the pair of them had put their faith in their own cool bravado and the legal legerdemain of Monsieur Mendy. Since the lawyer

279

would not yet have had an opportunity to visit his client – Madame Lucalle's doctor had only cleared his patient for visitors just a few minutes after Jacquot left *Maître* Bonnefoy's chambers at the Palais de Justice – it seemed surprising that she should know who her lawyer was. Or rather, not ask for his name or details. Had either one, or maybe the pair of them, been defended by Mendy before? He'd have Rully check.

But even with a lawyer less lethal than Mendy, Jacquot could see the problems the State prosecution might come up against. It all came down to the book matches, the car registration, the Ebel watch, and Madame Lucalle's mole. Nothing more. There were no crime-scene prints, no forensic evidence, and nothing to tie them directly to Dupay, Burak, or Laronde. Not even the jeweller in Aix, Lev Cahn, nor any of his assistants had been able to positively identify the woman who had brought in the Dupay jewels for a valuation from the photos in her passports that they had been shown, nor had any of them noticed the mole.

"Much older," one of the assistants had said, while Cahn studied the photo intently before slowly shaking his head. There might have been a more positive response if they'd been able to arrange an identity parade, as they had done with Duhamil, but with Lucalle hospitalised that wouldn't happen any time soon. At the very best the *Judiciaire* had a case that, without a confession, would go down to the wire. Whatever he could come up with, they had an answer.

The book matches.

The car registration.

The shooting.

The Ebel watch.

There was nothing he could find to link them with any certainty to the murders of Hakimi, Boultier, or Simone. Even with a good wind behind him,

280

he'd be lucky to get them more than a couple of years. If he was very lucky. But they were only a part of the picture. Who had employed them? They certainly hadn't done any of this on their own initiative. But there was no way, on current form, that he'd be able to do any kind of deal with them. Why should they give up their client for maybe two years at most in a comfortable prison. With a no-doubt substantial thank-you from said client when they'd served their time.

Back at police headquarters, Jacquot's mood was not eased when Luc confirmed that the guns found in Madame Lucalle's home were registered and fully licenced. "Apparently they're used for hunting. Rifles for boar and deer, shotguns for birds."

Jacquot held up a hand. He'd heard it already.

What he needed to do was find something.

Anything.

84

Jacquot hadn't made a call to arrange the meeting. He just turned up that Friday evening on the off-chance.

The address that Trudi Oberstock had given him led Jacquot to an ill-lit *impasse* off the buzzing night-time sprawl of Cours Julien. It was a narrow, cobbled alleyway a world away from the tutored lawns of Malmousque, and for a moment Jacquot was sure that he had misread the address. But he hadn't. He found the number on a dented steel door daubed with florid graffiti and pressed the Entryphone button beside it. A man's voice came over the intercom.

"*Oui?*"

"This is Daniel Jacquot, of the Police *Judiciaire*. I'm looking for Trudi Oberstock?"

"Trudi? I'm afraid she's not here right now. She just popped out, but come on up. She won't be long."

A buzzer sounded, and the lock clicked open.

On the other side of the door, a high-ceilinged hallway with a worn parquet floor led to a flight of bare wood stairs, a first-floor landing, and a second steel door that opened at his approach. A young man in his early thirties, dressed in jeans, sneakers and white t-shirt, reached out to shake his hand, introduced himself as Fabien Jobert, and ushered him in to a wide open-plan apartment that had clearly been some kind of manufacturing loft in the distant past. Worn wide floorboards spread with rugs, brick walls decorated with batik hangings and oriental masks, and the ceiling webbed with bare piping and redundant ventilator ducts. Beyond a nest of sofas and bean bags and a long dining-room table, a set of three tall windows overlooked Cours Julien. For all its worn look and manufacturing past, Jacquot had no doubt that this loft-style apartment would have come with a hefty price tag. Whoever this Fabien Jobert was, he was doing okay for himself.

"You just missed her. She ran out of cigarettes, but there's a *tabac* on the corner so she won't be long," Fabien told him, gesturing to the one of the sofas. "Please, take a seat, make yourself comfortable. Can I get you a drink? Some coffee?"

Jacquot was surprised to hear that Trudi Oberstock smoked. It was something he wouldn't have suspected, and he couldn't quite see her with a cigarette. "A beer, if you have it?"

"No problem," said Fabien. "I'll keep you company." Behind a breakfast counter, he went to a fridge and pulled out two bottles, levering off the caps with a wall-mounted opener. "Bottle or glass?"

"Bottle's fine," said Jacquot, looking around. "You have a fine place. Have you been here long?"

"Couple of years now," replied Fabien, handing Jacquot his beer and sitting on the sofa opposite. "The agent told me it was a sailmaker's loft, but it seems rather a long way from the port to be making sails."

"It's certainly big enough. But more likely a weavers' hall. Enough room here for a dozen or more looms. Back in the day, they'd bring in the cotton bales on donkey trains, and spin and weave. Marseilles drills were something to have if you worked the ships." And then Jacquot frowned, looked more closely at the young man. "Tell me, have we met before?" he asked. From somewhere Fabien's face seemed somehow familiar. The rangy line of him, the mop of curly blonde hair.

Fabien smiled. "We haven't actually met, no. But I saw you at Simone Laronde's funeral."

Jacquot sat up at that. "You knew Simone?"

"I worked with her. At DupayCorp. I was one of her team."

"Are you still there?"

Fabien shook his head, took a swig from his beer bottle. "Three years was enough for me. It may be all Christian names at DupayCorp, but that doesn't mean it's a friendly place to be. I'm at Borse now. Off Canebière?"

Jacquot remembered his evening with Simone at Chez Maman. How she'd leveraged their table from a group of Borse workers. Cokers, she'd said. He wondered if Fabien had been one of them?

"So how did you know her?" asked Fabien.

"We were friends. Not for long, but long enough."

Fabien started to shake his head. "When I heard about her death I couldn't believe it. Simone was tough, you know? It must have taken a lot to spook her into doing something like that."

"She'd been asked to go back to Aix to head up some back-office restructuring."

"Aix? No way? She was a lead analyst at DupayCorp. The best they had. And back office in Aix? No wonder she was pissed."

"That's how she felt about it."

Fabien frowned, thought about it. "But I can't see her being pissed enough to take her own life. That just doesn't add up. Getting even would have been far more her style. When I heard she'd hung herself I kind of assumed there must have been something else behind it. You know, something personal? A love thing? A break-up?"

For a moment Jacquot was tempted to tell Fabien about the autopsy result, that Simone had not committed suicide. But he held fire.

"I mean," Fabien continued, "she could have walked out of rue Vacon and pretty much asked for whatever she wanted at Borse. At any number of investment houses. They'd have laid out a red carpet. She had a fearsome reputation, and her clients loved her."

Jacquot took this in. Another argument against suicide. Simone had options. But he didn't mention that one particular client hadn't been too fond of her.

"How do you mean? A fearsome reputation?"

"She always got it right. I don't know how she did it, but it was like she had a magic wand. She'd go through the numbers and pick the winners. Long, short, didn't matter. She made serious money for her clients, and for DupayCorp."

"Maybe she'd started losing her touch," Jacquot suggested.

"If she had, it's the first I've heard of it."

"So when did you last see her?"

"Oh, a few weeks ago now. At Bar Léon on Dumas. Do you know it? A couple of blocks back from the port."

Small world, thought Jacquot. The place he'd met Simone.

"She'd just pulled off some big deal and was celebrating."

Jacquot nodded. Remembered. But he didn't pursue it. Instead, he asked, "So how long have you and Trudi known each other?"

"Eighteen months, give or take," replied Fabien, with a fond smile. "We met at a Dupay fund raiser, on Monsieur Dupay's yacht. For his wife's Down syndrome charity. Trudi was with Lucien, the star of the show. It was his birthday, and he had some friends to celebrate with. Along with a crowd of likely benefactors looking on. I thought she was the most beautiful woman I had ever seen. I couldn't take my eyes off her. Then I bumped into her about a week later, quite by chance, with Lucien again. They were shopping. I bought him a lollipop. It was the best investment I ever made," he said, with a chuckle.

But they got no further.

There was the sound of a key turning in the lock.

85

Trudi Oberstock pushed open the door, a carrier bag in each hand. At first she didn't see Jacquot, calling out to Fabien, "No Camels, so I got Marlboros instead. And some wine, and your favourite *rillettes* if you're hungry…"

Which was when Jacquot got to his feet and turned to her, noticing immediately how much more relaxed she seemed than the last time he had seen her; more colour in her cheeks, her hair glossier. A different person.

For a moment she seemed not to recognise him, so unexpected. But then, "Monsieur Jacquot. Chief Inspector…"

"I hope you don't mind my just dropping by. I should have called, but," he turned towards Fabien, "I was passing, and, well, I have been very well looked after."

She went to the kitchen counter, handed the bags to Fabien with a clinking of bottles, then came over to shake his hand. "It is good to see you again," she said. "And…" she paused. "I am so embarrassed about the last time we met. You must have thought I was a mad woman. It's just… I was so angry. So upset."

"There's no need to be embarrassed. And I quite understand how you must have felt. I'm only sorry I had to cut our meeting short. At least, now, there won't be any interruptions."

"I was the one who told Trudi she should go and see you," said Fabien, pulling a cork from one of the bottles and pouring her a glass. He brought it back to the sofa where she had settled, gave it to her, and sat down beside her. "When she read that story in the paper about Dupay selling his yacht, she just…" Fabien spread his hands. "Boom! Exploded!"

"You were very angry, I know. And I can understand that. But, as I said, there is no law against a ransom not being paid."

"But to pretend that he had? To know that he was putting a child in danger? Mortal danger. That can't be right?"

Jacquot shrugged. He knew there was nothing he could say that would comfort her, or cool her anger. Instead, he pulled out his cigarettes, offered one to Trudi. "Gitanes, not Camel or Marlboros I'm afraid."

"A real cigarette," she said, taking one, waiting for Jacquot to light it. He did so, and noticed her nails had been painted a bright, vibrant red; no longer the pale pink of Malmousque. Then he offered the pack to Fabien.

"A little too strong for me," he said, getting up and going to the counter. He dug into one of the carrier bags and brought out a pack of Marlboros. He came back to the sofas and laid an ashtray on the coffee table between them.

"I never took you for a smoker," said Jacquot to Trudi.

"I was a nanny. Nannies don't smoke."

"So you smoked behind the bike shed, or leaned out of your bedroom window?"

"At Malmousque? Not a chance. I'd have been sacked immediately. Just the smell of it – on my breath, my clothes." She took a drag, rolled the smoke in her mouth, and blew it out in a stream. A natural. "Which I understand, of course."

"Did Lucien know?"

She shook her head. "The darling might have said something, without meaning to."

"So, tell me," began Jacquot, steering the conversation back to the ransom. "If I remember correctly, when you came to police headquarters you said that when Monsieur Dupay paid the first ransom, you had seen the money, the briefcase, and Madame Dupay taking it to the car?"

"That's right. So much money. I remember it was difficult closing the briefcase. Trying to push down the lid so that the locks could be set." She gave a little laugh.

"But you didn't see any money the second time?"

"Because there wasn't any," Trudi replied, with an icy certainty. "I have no proof, as you said. But I just know it. After Madame Dupay's death, he could do what he liked."

"So, what happened that second time?"

"Nothing. There was no briefcase, no money that I could see. I just remember him getting into his car and driving off."

"This was shortly after my visit?"

"Maybe thirty minutes later."

"And he wasn't carrying anything?"

She shook her head.

"And when did he get back?"

"He was away maybe a couple of hours. I was in my room. I heard the car. Heard him come in."

"Did you see him? Speak to him?"

"Yes, of course. I went down and asked if there was anything I could do to help."

"And what did he say?"

"He told me not to wait up. That he would handle it. As though he'd be getting a call to say where he could pick up Lucien, and was staying up until he got those instructions."

"Was there any call?"

"I heard nothing. No phone ringing. Nothing."

"And how was Monsieur Dupay the following morning? And in the days that followed?"

"The same. Always, you know, very contained."

"Did you speak to him about it?"

"I tried, but he just closed me down."

"You must have been very upset by Lucien going missing. Did Monsieur Dupay comfort you in any way?"

Trudi shook her head, chuckled. "Not him. I was just the nanny. An employee. It was no business of mine."

"And how did his wife treat you?"

"Much the same. Always grateful for my help with her son, but a little distant, too."

"You told me the last time we met that they didn't get on...?"

"Like chalk and cheese. They just seemed like two different people who happened to find themselves in the same house. No love. Never a touch, never a glance. They could have been strangers. And separate bedrooms, too. It was like... a business arrangement. And a business that was in trouble."

"There were arguments, you said?"

"Just... this atmosphere. This... coldness. And do you know something else? In all the time I was there they never had a dinner party. Four years. Never friends around for supper, no lunches at the weekend. No drinks parties. It was always booking some table at a restaurant. Christmas, too. And New Year's Eve. The rest of the time they ate when they were hungry. And usually separately. Monsieur by himself, a sandwich or quiche in his study. Madame, a salad or fruit, an omelette, or a kiddie's meal with Lucien when she was home in time. So odd," mused Trudi. "Always these charities, these meetings, but never enough time to spend with Lucien, or each other."

"Was Madame Dupay happy with this arrangement?"

"I don't think she had a choice. Monsieur ruled Malmousque. Just like everything else. It was as if the house was just somewhere to come to, at the end of a busy day, somewhere to sleep. It was not – not ever, not once – a family home."

"But didn't Madame Dupay have friends? Girlfriends?"

"If she did I never met them. They never came to the house." She leaned forward and stubbed out her cigarette.

"Other mothers, maybe? With their children? For Lucien?"

Trudi shook her head.

"And this was because Dupay wanted it that way?"

"I would say, yes."

Jacquot looked at Fabien. "Does that sound like the man you worked for?"

"Nothing about Dupay would surprise me."

"You think he could do something like that?"

"Absolutely."

"You really don't like him, do you?"

"No, I don't. Not at all."

"Is that why you left DupayCorp?"

"Part of it, sure. But the truth is I got a better offer."

"But it wasn't just the money that made you leave?" pressed Jacquot.

"I had been there three years. I was good, but I wasn't getting the chances. It was time to move on. Even Simone said it was time to go, to take the offer from Borse."

"Was it Dupay who didn't give you the chances?"

"Pretty much from day one, as though he couldn't be bothered with me. Or didn't trust me. You work at DupayCorp, you're part of the family. And as part of that family you have to show loyalty, commitment and drive. In spades. Or else. And I was not a Simone. For me a job's a job, not a way of life. Which meant in his book, good riddance." Fabien tipped back the last of his beer, asked if Jacquot needed a refill. A couple of minutes later, he was back with another two bottles. "Don't get me wrong. He's a very canny operator. A real trader but, like Trudi says, there's no warmth there. It's the deal, and nothing else. Whatever it takes."

"Did Trudi tell you about her suspicions? About the second ransom?"

"Not until I showed her the story in the paper. About Dupay selling his yacht and giving the money to the Down syndrome charity. That's when it all came out." Fabien took a swig of his beer, and leaned forward to stub out his cigarette. "And I could see what she meant. Here was Dupay making the most of the situation. Turning what everybody considered a tragedy for him, into something of value. For him, and for DupayCorp. No money for a ransom, but this wedge for the charity. What a wonderful fellow he is. I agree with Trudi. The man has no moral compass. It is all about him. About money, reputation. Nothing else."

Beside him Trudi pursed her lips, shook her head. For a moment it looked as though she might weep with rage, but she gathered herself.

"He is a monster. I… I just… I just hate him so much."

86

Jacquot glanced at his watch. It was closing on nine o'clock and he began to think he might soon be out-staying his welcome, or already had. He'd arrived unannounced, and the last thing he wanted was to be a burden. Someone, a cop, they just couldn't get rid of.

It was a Friday night, after all. They might have friends coming over, or plans to be somewhere.

"*Alors*, I really should be going," he said, tossing back the last of his beer and putting the bottle on the table. "But, just one thing," he said, looking at Fabien. "Coming back to Simone. Did she ever mention a company to you called Burak Imports?"

"Burak Imports? The Turkish outfit? Don't tell me she got involved with that lot?"

"In Aix. Just before she came to Marseilles. Apparently, it was one of those times when that magic wand of hers didn't get the results they wanted, and the deal went south."

"Then she can be forgiven. She was starting out."

"Do you know them? Burak Imports?"

"Anyone in our business knows them. DupayCorp. Borse. InterMar. We've all had dealings with the Turk at one time or another."

"Doing what?"

"Trying to make money for them. Trading on their behalf. But they're difficult."

"How? Difficult?"

Fabien got up from the sofa, went to the fridge and came back with two more bottles of beer between the fingers of one hand, and the wine in the other. He refilled Trudi's glass, put the bottle on the table, and then handed one of the beers to Jacquot. "You go with an investment house, give money to be invested, you basically sign the responsibility for that money away," he said, dropping back into his seat. "You leave it to the experts, people who know the markets. But Burak Imports makes life difficult. It's real hands-on. They want to know what investments you're making and why. Or maybe they call and tell you to put money into this or that trade."

"And investment companies, like Borse, say, put up with that?"

"Hey, every change in the programme is commission-based. You want a broker to cut one bet and make another, it costs."

"So it's win-win for the broker."

"Until the first quarter's up and you get the figures. The gain not as high as it might have been. So, it's got to be the broker at fault, right? You didn't get me what you said you'd get, you didn't do what I asked in time. The thing is," continued Fabien, "it's like building a house. You give a construction company the brief, the budget, and you leave it to them. But once you start changing the spec, your budget's not going to go as far as you planned, and margins can take a hit. Potential profits get... watered down."

"But Burak Imports isn't that big, surely? It's a good business with a solid market base around the region, but it's not Elf or Renault."

"Small but effective, and they've been playing the markets for years. And, on the whole, done well. Re-investing their winnings, turning it all over. Long, short... depending on the advice they get. And from whom."

"You have any idea how much?"

"Medium amounts. Anything from a million, about the minimum requirement for most reputable houses, to maybe ten max."

"At a guess that would be a large slice of their operating profits."

"Some would say it's smarter to trade than bank."

"And how are the payments made? Cash, or cheque?"

Fabien smiled. "Bank transfer. From the client's account to ours."

"Does Borse deal for them?"

"We have, but not any more."

"How come?"

"I don't know. They maybe found a better dealer."

"Do you know who?"

Fabien shrugged. Shook his head.

"Could you find out?"

"Not easily, because it's not just Burak Imports. They have at least half-a-dozen subsidiary companies trading, investing. You'd have to know the names to check, and they change all the time."

Jacquot sighed. He couldn't quite understand what he was being told, but he had a sense that Burak's investment activities could do with further investigation.

"Another thing," Fabien continued. "They take losses badly. Personally. It's as if they don't understand that it's the markets not the traders that can bring a deal down. I mean, we don't take a client's money and deliberately try to lose it. But Burak Imports don't see it like that. They want refunds, they want discounts, they want guarantees. In short, they're a nightmare to do business with." He took a swig of his beer. "And sometimes they go further. Have you heard the story about the Aix book-keeper who got his figures wrong?"

Jacquot shook his head.

"He was really quick on the calculator. Went down the columns like a sprinter, but one time he missed a couple of lines. A week later he ended up in hospital with three fingers missing."

There was a moment's silence, and then, "We have *rillettes*," said Trudi. "If you're feeling hungry? It's no trouble."

Jacquot had no doubt that this was a genuine offer, and not just politeness. But he shook his head, smiled, and got to his feet. "You're very kind, and I am glad we've had this opportunity to talk, but it's getting late. Time to go."

87

Maître Bonnefoy was at her usual table, dabbing her lips with a napkin, when Jacquot stopped by at Bistro Savarin the following day. She had finished her lunch, but Jacquot joined her for a coffee.

"I'm afraid to say that your small deception at our last meeting, with regard to Duhamil wanting a deal, did not work. Unless you can come up with something a little more convincing than book matches and a questionable registration number Duhamil will be released on bail," she said.

"Mendy has submitted a formal request to the Procurator General, so as of last evening it's out of my hands." She gave him a stern, no-nonsense look. She was not pleased that supporting Jacquot had seen her authority and decisions put under scrutiny. "There's also pressure building that this Madame Lucalle should also be released, when she is judged fit to be discharged from hospital. Which, I understand, could be any day."

Jacquot shook his head. "She's been identified as being at Simone Laronde's apartment building immediately before and after Laronde's murder. She also wears a watch belonging to Madame Dupay, and fired a handgun at a colleague and I..."

"And a mole on the woman's neck?" *Maître* Bonnefoy turned down a point of her shirt collar to show a similar mark on her own neck. "And the watch? According to Mendy, she bought it at a market stall in Avignon... so good luck chasing that stall-holder down. Oh, and the gun? Mendy admits that his client was not registered to carry a handgun in this country, but that all the relevant documentation is in order in Lebanon, where she worked for a short time with the security service, the Amn Eddawla. Which may also account for the false passports."

Jacquot's eyes widened. This was news to him.

"And he also maintains that his client saw you coming out of her house when she returned home. Is that true?"

"There was a broken window in the kitchen door. We were simply checking the premises for a possible break-in. When we heard a car in the drive we came out to–"

"To introduce yourselves. Of course. But Mendy says his client was not to know that. That you were not in uniform and failed to identify yourselves as armed police officers, or explain what you were doing in her house. Daniel, you know as well as I do that, the cards are stacked against us on this one. And Mendy plays a mean game."

"She fired first. It was only luck we didn't get hit."

"What can I say? She felt threatened, outnumbered, with due cause to defend herself, and that's the defence that Mendy will use. And he'll play it like a pro."

"*Maître*, if they're released on bail they'll bolt. Can you at least try for a home custody order? So we can keep an eye on them. I mean, if they're whiter than white they have nothing to fear – maybe a slap on the wrist, or some short custodial sentence that Mendy will appeal and likely get suspended. So staying in the country can't be that much of a problem."

Maître Bonnefoy gave him a long, cool look. "I'll try, Daniel, but we both know that the evidence you have is thin. Right now, we simply don't have enough." She gave him a crooked little smile, and waved to Malherbe for her bill. "To frame it with a sporting analogy, they have the ball and a clear field. I'm sure I don't have to tell you that what we need is a tackle. And fast."

Outside the bistro on the corner of rue Montgrand and avenue Taillères *Maître* Bonnefoy cast around for a taxi.

"Is Alain Dupay still of interest?" she asked.

Jacquot spotted a cab and waved it down for his companion.

"Yes, he is. There is nothing definite I can give you, but I've been reliably informed that he did not make the second ransom payment. In other words, he condemned his stepson to death."

The examining magistrate looked at Jacquot in surprise. "You can prove that?"

"Regrettably not. Or at least, not yet."

The taxi pulled up and Jacquot reached forward to open the rear passenger door.

"It is not against the law, Daniel. Even if it's true."

"But it does explain why I still consider him a person of interest," said Jacquot, as *Maître* Bonnefoy slid into the back seat.

"Keep me posted," she said, closing the door and leaning forward to give the driver directions. With a final wave from the examining magistrate, the taxi executed a neat u-turn and headed back down Montgrand.

88

It took Jacquot a little over fifteen minutes to drive from rue Montgrand to the Accident and Emergency unit at La Timone hospital on rue Saint-Pierre, parking in the underground lot and taking the lift to the main reception. Weekends were never a good time if a cop wanted to interview a member of the Emergency nursing staff, but Daniel Jacquot took all necessary precautions. When he arrived at the reception desk he asked to see the senior nurse on duty, showed his badge, and told her that he needed to speak to trauma nurse Monique Fontaine as a matter of some urgency.

He was shown to a small waiting room behind the reception area and five minutes later Monique bustled in. She was wearing short-sleeved green scrubs and white plimsolls, and carried a plastic coffee mug. A surgical mask was looped beneath her chin, and her auburn hair had been pinned back under a green cap. When she saw Jacquot, her lips tightened and she gave a deep, disdainful sigh.

"What's so important I get pulled off a hard-earned coffee break to have a few words with the *Judiciaire*?"

"I think you had better sit down, mademoiselle. There is something I need to tell you, and I also have some questions I'd like to ask."

Monique took a chair, put down her coffee mug on the table, and rubbed her hands over her face. "I'm waiting."

"I am sorry to inform you that as a result of Simone's autopsy findings, we have been obliged to open a murder enquiry."

It was as if a bucket of ice-cold water had been poured over her. She jerked up in her seat. "What? Murdered?" she gasped.

"According to the state pathologist Simone was struck in the throat, at a point below where a hanging injury would show itself. At a guess, she answered the door and was hit before she could properly defend herself. After that, everything was stage-managed to make her death look like a suicide."

"But who would do such a terrible thing? And why?"

"That is why I am here, mademoiselle. I need your help." He dug into a jacket pocket and brought out blow-up prints of Duhamil's and Lucalle's passport photos. He handed them to Monique. She took the photos and studied them. After a moment she discarded the Duhamil photo, but held on to Madame Lucalle's.

"Yes. I know her."

"You've seen her before?" Jacquot couldn't believe his luck.

"In the apartment. Maybe two, three months ago. She was sitting at the kitchen table, like you, when I came home after a shift. When I arrived, she got up to leave. It was very quick. But I remember the face. And she was short, not tall. About here." Like the jeweller Cahn, she put her hand to her shoulder. "And very elegant. Like she had money. Why, do you know who she is?"

"Yes, I do. And she is currently in custody, in hospital."

Monique's eyes blazed. "She's the murderer? And she's here? At La Timone?"

"No, La Conception," Jacquot lied, taking the photos back and putting them in his pocket. The last thing he wanted was Monique going rogue, and confronting their suspect. Or something worse.

"Tell me, did Simone say anything about her? After she left?"

"Something to do with work, she said. But that was it."

"Someone from DupayCorp? A colleague? A client?"

Monique shrugged. "All they were doing was having a drink, like they knew each other quite well. But I didn't hear what they were talking about."

"And you never saw her again?"

Monique shook her head. "Just that once," she said, her voice low, unsteady.

Jacquot paused. He could see that Monique was still trying to come to terms with her lover's murder.

"But why would this woman want to kill Simone?" she asked at last.

"That's what we would like to know. But she is not co-operating. Indeed, she has stated that she did not know Simone."

"But that's crap. I know her. I saw them together."

"Which is good. She has been found out in a lie. And we now have a witness."

Monique frowned, thought about it. "Could I be in danger?"

Jacquot shook his head. "While she is in custody, you have nothing to fear. And if you are prepared to say that you saw her in the apartment, then she will not be going anywhere. For a very long time."

Monique sighed, reached for her coffee mug and took a gulp. "I could do with some fresh air. And a cigarette. Do you have any?"

Outside the A&E's main entrance, Jacquot cupped his hand around his lighter and lit their cigarettes. "Are you still at the apartment on Sadi?" he asked.

"Still there," she replied. "Took me a day or two to go back in the kitchen, but hey…" She shrugged; just something she'd had to do.

"Can you manage the rent?"

She shot him a look, like it was none of his business. But then, "No rent. Simone owned it. Just services and maintenance to cover."

"She owned it?"

"Bought it off the previous owner. Couple of years ago now."

Jacquot was surprised, though he knew he shouldn't be. If Fabien, working in the same kind of financial services business, could afford his loft off Cours Julien, then it shouldn't have been so surprising that Simone should own hers. But avenue Sadi was a whole different ball game to Cours Julien. By some considerable margin.

"So what happens to it now?"

"I'm staying put till someone moves me out. Simone had no family, so I'll carry on like it's mine. Of course, there's the will and all, but… well, let's see what happens." She shrugged. "What will be, will be. But, you know, it's a difficult place to be. It's not just the kitchen, it's like she's just… everywhere."

Jacquot nodded; he understood. "I can imagine it's very difficult."

"You can?"

"Cops have families, too. Loved ones. We're not immune."

She gave him a long shrewd look. "When I first met you, I didn't like you. I could see what you were thinking."

"I told you she made it plain what the game was. I knew I had no chance."

300

"No, you didn't. No chance." For a moment her voice had an icy, possessive edge. But then it softened, the tone more gentle, reflective. "It's funny, you know. Everyone thought I was the balls in the relationship. The tough one. The one in charge who decided who and what and where and how. But I wasn't. That was Simone. Always Simone. She was the one who made the rules, laid down the law. I just... did as I was told."

Which admission rather took Jacquot by surprise. Of the two women, he would have had no hesitation in picking out Monique as the dominant partner. But then he remembered what Simone had said to him, that evening at Paula's... that he was too trusting, that sometimes people were not who, or how, they seemed. And here was another perfect example. And he remembered the last thing she had said to him. Not just the words, but the tone. Soft and deadly. "Fuck you, Daniel."

"Tell me," asked Jacquot, "did Simone ever talk about her work?"

"Sure. But even if she didn't, you could tell. Like me. The good times, the bad times."

"Bad times?"

"Sometimes things didn't go to plan. Client stuff. The markets. And it made her mad. But it's the same in every job. You should hear me on a bad day, when some fuckwit junior doctor treats me like I don't know which end of the thermometer to put in a patient's mouth. Men. You just can't avoid them."

Jacquot chuckled.

"And the travelling, of course. She hated all the trips. Hated being away from home."

"Travelling?"

301

"You know, work stuff." Monique was softening, no longer the harsh one who'd give the King of Siam or the President of the Republic a run for their money, bound up in fond memory, almost warming in front of his eyes.

"I thought it was just a desk job in the office on Vacon?"

"Nope. All over. You guys didn't check her passport?"

Jacquot shook his head; knew they should have done.

"Well, there was Antwerp, Frankfurt, Beirut a few times."

"Beirut?"

"Which she hated."

"Did she say why?"

"Having to be a woman in an Islamic country for starters. Like, having to be some kind of second-class citizen. It made her mad."

"Just that?"

"I have a feeling the client was difficult, too. That they didn't get on. She was always tetchy before she left, and always seemed relieved when she got home. But hey, business is business. She had to do it."

"You know who the client was?" He knew he could ask Dupay, but this seemed the easier option.

Monique shook her head.

"Burak Imports?"

"Might have been. Can't say."

"So why would she need to travel when her job was looking at the figures and working out the best investments?"

"Hey, I'm a nurse not a trader." She took a last drag on her cigarette and stubbed it out with her foot, steered the butt to a nearby drain. Jacquot did the same. She glanced up as an ambulance, blue lights flashing, drew up at the entrance. "Break's over. Time to go," she said, watching the paramedics run out with a gurney as the ambulance doors opened.

"Thank you for your help," said Jacquot. "I appreciate it."

She shrugged, looked up at him and gave a tight little smile. "Guess we both want the same thing. Just make sure those bastards pay the price, is all I ask. For me, and Simone."

89

The first thing Jacquot did when he got back to police headquarters was call *Maître* Bonnefoy and tell her that he had a witness who would testify that she had seen Madame Lucalle in Simone's flat.

"The day of her murder?"

"A couple of months ago. But Lucalle has denied knowing Simone, and of ever being at the apartment. She lied to us."

It wasn't quite accurate, Jacquot knew, but Lucalle's silence when he'd accused her of killing Simone had been good enough for him.

"Whether she's a security service operative or not, I think we have what we need to keep her in custody, so she can answer more questions when she's discharged from hospital."

"You're sure of this? The witness?"

"Simone Laronde's partner. I showed her photos of Duhamil and Lucalle and she picked Lucalle. No doubt, no question."

"I'll let Mendy know. He'll be thrilled."

"And Duhamil?"

"More, please. Those book matches are still book matches. Otherwise, Monday lunchtime he walks."

After the call to Bonnefoy, relieved that he'd got a stay of execution on one of his suspects, and a day or two more to find something against Duhamil, Jacquot asked for Dupay's file on Burak Imports.

303

Chevin brought it in, dropped it on his desk. "It's all there in black and white. I had a chum on Fraud take a l-l-look and it all adds up. After a promising start, with some good returns, it was suddenly g-g-game over. A car crash. Pile-up, more like."

Jacquot flicked through the two pages, each with the DupayCorp letterhead, and the word 'Contract' beneath. Photocopying the documents had tilted and faded the text, but it was still legible: Client name – Burak Imports (Aix), address, tax reference, and total sum put under management. Beneath this was the account handler's name – in this case, Mme S. Laronde – with the rest of the first page and following page divided into four columns: A date, running down the left-hand side – a six-month run from January 26 to July 31 1986; the next column with the various amounts invested, a third showing percentage profit returns, and in the right-hand column a list of trading reference numbers, with a single company name for the last three entries. Soft-Com Enterprise.

The report was easy enough to follow. After reasonable gains on its initial investments – all of them emerging tech companies – the programme recommended by Simone had suddenly come a cropper, costing Burak Imports all but a fraction of its original investment. No wonder Burak was angry. Any investor would be. But how could a company like DupayCorp get it so spectacularly wrong, when the account had been handled by one of their star investment analysts – Simone Laronde?

"It was a s-s-slaughter," Chevin hissed. "How to lose m-m-money without really trying. Burak would have done better with a b-b-bank deposit. All your eggs in one b-b-basket comes to mind."

Jacquot closed the file and dropped it on his desk. "And your man says it's legit?"

Chevin nodded.

"So what happened? How come it went sour?"

"The last c-c-company she recommended, a computer software outfit called Soft-Com Enterprise, l-l-looked a hot bet after the tech industry press gave it one ringing editorial endorsement after another. So when S-CE offered a R-R-Rights Issue to raise further f-f-funding for the global launch of its latest software p-p-package – an operating system to beat all operating systems – DupayCorp went for it hook, l-l-line, and sinker, increasing their stake – or rather, Burak's investment – in what looked like a sure-fire money-spinner. Only it wasn't. If you look at the last two or three t-t-trading entries on the second page," Chevin continued, "you c-c-can see when and where it all went wrong. One day it's all sunshine and light, the next it's A-A-Armageddon. A series of unforeseen g-g-glitches in S-CE's state-of-the-art operating system threw its stock value into a tailspin pretty much overnight, and when a software competitor came along with a similar package that did work, the game was up. A ton of investors lost a p-p-packet, including Simone Laronde. Or rather, B-B-Burak Imports."

"Thanks, good job," said Jacquot.

"No problem, boss. Hope it helps." And with a loose salute, Chevin headed back to the squad room.

Jacquot sighed, put his feet up on the desk and tried to make sense of it all. Clearly Simone had picked the wrong horse, and what must have looked like a winner had gone down in flames. Which would explain why Burak was so angry – even years later. But if it was Madame Lucalle who had killed Simone for mishandling the Burak account, and losing the Turk millions, then what was Lucalle's link with Burak Imports? And what exactly had Lucalle been doing in Simone's apartment two or three months before the murder, sitting at the kitchen table with her, having a drink, like they knew each other quite well? '*Something to do with work*,' Simone had told Monique, after Lucalle had left. But what 'work', and for whom, wondered Jacquot? What had they been talking about, and just how long had they known each other? Was it something to do with Beirut, where Lucalle had worked for the security services, and where Simone had gone on business?

Or was it something else?

Maybe Burak wasn't the only DupayCorp investor who had lost out in the S-CE massacre? Maybe there were other clients who'd taken a beating, too, and decided that Simone was to blame? It was even possible, Jacquot was forced to concede, that Lucalle might not have murdered Simone, that she had turned up by chance at Simone's apartment and found her dead, just as he had.

Which would mean that someone else had killed Simone.

But who, and why?

Could it have something to do with Dupay, he wondered? It was worth considering, given that Lucalle had been wearing Madame Dupay's watch. She might swear that she had bought it from a market trader in Avignon, and Mendy would almost certainly make it stand up in court, but it was way too much of a stretch for Jacquot. If Lucalle had the watch, then he was certain she'd have had the rest of the Dupay jewellery, that she'd been the one who'd removed the stones from their settings and taken them to Cahn for a valuation. And if she'd had the Dupay jewels, then she'd have had the briefcase too, and the ransom money it contained, liberated by her brother at La Résidence des Cyprès.

But who had they liberated it for?

Dupay, or Burak?

Who had Lucalle and Duhamil been working for?

Burak, or Dupay?

It was time to make some calls.

90

Dupay was at home that Saturday afternoon, and opened the front door himself.

"Yes, what is it?" was all he said, making no attempt to invite Jacquot in, as though they could deal with whatever it was the *Judiciaire* wanted on the doorstep. He was wearing a pair of cream chinos, a red cashmere sweater, and tasselled loafers. He wore no shirt under the sweater, and no socks. He looked tanned and healthy, with a blank, expressionless gaze that held no warmth or welcome.

"I wonder if I could have a word?" asked Jacquot.

"About?"

"About your wife's murder, your stepson's murder, and the murder of Simone Laronde."

Now Dupay's expression did change. Complete surprise. A stunned look settling across his features.

"Simone? Simone was murdered?"

"So either we can talk here, monsieur, or maybe you would like to accompany me to police headquarters," said Jacquot, an icy edge to his voice. No more messing, was the message.

"I don't have long," said Dupay, turning back into the house, leaving Jacquot to close the door and follow him.

"You'll have as long as it takes, monsieur. Be under no illusions," said Jacquot.

Dupay spun round, fire in his cold blue eyes, as though he'd been waiting for this insubordination and would deal with it accordingly. "Is that a threat?"

"No, monsieur, a warning. A very serious warning."

When they reached the salon, Dupay settled himself on a sofa and crossed his legs; impatient, put out, not bothering to invite Jacquot to do the same.

"The last time we spoke you told me that Simone had committed suicide. And now it's murder? How? By whom?"

"We have a suspect in custody," said Jacquot, taking an armchair and making himself comfortable.

Dupay gave a disbelieving grunt. "You appear to be speeding up your investigations."

Jacquot ignored the jibe, reaching into his pocket and pulling out the two photographs he'd shown to Monique at La Temoin. He laid them on the coffee table and turned them for Dupay. The man leaned forward and looked at them. Shook his head.

"Do the names Edmond Duhamil or Marie Lucalle mean anything to you?"

"Nothing. Are those their photos?"

"Or Osman Muhtar? Fighen Muhtar?"

Dupay shook his head again.

Jacquot scooped up the photos and slipped them back in his pocket.

"I believe Simone's death, her murder, has something to do with her dealings – and your company's dealings – with Burak Imports."

"Not that again," sighed Dupay, a mix of irritation and impatience creasing his brow. "I employ more than forty traders at DupayCorp. If a disgruntled investor murdered every advisor for a poor performance, I'd have no-one left on the trading floor."

"Then maybe you could explain how one of your best analysts got it so wrong six years ago. Millions of francs lost in a single deal."

"The market dictates, it's as simple as that."

"So why did Simone take such a high-risk gamble?"

Dupay shrugged. "It was her call. She must have thought there would be a good return."

"Did no one at DupayCorp question her recommendations, given that she had only just started work for you?"

"The trade advice would have been scrutinised by a manager, of course, but since they went ahead there was clearly no sense that the recommendations were unrealistic. There was nothing suspicious..."

Jacquot nodded. And then, "Is it usual for an analyst like Simone to travel as much as she did?"

Dupay frowned, seemed not to understand the question.

"Antwerp, Frankfurt, Beirut on a number of occasions," Jacquot continued. "Business trips connected with her work."

"I had no idea that she travelled. And certainly not for DupayCorp. There was no need."

"So your analysts, your traders, never visit clients? They are never invited to see their clients' activities – factories, workplaces – for them to better understand their clients' requirements?"

"Why would they? It's enough for them to see a balance sheet, to know that the client is sound, and make the relevant judgement."

"And what about the companies – the stocks and the shares – that they recommend to their clients?"

"The same applies, of course. There is no need. I mean, when you go to Borély on race day do you only bet on those horses whose owners you know, whose studs you've visited? No, you check the form. In the papers.

How did your horse do the last time out. Our traders have everything they could want from reputable market sources. Past performance, future plans, current price. Will the shares go up, will they go down? IPOs and the like. Possible takeovers, or new management, that might affect the price. And political questions, too, of course. Elections, manifestos, judicial changes… You don't just lick the tip of your finger and hold it up, see which way the wind is blowing. Although, of course," he allowed himself a chuckle, "that can be useful, too."

"So let's move on, monsieur. Why did you decide to move Simone back to Aix?"

Dupay sighed. "You have asked me this before, and I told you then. She was the perfect fit for the job."

"No other reason?"

"None."

Jacquot nodded. He could tell that, for all the blameless, blasé show, Dupay was uncomfortable, a little unsettled. Something wasn't right, and Jacquot knew he was getting closer.

"I understand from those who knew her well that Simone Laronde was gay. Might that have had something to do with your decision to move her from Marseilles?"

"You didn't know that yourself?" replied Dupay, with what looked close to a sneer.

"What I asked, monsieur, was if her sexual preferences might have influenced your decision?"

"A good analyst is a good analyst. I don't need to know if they have a balanced diet, or go to church. And I wouldn't dream of asking."

"If it is clear that someone applying for a job with DupayCorp is gay, would that affect the offer of a position?"

"Of course not. This is the twentieth century, Chief Inspector. We have moved on."

"So you have no problems with homosexuality?"

"I have friends in both camps, so to speak. So, it is not important. And I would never make judgements based on sexual preference. Certainly not a good judgement."

Jacquot gave Dupay a long, amused smile, knowing what he did about Dupay. But Dupay held his eye, didn't flinch. But for Jacquot it was enough. He knew, under that urbane, cosmopolitan mask, the discomfort would be growing.

"So, let us move on to the murder of your stepson, Lucien?"

Dupay nodded, took a breath, as though the change of subject was a comfort to him. He had headed off an assault, and Jacquot could see that it had given him confidence.

"Tell me," asked Jacquot. "The money you raised for the first ransom payment came from where?"

"My own personal account. Or rather, a deposit account I keep for emergencies. In my business it is a wise precaution to have such a safety net."

"And that withdrawal would show, in your bank records?"

Dupay nodded.

"Did you use all of that emergency money to pay the ransom?"

"A sizeable proportion."

"Leaving enough to pay the second ransom demand? The same amount again, plus the surcharges, of course."

Dupay tipped his head from side to side – neither a yes, nor a no.

"And that second withdrawal, whatever it was, would also show? In your bank records?"

Dupay's face hardened. "I fail to see where this is going, Chief Inspector? Why there should be any question about how, and from where, I raise money. It is what I do, after all. And in that regard, you may also be aware that I have just sold my yacht, for much more than both ransom demands put together. And given the proceeds to charity."

He glanced at his watch, as though he now realised that his time was being wasted, for no good or obvious reason. He was Alain Dupay, after all. He had places to be, people to see. It was time to flex some muscle. He had accommodated this hapless policeman long enough. Jacquot saw it all in that single glance at his watch.

"Tell me, monsieur, you said that you were instructed by the kidnapper to leave this second payment in another bin on rue Honnorat?"

"That's correct."

"And how did you carry the money? Another briefcase?"

"No. In a bin liner."

"A bin liner? Extraordinary. To fill a bin liner with ten million francs and just leave it in a pile of other bin liners. When every bin in the city was pretty much hidden under a load of uncollected rubbish."

"I assumed I was being watched. That they would see where the bag went, and pick it up after I left." His delivery was smooth, easy. It could have been true.

"So, there was a pile of rubbish there?"

"You're quite right. Huge. You could hardly see the bin."

"And you think you were being watched?"

Dupay shrugged. "I didn't see anyone. The street was deserted. An *impasse*, as you probably know. So, yes, I assumed someone was watching me. I mean, it wouldn't do to leave that sum of money lying around in a bin liner for any length of time. In case the strike suddenly ended, and everything was picked up, or for the bag to be covered by other bags and lost."

Jacquot nodded.

"Tell me, how did you get on with your stepson?"

"Extremely well. He was the sweetest little boy. There was nothing I wouldn't have done for him."

"You spent time with him? Played with him?"

"When my work allowed it, of course. Regrettably, late nights at the office often meant I missed him when I came home. He would be in bed, asleep. So our time together was usually limited to weekends. But every summer he would come to my yacht with others with his affliction... condition, I mean. With their parents, and they would have a cruise along the coast. He always loved those cruises. Such fun for all of them."

"And you would go with him?"

"Not always, no. As I said, when my work allowed..."

"So, just now and again?"

Dupay nodded.

"I understand that your nanny, Mademoiselle Oberstock, is no longer at Malmousque? That she is no longer employed by you?"

The face hardened again. "That is correct. After the funeral, there seemed little point in her remaining here. And, frankly, I found her presence painful. Memories."

It was plain to Jacquot that Dupay now suspected that he had been talking to the nanny without his knowing. To cover for her, he asked. "I wonder, do you know where she might be?"

"She said she was going back to Switzerland. To her family."

"Would you have an address for her?"

"Of course… somewhere." He cast around, as though he couldn't be sure where he might find such a thing, without a further waste of his time. "Why don't I have my assistant call you on Monday with the details?"

"That would be most helpful, monsieur."

"But right now," he continued, looking again at his watch, pushing back the cuff of his sweater to make a point of it, "you really will have to excuse me." He put his hands on his knees and pushed himself out of the sofa. "I'm sure you'll agree that I have answered your questions to the best of my ability, that I have given you as much as I can, but I'm afraid I must now bring this meeting to an end."

Jacquot nodded, rose from his seat. "Just one more question, monsieur."

Dupay sighed. "What now?"

"I just wondered how a gay man might feel when he knowingly condemns a ten-year old Down syndrome child, his own stepson, to death?"

91

It had been a deliberate move on Jacquot's part to rattle Dupay, to see how he would respond, and it had paid off in spades. But for all the anticipated threats and colourful cursing that had followed him out of the house and off the Dupay compound in Malmousque, Jacquot was certain of one thing. If he was wrong, and Dupay had paid that second ransom, a complaint in the strongest possible terms would be lodged by Dupay with the Procurator General, with *Maître* Bonnefoy, and with anyone else with enough *piston* to see Jacquot on the carpet and off the force.

With the gay reference, of course, not mentioned.

But if Jacquot was right, and he had not paid that ransom, then there would be not a word. Dupay would have to prove that he paid it and Jacquot was certain he couldn't, and hadn't. He would find out one way or the other on Monday morning – or even sooner – but until that time… well, there was work to be done.

Back at police headquarters Jacquot crossed the reception area to the lifts and pressed for the third floor. The lift arrived, from the basement, and the doors slid open. Rully, in an unbuttoned white shirt over a round neck blue t-shirt, broke into a smile when he saw Jacquot, a smile framed in dark stubble, his eyes tired, his hair awry. He looked like a student being woken too early after a late-night session.

"I was just coming up to see you," he said, as Jacquot stepped into the lift, reaching forward to press for Three. "But now that you're here, maybe we should head back down." Leaning past Jacquot he pressed for the basement. The doors closed with a shudder and, with a single jerk from the cabling overhead, they slid downwards.

Under Sergeant Lefèbre's tenancy, the basement Records Office had always been scrupulously clean and ordered, but this evening it was a picture of disarray. The linoleum tile floor was piled with straggling islands of print-outs, spread in a rough semi-circle around Lefèbre's desk and arranged into three different groups. Each group had a name, written on a sheet of paper in black marker: Burak, Dupay, Laronde. Burak's pile was the biggest, six or seven seperate islands in its particular archipelago. Dupay's was next with just four islands, and Simone's with three. Beyond these piles three blackboards had been set up on easels, their surfaces scrawled with chalk scribblings, many of the notations circled or underlined or ending in multiple exclamation or question marks, with various arrowheads between them indicating some kind of link or progression. All the major players were

315

featured – Dupay, Burak, Laronde, Duhamil, and Lucalle – but quite a few of the names were unfamiliar to Jacquot: Medea, Beqaa, Tage, Seljuk, Elias.

Rully noticed Jacquot's puzzled expression as he looked around the room, trying to make sense of it all.

"I know it looks complicated..."

"Looks complicated! It is complicated," said Lefèbre, hauling himself off a camp bed in one of the unlit passages behind his desk. "I thought if I sent him up to you, I might be able to get a little shut-eye," the old sergeant continued, hoisting his braces back on. "It appears I was wrong."

"He looks like he's been keeping you busy," said Jacquot, noting the two chairs drawn up at the desk in front of the computer screen, the desk's surface cluttered with ashtrays, coffee mugs, and sandwich wrappers. Wires snaked across the floor from desk lamps, the computer, and printer.

"A whole new world," said Lefèbre. "But sometimes it's hard to keep up with him. He moves too fast."

"But you've got something?"

"More than something. You won't believe it," said Rully.

"Right now, I'd be happy to believe anything."

"Except there's nothing on Dupay. Just a hefty insurance pay-out on his wife and, with her stepson out of the frame, the bulk of her estate."

Jacquot sighed. Not what he wanted to hear. He would have liked a great deal more.

"So where would you like me to start?"

"With something interesting."

"Oh, we've got a lot of that," said Rully, and taking a stick of chalk from the desk he went to the blackboards. "Why don't we start with passports. Duhamil's, Lucalle's, and Laronde's. As you suggested, they were certainly worth a look. Same destinations, around the same time. And it wasn't difficult to track where they stayed. Would you believe the same hotels?"

"I'm listening," said Jacquot, feeling his blood start to warm.

An hour later, he stubbed out a cigarette and stretched his arms above his head.

"*Im-pecc-able,*" he said, and looked at his two companions. Smiled. "So, let's go through it one more time."

92

With Duhamil's bail hearing set for 2.30 that Monday afternoon, Jacquot finished a final briefing with his squad over an Al-Andalus take-out breakfast of strong coffees, croissants, and rings of sugared *churros*. He had already spoken to *Maître* Bonnefoy and obtained the necessary permits and warrants, without her mentioning any serious complaints being levelled against him by Alain Dupay, and he had ended the call with an assurance that he would have everything she needed by lunchtime at the latest.

"You're cutting it fine, Daniel," she'd told him.

"Whatever it takes," he'd replied.

They took three unmarked cars for the drive to rue d'Académie and Châteauredon, followed by an SOC van and two squad cars, while a second contingent of uniformed officers with Peluze and Grenier in charge had already been dispatched to Joliette's Quai du Lazaret. The journey across town was a slow one, the usual stop-start crawl through rush-hour Monday morning traffic, but Jacquot remained silent, going through the game-play he'd put together as they drew closer to their destination. What he knew, and what he didn't know. And how to work whatever happened to his advantage, joining the dots that Rully and Lefèbre had provided.

The turn of the cards.

It was time.

Jacquot and Rully in the lead car reached rue d'Academie first and Jacquot turned back in his seat to watch Bernie Muzon and the stutterer Chevin make the left, followed by Charlie Serre and Luc Dutoit, with the SOC van behind them and one of the squad cars. Fifty metres further on Rully did the same, followed by the second squad car, swinging up Châteauredon and stopping outside Burak's office and residential entrance. The shadowy lane was now effectively blocked, with maybe enough room for a scooter or cyclist to squeeze past, and the uniformed officers in the second squad car taking up positions at both ends of the cut-through.

As he had done just a few days earlier, Jacquot pressed the doorbell and they waited for Javad Dalan to answer. There was no response. Jacquot pressed the bell again and tried the handle. The door opened and, without any invitation, they crossed the courtyard and knocked at the screen door. For a moment it seemed there was no one in the house to answer, but then, without warning, the door swung open and there was Dalan.

"Chief Inspector, I'm so sorry. I do not hear the bell." He stood in the doorway, but made no attempt to invite them in. "We have busy, busy day today, and I am in the yard. New supplies coming in, space to be made, deliveries to be arranged."

"I'd like a word with Monsieur Burak," said Jacquot, gently, with a smile.

"Today will be difficult, Chief Inspector…"

"We really need his help on a matter of some considerable urgency. Just a few minutes of his time?"

"If you will wait here, I see what I can do." And with that Dalan scurried back down the passageway and they watched him hurry up the stairs. A minute or two later, he returned. "Please, to follow me. Monsieur Burak will be happy to see you but, as you say, for just a few moments, isn't it?"

With Dalan leading the way Jacquot and Rully walked down the passageway to the stairs. Beyond, came the sound of fork-lift trucks manoeuvring and the muted shouts of workers. As they turned to climb the stairs, Jacquot caught a glimpse of a busy working yard. The gates on rue d'Académie were closed and he was pleased to see that his team were out of sight, probably parked somewhere close by and waiting for his signal. All was going to plan.

With a tap at Burak's door, Dalan ushered them in, announced them, and then departed, closing the door behind him with a soft click.

The room still smelled of sandalwood, and the sparrows on the balcony beyond the open widows chirruped as busily as before. But it was Burak who drew their attention, standing behind his desk, leaning forward on pudgy pointed fingers, the divan where he had sat on their last visit now covered in box files and papers. Gone, too, was the *jubba* gown he had worn, its scooped lap filled with cast-off pistachio shells. This morning he was dressed in a tightly-buttoned black double-breasted suit with bold white pinstripes, its wide reveres pointed and drooping. He looked like a vast sailing ship with a wind stretching its canvas sheets. To complete this extravagant display, a scarlet tasselled fez the size of an upturned flower pot sat on the edge of the desk. It would be, thought Jacquot, a remarkable sight to see that fez on Burak's stubbled, scarred head.

"Chief Inspector," said Burak, nodding at Rully, whose name and rank he could not possibly be expected to remember, so a nod would do, "as you can see, you catch me on the busiest day of the month. So much to do, so little time, but, for the *Judiciaire*...? What can I say? Please, do be seated. Some coffee, perhaps? Pastries, dates?"

Jacquot shook his head. "As you say, monsieur, time is short and I do not want to hold you up any longer than is necessary." The words came easily, and Jacquot felt a strange calm settle over him. He reached for his pocket and pulled out two photographs, spread them on the Turk's desk. "I'd be grateful if you could look at these photos and tell me if you recognise either of the people in them?"

Burak picked up the photos of Duhamil and Lucalle, one in each hand, and peered down his nose at them as though to bring them better into focus, eyesight not his strongest suit. It would, Jacquot knew, be a difficult moment for the Turk. A hard choice to make: yes, he did know them; or no, he didn't. Jacquot wondered which way it would go.

After what seemed like an age, Burak began to shake his head.

"Their names are Edmond Duhamil, and Marie Lucalle," said Jacquot, so there could be no come-back, no denial, the old Turk's eyesight not what it should be.

"No, no. Neither face, nor name."

"Or what about Osman Muhtar? Or Fighen Muhtar?"

Again Burak shook his head, though Jacquot sensed a tightness grip the movement, a more thoughtful shake this time. Either the old Turk knew that they were currently in custody, but wanted to keep any criminal activity they may have been involved in at arm's length, or Duhamil and his sister had stayed silent, betting that their lawyer would secure their release without Burak finding out what had happened. Of course, there had always been the possibility that he would confirm that, yes, he did recognize their names and photos. But he hadn't. He'd chosen the bluff. Because he could not know what Jacquot knew, what Rully and Lefèbre had uncovered. Which was how the team had called it in their early morning briefing at police headquarters. A punt. Just to see how the man reacted.

And it couldn't have gone better.

Reaching for the photos and sliding them back into his pocket, Jacquot nodded.

"Such a strange coincidence, don't you think?" he said, at last.

"Coincidence?"

"That your own sister should have the same surname. Muhtar. Married to the late Elias Muhtar, a trader in Beirut whose shipping company, Fleet Seljuk, you took over just four years ago."

Now Burak really did stiffen. He'd made the wrong call, and now he knew it. His bluff had been called.

"You will also know that Elias and your sister had two children. Osman and Fighen, would you believe? Names you would certainly know, their photos, too, since they're your nephew and niece. Yet, here we are, and you tell me that you know neither of them. And both living so close to you as well, just outside Aix in fact, in a house owned by another of your companies, Koza Han Holdings. And both of them co-directors of an import-export company in Beirut in which you also have a considerable stake."

Burak said nothing, just raised a hand and ran it over his head.

"And both, of course, currently in police custody for a range of serious offences, including murder."

Without waiting for any response, Jacquot turned to Rully. "You can give them the go-ahead," he said, and Rully pulled a walkie-talkie from his pocket. As he issued instructions to the teams waiting outside the gates on rue d'Académie, Jacquot slipped the various permits for a search of the property and an arrest warrant for Burak from his pocket and laid them on the desk. "I think you will find these in order, Monsieur Burak, as will your skipper on Fleet Seljuk's MS *Medea* at Quai du Lazaret. Regrettably, your colleague Sergeant Ahmed Tage of the Marseilles Customs Office will not be on hand to assist in the clearance of any goods being brought ashore. So," said Jacquot, "if you would be so kind as to accompany us to police headquarters, monsieur? There are certain questions that will need to be addressed."

93

When five kilos of heroin were discovered in the first three pallet-loads craned from the hold of MS *Medea*, along with more than fifty kilos of hashish in the next four loads, the first hidden in sealed bags of Iranian pistachios, the latter in plastic tubs of sumak, the entire load registered to Beqaa Trade of which Duhamil and his sister were directors, *Maître* Bonnefoy had all she needed to have their bail applications summarily overturned. Duhamil and his sister would remain in custody, much to the tight-lipped irritation of *Maître* Mendy.

But dealing with Nakim Burak in an interview room at police headquarters was not quite so straightforward. Sitting sideways on to the table, hands loosely clasped over a bulging stomach, legs stretched out, ankles crossed, Burak refused to acknowledge either his new surroundings or the questions that Jacquot asked.

About the kidnapping, ransom demands, and subsequent death, either deliberate or accidental, of Lucien Dupay.

About his involvement in the murders of Boultier and Hakimi.

About his dealings with Duhamil and Lucalle.

About Alain Dupay.

About Simone Laronde.

And, when the news arrived of Grenier and Peluze's discovery at the Lazaret docks, questions about his drug-smuggling activities, and distribution network.

But Burak showed no emotion. Throughout that first session, like Duhamil before him, Burak simply stared at the tips of his shoes, turning them now and again in the light as though to check the shine, or inspected his fingernails, or gazed blankly at the mirrored observation panel.

Even when the SOC team reported later that day that they had found a blue trainer wedged under Burak's office divan where he'd sprawled with his pistachio box when Jacquot first came calling, a trainer subsequently identified by Alain Dupay as one of a pair belonging to his stepson, Burak still said nothing.

In the end it was his assistant Javad Dalan, in the interrogation room next door to his boss, who started to sing.

"What can you give me?" he asked Jacquot.

"Give you? What for?"

"I tie up loose ends for you."

"There are no loose ends."

Dalan gave him a look, a trader at a market stall sizing up a customer. "Oh, Monsieur Chief Inspector, there is lot you don't know. Can't know. Things that could prove utmost importance in this investigation. Things that could see this evil man, Burak, put away for long, long time."

Jacquot did not reply, just returned Dalan's look, cool and level. As though to make it clear that so tight was the *Judiciaire*'s case that it was highly unlikely he would be surprised by anything Dalan had to say.

But he was wrong.

Dalan did surprise him.

"Do you know how Burak find out about Boultier? How he the one who take the money?"

Jacquot said nothing.

"A mechanic at Faranese, the Alfa dealership on Plombières. He recognise Boultier, see him buy some sporty car for cash. So he pass it on, and by the end of the day we know about it."

"And Osman Muhtar was sent to get it back. We know that."

"Ah, pretty boy Osman. Another nasty piece of working. It run in the family. He Burak's main enforcer. You don't mess with him."

"The man who took off those book-keeper's fingers in Aix," said Jacquot. It was a guess, but a good one.

Dalan look startled. "You know about book-keeper?"

"As I said, there's not a lot we don't know."

"Did you know he kill Hakimi, too? Shoot him dead. After finding out where Boultier was."

Jacquot said nothing.

"So you have gun, yes?"

"We don't need a gun. We have enough," Jacquot replied, knowing that the gun would be a clincher.

Dalan beamed. "But good to have, all the same? Another piece of jigsaw."

"It might be helpful, nothing more."

"So, you search Osman house in Aix and not find it?"

"As I said..."

"He keep it clever. You never find. Behind fusebox under stairs, a space built into wall. I give you that for free."

"I'll have someone take a look," said Jacquot, downplaying the information. "But how would you know something like that?"

324

"Like I say, I know lot of things." He tapped the side of his nose, and smiled. "For example, there is his sister, the evil running in the blood. Did you know she the one done that Dupay girl."

"Simone Laronde."

"That her. Young and pretty."

"Which we know about. We already have Marie Lucalle, or Fighen Muhtar, in custody for the murder. She's made a full confession."

Dalan looked at Jacquot for a moment, then chuckled. "Told you, man. You don't know everything."

Jacquot did not respond.

"If you know everything," Dalan continued, "you wouldn't tell me lie. But you just did, and such a terrible big one. Because I telling you this for absolute certainty, that Fighen and her brother would never say a word. Full confession? You joking me."

"Confession or not, she'll still go down. We have witnesses that put her in the frame. The same with her brother."

"But you still don't know why she do it, do you?" Dalan gave Jacquot a sly look. "Don't you want to know? You knowing Mademoiselle Laronde the way you did."

Jacquot felt a shiver down his spine, but didn't let the chill show. How could this man possibly know about him and Simone?

"Young, pretty, like I say, with real gunslinger brain," said Dalan. "She was good. Know everything. No one like her when it come to names and numbers."

The phrase jolted Jacquot. He could hear her saying the same thing, sitting with him at Bar de la Marine.

"That how she sell herself to Burak, you know? Look what I can do for you. No one like me. And that why the boss like her. Back when she lost him the money he wanted pay-back, and she was top of list. But soon as we get her in and he start talking to her, when he see the kind of woman she is, hear her proposition, well, he give her the second chance. How good for Burak to have a DupayCorp insider, and get his revenge. And she pay him back big time, play good game for them both. But then she get greedy."

"How? Greedy?"

Dalan chuckled, slapped his hands together. "See. Again, you not know everything. But I do. And that's what I offering. The inside story. But what I get in return?"

"Nothing. Because I don't need you, or what you know. We have everything we need against Burak, Osman, and Fighen to put them away for a very long time."

"It good bluff, Chief Inspector. But I know there things you want to know. You yourself. Those loose ends."

"I'll talk to the State Prosecutor…"

"No, no. That far down the road, when I don't have no way out. And don't think to get me testify. It not happen, I'm telling you. I need the paper now. I need the pass. I need that… understanding."

Jacquot knew he had nothing to lose. Dalan had been brought in for questioning as part of the Burak raid, but there was no real evidence that he could be charged with anything substantial. As Burak's personal assistant he had probably been involved in much of his boss's illegal activities, but it was unlikely that Dalan was in any real sense a principal, or had done anything seriously illegal. And there was no reason why he would ever need to testify against his boss because, thanks to Rully and Lefèbre, they already had all they needed. Unless something came up that particulalrly incriminated Dalan, it was unlikely that he would serve any time, no more than a couple of years behind bars for some kind of complicity that had yet to be determined. But it was a possible term of imprisonment that Dalan was clearly not prepared to serve. And Jacquot knew that Dalan could tell him a great deal, fill in the gaps. The insider's story.

About Simone Laronde, for starters.

A word with *Maître* Bonnefoy and Dalan would walk. It could easily be arranged.

"Tell me everything, and you disappear. No charges, no follow up."

"No good enough. I want paper."

It took a call to *Maître* Bonnefoy, and some persuasive arguments, to secure her agreement, but the relevant *laissez-passer* document was delivered within the hour.

When Dalan was brought up from the cells and taken to the interview room, Jacquot pushed the document across the table. Dalan opened it, read it, and was about to slide it into his pocket when Jacquot reached forward and snatched it from him.

"Only when you give me what I want."

"So where you like me start?"

94

"Burak buy car for her. He buy apartment for her. She do so good for him. Pay back big time, like I said. First she start milking DupayCorp accounts, small to start, and then begin moving client funds into new arrangement with some of Burak's companies. One after another she bring them in, but slowly, slowly so no one notice. And cleaning money, too. All Burak cash. Knowing how to do it, so no one see. And always on the bullseye target she is, and taking big cut."

It was then that Jacquot remembered something else that Simone had said to him. *'There's always someone trading somewhere. Always a deal to do.'* And Dupay must have found out about it, Jacquot realised, and sidelined her, posted her back to Aix, away from the action. No wonder she was so angry.

"But it the funny boy, Lucien, when everything go wrong," continued Dalan. "Somehow this young woman, Simone, she find out about it. Don't ask me how, I don't know. But next thing she tell Burak she spill bean if he don't make it worth her while. And spill bean to this *flic* she know… You."

"You heard her say that?"

"I did."

"You were in the room?"

Dalan shifted his shoulders, smiled coyly. "Sometime office door don't shut so good."

"So what did Burak say?"

"He tell her it accident. He meant to return boy, but when first ransom not get paid, he hold on to him."

"So you knew about it? Knew the boy was there?"

"Between you and me…" Dalan replied, the coy smile turning crooked. "But to start he in Aix, after Osman snatch him at Prado. All set up with carousel man. So easy."

"The carousel operator refused to identify him."

"And you surprised? Everyone know Osman, everyone watch their manners. He don't dare say nothing. But now Osman inside, maybe the bird change his pretty tune."

"And after being in Aix, Osman brought the boy to Marseilles?"

"That right. And if second payment come through, Burak maybe say there not any problem, the boy given back." Dalan shrugged. "Course, you and me both know he never go home. Aix, maybe. But here, Marseilles, he see, hear too much."

"But by then Burak had got the initial ransom back."

Dalan chuckled. "But Dupay don't know that, did he? And Burak not one to tell him."

"So when the second payment failed to arrive…"

"Like I say, first payment, second payment, make no never-mind to Burak. The boy not going anywhere. But what happen was accident. Burak give the boy ice cream. It was…" Dalan paused, and for the first time he looked uncomfortable.

"It was… what?" prodded Jacquot.

"It is not good thing, I know, but Monsieur Burak have certain tastes, certain appetites," he began again. "And I not talking just about food, you understand. The pistachio, the baklava, and all that kind of thing. For instance, he like to sit his little boys on his lap, and play with them, and give them ice cream, spoon it into their mouth. Feed them. Like, a treat. For being… good."

"And Lucien had an allergic reaction."

"Yes, yes. Oh, so bad. I am in my office, getting ready for home, when Burak call down. 'Hurry, come quick,' he say. So I go there, to the office, and the little boy is on the floor… Choking, so bad. And shaking, going blue. His tongue, so swollen. You won't believe."

"But why did Burak do it? Why kidnap Dupay's stepson in the first place?"

Dalan beamed. "There, you see. You don't know everything."

"Losing that money in Aix?"

"That what he tell you. I'm listening when he say it. But I know it not the truth. Just a cover."

"And the real story?"

"Ah, such a sad love story. A young man called Samir. He work with shipping agent in Beirut and Burak meet him, invite him to Marseilles. So he come, spend year with Burak. Like special son to him, he is. Very loving, very tight. But then one night, Samir go to Opera and meet Monsieur Dupay. And in no time, Samir in Dupay's bed... not Burak's. And if that not bad enough, Samir die in car crash, going to pick up Dupay from airport. For Burak, it is enough. Too much. Dupay must pay."

Jacquot worked it through. It all made absolute sense, but something they had never seen. Something that Rully and Lefèbre had failed to find, could never have found.

"Tell me," asked Jacquot. "Was it you who kept Lucien's trainer and put it under Burak's divan?"

Dalan smiled, a warm, complicit smile. "You got fingerprints? I don't think."

And he winked.

95

Javad Dalan was released without charge two days later, at about the same time that Nakim Burak was transferred from his holding cell at police headquarters to more appropriate accommodation at Baumettes Prison. Standing in his office, watching the seagulls wheel silently around the cathedral domes of St-Majeure, Jacquot wondered whether the two men might see each other on rue de l'Évêché – Dalan standing on the pavement looking out for a cab when the *Administration Pénitentiaire* prison van drove past carrying Burak off to his new address. He was trying to think what kind of look they might exchange – Burak bitter and frightened, Dalan triumphant and free, maybe lifting a middle finger to his old boss – when his phone rang. The voice on the other end of the line was immediately recognisable, a slow, amused drawl.

"So, book matches really do work?"

"And the gun. And the trainer," said Jacquot, pulling out his chair and settling himself.

"But still…"

"I was fortunate, *Maître*."

"I like fortunate. And your first case as Chief Inspector. A good start. Long may it continue."

"I had help, too."

"Your predecessor wouldn't have said that. And it didn't take help to come up with book matches. Among other things, it took a certain kind of… instinct. And nerve. I like that."

Jacquot smiled, said nothing.

"So, I assume you will be celebrating?"

"I have a date. Long overdue."

"I trust you'll enjoy it. You deserve to."

"I will try my hardest."

"I have no doubt that you will."

Later that day, with a warm spring breeze filling their sails, Jacquot and Salette headed east with the chalky cliffs of the Calanques on their port side and the ocean glittering to starboard. Jacquot had the wheel and felt the wind on his shoulder, felt the yacht dip and surge forward, the wheel tug at his hands. But he held his course; any luffing, even the slightest ripple in the canvas, and Salette would laugh and scoff, or read the riot act.

They anchored in a small cove past Cassis, and the first of the wine was opened, a warm baguette from Boulangerie Desaintes torn up and passed between them, with a wedge of goat cheese cut into chunks and drizzled with honey.

"For a *flic* who wins his first case, you seem a little down," said Salette, tipping back his glass and reaching for the bottle.

"I couldn't get the man I wanted."

"Dupay?"

Jacquot nodded. "He's as bad, maybe worse than Burak. But he walks away. There's nothing we can pin on him."

"So what did he do?"

Jacquot explained about the second ransom; how, with his wife dead, Dupay had refused to pay another ransom for his stepson's release. As Dalan had said, the boy would have died anyway, but Dupay wouldn't have known that. Or cared.

"Why am I not surprised?" said Salette. "Once a *con*, always a *con*. But his time will come, my friend. One day the dice will roll and the numbers will go against him. Maybe tomorrow, maybe next year. But that day, believe your old friend, will surely come, and justice will be done."

Marseilles
Three months later

96

It was the best car. Brand new. Among the first of its kind. Ten days off the assembly line and brought out from the United Kingdom in the company's own liveried transporter. Delivered that morning, rolled down the ramp, and parked now at the bottom of the front steps. A two-door Aston Martin Volante, its soft top neatly stowed, black bodywork smooth and muscled, its windscreen a steel-framed mirror of blue sky and rippled cloud.

Alain Dupay allowed himself a soft hiss of pure, unadulterated pleasure. Standing on the top step of his Malmousque home, he just stared at it, gloried in it. Waiting for him. Ready for his touch. He could almost smell the oil and leather.

And the Mercedes? The Jaguar? The family SUV? No place for them in the new order. Just this one superb model, its growling, five-litre V8 engine block concealed beneath a curved, voluptuous hood, its plush interior a soft ribbed hide and polished walnut burr. And he was going to be the one behind the wheel. His to control.

This was the new Alain Dupay.

He went down the steps, walked towards it, gravel crunching underfoot. Fingertips to the handle to open the driver's door, closing it with a soft clunk as he settled behind the wheel, pulling on his seat belt, reaching out his toes to rest on the pedals, hand cupping the gear lever.

Holding his breath, he turned on the ignition and felt the engine roar into life. Eased his foot off the accelerator for a low, chortling purr. Then touched it again – another rising bellow, the rev-counter needle oscillating like a manic wand.

There was no need to turn the brute. The car had been left facing the driveway and distant gates; ready to prowl, to eat up the road. So he slid the gear stick into first, released the handbrake and, easing off on the clutch like a learner-driver frightened of a stall, he let the transmission engage.

Oh, oh, oh, this was something, he thought, as the car moved forward as instructed. Solid. Sure-footed. A true thoroughbred. Trees and lawn sliding past either side of him, just the softest growl of impatient intent from beneath the hood. I'll do what you want, he could hear the engine telling him, but when we're out on the road I want you to loosen the reins, give me my head. Thrash me. Which he knew he would do. Couldn't wait. Down to the Corniche carriageway for a first blast out to Prado, and then back to the city.

He reached for the remote on the passenger seat and bleeped the gates open before he could see them, the wooden panels neatly housed by the time he reached the final curve of the drive. Allowing for the dip between kerb and road he slowed to avoid any contact between the low-riding spoiler and tarmac, and as the threat passed he sensed, then saw, someone standing by the wall, and now stepping forward.

A woman. Immediately familiar. But something more. Something unsettling. Some planned intent on her part as she came towards him, flicking a lighter in her gloved hand, and setting it to the wadded cloth 'cork' of a bottle.

It made no sense, and Dupay wondered for a second whether he was imagining it. The cool determination of this unexpected presence. Stepping forward, and now raising the bottle to throw at him.

Jesus, she was attacking him.

He was in danger. Real danger.

On such a bright and wonderful morning.

And in his new, gleaming car.

It couldn't be. It wasn't right.

He flung up his arm as the bottle left her hand, and wrist and glass connected, enough to deflect the bottle's trajectory, snuffing out the flaming cloth, and sending it tumbling over his shoulder. He heard it clunk down somewhere behind him, and he hoped it wouldn't do any damage, stain the Aston's cream hide upholstery or thick-pile carpeting.

But there was no time to check. He could see her reach into her bag and bring out another bottle, flick the lighter again, put flame to the cloth and, once lit, just lean forward to drop it between his legs.

Shit, he thought, smelling petrol.

She was trying to kill him.

Shit, shit, shit…

97

Trudi Oberstock had not expected to see Dupay in a convertible. She'd imagined him driving the Jaguar or Mercedes, with the driver's window down and his arm on the sill. Which was why she had brought two bottles, in case there had been a problem getting the first one through the open window.

But the convertible made everything a great deal easier, even if the first bottle had been knocked away by Dupay, its flame extinguished, the bottle landing behind the passenger seat where the petrol pulsed unlit and unseen into the richly-carpeted footwell.

Her second bottle, its 'cork' aflame, found a more secure destination, dropping between Dupay's knees and the steering wheel, and rolling between the clutch and brake pedals.

As she stepped back and away from the car, she could see Dupay trying desperately to find it, retrieve it, and throw it out; then giving up, deciding to get out of the car as swiftly as possible, but held back by his seat belt, struggling now to unbuckle it.

She was twenty steps away when the petrol pouring from the first bottle in the rear footwell finally came close enough to the still burning fuse from the second bottle to have its fumes combust with a mighty whoosh. Even at that distance from the car she could feel the gust of hot air flatten the back of her blouse and whisper past her ears.

And just seconds later came the next blast as the second bottle did what it was meant to, engulfing the car's open cockpit and lone driver in a blazing inferno.

She turned then, and could see the flailing arms and hear the agonised screams until there was no breath left to make them. Then came a strange tap-tap-tapping sound as the windscreen started to crack and craze, until the whole panel of tempered glass exploded in a shower of crystal shrapnel that spattered around her feet.

She watched a moment more, was about to turn away, when the car's petrol tank caught and blew, lifting the car off the road, dropping it back amongst the flames, the stink of burning petrol and melting rubber streaming out from the column of fire, a muscly cloud of orange flames and black smoke roiling up into the morning sky.

It had been so quick, she thought, turning away at last and hurrying to her own car.

If only it could have taken longer.

If only he could have suffered more.

He deserved to. For what he had done.

And as she opened the door and slid in behind the wheel of an ancient Deux Chevaux she thought of the little boy, his soft blonde hair, his wide smile, and his bright, laughing eyes.

Lucien.

Oh, Lucien.

Other 'Jacquot' titles by Martin O'Brien

THE WATERMAN
They say drowning is easy...

Daniel Jacquot always jokes that he joined the police so he could earn a living and still play rugby. And play he did, for France, scoring the winning try in a Five Nations final against the English at Twickenham. Twenty years on, Daniel Jacquot is still remembered for that mighty try. But now he's a chief inspector, working homicide with the Marseilles *Judiciaire.*

Like playing rugby, tracking down killers is a game that Jacquot understands. And Marseilles just happens to be his own home ground. Every brash, bustling, sun-splashed square centimetre of it. It's here, in this city by the sea, that a shadowy, elusive killer steps onto the field of play, drugging, raping and drowning three young women in as many months.

With a new partner, a rising body count, and only a three-word tattoo to work with, Daniel Jacquot tracks down his quarry, gradually closing in on a methodical, yet sometimes whimsical killer the Press have christened *The Waterman.*

*

"British writer O'Brien makes an impressive debut with this gritty procedural set in the south of France."
– Publishers' Weekly (US)

"Chief Inspector Daniel Jacquot of the Marseilles PD is a marvellous invention and deserves to be discovered quickly. The characters and plot are great, but the real hit is Marseilles. It's gaudy, loud, filled with exotic people and loaded with mystery. All that, and rugby too."
– The Globe and Mail (Canada)

"Lovers of thrillers will welcome this new voice."
– Irish Examiner

"Tightly written and engrossing, Jacquot is someone we hope to meet again, soon."
– The San Antonio Express-News (US)

THE MASTER
Death is just a brush stroke away...

In the heat of a Provençal summer, Chief Inspector Daniel Jacquot is called to a luxury hotel on the slopes of the Grand Lubéron. One of the guests, a high-class call-girl from Marseilles, is missing. Her bedroom is drenched in blood, but there is no body.

Jacquot quickly discovers that among the remaining guests there are those who have both the means and motive to be her killer, people with personal secrets, hidden agendas, and their own dangerous liaisons to protect.

When a summer storm and raging flash floods isolate the hotel, passions start to run high when not one but two bodies are found.

*

"Well written and compelling. Tight plotting, lyrical descriptions, and excellent characterisation mean Jacquot is here to stay."
– The Daily Mail

"A strikingly different detective, Jacquot walks off the page effortlessly. And O'Brien seems to bend the plot at will, each time leading readers up an alley only to dart away into the shimmering heat."
– The Good Book Guide

"O'Brien is an elegant writer, and he's particularly strong on his scene-setting – you really will believe you're in Provence, admiring the scenery and partaking of some sumptuous meals."
– reviewingtheevidence.com

"A wonderfully inventive and involving detective series with vivid French locales creating the perfect backdrop. Jacquot is top of le cops."
– The Daily Express

THE FIFTEEN
On the Côte d'Azur,
jealousy is a hot-blooded killer...

Pierre Dombasle is the billionaire owner of SportÉquipe, the world's leading sportswear manufacturer. Twenty years ago, he was also captain of the French rugby team that beat England at Twickenham. To mark the anniversary of this famous victory, he organises a reunion for his old team-mates.

At Dombasle's luxurious Côte d'Azur residence, Daniel Jacquot meets many old friends from his playing days – and enemies, too. In the years since they hung up their boots some of them, like Dombasle, have become hugely wealthy and successful. But others have not.

Old rivalries and dark jealousies soon re-surface, and when one of the team is found dead Jacquot starts looking for a killer.

*

"Martin O'Brien's books featuring Chief Inspector Jacquot are fast becoming detective classics."
– Crime Squad

"A French counterpart to Ian Rankin's Scottish Inspector Rebus, with a tough authentic voice, and deft plot."
– The Cleveland Plain Dealer (US)

"Fans of Agatha Christie's technique in And Then There Were None, *in which trapped characters are thrillingly knocked off one by one, will appreciate the strategy. O'Brien, as always, makes effective use of his chosen setting – a sunny place for shady people."*
– The Daily Mail

"Exotic and different, exceedingly well-written and entertaining."
– Huddersfield Daily Examiner

THE ANGEL

Long-listed for the Theakston Old Peculier Crime Novel of the Year 2007

A small town, a beautiful stranger
and a crime no-one can ever forget...

When three generations of a wealthy German family are brutally murdered in their Provençal home, Daniel Jacquot heads up an investigation that rapidly turns into one of the most baffling – and personal – cases of his career.

After a local man is arrested for the murder Jacquot cannot shift the feeling that there's something wrong, something they've all missed. His suspicions are confirmed when a mysterious young woman arrives in the village claiming a special insight.

With her help, Jacquot follows a trail that leads back more than half a century – a story of love and betrayal, hatred and blackmail, in which Jacquot's own family had a tragic part to play.

*

"Martin O'Brien creates a sexually-charged atmosphere that is as chilling as it is engaging."
– The Sydney Morning Herald

"French country life has never been so fraught with sinister atmosphere, and it is only a matter of time before readers will be eagerly anticipating each new trip to Daniel Jacquot's France."
– Barry Forshaw
The Rough Guide to Crime Fiction

"This is a rich, leisurely read. Jacquot's not a cop to be rushing around – he enjoys his food and his cigarettes and the occasional joint. So relax and enjoy what's turning into an impressive series."
– reviewingtheevidence.com

"Only an Englishman could set his detective fiction in France and infuse it with such passion for the place and its people."
– The Daily Mail

CONFESSION

Jacquot's back,
working the mean streets of Marseilles...

Daniel Jacquot knows Marseilles better than most. He ought to, he was born there. And Marseilles knows him, as the rugby hero who once scored the winning try for his country at Twickenham. But now he's a cop – passionate, incorruptible, and often inspired.

When the sixteen-year-old daughter of wealthy Parisian parents – the niece of Marseilles' Chief Examining Magistrate – goes missing, Jacquot is brought in from a dead-end posting in the Lubéron to find her. With no ransom demand forthcoming, the authorities fear the worst.

Working undercover for the first time in his career, Jacquot finds himself in the dark and dangerous underworld of his beloved city, locked in a deadly battle of wits with a woman whose long and unforgiving memory is matched only by her taste for pain.

*

"The Marseilles scene seems to be written by a native. O'Brien's ability to deliver a sense of place makes him worth watching."
– The Washington Post (US)

"Jacquot is an excellent character, no doubt set for a long and entertaining career, and the scenery of corruption in the South of France is very well painted indeed."
– The Birmingham Post

"O'Brien's portrait of the Marseilles underworld is deliciously dark and shadowy."
– www.curiousbookfans

"Murder, mayhem, and the seedy side of Marseilles make for a mesmerising mix."
– The Northern Echo

BLOOD COUNTS
Vengeance is mine...

Daniel Jacquot doesn't know it yet, but someone is after his blood.

When you're a cop in Marseilles, threats of violence and revenge go with the territory. Usually they come to nothing, but when friends and colleagues start turning up dead it soon becomes clear that someone from Jacquot's past has a score to settle, and intends to see it through.

But this killer is different. To sweeten the revenge, and cause the greatest pain, it's always the target's nearest and dearest who die. When Jacquot discovers that he's in the firing line, he knows that unless he can track down the killer then someone he loves will pay the ultimate price.

*

"You can practically feel the sun of the Mediterranean beating down on your head as the mystery unfolds."
– Time Out

"Chief Inspector Daniel Jacquot of the Marseilles Police is fast becoming one of my favourite fictional cops."
– Henry Sutton
The Daily Mirror

"O'Brien does a good job in conveying the atmosphere of the place; above all, he manages to portray his characters without resorting to the stereotypes and caricatures that so often spoil Brit-written novels set in France. Blood Counts *is an entertaining read, and Daniel Jacquot an appealing cop."*
– Marcel Berlins
The Times

"Well-drawn, strongly flavoured setting in Marseilles... with grisly forensics offering vital clues as to the nature of the crime while skillfully concealing the whodunit. Rich, spicy, and served up with unmistakeable relish."
– The Literary Review

THE DYING MINUTES
Some people take their secrets to the grave,
but some people don't...

In 1972 a gold bullion convoy is hijacked on the outskirts of Marseilles. Within hours of the robbery the security trucks and hijackers have been rounded up, but a ton of gold has disappeared. Neither the authorities nor the hijackers have any idea where it is, or who has taken it.

More than twenty years later Daniel Jacquot receives an unexpected gift which points the way to the missing gold, a gift which pits him against the Polineaux and Duclos *familles*, two of the most feared crime syndicates on the Côte d'Azur.

When the Marseilles police become involved, following a series of gruesome murders, the investigation is headed by Chief Inspector Isabelle Cassier. A one-time lover of Jacquot's, she quickly discovers that the years haven't lessened her longing for the maverick Marseilles cop. Together they embark on a cut-throat hunt for the missing gold, with Polineaux and Duclos hitmen hot on their heels.

*

"An exciting, occasionally brutal caper. Unlike so many English writers O'Brien excels at depicting real life in a foreign city."
– The Sun

"A rich, colourful setting... O'Brien truly makes us feel, smell, hear, and see Marseilles. He writes skillfully, and the city setting simply reaches out and surrounds the reader. Definitely recommended."
– Mystery Scene

"A tense and thrilling read that had me on the edge of my seat all the way through."
– Bookbag

"The Dying Minutes by Martin O'Brien is a Château Lafite novel – high-end, literary, well-crafted, and beautifully written."
– It's a Crime UK

KNIFE GUN POISON BOMB
For a cop in Marseilles,
Christmas is just another day...

A Russian arms dealer is on the run. He has money, he has secrets, and powerful enemies who want him dead. Three hired guns are sent to track him down and kill him. They find him in Marseilles where Chief Inspector Daniel Jacquot is investigating a series of deadly knife attacks.

As Christmas approaches and Jacquot closes on the killer, his pregnant lover, Claudine, is rushed to hospital. Jacquot hurries to her bedside, but he soon discovers that a hospital is not the safest place to be.

Jacquot may be off duty, and about to become a father, but for a cop in Marseilles Christmas is just another day.

*

"O'Brien's evocation of the hot, vibrant, and seedy port in which everyone seems to be either a cop or a criminal, and sometimes both, is as masterly as Ian Rankin's depiction of Edinburgh."
– The Daily Mail

"Tall and tough, smart and sexy, Jacquot is a first-rate series hero."
– Kirkus Review (US)

"This is top quality crime writing that combines the key elements of plot, pace, characterisation and location, making a rounded novel that engages right to the last page."
– www.curiousbookfans

"J'adore Jacquot."
– Amazon Reviewer

TALKING TO THE SHARKS
They tear you apart,
they leave no trace...

Jacquot has retired from the Marseilles *Judiciaire* and has started a new life with his two young daughters on Île des Frères, a small Caribbean island off the coast of Martinique.

But the good life is put at risk when an ex-lover, Boni Milhaud, (see *The Waterman*) arrives on the island to ask for Jacquot's help. Her husband, Patric Stuyvesant, a professional gambler and the owner of private gaming clubs in the Bahamas, has gone missing with a girlfriend. To make good their escape he has stolen ten million dollars from gangland boss, Ettore DiCorsa, who runs a money-laundering syndicate based in Nassau. All Boni wants is for Jacquot to find her husband before DiCorsa catches up with him.

At first Jacquot wants nothing to do with it, telling Boni that he's retired and cannot help her. But in the days that follow he is given no choice but to take on the case, following Patric's trail from the gaming tables of Nassau to the distant vineyards of Provence. What he uncovers on this journey is a deadly conspiracy that threatens not only DiCorsa's syndicate, but everything that Jacquot holds dear.

No one is who they seem, and nothing is how it looks.

*

"One of the very best books I've read in a long time... Utterly and brilliantly entertaining."
– Goodreads

"This exceptional writer has yet again penned an absolutely brilliant novel which had me hooked from the first page. Recommended very highly."
– Terry Halligan
Eurocrime

"Atmospheric and enthralling."
– Lancashire Evening Post

Writing as Jack Drummond

AVALANCHE
It begins with a single flake of snow,
and ends in disaster…

Every winter thousands of people flock to the exclusive ski resort of Les Hauts des Aigles in the French Alps. The highlight of the season is the Course du Diable, the most thrilling and dangerous downhill race in the world. This year six champions will compete for the prize, a rare diamond worth twelve million dollars donated by a mysterious Russian billionaire.

On the day of the race, as crowds gather on the slopes and line the route, competitors, visitors, and townsfolk alike are oblivious to the silent killer waiting for them in the mountains.

When the avalanche comes only three things can save them.

Luck, courage, and the will to survive.

*

"Big, high-pitched disaster novels don't come much more thrilling than this."
– The Daily Mirror

"A top thriller for all fans of the white stuff."
– Closer

"Gripping stuff, though not recommended if you have a ski-trip booked."
– Choice

STORM
No warning, no escape.
So who will survive...?

It's late summer in Melville County in America's wild north-west, a land of fog-shrouded coastal cliffs and wave-pounded beaches, with a backwoods interior that rises up around the twisting course and echoing canyons of the Susquahannish River.

Up in the highlands, the first of the season's fishermen are casting for steelhead salmon and cut-throat trout, and despite the cold seas wet-suited surfers are gathering to ride the breaks on Melville Bay.

And then the rain begins to fall... And the rivers rise...And the tide begins to turn... And the sharks gather...

In a single day, a vengeful Mother Nature will change lives for ever.

*

"A classy old school thriller."
– Daily Sport

"Jack Drummond's second rollercoaster ride is gripping stuff. Exciting and enjoyable."
– Amazon Vine Voice

Writing as Louka Grigoriou

IN THE HOUSE OF THE LATE PETROU
A story to haunt you…

When journalist Electra Contalidis returns to her island home after a long illness she resolves to finish her biography of the nineteenth-century freedom fighter, Admiral Ioannis Contalidis, the family patriarch who built the house she lives in.

But it's not this celebrated hero of the Greek War of Independence who fills her days, and haunts her dreams. It is someone else. Someone who hates the family she married into… Someone determined to have his revenge… And someone who sees in Electra the fragile, fractured means to his murderous ends.

Electra may find refuge and comfort in the past, but there is only pain and betrayal in her future.

In this modern Greek tragedy there is only one winner.

And he's dead.

*

"A captivating story and a real page turner from start to finish, with a twist when least expected."
– Amazon Reviewer

About The Author

After graduating from Hertford College, Oxford, Martin O'Brien was travel editor at British Vogue for a number of years, and as a travel and life-style correspondent he has contributed to a wide range of international publications.

As well as writing the Daniel Jacquot detective series (*"Rich, spicy, and served up with unmistakeable relish"* - The Literary Review), he has also written straight-to-paperback thrillers under the names Louka Grigoriou and Jack Drummond (*"Big, high-pitched disaster novels don't come much more thrilling than this"* - The Daily Mirror).

Martin's books have been translated into Russian, Turkish, French, Dutch, Spanish, Portuguese, German, and Hebrew.

He lives in the Cotswolds with his wife and two daughters.

www.martinobrienthrillers.com

Printed in Great Britain
by Amazon

74283344R00210